VIA Folios 160

What She Takes Away

Cover photo from the author.

Library of Congress Control Number: 2022918049

Published by
BORDIGHERA PRESS
John D. Calandra Italian American Institute
25 W. 43rd Street, 17th Floor
New York, NY 10036

VIA Folios 160
ISBN 978-1-59954-194-5

What she takes away

A NOVEL BY ADELE ANNESI

BORDIGHERA PRESS

For my mother

Chapter 1

Gia peeled the swatch from the padded mailer and examined the sample, the muddy shades and inarticulate pattern, the transparent uneven weave. Who would want a dress made of this? Certainly not a women's wear house that prided itself on quality. She checked her laptop—seven minutes to the video meet with Martell. She looked down at her carryall, inside it the scarf her father sent. In the forgiving natural light of her co-op, the material had fairly glowed. What about here in her office, under the fluorescents?

Taking the poly mailing pouch from the carryall, she removed the scarf and checked the time. Six minutes. She held a section of the scarf under the magnifier. The material had a natural hand-woven quality, a tight even weave. The paisley mosaic in chiaroscuro shades spoke of changing seasons. At the center of the repeat, the lustrous yellow gold of sunflowers. She drew the fabric over the uncut diamond on her finger to her wrist above the palm. The translucent border threads shimmered, absorbing the light. The material's hand against the skin was supple, breathable, a gracious covering.

Well, she thought, her tailor father had outdone himself, assuming he somehow created the piece. She turned it over and examined the underside, the narrow rolled hem, the familiar baste-style lockstitch in invisible thread a signature, one her mother had never cared for, having branded it common.

She laid the scarf on her desk and pushed Adrian's sample away with the heel of her palm. How she hated handling the wholesale stuff Fiber carried now, synthetic blends whose flypaper stick instantly made her want to wash her hands, lifeless poly that drooped on hangers and shoulders and pilled after a first wearing—*stracci,* her mother had called them, rags.

She heard the buzz of the downstairs door. Not even downtown Boston traffic on a Friday afternoon could keep Rafael Bautista from the meet with Martel. She heard Bautista's step shuffle up the cracked linoleum steps and slipped the scarf back in the pouch.

Bautista stood in her doorway. "So, Adrian sent the sample? It got here okay?" He dipped his mirrored shades, revealing bloodshot eyes.

She nodded at her desk. "He sent something." At least this time the sample arrived before the meet.

Bautista raised his hand and waggled thick fingers. "Let's see it."

She stared at him. "You can't see it from there?"

"Ha, funny. Let's see what he sent."

She nodded at the swatch. "Try and pick it up."

Assailing her desk in short strides, he grasped at the thin cloth. Permeated with static, the fabric clung to the desktop. "Damn thing," he muttered. He bunched the cloth and held it to the light. "So it's sheer, so what? It's for dresses next summer, not suits."

"Expensive for disposable, don't you think?"

Bautista shook his head and tossed the swatch back on her desk. "You think your contacts can do better? You can't—not for this price."

She studied him a moment then glanced at the laptop. Five minutes. She reached for the pouch. Even under the fluorescent glare the scarf's material was suffused with color, vitality, inviting human touch.

"Ho, and what's this?" Bautista looked at her over his glasses. "You been holding out?" He opened his palm. "Let's see."

She held onto the scarf. "I thought Adrian was a colleague—with benefits."

"Adrian is a toad. But a toad with good prices. Where'd this come from, anyway?"

"Italy."

Bautista gave his head a hard shake. "Uh-uh, sorry, no. We gotta go global, we deal Asia, Indo—places I know people."

She glanced at her laptop. "I have Martell in four." She pealed the swatch from her desk. "I'm not showing him this."

Bautista snatched the cloth. "I can talk to Martell, too, you know."

"You have his number?"

"Well, aren't you all that cause you know somebody."

She draped the scarf lightly over her arm.

Bautista grabbed the swivel chair and shoved it against her desk. "Fine, make the call. I like to hear what he says."

She laid the scarf beside the laptop and clicked the live meeting link. Three minutes remaining. The display gave a passcode prompt. She moved the cursor to the side of the screen.

Bautista leaned forward. "So, is he there?"

"We're waiting for him to enter." She crossed her fingers under her desk. The electrician was supposed to call with a verdict on rewiring. She glanced at the laptop. Three minutes. No, two.

The cell in Bautista's shirt pocket vibrated. He stared at her, ignoring it.

"Are you going to answer?" she asked calmly, her legs jiggling.

"It can wait."

"Isn't Walsh supposed to call?"

"I said it can wait." Bautista's cell sounded an upbeat Pinoy pop ringtone. He slipped the phone from his pocket and squinted at the display. "Dammit. Walsh. Says it's urgent."

She held out her hand. "Want me to talk to him?"

Bautista stood and aimed his cell at her laptop. "Better you do what you supposed to." He pressed the phone's display and held it to his face. "Now what?" He moved to the doorway.

She waited until she heard the scrape of chair rollers in the adjacent office. One minute. She got up and quietly closed the office door then moved the dressmaker's form nearer the laptop.

Angling the computer away from the wall, she entered the passcode. The live meeting window opened, revealing James Martell's profile, black horn-rimmed glasses stationed on a broad, hooked nose magnifying lateral eyes sharp as an eagle's.

Chapter 2

"Mr. Martell, good to meet you. Thanks so much for your time."

Martell faced the screen. "You have five."

"Don Roccia sends his greetings."

"He says you have something to show."

She moved the laptop around and stood. "Normally, I would send the sample, but I wanted to show you what this does on."

She took the scarf and draped it across the dressmaker's form. "Even on this." The fabric's vibrant shades made the tattered shoulders of the form appear broader, the dull cloth body more like human skin.

"And here's what it does off." She tossed the fabric onto the cutting table in front of the screen. The piece drifted downward, holding its shape.

"I know we don't usually show samples this way, but I wanted you to see how the material moves and traps color even in an intricate pattern and saturated shades."

She laid the scarf across the laptop near the screen so the fibers caught the light of her desk lamp. How she would love to pitch to Martel's interest in an organic line. But first she needed the material's fiber content—and its source.

Martell's hand flexed as if to reach through the display. "Don told you we're already into next summer?"

"Fiber is agile. We can turn on a dime." Or less, she thought. "You'll be in Milan next week? I'd like to show you this in person."

"After the shows."

"Perfect." The later the better.

Martell peered into the screen. "I don't do this for everyone."

"I know, Mr. Martell, and thank you. You won't be disappointed."

"Good. There isn't time." Martell glanced to his right. "David will set it up. Tell Don I'll see him in Maggiore."

The jangle of her nervous energy rushed to her belly as she worked with Martell's assistant to set a meet for next Friday evening, a week from tonight.

Closing the live link, she felt lightheaded, disconnected, as if gravity had failed to hold. She sat back in the chair with a creak and gazed at the dressmaker's form.

This was the connection she had hoped for, longed for even before leaving Boston School of Design and that unfortunate project for Roccia's course. It was the only class she hated leaving. Don had stopped in again last week to wheedle her into finishing the degree.

"Surely you're not staying here forever?" he asked while Raf was out having his grays retouched.

"I like it here, Don," she answered. "It's comfortable."

Roccia looked across the showroom, his tall trim form in black jeans and a white button-down shirt in stretch poplin. "You believe this suits you?" He stared with tawny, almond-shaped eyes at the corner of the ceiling where a leak had discolored the tiles.

"I have a place here, Don, stability."

He looked at her. "And inspiration?"

Her smile felt stiff, unnatural. "Why not," she answered. "I'm needed here."

Roccia shook his head. "Not the same." For a moment, he looked as if he wanted to say more. "Well, contact James, anyway. We're out at Maggiore until the end of the month so I'll put in another word. Now let's see that little stone you're wearing."

She nudged the band, still in need of sizing, with her thumb and glanced at the phone. She dreaded the next call like an internal. How to approach a man after sixteen years and half a lifetime? Ask for an audience and the proprietary, step-by-step of the scarf's creation? Please, God, it hadn't come from that flyspeck of a mill near him in Italy whose name she couldn't recall. And if he said no? The fact that this year he had sent a birthday gift might only be a more elegant form of apology.

The brow over her left eye pulsed. She pressed it down with her thumb. Maybe she should do a search for the mill first and talk with Peter at dinner, make the call in the morning.

From the adjoining office she heard Bautista's voice getting louder. It was a small but saving mercy that the walls of this decrepit space were plaster and not sheetrock. She opened a document on her laptop and quickly made a to-do list. Next door Bautista burst into a torrent of protests that ended in an oath. She slipped the scarf back in her bag and nudged it under her desk with the toe of her ballet flat.

Her office door opened. Bautista hovered in the threshold. "Walsh. That butt end of an ox. Says the electrical has to be to code next month or they shut us down. I told him lower the cost or we go someplace else." He came and draped himself over her chair, the black hair of his forearms on end.

"We knew it would happen eventually." She made a note. "Meanwhile, good news. Martell wants to meet."

Bautista stared at her. "About?"

She stared back at him. "What do you mean, about? The new fabric."

Bautista's mouth hung open. "He was just in front of you. You didn't pitch him?"

She gave a laugh. "Without the numbers? Please. I demoed the material. He was impressed. The next meet is in Milan."

Bautista's foot slipped from the chair rung. "I said no Italy. Didn't I say we don't deal Italy?"

"It's not we, Raf."

"You think you're going? No—not to Italy or Europe anyplace. Time was you could get the Romanians cheap. Now not even that."

"But we can get the process and the fiber content." Her father owed her that at least. "Then we can have another mill produce it cheaper, maybe through your contacts."

Bautista blinked through heavy lids. "Well, now that could be something."

"What we can't afford, Raf, is to hand the head of an international woman's apparel house cheesecloth. Besides, I have contacts where this was made so the trip won't cost more than airfare." She recrossed her fingers. She'd be lucky not to end up on the street. "Besides, what choice do we have?"

Bautista scratched at his bald spot with his pinky nail. "So, who are we dealing over there?"

"Relatives."

"These relatives have a name?"

"Same as mine, Falcini."

Bautista threw back his head. "I can't take another of you."

"You won't even have one of me. I won't be here. It'll give you a break."

"It's giving me a headache. You're sure Martell is interested?"

"Why else would I go?"

Bautista took his foot off the chair. "Then find out how those *tanga* make this stuff. Don't let them get up cause they know you. And I want to hear you every day—before you pitch Martell, not after. I know you, you know. Without me you'd give away the store. So no deals, no percentages, nothing without my approval. We need the order but for the right money." He rolled up the sleeves of his checkered shirt and went to the door. "You hear me, *tama?*"

"How could I not?" she said, her jaw clenching.

"Good. Be back in a week."

He swung the door so hard the knob smacked the wall, another ding in a structure that despite its walking distance from Faneuil Hall needed painting, new flooring and the repair of a roof leak that not even the prior owner could find. The electrical, by comparison, made the rest seem livable. She hated to admit it, but her mother had a point about this place.

"You're just like your father," she said shortly after the second heart attack. "The minute I'm gone you'll buy into that sinkhole. Why can't you be happy with what you've got? An education and a name for yourself at that nice Italian company with the good material. Okay, it's a little she-she, but so what? They pay you decent."

She had just started working at Tessero and hadn't had the heart to tell her mother college was over. Yet, in the end, it was hard to know which accusation had stung more, that she was a spendthrift lurking at her mother's deathbed for funds or that she was like her father.

She checked online for flights of out Logan to Malpensa and found one late Sunday afternoon that gave her time with Peter and time to pack. She keyed her credit card into the airline website, opened another browser window and checked email. A confirmation appeared in her inbox. For this price, she would stay on Don Roccia's floor.

She clicked Trenitalia for rail schedules then a newsfeed of Milan. An afternoon protest had fulminated from downtown to the Rho fairgrounds where the textile shows were held. A journalist held a microphone under the nose of a young man wearing a form-fitting leather jacket ripped at the shoulder. He hadn't planned to join the rally, he told the interviewer, but with the rising tide of immigrants threatening more than just the country's economy the time had come.

She added the Trenitalia site to favorites and closed the browser. She had kept up with news from *il bel paese* via cable at her North End co-op until the provider axed the free Italian station from its lineup.

"That's not the place to save money," her mother had surprised her by saying. "Pay for the better menu and keep up your Italian. You had my language first."

She took the carryall from under her desk and moved the tattered dressmaker's dummy to the corner by a teetering tower of sample books. Why was it that no matter how often she tidied the space it still looked shabby?

She switched off the desk lamp, shoved the pouch and laptop in her bag and went downstairs past a protruding bolt of duck cotton in garish geometrics that would make better slipcovers than dresses. Through the front window, Atlantic Avenue sparkled in sunlight that glinted off the wharf, the morning's thunderheads swept away by the wind. She buttoned her denim vest for the trek up the uneven cobbles of North Street. For now, she would have to table the question her attorney had asked when she signed the papers for Fiber, whether or not she wanted to walk away from this.

Chapter 3

Outside the darkened windows of the Top of the Hub the night sky hung over the city like muslin, the pale sliver of moon a cutout against the silhouette of buildings. If stars glittered in the opaque tapestry, Gia couldn't see them in the haloed glow of streetlamps, lighted office windows and commuter traffic. How seldom she saw the outside world at night.

She looked across the room at Peter talking to a thickset man with coarse graying hair combed back from a podgy, animated face. The man stopped and shook Peter's hand. He nodded in her direction and started back toward the table. She couldn't see the deep-set blue of his eyes from here or the crescent-shaped scar over his left cheek from a boating accident in youth, but even at a distance she felt his warmth.

A doyenne sitting at a center table, her chestnut hair in a chignon, sleeveless square-neck black dress accentuating toned shoulders, turned to watch him. As he neared the table, the woman looked at her. What was it she saw in the woman's eyes? Doubt about the younger female sitting alone at a table for two whose ginger hair needed a trim and a warmer shade, a woman whose comparative youth only underscored that she wasn't on quite the same footing as the son of William Litton, founder of Litton Learning?

She reached for the dessert menu and looked down the list. Maybe it wasn't too late for something sweet.

"You won't need that." Peter took the padded holder. "Don't look so worried, I promise I won't sing."

She grasped his hand. "No candle either."

"Not even one?"

She squeezed his fingers.

He nodded to a nearby waiter who disappeared around the cherrywood wine cabinet.

She folded her napkin. "Who are those people?"

"Friends of friends."

"So, strangers, then?"

"More like potential contributors."

"Perfect, you can write off the dinner."

He smiled and turned her hand under the table lamp. The uncut diamond caught the glow of the lamplight. "Do you like it?"

"I'm getting used to it."

"It's a tribute, you know."

She smiled. "So you said."

He pressed her palm. "Well, are you going to tell me?"

"Tell you what?"

"What you've been mulling all evening."

She sipped the last of the Brunello. "I heard from my father yesterday. Another letter—and a gift."

"Really, what did he send?" He dandled her fingers.

"A scarf."

He glanced at the black swing purse on the back of her chair. "Did you bring it?"

"It's at home."

"So how is he?"

"Well, I guess." Her father had made it sound in the letter like everyone was quite well—he, his wife, her sons.

He leaned closer. "And?"

"I have to make a trip."

He sat back. "To Italy?"

"For work." A wisp of cloud obscured the sliver of moonlight. "A meeting, with a prospective client about a new fabric. The scarf, the material, really, it's—there's something different about it." She looked at him. "Don Roccia got me a meet with someone who may be interested."

He tilted his head. "I thought Roccia was persona non grata."

"He knows a lot of people. And he and the client, prospect, are in Milan for Fashion Week then Maggiore till the end of the month. He promised to put in a word and got a ticket to a preshow."

He took her hands in his. "Why don't I go with you? It would give us time away. I could meet your father—"

She couldn't help but smile, struck afresh by the candid eyes, wavy brown hair and olive complexion, darker than hers and a testament to his mother's black Irish heritage.

"I leave Sunday."

"This Sunday?" The crescent-shaped scar looked more pronounced. "You'll miss the fundraiser. Can you change the date?"

"Don's contact is out of Santa Barbara—next week is the only time we can meet. And I have to call on some people first."

He shook his head. "You've phoned your father?"

"First thing tomorrow. I—couldn't manage it today." She ran her thumb over his fingers.

He smiled. "But I'm still staying over, right?"

"Long as you don't mind the double bed."

"Not if you're in it."

"Your dessert." The waiter stood at the table bearing a white ironstone plate with a slice of Blackforest in brandy sauce.

Peter nodded at her. "For the lady."

She looked at him. "You're not having any?"

"I'll just watch you."

She turned to the waiter. "Could we get a second fork, please. And an espresso?"

Peter grinned. "Does that mean we'll be awake a while?"

Chapter 4

A film of gray light filtered through the bedroom shade. Beside her under the white down comforter, Peter slept. He could sleep anywhere, anytime, a trait she envied, even if she prized the early morning hours to plan, get a drop on the day.

Turning slowly, she reached for her carryall under the nightstand and took out the letter, her father's looping scrawl partly in English, partly in Marche dialect, his account of the central hillside province where the poppies were sparse this summer, the Cesano had disgorged more of its riverbed, and the museum in the decaying bastion from which the village of Castel Barberini derived its name had closed its doors for lack of visitors. The sausage festival, however, was well-attended, with people streaming in despite a heat so scalding the grain had all but withered in the fields. Absent was any mention of the abysmal economy, the exodus of villagers in search of a better life. Where was that fruitful labor, she wondered.

She looked down the page. Was it her imagination, or had his handwriting become thinner, less decipherable? She could compare the letter to last year's but had tucked it away with the rest in the nether regions of the bedroom closet. In a box that once held a pair of ankle boots she bought on a Saturday in Haymarket two springs ago.

She looked down to the close of the letter, this year only a page, and read again where he spoke as in prior missives of his family, his wife and Gia's two stepbrothers, all strangers, and at the end the usual close—*un'abbraccio forte, Babbo.* Had she missed the customary invitation to visit that over the years had become ritual? She looked again but found nothing. She folded the note and tucked it back in her bag.

She turned and looked at Peter, his face half-buried in the feather pillow. She slipped her leg from under his. How easily their comfort in each other's presence had grown over the nearly two years they had been together. She held up her hand up in the diffused light and turned the band on her finger to surface the uncut stone.

"Just think about it before you say no," he told her, to fill the silence of her hesitation.

She wanted to say, yes, of course, she would pledge her troth or whatever people were to say on such occasions, believing it was what they both wanted, how she should feel.

"You're always quick to say no when you're not initiating," he added. "Give yourself time to get used to it."

She nudged the band with the tip of her thumb. At times it was annoying, his ability to read her, which also had been there from the start. She would never willingly admit it, but the tendency toward the negative in the face of uncertainty was inherited, and not from her father.

Peter stretched under the length of sheet and rubbed his eyes, squinting as if the room were bathed in sunshine. As he stretched again, she caught a whiff of his scent, a woodland in early spring.

He blinked and squeezed her thigh. "So, are you calling?"

"In a few minutes." She tugged the threadbare white terry robe from the bedpost.

He sat up against the pillows and pulled the comforter to his chest. "Mind if I ask—why now?"

She turned and stared. "What do you mean? I have to go over, why not call now?"

"I mean, why not before? Why so long after your mother passed?"

"How should I know?"

"I'm asking, Gia, not judging."

"I don't know. Maybe because he owed me a better explanation— and not in writing." She pulled the robe around her. "Before Mom died, he used to call. What parent waits till the other dies to stop calling and write?"

"Maybe he wanted to give you space, time to hear what he had to say when you felt like it, whenever that might be."

She shook her head. "This isn't like your father. The two of you had something." She sat back against the pillows.

He nudged her arm, his smile soft, indulgent. "Don't think because my father's gone I have him on a pedestal. He and my mother—" He shook his head. "They had each other, the cottage, a shared history. It bonded them but not to me." He tilted his head back. "Then when Mom got sick, she needed someone. But it was still him." He pressed his leg against hers. "All I'm saying is, don't see it as weakness if you feel something. Most of the time it's the other way round."

She belted the robe and sat back. "I should call, get it over with."

"I'll make coffee." His forearm brushed her breast. "I could still go, you know. To Italy, I mean. After the dinner next week."

"And miss the board meeting, the pledges coming in? The school can't afford it."

"There are a lot of things we can't afford." He pressed his cheek to hers.

She could feel the gentleness in him, the inherent kindness that made him want to do things for her like staying at her small functional place on weekends instead of the cottage on Scituate Bay.

He grinned. "I like it when you look at me like that."

"How am I looking at you?"

"Like you want to know me better—say, over a lifetime?"

"I already know you. That's why I'm wearing this." She held up her hand and gave him a nudge. "Go make coffee."

He pulled on his pajama bottoms. "Fine, but don't think of me as an easy mark."

Grabbing his pillow, she clasped it to her belly and snatched the scrap of paper from under the clock on the nightstand. She reached for the phone, and quelling the impulse to cross her fingers, pressed the digits on the dial pad.

The receiver emitted a low hum and a series of staccato rings.

"*Residenza* Falcini," said a woman's voice. She sounded annoyed.

"Please—*per favore,* Giovanni Falcini."

In a tone clearly suspicious of the female on the other end, the woman asked who was calling.

"Gia," she answered. "Falcini—*sua figlia,*"she said. His daughter.

She heard what sounded like an intake of breath and shuffling then silence.

"*Pronto,*" she said, instinctually resorting to the customary greeting of readiness. How seldom anybody was really ready for anything anymore.

Closing her eyes, she looked down the length of a long passageway to the kitchen of her father's ancestral home. He had settled there after she and her mother returned to the states, after his many prior pilgrimages to the Marche region had failed to yield a place he could hang out a shingle and they could live.

"Now this is a good location," he said of the last property they surveyed, a shabby brick affair situated along the Adriatic shoreline he'd fallen so in love with. "Right on the main road."

He parked the battered blue Fiat rental at the end of the weedy gravel drive, got out of the car and strode to the front steps while she waited, staring at the faint outline of mountains and a stroke of heat lightning that flashed across the gray horizon. It rarely rained in this part of the country in summer, but they had overstayed the season and with October came the rains.

Wearing a rumpled golf hat to shield his balding head, her father stood sweating on the bare cement step under the awning and waved to her to get out and see the place on which he had set his hope. All she wanted was to go back to Boston and a junior year of high school that had already begun. Back to the boy she'd met just before classes let out for summer, an Irish kid with straight black hair and big blue eyes who aspired to follow in his father's footsteps and become a cop. Her father waived again.

She rolled the window partway up and got out of the car. The afternoon heat was oppressive.

He took a key from his pants pocket. "Let's take a look around. But let's don't say anything yet to your mamma, eh, Gia—"

"*Pronto,*"said a hoarse voice on the other end of the line.

"*Pronto,*" she echoed.

"Gia? *Tutto bene?* Everything okay?"

She stared at the phone cord. How casual his tone sounded, how disturbingly false the sense it created that they had only just spoken, the other day or last week. He couldn't be that callous, could he? Maybe he was worried she was calling with bad news, an illness perhaps, hers this time. Last time they spoke was after her mother died.

"She always had a weak heart," he said, whether by way of consolation or indictment, she couldn't tell.

"I have to make a trip," she answered. "For work, I'm in fabric sales and have a meeting in Milan with a client. I thought I'd stop by, see you, the family."

She could also see firsthand what that miniscule mill near his village could produce. She had located Ordito Trama online, and while the website affirmed the mill's ability to weave quality fabric, seeing was believing. The down pillow she was strangling emitted a small white feather from a side seam.

"*Certo,* certainly, yes, do come. We would love to see you. Just say when and we will get everything ready."

She nodded, realizing he couldn't see her nodding, sitting in bed wearing a tattered robe, with a potential fiancé he didn't know making coffee in her galley kitchen. And how convenient for him to hide behind the plural in accepting her request for a visit. There was no, "I would love to see you," only the safe multiplicity of his family.

"I leave tomorrow afternoon," she said, willing herself to believe it was real. "I'm in Milan Monday night." By then, the Fashion Week previews would have started, so why not get the lay of the land? And the extra day would shorten the visit with him while giving her just enough time to get what she needed and get the hell out. "There's a train at noon Tuesday. With the transfer in Rimini, I should be in Marotta around three-thirty."

"Wonderful, *perfetto.*"

"Are you, I mean, can someone pick me up?"

"I am happy to come get you."

"Then let me give you my cell. I'll call again when I arrive. Do you have a mobile?"

He laughed and coughed a little. "Stella is the one with the know-how."

"I'll give you the number anyway."

"Yes, fine—just let me find something to write on."

In the scratchy static of the overseas line, she could hear what sounded like the crackle of paper being uncrumpled and smoothed. How easy it was to reconnect after so long a time when the only thing needed was to ease a few creases.

Chapter 5

Giovanni stood at the cutting table gazing down at the phone, an ancient red affair whose soiled finger holes and rotary dial had seen decades of use. Stella had tried more than once to replace this relic, but he wouldn't have it. It was solid, reliable, an anchor that kept him from drifting away on a tide of hopes, longings, even possibilities. And now, finally, his daughter had called.

Perhaps he had dreamt it, imagined their conversation as he had countless times, seemingly endless hours over and over in his mind's eye so that on more than one occasion he had thought that what he imaged, yearned for, was real. In one particular instance, he had turned to Stella and started to say wasn't it something Gia had finally gotten in touch? Then he caught himself and scolded himself that if he kept this up he would shortly go quite mad.

He looked out the open workroom window at the viale, the cobblestones polished by centuries of footsteps glistening in the afternoon sun of a warm autumn day like so many other warm autumn days. Perhaps he had imagined the call this time, too, he thought gloomily, just as he had before, since the call carried none of the sequined sparkle he envisaged, dreamt of, in all those illusions.

He took the stub of pencil from its holder on the small pad of unlined white notepaper he still kept on hand for suit measurements. Looking down, he saw with a start the writing there—Gia's flight number, the arrival date here, Tuesday via Eurostar from Milan with a transfer in Rimini to Marotta . . .

"Giovanni! What are you doing?"

He looked up to see Stella standing in the workshop doorway, the ends of her hennaed hair frizzled in the humidity. She must have washed that yellow button-down dress in hot water again for it seemed to have shrunk another half-size.

"Can you explain to me, please, what the devil is going on here?" she said, panting, her perfume too musky for the season, any season. "Was that your daughter on the phone?" She stared at him. "What's wrong? Why don't you answer?"

She wanted his confirmation, he realized, because she couldn't believe it either, that after half a lifetime his daughter had indeed called. But now he did believe it, now that she reproached him for it.

"Well?" she demanded with the same asperity as his deceased his ex might have done, the same inescapable tendency to overpower a room to he was still perversely drawn.

"It was Gia, apparently."

Stella's mouth dropped open. For once she was unable to speak, though she was clearly filled with questions that had risen silently in her eyes. Why had his daughter called? What did she want? Was she all right? Don't tell me she's coming here now …

He could just see it, his head on a platter like Giovanni Battista, and although in this moment the room was still calm he knew better than to believe there wasn't more to come.

"She arrives by train in Marotta on Tuesday," he answered. Why mince words.

Stella's hands kneaded the air, her breasts straining against the shirtdress. As predicted, she pelted him with queries.

Who did that young witch think she was, might she ask, intruding upon their lives after so long without a word, expecting them all to roll out the red carpet? And who would help them roll out this carpet on such short notice? And what hostess with any integrity could put together a feast on the fly. This question she addressed to the face of the tarnished brass mantle clock that stopped ticking ages ago. And what about her sons, Massimo and Paolo, who lived in Rome but must be apprised of this latest shock? And, face it, how many more shocks could anyone here handle, anyway?

Most of all, she asserted, the back of her hand plastered to her forehead as she motioned to the door and the rooms beyond with fresh worry, how in the balls could they get the place fixed up in time? She gazed up at the ceiling and the second floor where, of the two bedrooms, theirs and boys', one room would quickly need to be outfitted for a guest.

"The boys will just have to sleep in the TV room on the pullout," she said, still staring heavenward.

Moving toward her as she swirled the air overhead with her hands, he cupped her breasts straining against the shirtdress and heard her gasp. As she started to pull away, he cupped her underneath and massaged a bit.

"We'll manage," he said, feeling her respond. "You know how much you like a party." He put his arms around her and lowered his hands to her backside.

"We'll order the food from Carlo's," she continued, ignoring him. "The *trattoria* outside the village went to the dogs the minute they sold it to those *Marocchini,* though maybe we'll get the bread from there. It's good to keep a few local contacts." She looked at him. "You still haven't said what she's coming for."

He scratched the cleft of his chin and felt the stubble where he had missed a spot shaving. Gia had been quite matter of fact about why she was coming. The trip was for work, a meeting in Milan. And he had been right in surmising with his gift that she was still in fabric. Then equally offhandedly she had mentioned stopping by to see them. The reasoning was compact as a ball of yarn, with as many potential tangles.

"Giovanni, O!" Stella gave him a shake. "Where are you? I'm asking, what does your daughter want after all this time?"

He flapped his hands. "What do you mean, what does she want? She is my daughter."

The light through the open window pooled on the floor where over the years it had dulled the terrazzo. Even now Stella nagged him to close the shutters since the house sat right on the main street. But who wanted to keep out the sun?

Stella waggled her head. "Well, she must want something, to be coming on such short notice. Didn't she say?"

Anger shot through him like a current. "She wants to see her father again. That's what she wants." He pushed her away. "Now leave me in peace. Can't you see I have things to do?"

Stella laughed and gave her head a shake. "And what have you to do? Prepare this junk room for guests?" The frayed ends of her hair streaked the air like light trails. "Well, maybe you're right," she said, looking around the workspace. "We don't want the place looking like a pigsty. Though why we should fuss for a truant who deigns to look her father up only after a dog's age is beyond foolish." Catching a glimpse of herself in the three-way mirror, she sucked in her stomach.

"Maybe I should stop in at Bernadetta's, see if the new dresses are in." She turned with a coquettish smile. "I can afford a new dress, you know, since I did her books last month."

He waved her off. "Get whatever you want. But no yellow. It makes you look sallow."

She tossed her head. "A lot you know about it." She went to the door. "So, what does this absentee daughter do for a living?"

He took a remnant of material from the scarf and held it under the extension lamp. The fabric was good, he thought, very good. But what had she thought of it?

"Giovanni, good God in heaven, why don't you ever answer?"

"Christ, woman, give a man a chance to breathe. You're like a taxi with the meter running." He put the scrap under the presser foot of the Pfaff. "Gia works in fabric." Just like her old man. He closed the pinking shears and set them, handle down, on the cutting table by the pin cushion. "I think I'll go for a walk."

Stella paused at the door. "On a Saturday afternoon? You won't find a soul on the street. Anyone still left around here is at the beach."

He brushed past her to the foyer. "Well, I don't like to waste a nice afternoon either."

"What you don't want is to waste a chance to spread the news. Though what you have to spread in this situation, I can't imagine."

"Can't you?" he said, pinching her.

She gave a wave. "Uffa, off with you, then. Some of us have work to do." She nudged the kitchen door open with her hip and let it swing shut behind her.

He unlocked the front entrance of the row house and stood out on the hushed sidewalk. Stella was right, he thought, closing the door behind him. Via Barberini was empty. Why had he thought today would be different just because he had news to tell?

The only prospective audience was Girolamo Caspretti, who sat in front of his three-room flat on a frayed green lawn chair. The old stone mason had gone to America more than half a century ago nearly penniless and had returned nearly the same way and blind besides. Ah, well, the nonagenarian never complained. Nor did he resent what he still referred to as his adventure.

He strolled across the street, leather mules clacking against the cobbles. Caspretti cocked his head. It looked as though he hadn't shaved in a week.

"Is that you, Don Giovanni?" he asked, with tilt of his head. "You should see a cobbler about those damn shoes. I can hear the sole on that right one from here, flapping like a sail."

"I see you're still flying the flag," Giovanni responded.

Caspretti tapped his gray laborer's cap, the faded snippet of red kerchief tacked with a rusted safety pin. "We could use another Garibaldi around here, give these radicals some focus."

Giovanni went to the overturned barrel the mason used as guest seating. "I had a call today," he said, repositioning the cask.

From this angle he could sit with his back against the sunbaked brick and gaze out at the sea where a sun partly eclipsed by clouds had turned the Adriatic a rich shade of ultramarine just right for the lining of a coat.

Chapter 6

The wind raced in gusts across Scituate Harbor, whipping the surface of the water to froth and rattling the windows of the cottage that had been in the Litton family a generation. A bank of thunderheads hanging the bay obscured the sun.

"Looks like rain," Gia said.

If she had a nickel for all the times the North Shore looked that way, she could fix Fiber's electrical. Though money wouldn't offset the need for a breath of new life.

Peter put his arm around her. "Excited about leaving tomorrow?"

She leaned against him. "Haven't had time to think about it."

In truth, she had sought refuge in planning precisely to avoid thinking about it. Yet, each time her imagination spun round to the reality of returning to her mother's birthplace, her father's idyll, queasiness churned her stomach.

Peter tightened his arm around her. "My parents went to Italy once. Lake Como, as I recall."

She glanced at the Irish white pine hutch, the pewter frames with their black and white photographs, none of Italy. In the center of one hand-carved shelf, a photo showed William Litton standing on the jetty gazing out at the bay, dark wavy hair blown back from a lean squarish face. In the next photo, Peter's first wife, Maddie, lounged in an Adirondack chair on the back porch reading, her fine fair hair loose at the shoulders. On her other side in profile, stood a tall woman, straight black hair tied back from an elegant oval face, dark eyes glittering above high cheekbones. Too bad she hadn't met either of Peter's parents; it made them both seem so alone in the world.

"That other shot is from before my parents left England." Peter nodded at an image to the right. "Dad had finished his second year teaching at university and they had free time before fall term. They were both so young," he said, staring at his mother's image. "Dad's family were Protestant. They could never quite accept that he'd married an Irish Catholic."

She looked up. "Did it matter so much what other people thought?"

"Not enough to stop him." He pressed her hand. "He knew a good thing when he saw it." He gazed out the window. "Of all the places they visited in Como, my mother especially loved Bellagio. Said the cottages cascaded right down to the water, bougainvillea in every color framing the doorways. 'This must be what heaven looks like,' she said." He pulled her close as if seeking her warmth. "You're lucky for the chance to experience it."

"The Marche region is in the middle of the country," she answered. "A lot of working farms, not a lot of beauty." At least not the ancient, dramatic type found in the cities and northern alpine peaks. "You can't even see the mountains there."

"It's still Italy," he said softly.

"Problems and all."

He looked at her. "Worried about seeing your father, or the meeting with Martell?"

She shrugged. "Both, I guess."

She looked out over the bay at the gunmetal clouds now edged in gold by the sun. The meeting with Martell was later in the week, after the visit with her father. The start of the trip was the pre-show in Milan. Italy had always had strikes and protests over everything and nothing, but the news clip of the demonstration wasn't just for effect. Milan was industrialized, with people from everywhere, and too sophisticated to become embroiled in marches and rallies. She watched a gull hover over a pylon. Whatever happened this trip, it would be different from other times, and not just in Milan.

Peter squeezed her waist. "Let's go for a walk. Fresh air will do us good." He went to the mudroom and brought out a plaid flannel jacket. "This will keep out the chill."

She took the jacket, whose quilted material smelled of mold and damp. She had little interest in a walk but less in small talk and staying inside. She stuck her arms through the sleeves and latched the leather toggles, worn smooth at the tips.

"After you," he said, closing the backdoor behind them.

Out on the hard-packed sand, she turned her face to the sun, the jacket's scratchy collar to the wind. Gust after gust swept in from the bay, creaming its surface and tossing the glittering sand in the air.

He linked his arm in hers. "We'll go inside if it gets too much."

"It's fine," she said, pulling her hair back from her face. "Let's walk out to the jetty."

The bracing wind coated her cheeks with saline damp as the changing tide filled the air with the briny smell of seawater. Her sneakers sank in the ridge of broken shells that crunched underfoot. How many times had William and Isobel tramped this narrow strip of beach? Peter was right. They had always had each other, unlike him, who when the boom of the Sunfish struck him had been out on the water alone.

"That part looks dry." He pointed to a section of the rocky abutment and a weathered boulder with a leeward indent just right for two.

As he drew her down beside him, she had an instinct to draw back, but he folded her arms in his.

"Now hear me out before you answer." He took her hand. "I know you can't change the trip dates, but I could still get a flight out Friday after the fundraiser, get into Milan Saturday, come back Monday or Tuesday. We'd have time together, and I'd have a chance to get away." He gazed out at the bay. "I could use a break—"

She looked at him. "Is there a problem?"

She could see in his expression he wanted to unburden himself. But his eyes held the habitual wariness, as if he first wanted to gauge how she would respond.

"I'm . . . not sure how much longer I want to keep the learning centers going. I know I can't shut them down now. I wouldn't, anyway, they're my father's legacy. But they are his legacy, not mine, not in the long run." He looked at her. "I know now isn't the best time for all this, with you leaving . . ."

She shrugged. "So you want a change. What's wrong with that?" Relief at her acceptance flicked across his face and was gone. She squeezed his hand. "Maybe you didn't feel you could tell me before now." She touched the scar on his cheek. "I haven't been a good listener lately, have I?"

"No, you're—you've been fine. You've had Fiber to think about and now the trip." He gazed out at the water. "And this thing with me isn't easy to admit, even to myself. In a way, it feels like a betrayal, like I'm turning my back on family, what they started."

He held her hands. "When Dad died, the centers were all my mother focused on. It was unexpected, you know, his passing. Sometimes I'd see her standing at the dining room window staring out at the water, her hand on her chest gulping air like she couldn't breathe. I took over managing the centers to give her a break. It seemed the best way to keep my parents close. For a while, it even worked." He drew nearer. "Did I tell you they met at the university?"

"No," she said, drawing her arms around him.

"Mom was in administration, Dad was a professor. They loved each other from the start, I think, maybe not in that consuming way some people do but with a kind of totality and their heads on straight." He looked at her. "That's what I like about you. From the moment we met, the lights were on."

She smiled at the memory. "I was with Tessero then, trying the sales end of the business."

Don Roccia had told her after she dropped out of design school that if she wanted a future in fabric she should try sales, learn about the material. She could have tried working as a converter, buying greige goods directly from mills. But the process was intricate and being a jobber meant constantly roving for excess fabric and seconds. In sales, she could show fabric and work directly with the mills, even overseas. But it was a grueling business, too, and the material she had worked with wasn't for women's apparel. In the end, she consoled herself that at least she'd gotten Peter out of the deal.

She grinned. "You liked that nubby gay upholstery I picked for the office chairs."

"And just in time for the annual dinner that year."

He held her hand to his chest. In his eyes, she saw a flicker and had the sudden sensation that the rock under them had cracked loose from the rest and gone adrift.

He pressed her hand with his. "My father didn't leave England just because of my mother."

"I figured they came for a better life." Like everybody else.

"That's the party line, isn't it?" His smile was quick and gone. "My father was keen, well-educated and, at the time, well-liked. Then came this student, an undergrad who made accusations." He shook his head. "They were false but he spread his lies, and his family backed him. The kid wasn't doing well. Lazy, my father said. And Dad wasn't the type to let indolence slide. He told the kid he wouldn't pass him, that he could do better. And he wouldn't be doing anyone any favors letting him go on. The boy turned around and said my father—" He shook his head. "It didn't matter the kid was lying. It was the kind of accusation that sticks."

He held her hand tighter. "My parents left the country. Though I think later my father regretted not staying to fight the charge. But by then any family support he might have had was gone. Only one cousin was sympathetic. But even he advised Dad to leave and not look back. Lot's wife and all." He looked at her. "Sometimes I think my coming into my parents' lives was an intrusion, almost like a reminder of that other boy."

She felt herself stiffen.

He smiled softly. "I've shocked you."

"No, it's—I'm just—this is the first time you've said anything."

"And, of course, the timing is wrong." He looked away. "I shouldn't have mentioned it."

"No, it's fine, it's—what made you decide to tell me?"

She hated how she sounded in asking, the hesitancy, the obligatory tone in the question. But she couldn't help the feeling of overload, with Raf and Fiber, her father. And she'd never seen insecurity in Peter before, vulnerability, really. He had always been self-controlled, even-keeled. But as he'd said just this morning, feeling something, even vulnerable, didn't necessarily equal weakness. She wanted to believe him. And she did, in theory. It was the practice of human relationships in daily life that was giving her trouble.

He looked at her, the blue gray of the sea in his eyes. "I never said anything before because you were never leaving before. I guess … I thought you'd always be here." His smile was wistful. "That's not fair, is it? I know the people we love can't always stick around." He looked down along at the rocks. "What bothers me is when they don't seem to want to."

He was recalling first wife, she knew, maybe Isobel, too. Both his wife and his mother had succumbed to illnesses they'd been unable fight. Isobel to sepsis, a complication from multiple sclerosis, Maddie to ovarian cancer, uncovered during testing to learn why she had such trouble carrying a pregnancy to term.

"After Maddie and your mom, you feel I'm leaving you, too?"

He shrugged, his shoulders set.

"This departure is temporary. I am coming back."

He looked at her. "What if we set a date now, before you leave?"

"You mean a wedding date?"

There was a sort of flame in his eyes, a fire and a hunger.

"But you haven't really asked—"

"I wanted to. But I wanted to give you time, after the ring. But would you? I mean, we could go to Italy for the honeymoon. I could meet your family—" He paused, smiling. "I'm getting a little ahead of us."

She grinned weakly. "Just a little."

"Then let's just pick a date, put a stake in the ground. March maybe. It's spring, my birthday—"

March was just six months away, hardly enough time to plan. Though given his enthusiasm and ready suggestion, she couldn't help wondering if he'd had this in mind when he gave her the diamond.

He put his arms around her. "Listen, I'm not trying to pressure you, really. It's just, we've talked about your moving in, but it's a long commute from here to the city. And a new living space would be better anyway, a place that's yours and mine. We could rent the cottage, use the income for mortgage payments." His unfeigned eagerness belied his thirty-eight years.

She took a breath. "March 30," she said, as a gust carried the words away.

He leaned closer. "What?"

"Let's set March 30 as the date, after your birthday but still spring—St Peter's Day."

"St. Peter has a day?"

She squeezed his hand. "Listen, if you want to be part of an Italian family you need to know, it's the saint's day that matters, not the birthdate. March 30 is San Pietro Regalado."

If she remembered correctly, the saint's name was Spanish, not Italian, and *regalado* could mean anything from gift to theft. She had heard of this particular cleric from a colleague at Tessero who had used each day of the year as an excuse to proffer gifts to prospective clients.

"Sounds perfect." He pulled at her collar. "Why didn't you wear the new scarf? It would have made a good buffer."

"That piece is for work, not wearing." She drew nearer. "Now let's decide when to leave for the airport."

Chapter 7

"You're checked in?" Peter asked, sunlight streaming in behind him through the windows of Logan's international flight area.

"All set." In the comparative calm of Sunday afternoon, the antsy feeling in her gut had intensified. "If you don't want to wait—"

"Don't you want me to?" He looked at her, in his eyes a mix of uncertainty and caution.

"No, I mean, yes, of course. It's just—there isn't much to do." She looked around the waiting area. "And no comfortable place to sit."

"We could grab a bite," He reached in the pocket of his gray flannel trousers. "Are you hungry?"

"Not really." She couldn't bear being confined between fast food and forced stillness.

He nodded at her bag. "You have the scarf?"

"Right here." She patted the carryall. She had the padded pouch tucked in the center compartment with her father's letter, though it was hard to say why, since he seemed to have nothing of import to say.

A buzzing emanated from the breast pocket of Peter's blazer. He took out his cell and glanced at the display. "It's work. Do you mind?"

"Go ahead." She took the cell from her bag. "I'll check email."

"I don't understand," he said moving away a few steps. "We confirmed the date three months ago—and paid the deposit." He tapped her on the shoulder and shook his head. "I'm at Logan. Gia's leaving for Italy."

She dropped the cell back in her bag. "Something with the caterer?"

He pressed mute. "They installed a new booking system and lost the dinner reservation. Now they're saying Thursday won't work. Olivia wants me to make a few calls, sort things out."

She nodded at his phone. "Then you should go. The flight doesn't leave for an hour. I could use the time to prepare."

"I don't want to just leave." His phone buzzed again.

She put her hand on his arm. "Go help Olivia. I'll be fine."

He pressed his palm to her cheek and unmuted the call. "Liv? Give me twenty and pull up the payment records." He slipped the phone back in his pocket. "I'm really sorry."

"Don't be, you're needed there."

He shook his head, the blue eyes like slate. "I'm the glue that holds everything together—where's the fun in that?"

"Then teach Olivia what you know so she'll gain confidence." She hitched her bag up on her shoulder. "That way if you decide to sell or take a backseat she can do more, be more valuable, and you can ease your way out."

He put his arms around her. "You'll call when you get there?"

"Of course," she said with a grin. "They've had cell service for a while." The image came to mind of years before and a trim man in a fitted, gray summer-weight suit dashing down Via Veneto, flip phone pressed to his ear.

He drew her close. "Sure you don't need anything?"

"Really, I'm set. And tell Olivia she's lucky to have someone she can count on." She touched the small scar. "Let me know how the fundraiser goes."

He held her tight then let her go and touched his fingertips to her lips. "See you," he said softly.

She would only be gone a week, not even, she reminded herself as she watched him turn and walk down the terminal and under the flag through the exit.

Down the corridor of memory she heard her mother calling . . .

She was eight years old and elated over the green matelassé spring jacket with three-quarter sleeves she had badgered her mother to make from a remnant.

"Come, Gia, we'll miss the flight," Antonia admonished, grabbing her arm. "What's wrong with you, anyway? No one will wait for you if you don't keep up."

An elderly American couple waiting on line had turned with a scowl as if to say, "You're the mother. Why don't you slow down? Can't you see she's only a child?"

Where was her father at that moment? In the men's room, or the duty free buying a pouch of Amphora? Or was it Borkum Riff tobacco he favored then?

The memory of her return from Italy alone with her mother eight years later remained a blur. Except for the perpetual chill that had arrived with the rains and stayed the whole of winter despite the blue angora cardigan with pearl buttons she wore every day for months.

She looked around for a leaderboard. There must be one somewhere showing departures. She walked to the end of the terminal and saw the Lufthansa flight listed on-time. She went through to the gate and down toward an empty seat near the wall.

She stepped over a backpacker in a Rasta cap zonked out on a rolled-up sleeping bag and took out her cell. Too keyed-up to plan the meeting with Martell, she could only hope her work in design school and at Tessero would serve her well despite her exit from both.

"I'm not surprised," Don Roccia said when she told him in his office at Boston School of Design that Tessero was over. "But I think the fabric shop is a mistake. In a few years, the mom and pops will be out of business, and I can't see you with a chain. And don't you want more experience before making a change?"

"I have experience," she answered. In some ways, anyhow.

Roccia had been her professor and advisor while in design school, and she still went to him for advice. But she could see he had no intention of conceding that he might have at least tried to step in when her classmate at BSoD used her fabric design to win a competition sponsored by a Dutch energy firm expanding its offices in Europe.

"And experience is a good teacher," she added to fill the void. "Maybe better than most."

She could tell by the narrowing of the almond-shaped eyes the remark had stung. Roccia didn't just pride himself on his instruction but on his integrity and on his fairness in every step of the design process. And if he warned his students once, he warned them a dozen times not to skip a step.

"To learn textile design you must understand fabric. To understand fabric you must understand yarn and fibers. And to design, you must learn to weave," he repeated ad nauseum.

After this, he avowed, came understanding and interpreting woven structures. But for all his ability, and he had more than most in the Northeast, he hadn't been such a good example. Was it this that prompted him to keep encouraging her to finish school? Guilt wasn't a great motivator, but if it had yielded the meeting with James Martell, it was worth it.

Over the loudspeaker came the call for Lufthansa boarding all rows. She shouldered the carryall and trailed the herd of economy passengers through the check-in and down the jetway.

She found her place two-thirds of the way aft, in the middle row of noble-looking seats in blue and gold. Stepping quickly over an older couple, she stowed her bag under the seat in front. Across the aisle, a flight attendant in a navy uniform and modified pillbox hat paused to help a middle-aged man who flashed her an indulgent smile.

She adjusted the backrest and reached in the center compartment of her bag for a piece of gum. She unstuck the pack from the pouch that held the scarf and took out the envelope. Had she missed something in her father's letter after all? Maybe it was buried in the local news or family update, the description of daily life, which in her memory had taken on the grainy quality of a 1920s silent film. Calling for attention, the flight attendants explained the safety procedures to follow in case of emergency. Fastening her seatbelt, she felt a prickling nervous excitement as she unfolded the letter on her lap.

Chapter 8

Late Sunday night, Giovanni lay in bed beside Stella watching one of those outrageous talent shows that had her laughing like a red-haired hyena. When she was excited or in a fit of anticipation, such exhibitions freed her nervous energy and channeled it into the activity at hand, the livelier and more inane the better. His nerves, on the other hand, had wound him so tight his imaginings twisted around and around in his head until they spiraled down into thoughts of his letter to Gia as if it were still before him.

Cara Gia:

I hope as always that this finds you well and making a life for yourself in the little place on Fleet. It was probably for the best your mother held onto the co-op and didn't saddle you with a house. Though by now you must have security of your own and even a man in your life. Someone trustworthy, I hope, who will care for you and maybe give you a home and *bambini,* though it is hard to imagine you with children tripping your feet. You will forgive, I hope, this lack of vision in an aging fellow who no longer sees so much of the world.

As I have told you perhaps too often, our life is small here in the province, where the summer heat and drought have driven the villagers to the shore and shriveled the poppies in the fields. Even the banks of Cesano look like the ribs of a skeleton, and the quail peeping out from the underbrush can barely wet their feathers. Castel Barberini is also sparse, though of people, and closed its few renovated rooms to tourists. Perhaps this is just as well since old Alberto, the caretaker, has such arthritis in his hip he has trouble walking more than a few paces.

On the lighter side of our lives here, last month's *salsicciata* was a success, with many visitors coming to the festival to gorge themselves on sausage. You should have seen one fat old German sweating and eating himself into an early grave, though in reality it was not such an attractive sight.

Otherwise, we are generally well, Stella and the boys and I. Massimo is in Rome working as an engineer. Paolo graduated with a degree in architecture from Milan Polytechnic. He's a dreamer, that one, drawing idealistic renderings for whatever clients he can get wherever he can get them even if it means more than a few nights on Max's couch. Neither of the boys calls or visits often now, though perhaps this is just as well, too, since Stella and I have reached a stage of life where we find that no news is generally better. These days we content ourselves with being all together at the holidays. After all, Max and Paolo have their own lives, as they are fond of reminding us.

I suppose it is time now to close but not before telling you I think of you daily and long always for the best for you, and that I hope you enjoy the little gift.

Un'abbraccio forte,

Babbo

He had revised and revised the letter, cutting it back and back so often he could summon it to mind as if it were still in composition. Yet, even after the varied drafts, he had been plagued with doubt. He hadn't expressly asked Gia to visit this time but had proffered the invitation in a different form. And if there was a God in heaven, a form that would prove more alluring.

Had she noticed the scarf hadn't been purchased, that the fabric hadn't been created on a high-speed loom? If she noticed all this, she might realize the time he had taken, that others had taken, too. But he mustn't put too much hope yet in how their lives might be mended.

And what was her life like now, anyway? Each time he wrote, and often in his imagination, he saw the red brick buildings on the narrow North End streets wound tight as a skein of yarn, the festivals on the saints' days and the little North Square in the purple flowers during summer, the grass poking up through the cobbles he had trod from early morning to late evening, going from one tailor shop and men's store to another to earn a living wage.

Each time he ventured to whatever shop had hired him, or to the home of a patron to fit a jacket or hem a pair of pants, he had felt a longing for a place of his own that grew more incisive with every passing season so that he could barely stand it in a place so deep he might have said it was his heart but knew on instinct it was his soul.

One day he finally summoned the temerity to poke his head into a shop near Haymarket that had been around since Moses to inquire whether the owner might one day sell. Initially, the man was noncommittal, saying he might be willing if Giovanni would come a few days a week to prove he not only knew how to tailor but also how to fit garments—men's and women's—how to content the customers and keep the shop's good name.

"Of course," he had responded, lunging inwardly at the longing that pricked him at unexpected moments like a pin.

"You do seem a serious fellow," the old shop owner said on seeing that Giovanni was wholehearted in his response. "I may even put the place up for sale before the year is done and you can buy me out."

It was then that the very depths of hell had erupted. How in God's name had Antonia gotten wind of his interest?

He looked at Stella who was still staring at the television as though she might climb into it. He shook his head. Grown people dressed as zoo animals—that one in particular with a lion's mane. The fool. His costume didn't even fit properly.

He stared at the assorted buffoons. Antonia, he eventually learned, had found out about his interest through the gossip of another seamstress. He certainly hadn't let it slip, knowing only too well what would happen.

"Don't even breathe a thought of buying that place," Antonia had leveled at him, her short curly black hair bristling, slender frame taut as a wire. "Not after that first fiasco. *Dio,* Giovanni, what were you thinking? The place was twice what we could handle. Well, there will be no more of that."

He still felt the pang of that first failure as if it were happening all over again. They had almost gone bankrupt and became, as Antonia framed it, a laughingstock.

"Think of your daughter, if you can't think of anyone else," she said when she saw he was still silent about the prospect of buying another place. This while Gia sat placidly watching Saturday morning cartoons, preferring Looney Tunes to the more popular purple dinosaur.

He glanced at his daughter, who on mention of her name had looked questioningly in his direction. He smiled weakly, and she smiled in return, guileless and completely unaware, while behind her Bugs Bunny again outwitted a lesser compatriot.

"It's not as bad as all that, Toni," he answered, gaining sustenance from his daughter's lopsided grin.

"Not as bad as all that—"

Involuntarily, he covered his ears to block the now silent tirade in his head, though the visual remained.

Stella turned. "What, is the TV too loud?"

He looked at her, keenly aware that it was now she now sat beside him. He smiled with relief at her lack of concern for certain things he preferred to keep in the past.

She shook her head. "You're worried about the visit."

He wanted to embrace her for making it safe to feel the old pain, see the memories and feel the attendant paroxysms that still rippled jarringly through him.

"I was just wondering if I did the right thing," he said. "Encouraging her to come."

"You wonder if you've done right? She's the one who should wonder, all these years and nary a word."

He would have accepted his wife's support with glee, except that in truth he hadn't told her exactly why he had sent the scarf. How he had worked to have it made for Gia's coloring, her partiality for autumn and the academic year, long as she liked the course of study. For it was in autumn that things had gone so very wrong.

"You know after Antonia died I stopped calling."

"And who could blame you?" Stella asserted. She muted the television. "It's not as if anyone over there ever called you."

He smiled again, weakly. "I never visited."

"Did anyone invite you?"

Antonia had wanted never to see him again, had threatened him within an inch of his miserable life with a custody suit if he returned. But Gia had asked once, or started to, when he would come back, hinting in her own way that she still wanted him in her life. He could still hear Antonia in the background.

"Give me the goddamn phone," she charged. Then click. The connection was severed.

After that, whenever he called, his daughter was never the one to answer. A few times he heard her voice in the background. Then Antonia warned him not to call again. The prospect of the courts again.

"Well, did they, ever invite you?" Stella poked his side with her elbow, the ends of her hair in the damp night air standing out as if electrified so that he felt like laughing. Almost. But this sort of relief was too free, too easy. Even if her thought did reflect his.

He took her hand. "I was angry," he said, rubbing the blue vein that slid over the bone from her forefinger. So angry. Angry and afraid. But he had intended to go back, at some point. If only for Gia. "I did intend to return, you know."

She stared in surprise. "I thought you said you never wanted to go back while that *strega* was alive. And then not after because your daughter wouldn't have you."

"Well, maybe I didn't *want* to." He steadied himself against the headboard. "But I intended to." Or so he told himself. His mistake was not returning immediately. "I planned to open a shop here, make a go of it then return and say, 'Ha! You were wrong, *cara* Toni. You called me a failure, but you were wrong.'" He looked at Stella's wide-set eyes the color of hazelnuts. "As we know, I didn't quite make it." A recollection of the three strikes rule of American baseball came to mind.

Stella slid nearer. "I don't know how they compute failure in America. But to me, the real shortcoming is not standing by someone you say you love." She peered at him with heavy eyelids. "I know maybe you wouldn't have gone back even if that woman asked. But what about Gia, what if she asked?"

He brushed at the dampness on his cheek with the back of his hand. "I don't ... To be honest, I'm not sure." At the time, he had felt an odd sense of reprieve that no one had come right out an asked him to visit. Or worse, ordered him to. But his freedom had come at such a cost that now with his daughter's impending visit, he wondered if the comparatively brief feeling of amnesty had been worth it.

Stella put her hand on his arm. "Some questions, they're impossible to answer. We can only hope now that that woman didn't raise Gia to follow in her footsteps."

Giovanni ran the edge of the sheet over his face. "Don't talk so. Gia isn't like her mother." Not that way, anyhow. At least, he hoped not.

Stella softened. "Good. Because if your daughter takes more after you in this way, the two of you could have a chance."

He brightened. "This is my hope."

This was partly why he had written to Gia of the beauty he still found here, the patchwork hills and winding country lanes. The lone olive tree in the field on the road out of the village to the hill country whose leaves bent back to silver in the wind. The azure of the Adriatic, the silhouette of the Apennines in summer. And there was still family, her family, theirs. These were the compass points that guided him. And if he were honest, he must admit that he still hoped that in his daughter's heart there was still a soft spot, too, for this place, if not for him.

He smoothed the few strands of graying hair around his head. *Dio,* what would she think when she saw him? And how would she look? He hadn't a recent picture of her, nor she of him, not one.

Chapter 9

Gia closed the file with the designs for a new swing dress and powered off the laptop, now low on battery life. The sketches were for a natty piece with full sleeves and a flare skirt to showcase the lightness and movement of the new fabric. She needed distance before choosing from among the varied sleeve styles and lengths. If she could get hold of enough material in time, she might find a way to make the dress and wear it so that Martell would see the material on a live model.

Looking across the center aisle and out the window, she saw the Airbus approaching the runways of Malpensa. A ripple of anxiety and nausea filtered through the fatigue. She gripped the padded armrest. Maybe it had been a mistake not to take another Dramamine.

With a whirr and a thud, the landing gear lowered. The aircraft dropped nearer the ground. As they approached the tarmac, she felt another dip and heard the roar of the engines, the rumbling strain of controlled acceleration as the wheels slammed the tarmac and bounced. The plane leveled, then slowed to a long rolling stop near the end of the airstrip to the sound of clapping, albeit with little enthusiasm.

She peered out the bright cabin window at the chain of baggage carts and ground crew already nearly the aircraft like columns of ants. Inside the plane, the passengers ignored the blinking overhead caution signs and unbuckled their seatbelts.

"Velcome to Milan," the flight attendant announced in a guttural tone.

A middle-aged woman with straw-colored hair gave a tsk of discontentment, silver and gold bangles jingling on thick wrists. The flight had been bumpy, she complained in a flat Milanese accent, not to mention downright unsettling with those cabin lights flickering off and on. What was wrong with the Germans, anyway, she asked of everyone and no one in particular. All that engineering knowhow and they still couldn't manage a better flight?

Welcome to Italy, Gia thought.

She stretched her legs and waited for the rows ahead to empty then reached under the seat in front and pulled out her bag. As the older couple beside her rose, she got up and filed out past the stilted farewells of the cabin crew to the exit.

Shielding her eyes from the jetway glare, she followed the human tide to a glistening glass and metal exoskeleton that hovered over a shimmering open space like the showroom of a Maserati dealership. Drawn in the wake of those in front, she followed the signs and yellow caution arrows to customs. Finally, she thought, a chance to use the Italian passport she'd gotten after having been granted dual citizenship.

"Always stay close to your roots," her mother had exhorted. "You may want to go over once in a while, just for yourself. Who cares about that swine?"

The lower-level baggage area had two active carousels, the last marked for her flight. She went to the far end of the area, away from the other passengers. After the same assortment of luggage circled the conveyor belt, a new selection dumped out, among them her black suitcase, still sporting the giant red plasticized Christmas bow she hadn't had the heart to tear off after her mother died.

"Don't you dare take off that ribbon," Antonia said when they left Italy for the last time, over Gia's protests that the bow was a glaring eyesore. "I said leave the damn thing," Antonia warned as Gia started to yank it. "All those other black bags—how else can we tell what's ours?"

She maneuvered toward the conveyor and planted her foot on the carousel. Hauling the suitcase off the conveyor, she thumped the case onto the terrazzo in front of two men in matching black leather shoulder bags. The pair glared at her as if she'd dinged their dining room floor. She regarded them briefly then nodded at the shorter man with bleached blond bangs. The ribbed collar and cuffs of his leather bomber jacket were maroon, not the red of the designer original.

She smiled sweetly. "You realize that's a knockoff," she said in practiced Italian.

The man's mouth gaped. He must know the piece wasn't designer, but to have it announced by someone he had clearly taken for a foreigner wouldn't soon be forgotten. His mate scowled at her as if she were something to be scraped off his Bruno Magli's. Holding his gaze, she arched an eyebrow.

He turned and lambasted his companion. "Didn't I tell you not to buy that cheap piece of crap? Now you wear the thing in public and embarrass yourself. Will you never learn?"

She turned to hide a smile and went to the exit, the verbal exchanges of *stronzo* echoing behind her. She rolled her bag to the escalator, then for what felt like miles along the upper level. Through the surrounding windows a pale blue ring of alpine peaks etched the distance a chalk outline in the distance. What would it be like to see more of the white-capped summits and Maggiore, which locals avowed was less of a tourist trap than Lake Como? But each day here was numbered and fleeting, with zero time to think of anything but one thing. Tightening the strap on her bag, she tugged her suitcase to the bus ticket window then out to the terminal.

At the front of the center median, an autobus was boarding passengers for Milano Centrale. She hurried down the walkway.

"Attenti," shouted a baggage handler who motioned her away from oncoming traffic and over to where he stood.

She rolled her suitcase down the curb and started to lift it.

"We don't do," the handler said in English, waggling his forefinger. The driver standing beside him looked down the sidewalk for other passengers.

"Sorry," she replied. "This bus goes to Milano Centrale?" Even with the placard over the bus's front window, one could never be sure.

The handler nodded and tossed her bag into the bowels of the coach.

She gave her ticket to the driver and went up the steps. Inside, she found an empty row of seats near the front, climbed in by the window and propped her bag between her torso and the glass The smell of cleaning fluid rose from the scratchy blue seat cover. She felt a spurt of panic. She did still have the scarf, didn't she?

She glanced furtively at the mostly empty seats and unzipped the center compartment of her bag. Peeling back the flap of the bubble pack, she slid her hand inside. The material felt thin, flimsy. She opened the pouch and peeked in. The scarf seemed to have shrunk. Did the material fail to hold its form when folded?

Wiping her fingers on her shirt, she carefully removed the piece. The sprightly, unwrinkled fabric had held its shape. Blocking the aisle with her shoulder, she held the material to the window. The russet and amber paisley, agleam in the center with yellow gold, had a rich luster even in the diffused light that filtered through the tinted glass. With her fingertips, she smoothed the fabric and found it still soft to the touch. She glanced around again then slipped the piece back in the pouch and wedged the bag between her and the window.

The bus driver came up the steps and looked down the rows of seats, made a note in his pad and taking his place at the wheel put the vehicle in gear. She stared out the window at the crush of Monday morning traffic as they roared out onto the autostrada. How strange it was that it didn't seem strange to be here, she thought. But, then, the anonymous highway that stretched out before them with speeding lorries and autos could have been almost anywhere, until the sign for Milan city center.

She pressed her back against the seat. After sixteen years, she was here, back again to where life had begun and ended in a place that whether she liked it or not was still within her.

As they neared Milan center, the bus turned onto the main boulevard then around the back of the train station. The day after tomorrow she would leave again, for the March region. But that was tomorrow. Today she was here, for a pre-show. She got up and followed the other passengers down the autobus steps to the curb.

Despite seemingly endless renovations, the Milan Train Station in the Piazza Duca d'Aosta retained its imposing stone façade, the muscular architecture still evoking Mussolini's favored style.

"Fascist dictator," her mother had called him. She had also pronounced him a liar and a closeted gay who let himself be "led around by the nose by that damn Itler," from whose name she perpetually dropped the H.

"Where do you get your information, Toni?" her father queried.

"Do you deny that Mussolini was as weak as a woman when it came to the Germans?" Antonia had accused during a family debate over why the country was still beleaguered by a revolving door of ineffectual leaders.

"More than one reason, I suppose," her father had replied before getting up from the lunch table and going into the bedroom to nap.

The white stone exterior and red shutters of the Excelsior Hotel across the boulevard still gave the impression of an embassy, a place of neutrality, safety. Like the pull of an outgoing tide, she felt the old longing to stop and rest, if only for a night.

"What are you about that you think we could afford such a thing?" her mother declared when she had expressed this desire. "We'll be lucky to keep a roof over our heads when we go back. Now stop dragging your backside and come along with that bag."

At this, Gia had turned her suitcase over on its wheels and dragged it, canvas side under, down the station steps. At the bottom, Antonia had stood waiting, ostensibly to recompense her bad behavior. Gia paused halfway.

"Have it your way, little girl. Ruin the last decent suitcase you're likely to have," Antonia asserted, defaulting on instinct to aim an arrow of guilt that usually found its mark.

She went past the Excelsior and down the thoroughfare. On this side of the boulevard, people stood queuing for taxis in a line that stretched around a grass-lined square. She turned and spotted a cab coming in from a side road. It stopped at the light.

"*Tassi!*" she called out.

The cabbie looked out, nodded then popped the trunk. Dragging the suitcase behind her, she rushed to the curb. Those waiting in line nearest the roadway started yelling. She rolled the suitcase to the back of the cab, hoisted it into the open trunk and slammed the lid. Hurrying to the passenger door, she got in the backseat.

"Eurotel Rho, please."

The cabbie nodded in the rearview and turned into traffic.

She ducked down in the seat as he zoomed past the square and the queue of waiting customers, some waving and yelling.

"Busy with Fashion Week?" she asked.

The driver shrugged. "Same as usual this time of year," he said, cutting off a cyclist who rode up onto the sidewalk to avoid being hit.

They weaved down the busy thoroughfare past elegant second-story flats with Palladian windows and French doors that opened onto wrought iron balconies with corpulent earthenware pots of red geraniums. The heart of the city, undergoing renovation, was flanked by scaffolds.

The cab rounded a corner in front of the massive fountain of Castello Sforzesco, the fifteenth-century fortification crisp-edged under an enameled vault of cloudless blue. Her breath escaped in a shudder. How beautiful a citadel could be when it carried a rich history into the present day.

The cab wound along the roundabout to the far side of the fairgrounds and stopped. She glanced up at the hotel entrance and grabbed her purse. The cabbie opened the door, went around to the trunk and set the suitcase on the sidewalk. She took the fare plus five euros from her wallet.

He stared at her momentarily then reached for the case to help her to the hotel door.

"No, *grazie,*" she said. "It's all right, really. I can get it. I'm late for a meeting," she added to explain her haste.

As the cabbie went back around to the driver's side, she turned and took her things inside the hotel to the concierge desk. A slender woman with tawny hair stood at the marble counter wearing a lilac angora sweater, creamy wool crepe peg trousers and patent leather stilettos in nearly the same cream shade.

"Falcini, Gia," she said. "I have a reservation."

The woman glanced at the computer screen, amber eyes swathed in shimmery lilac shadow a shade lighter than her sweater. "Room two-thirteen," she said in perfect English. "The porter will bring up your bag."

Chapter 10

After a quick shower, she changed into a pair of cropped straight-leg, stretch-cotton pants in black and a long-sleeved men's Henley in a rich cognac shade that set off her hair. She had been teased in design school for mixing women's clothing with men's, but who cared? What mattered was comfort and clothing that was functional and held its shape without pilling. She fluffed her fine straight hair in the mirror. She really did need to touch up the roots, maybe get a trim. She stood back. Normally, she would wear a jacket, but the early afternoon weather was fine and warm with no hint of rain. She reached for her bag then went down in the elevator to the hotel lobby.

She took a cab to Via Pontaccio, near the Pinacoteca di Brera, home to the country's most elite cultural, science and art institutions, including the Academy of Fine Arts and the Brera Gallery. She paid the cabbie and hurried into a lower-level event space in the former galleria whose inner portico was cleft in two by a makeshift runway. Showing the ticket from Don Roccia, she found an empty seat beside an older man sporting an immaculately groomed goatee, a black dress shirt and knobby knit trousers in a smoky shade of gray tweed.

The shared mini-show featured two of Roccia's former students, new designers who hadn't quite made it to Fashion Week and whose names she didn't recognize. She put her bag down in front of her and took out her sketchbook for notes. She moved the scarf sideways so that the loosely knotted section sat on her lower shoulder.

The houselights went down. Tinny notes of music twanged from slim black speakers and echoed through the gallery. Spotlights like lasers shown on the first bladelike body undulating up the catwalk amid the murmur of the small but attentive crowd. She sat up in the padded folding chair. If the rest of the trip was this intriguing, it might not be so bad.

The first of the two collections featured shimmery georgette, voile and organza fabrics that flickered with iridescence at the tip of a collar, the cuff of a sleeve—the glitter an homage to seventies glam rock. Cloudlike dresses in varied lengths drifted past in metallic shades of silver, platinum, pewter and gold, copper, nickel, cobalt and bronze. The last wraithlike figure moved down the platform in a sheer, silvery striped voile blouson shirtdress gathered at the waist with a wide matching belt. Pausing briefly before the onlookers, the model spun once then moved off.

She glanced down at the empty sketchbook, within her a growing sentiment she hated to acknowledge. The dresses, with their ethereal colors and styles, were captivating and refined. But how could a woman with little time, energy and budget buy and care for a closet full of such impractical clothing? And why should she, when the designs' lack of utility implicitly denigrated her working lifestyle?

Here she agreed with her mother. A woman who out of next to no fabric could make a pair of shorts and top that had outlasted her daughter's adolescence. "The clothes need to do what you tell them, not the other way around," Antonia had affirmed.

She reached down and took a pencil from her bag. Too bad she had arrived too late for the textile shows. How she would have loved to discover fabrics that held at least some reverence for the composition of daily life—the warp and weft of family, the inspiration of creativity.

The music for the second collection shifted to the soothing sunny sounds of Trinidadian steel drums. The arm of the man beside her pressed against hers. She leaned forward. A dark angular model with slanted cheekbones sauntered past on legs like stilts. The semi-sheer blouse in saturated midnight blue billowed at her torso, the lightweight woven trousers in a soft pumpkin shade were fitted at the high waist, softening the curved hips and accentuating the small midsection with a short sash in the same shade of blue as the blouse.

She leaned around the woman in front of her. The ensemble slacks were perfectly tailored, escaping the masculine to respect the female form, the wide trouser leg slightly more tapered than the full palazzo breadth of seasons past. The next model wore an A-line skirt of buttery woven fabric and a boat neck top in midnight blue that emphasized her straight slender shoulders. The slim figure that followed sported a pencil leg pant in midnight blue with a chiffon blouse in canary yellow. A dark-skinned blonde with a childlike face flounced down the walk in a short, sleeveless canary yellow dress fitted at the bodice, flared from the waist, the dress's neckline and hemline bordered in ribbons of navy and cream.

Even as she scrambled to take notes she could guess the reviewers' likely verdict of the collection—wearable. Given the altitude to which the designers aspired, such a pronouncement was deadly. Unfortunate, she thought, as the last model walked the runway in a short woven skirt in midnight blue and tailored voile blouse. For women's wear, the label of wearable seemed the best of all attributes.

For the finale, the designers of both collections took their bows, their respective models lined up on either side. She looked out at the stark but still hypnotic catwalk as the music faded, replaced by the murmur of observers as they rose to exit.

Her cell emitted a majestic tune. She reached down and looked at the display. Oh, dear. She pressed the icon. "Peter, I'm so sorry."

"I was worried."

"I know. Sorry. I was late to the preshow. Everything okay?"

"Everything's fine here. Everything okay there?"

"Well, it's Italy so you know …" She smiled. "Yes, everything's fine."

The man beside her with the goatee turned and stared. Sorry, she mouthed then instantly felt annoyed. The show was over. Who cared about phone calls now? The man stared at her neck.

"Listen, Peter, I'm just finishing a few notes. Let me reach out with video when I get back to the hotel."

"Sounds good, now that I've heard your voice."

She could hear the smile in his tone and the relief. "It's good to hear you, too, really good. Talk soon." She pressed the red button and dropped the phone in her bag.

She looked at the man with the goatee, who still stared at her neck. "Sorry. My fiancé."

He nodded. *"Signorina,"* he pronounced in a guttural tone.

Northern Italy, she thought, German border.

He gazed at her neck. "Interesting accessory, well cut on the bias. It hides quite nicely your lower shoulder."

Her hand went to her neck. God, who was this person? She felt her face color. "Well, it must not hide it that skillfully if you can tell."

"I am head *stilista* for Trentino Alta Moda, a design house up north," said the man with a half-smile. "It is my business to tell such things."

He moved closer. "May I?" He fingered the rolled hem of the scarf where it draped on her right. "Intriguing fibers, supple hand. Unusual dye cast. Quite original, overall. Someone knows material." He stood back and gazed at her face. "And understands your coloring. It wouldn't be your work, by chance?"

Unnerved, she shook her head. "I'm in distribution. The fabric is ... new."

The man gave her a quick once-over. "Hmm, I can see. It has a classic quality, protective in a way. Have you family in the business?"

"My father," she said. "A tailor, down in the Marche region."

"A good region for fish." The man produced a black suede clutch and took out a business card. "Erno Prati, perhaps we can chat sometime."

"Yes, sure." She slipped the card in her bag.

"Look us up if you come north. Trento is breathtaking in autumn."

"Yes, thank you, I will."

She watched him walk purposefully away down the center aisle to the exit, the knobby trousers emphasizing heavy thighs. She waited until after he exited the space then followed, anxious to get back to the hotel for a call and good night's rest, if she could manage it.

Chapter 11

She rolled her suitcase quickly up the stone steps of the Milan train station, whose high walls and vaulted ceiling with skylights made the space appear larger and grander than she recalled. She strode down the great hall under chandeliers that hung like censers, past banners depicting Fashion Week exhibits, most of which would be over by the time she returned. Dodging one clot of travelers then another, she rushed past the varied shops and kiosks to a ticket window.

"One-way to Marotta, *per favore.*" Breathing hard, she handed over the requisite euros. "The Eurostar leaving at eleven thirty-five—it arrives in Marotta around three-fifteen, correct?"

The agent nodded. "Change trains in Rimini to arrive Marotta fifteen-sixteen."

"Grazie," she said, struck afresh by the continued use of military time.

She stuffed the ticket in the side pocket of her bag. Turning her suitcase, she queued in the slow-moving security line then rushed out to the platforms where the air was warm and thick with the odor of hydraulic fluid and diesel. The thud of her steps on the concrete slab reverberated up through the thin soles of her black ballet flats to her shins. She was still jetlagged after a light night's sleep disrupted by distorted fragments of the video call to Peter, the call to her father.

Talking to Peter, the call was so clear she might have been at Rhode Island School of Design for a seminar or in northern Connecticut visiting a mill. And she hadn't been surprised to learn that the caterer had come around on the fundraiser.

"It only took reminding them Litton Learning still has a name in this town," Peter asserted.

She smiled. He rarely reminded people who his family was so when he did they took notice. "Well, that's one caterer we're not using for our—next March."

She heard Peter's happy laugh and knew that even if she wasn't yet sure what to call it he was glad she had raised the subject.

The call to her father was another story. She had the distinct impression he wasn't alone in the room when he answered. His only comment on her confirmation of the arrival time was to say yes, of course, that was still fine.

Out from under the Milan station's great canopy sections of track splayed out to points south throughout the country and up into northern Europe. Quickening her pace, she raced toward the high-speed White Arrow, slowing only momentarily to view the shuttering schedule board, a throwback to when public restrooms were little more than latrines and yesterday's newspaper often did double duty as toilet paper.

"We're bringing the Kleenex," her mother said before one of the early visits. "I don't care how modern they say it is now, the toilets are still back in the war."

She hoisted her suitcase up the White Arrow's steps and into the railcar. Taking her ticket, she stowed her case in the nearest baggage area appointed for larger pieces and went down the aisle. The train was more commodious than the cattle cars she and her parents had taken in the searing heat of summers past, and air-conditioned besides.

She found her seat and leaned over to look out the window. The automated announcement noted the train's departure.

Behind the cement barricade running alongside the track were rows of low-rent buildings, their outer walls obscured by graffiti and overhung with enough wiring to light up Back Bay. If only the electrical at Fiber could be jury-rigged a little while longer. Above the tenements and interlacing grass courtyards, the skyline of the country's major industrial city was lower than she recalled.

Reaching in her bag, she took out her cell and tapped the display. Nothing. She tapped it again and shook it. Still nothing. She must have left it on last night. Rummaging in her bag, she found the adapter. When she went to plug it in, she realized it wouldn't work with European outlets, and Italy's were different again from those. Her first free minute she would have to buy one, since she would also need it for her laptop.

She glanced across the aisle as the cool, clean conjoining railcars glided out from the netting of inner tracks and picked up speed. She shoved the cell back in her bag and took out the Fashion Week schedule she printed before leaving.

"Permesso?" A young man wearing a tweed cap, a camera bag slung over his shoulder and a black portfolio under his arm, pointed to the opposite *sedile.*

She moved her legs. "Yes, *si.*"

He put the camera bag on the aisle seat and took the cap from his pale hair. He glanced at her brochure. "Speak English?"

"Yes," she answered.

"Bene, I am Marcello."

"I'm Gia."

He heaved an exasperated sigh. "Just finished sitting for law finals. What a pain in the ass." He took his seat as the train glided along the sunlit tracks. "Now I'm pursuing what I want—photography. Shooting stills for a film in Rome next month." He looked at her bag. "What is your work?"

"Textiles, fabric. Just got in from Boston. I'm back in Milan Friday for a show."

Down at the end of the row the conductor slid back the railcar door and moved up the aisle. She dug in the side pocket of her bag for her ticket.

"Are you at the Rho? I shot the Euroluce there. All that glare." Marcello shook his head. "A real ball buster to photograph." He reached under the flap of his portfolio and handed the conductor his ticket.

She handed the conductor hers.

He turned it over. "This is not stamped." He turned it again.

"I'm sorry?" she queried, staring.

Marcello pointed to the voucher. "You're to stamp the ticket before you board."

She stared at him. "Before you board?"

Seeing the conductor's scolding expression, she recalled an instance when her father had forgotten to stamp their tickets on leaving Naples. When the conductor called them to account for themselves, her mother heartily challenged this ridiculous rule and the man's questionable heritage until in exasperation he moved to the next row of passengers.

"Sorry," she said. "I didn't realize."

The conductor took a card from his shirt pocket. "There is a fine for this."

"Give the young lady some leeway, can't you, sir?" Marcello advocated in cultured Italian. "She has just arrived from the states."

"Actually, I'm a citizen." She took out the Italian passport. "I just … haven't been here in a while."

The conductor frowned at the maroon booklet and shook his head. "These days they give those to everybody." He slipped the warrant card back in his pocket and went to the next seat.

Marcello nodded. "You speak Italian well."

"Not as well as I'd like." She tucked the passport back in her bag.

He smiled. *"Perfetto,* then you speak Italian and I will speak English. We'll practice."

He was nice looking, Gia thought, as he talked of the prelaw education forced on him by his father, whose years of hard work he was glad beyond measure to be free of. She gazed at the straight blond hair, hazel eyes and fair complexion, none of which immediately conveyed Italian heritage. Yet, as he spoke, she heard the inculcated sense of entitlement, the great expectations that came from an inherited social position, if not always the money to back it, the smooth diction and absence of dialect the result of an urban education begun at an early age.

He was en route to celebrate his graduation with friends in Pesaro, he said, but hailed from Rimini, a provincial capital and resort city on the Adriatic whose hotspots she recalled as glittering garlands along the shoreline. He was smart, too. Young, but not unknowing. Yet, he was naïve in that way some young people had of warning themselves about the facts of life in advance of actual experience so as not to be surprised or pained when problems arose. But he would be surprised, she knew as she listened to him speak of his plans, his future and dreams, never mind his father's goals, which he dismissed in tone, if not words, and all with a certainty that allowed no space for disappointment.

Yet, he would be disappointed, somewhere along the way. Everyone was. What would he be like then, she wondered, after the inevitable shortfall in his aspirations to become a filmmaker, even if he eventually found success? Or was it an actor he wanted to be? Perhaps both. She tried to gain a sense of which was most important, if there was an order, as he spoke of Rome, the eternal city, and what sounded more and more like a dubious film. Would he become bitter when life failed conform to design, she mused, admiring the gold flecks in the amber eyes? Or would he retain his exuberance? She felt not, somehow, seeing his young beauty absent of acrimony. She hated to imagine what the unlined face would look like when life set in. His kind of edgy determination didn't usually rebound well. What would he do then in whatever relationship he found himself—succumb to disappointment, close himself off?

These were snares to which Peter hadn't yielded, she realized. And it was his openness that had drawn and held her. Though he, too, had a kind of naivety, a hopeful, fragile quality. As if in losing both parents, his wife, Mattie, and their unborn child he'd gotten the worst of life's disappointments out of the way. Though he hadn't said so, he really seemed to believe this. She sensed it in the way he pinned his hopefulness on their relationship, on her, with a cautious but persistent expectancy that was more burdensome for being unspoken.

Marcello was looking at her as if awaiting a response.

"I'm sorry?" she said in Italian, recalling then their pact to practice each other's language. "I missed that last part," she added in English.

"I asked if that is your only bag. If not, you'd better get your luggage. Rimini is the next stop."

She felt a jolt of what might have been enthusiasm, but like cold water on a live coal it was doused by apprehension.

"Oh, yes, I do have another bag."

She got up quickly to follow, but he was already walking down the aisle. She glanced back at the seats to make sure she hadn't left anything then turned and moved past the rows, hauled her case from the baggage section and went hurriedly to the exit.

"Remember," Marcello said over his shoulder as they descended the steps. "It's this side of the platform for Marotta." He turned. "What did you say you were planning to do when you arrive in Castel Barberini?"

Get out fast, she wanted to say. "I have work there," she answered.

"Ah, work. I thought a visit to such a remote village must be for family. What kind of work is there?"

"My father's a tailor," she said and saw the change in his expression. "We—I have to pick something up from him."

"A tailor, well, isn't that something?" He shook his head. "I didn't realize there were any working tailors left in Italy." He stepped out onto the platform and took a card from his bag. "My cell. Let's keep in touch."

"Yes, let's." Maneuvering her suitcase down the steps, she fished in the pocket of her bag for her business card and scribbled her cell under the name. "In case you're in Boston."

He nodded. *"Allora,* welcome again to Italy, *auguri."*

"You as well," she said, instinctually lapsing into formal Italian.

Tipping his cap, he strode down the platform, camera bag over his shoulder, portfolio under his arm. Whether or not he ever came to Boston, he seemed certain to at least make it to Rome.

She went and stood out on the open platform. The heat of the searching sun in the glare of late afternoon quickly sapped her dwindling energy. The cost of splendid autumnal weather and company but without opportunity for rest.

Down the curve of track in the distance came a line of matchbox cars. Now this was how she remembered the rail system—rusted blue carapaces with stuck-open windows clacking into the station and shuddering to stop without preamble of announcement or a conductor. She tugged her suitcase up the worn metal steps and down the aisle past faded seats the texture of indoor-outdoor carpet that smelled like a litter box.

She found an empty row, rolled her suitcase to the window and tucked her bag under her arm. Unable to keep her eyes open, she closed them against the brilliant sun. Across the dazzling panorama, a field of sunflowers glowed in the precise vibrant yellow shade of the neck scarves of the Lufthansa flight attendants …

When she opened her eyes, the train was slowing to a stop. *O, Dio,* had she missed Marotta? She leaned over the seat in front and tapped the shoulder of a young woman in a white cotton sweater with straight brown hair pulled back in a shiny black banana clip.

"Per favore, is this Marotta?"

"Yes," said the woman. She turned further around and looked closer. "You are French?"

"American, my parents are Italian. My father is from these parts."

The young woman stared a moment then looked out the window.

She sat back against the seat. Too much information, she thought, recalling with a prick of embarrassment that Italians preferred to initiate nosiness and the proffer of information rather than having either thrust upon them.

The train rolled toward a compact but bustling city center past a parking lot jammed with cars and motorbikes into a miniscule station whose barrel tile roof suddenly felt more familiar than her own brick co-op. She rose, hoisted the orange bag up onto her shoulder and maneuvered the suitcase down the gritty aisle into the vestibule. With an unsettling shot of excitement that made her legs quiver, she waited until the train came to a stop then bounced the suitcase down the steps to the platform.

The late afternoon sky was clear and bright, white gulls soaring in the distant blue. In the offshore breeze, she caught a whiff of brine that recalled a nearby flat her father had rented—where had it been? Al Cesano, she thought, recalling the noonday heat and her father and mother sitting across from each other at the lunch table.

"You remember the film, Antonia," her father was saying. *"Pane e Tulipani*—about that woman who started a new life? You said she had guts, remember?"

Her mother snapped to attention. "You bought that damn place in Marotta, didn't you?"

Gia slid closer to her Uncle Paolino, who sat stirring sugar into a thimble of espresso.

"No, Toni, I didn't," Giovanni answered.

Antonia glared at him. "So what are you telling me, then?"

"What the hell do you think I'm telling you?"

Her father wanted to return to Italy, everyone in his family knew it. Strangers in Rome knew it. In awe and the idealistic notion of paying homage to a legend, he had run down Via Barberini after Brioni himself for God's sake.

"What you must do here, Giovanni, is consider the future," Paolino had cut in. "The property is available at a decent price. It's on the main road with good access. And we all want you to stay, you know that. But what you must realize, Gi, is that there are a lot of tailors in Italy."

"Exactly," her mother said. "And they're artists."

Whether her father had been stung by this comment or not Gia had found it hard to tell. He turned to her.

"Beh, Gia, what do you think?"

She froze. It wasn't just that no one had asked her opinion on anything important before, though no one had. It was that her father seemed ready to pin his decision entirely on hers.

Staring down at her lap, she fingered the gold vermeil heart necklace, a gift from her boyfriend, that high school junior who aspired to become one of Boston's finest like his father.

"Well," she said slowly. "If I go to school here, I have to buy my own books from that cooperative in Fano," she said in the direction of her knees.

She had seen the massive bookstore in Fano exactly once, with a cousin who had navigated the dizzying, ceiling-high shelves with ease while she stood with her mouth gaping at more books than the Coop at Harvard Square.

She could feel her mother's disapproving glare from across the table. "And everybody keeps saying the government is about to collapse." She looked up, avoiding her mother's glower. "I—just don't think this is a good time for a change." Unable to hold her father's gaze, she looked away.

"It's all right," she heard him say, after the briefest pause. "I understand."

There had been understanding in his voice, empathy even. Then all on his own he decided to stay here. And although her answer had earned her mother's favor, her acceptance was transitory. In the days and months and years that followed, Antonia questioned her daughter's loyalty so often that the perpetual agitation in Gia's belly never quite left.

Out on the platform she shielded her eyes from the probing sun as the train rumbled away from the station and down the curve of track that shimmered in the heat like a mirage. Would her father still know her after so many years and so many forfeited moments and not even a photograph?

In the distance another line of matchbox cars on the opposite track clipped along at a good rate. A high whistle pierced the air as the next train in cleared the streets that separated the municipality of Marotta from the Adriatic. She stepped back and heard the ping of the loudspeaker and the predictable lack of a following announcement. Good luck to any visitor who didn't have a schedule or know the language, she thought. The incoming train squealed to an unsteady stop.

A woman descended the railcar holding the hand of a child who wriggled like a puppy on a leash. *"Fermati,* Elisabetta." Be still, the woman said to the child, who ignored her mother's plea and dragged her along behind.

A businessman in a drab, ill-fitting gray suit stepped down and gazed around the platform as if waiting to be seen. People should check themselves in the mirror before they left the house, she thought, noting the man's rumpled jacket. An older woman with black hair and white roots paused on the last step.

She turned and looked around for a station clock, her forehead damp. Had she given her father the wrong time, which would mean trying to reach him at home …

As she started to turn back around, she saw an older man in a twill cap walking past the stationary train. Her father always wore a sporty cotton golf hat with a tricolor band. The man produced a half-smile that crinkled his pale face under thick dark sunglasses. How could he see in those things, she wondered, looking at the slightly crooked lips she had inherited along with the chestnut eyes she couldn't see.

She heard the whoosh of airbrakes and the high whine of steel as the outbound train began moving out of the station. The older man came toward her, his face a panoply of expressions like passing seasons. A younger man came up alongside as if to pass him, but the older outmaneuvered him until the younger fell away. The train blew its whistle. Picking up speed, it pushed past the station. The man slid his sunglasses down and extended his arms.

Chapter 12

The day had dawned as bright and clear as any he had seen of late. His daughter had chosen the perfect time of year to come, he thought, as he drove to the train station past the close-cropped hills to a sea that glimmered in the sunlight like that gold lamé Stella wore whenever she had the chance, though it, too, invariably made her look sallow. She should get some sun, wear silver, avoid yellow, something. But no one listened to the counsel in his own household.

He stood at the station end of the platform in Marotta listening to the cry of gulls. Inhaling deeply the salt air, he recalled with renewed conviction why he had stayed here despite the persistent agitation in the pit of his stomach like a washing machine spinning, spinning, spinning.

He turned and looked down the snaking line of track undulating like a mirage in the heat. Would he know her, after so many years and so much time and not even a picture, not one? No, but he would know her. What did photographs matter, anyway?

Down the track a dark line of matchbox railcars hugged the sandy curve of shoreline. The crescendo of the train whistle pierced the air as the InterCity from Rimini clipped along at a good rate of speed. He stepped back to the middle of the platform and heard the ping of the loudspeaker followed by the usual dead air. Ah, well, people used their cell phones now for timetables. Looking up for the tenth time to check the track number, he waited until the train passed the city streets and squeaked to an unsteady stop.

The conductor eased himself down the steps and stood to one side to let the passengers exit.

A woman holding the arm of a squealing, unruly child descended the railcar. "Stop fidgeting, Elisabetta," the woman said to the tot, who ignored her and dragged her along like a ragdoll.

A man in a rumpled, dun-colored suit stepped onto the platform and gazed around with a sense of importance. He would have fared better wearing a casual outfit, Giovanni thought, a shirt and pants he could afford to have cleaned and pressed on occasion. An older woman, her black hair in a tight bun, gripped the handrail of the coach, eased down the steps and followed the other passengers alongside the platform to the station house.

Dio, he thought, his head sweating under his cap. Had Gia missed the connection in Rimini? Well, who could blame her, with these crazy schedules? Now he would have to try her mobile, devil take the confounded things.

He turned to see a woman step from the railcar, a girl, really. No, a young woman, a young man at her side. But his daughter had mentioned no man, had seemed in fact to emphasize that she was coming alone. Yet, in the young woman's smile, the toss of her ginger hair and dismissive gaze was something of Antonia, in the slightly crooked smile on her thin lips something of him. She stopped, glanced around him down the platform then looked at him again. The deep chestnut eyes that once matched her hair loomed from the narrow, lightly freckled face that came to a point in a slightly jutting chin.

He heard the whoosh of airbrakes, the high whine of steel wheels turning. With a businesslike expression, the young woman moved toward him, the man beside her walking past as the train blew its whistle and pushed out of the station, picking up speed. The young woman planted her black suitcase with its garish red bow, hiked an orange bag up onto her shoulder and extended a hand.

Unable to control his nervous excitement, he gripped her arms and folded her into a strong embrace. Under the bright blue of an endless sky that made him want to hang on and on and on, he felt her letting go, too soon, took quickly. He stood back and met her eyes. He saw nothing there of what he wanted, nothing of what he had unreasonably hoped for. It would take time, he told himself. All of that would take time ...

"You are—lovely," he said, meaning it. She was no classic beauty, that was clear. But she was interesting, which had much more going for it, he felt, limitless, a face one could take in and savor for a lifetime, maybe two.

She gave him a dubious look then smiled, an ironic twist to her lips. In her eyes, the shake of her head, he saw that she thought he had only noted her appearance because it was expected, something any Italian man might say to any woman. Yet, in the same eyes, at the same moment, he saw that she had laughed because she didn't believe in herself.

"Truly, you are lovely," he repeated, though he knew on instinct that the more he pressed the less she would believe. "You're staring." He smiled to change the subject, his turn under the microscope. "I'm older, I know," he said before she could speak. It was easier, less painful, to volunteer the obvious than have someone else extract it.

"And you look—well," she answered.

He sucked in his breath, only just managing to suppress the exquisite pang in his chest that she had not called him Dad or Papa or *babbo,* or anything. While he might not expect her to use such words at the start of a visit, he had hoped she would call him something endearing. When had she let such appellations go? Were these treasures he would never get back?

"Good to see you," she answered, apparently sensing the void.

He nodded and clung to the words and the ephemeral hope that someday she might mean them. He squeezed her arm. "It's wonderful to see you, too."

Dio, would they ever at any point rise above banality? He shook himself into the innocuous role of host. "Just the one valise?"

The black case on wheels with the gawking red bow, which, dear heaven, must have been there since Antonia, was just large enough for a few days' gear. However, the orange plastic carryall slung over her shoulder, which looked to weigh ten pounds empty, seemed a more tangible sign of her stay.

"I go back to Milan Friday," she advised. "Remember, I told you?"

"Yes, of course." But she was here now. "For a meeting to do with your work. Am I understanding that correctly?"

She smiled. "Your English is atrocious."

He grinned. "Ah, really? Let's hear your Italian."

She flushed a deep shade of coral. "In truth, I remember quite a few words," she responded formally.

"Ah, good, very good." He tipped his cap. "A good start."

And a load off, he felt, since it meant that she could communicate with Stella and the others he wanted her to meet without his having to translate every word. He swiveled her case. Though smallish, it was dense as lead. "Let's stop for a coffee before we go home."

She stopped in the middle of the platform, blocking an older man with a briefcase who glared as he brushed past. His first mistake, he chided himself: conferring home to a town she hadn't seen in a dog's age. He started to reach for her hand to say he was sorry, as he had said in all the letters she had never answered. But this was no time for apology, a tack he had taken often enough in sixteen years to know wouldn't work. He saw her face soften briefly and thought his mood must reflect in his eyes.

"There's a place nearby with very good *caffè latte*. And we can get a brioche." Her expression wasn't a smile, really. Just a willingness to suspend hostility and accept as a sort of bribe the breakfast she loved as a child.

"I could use the caffeine," she answered. "And fresh air after that train ride. A generation later and the Intercity still doesn't have air-conditioning?"

"Not a high priority, apparently, with everything else to consider." He moved down the platform. "The car is this way."

He led her down the steps of the underpass. The sound of her suitcase banging against the cement echoed off the tiles in a space empty of words. Yet, within him, was a void that needed words. But what to say, since the usual small talk felt forced?

"This way." He nodded at the stairs leading up to the street level. "I don't know if you remember the station before, but they've remodeled."

He turned to watch her take in the small tidy lobby in sea green and auburn tile, the new ticket agent's booth.

"It's nice," she said. "Clean," she added, though he saw she was looking out the open doorway to the street where the first stage of rush hour traffic had already clogged the main thoroughfare.

Chapter 13

Gia followed her father across the cracked asphalt lot to a shabby white Fiat Punto. She watched as he opened the hatch and fumbled to lower the extension handle on the suitcase.

She stepped in front of him. "This way," she instructed, squeezing the crossbar.

"Your old man can still manage a bag," he cut in. Hoisting the case, he shoved it in the empty trunk wheels first. "Now to get out of here," he muttered. He wiped his brow and stared at the street. "Good thing you didn't come during the lunch hour."

"Isn't this worse—the afternoon crush after naptime?"

He laughed and coughed slightly. "Who takes naps anymore? People are either rushing home from an early shift or out to the late. Those out of work just rush not to lose the habit. It's unlocked." He nodded at the passenger door and went around to the driver's side.

For a moment, she stood listening to the sound of the traffic like a song, the grinding beat of truck gears, the counterpoint meep of horns. A current of air carried the aroma of roasted garlic and rising dough from the pizzeria across the road where two crusty old fellows sat on rickety stools drinking Peroni. Beside them, a young student nodded to an unheard rhythm, minuscule white earphones threads dangling past earlobes.

As much as the North End might remind her of here, it wasn't the same, not even the scent of herbs and yeast or the sight of old and young together. Yet, looking closer, she saw that the elders faced the street and the student was staring at nothing in particular, his book bag zipped shut, the iPhone an older model.

"Get in," her father said. "The café is just up the road."

She got in the car and closed the door. As she grasped the seatbelt, he shifted into reverse. The Punto lurched and sputtered. She pushed herself back from the dash and quickly buckled the seatbelt. In Boston, they hadn't owned a car so her father rarely drove. As a result, his piloting of rentals here had produced tight-knuckled excursions along hillside roads wound tight as clock springs, with barely room for one car and a practiced driver. The dizzying expeditions from his village to the sea had nauseated her mother and forced her to focus on the floorboards.

Her father punched the gas and jiggled the shift. "Piece of crap," he muttered, maneuvering past the other cars and out to the street.

"The A14 is busy," she said, watching the exasperated care and moped drivers cursing and gesticulating to each other along the formerly sedate route. "And there are sidewalks."

He looked over. "They've been here a while, along with the traffic lights they put in every few meters."

They swirled around a rotary that managed the flow of vehicles in front of a broad, white two-story structure that recalled the shopping plaza in Burlington.

She stared out the windshield. "Is that a mall?"

Her father threw up a hand. "Yes, the thieves—taking all the business from the shopkeepers."

"It's the same in states," she said.

"Ha!" He shook his head. "It's worse here."

She looked at him. Why was it worse here, because it was happening to them?

Her father turned left under a railway overpass and down the beach road along the seaside. Devoid of tourists, most shops were closed, sliding doors secured with weathered two-by-fours. They made a quick U-turn and coasted into a parking space in front of a small café with a boarded-up front window.

"Now here is a place that still makes a good *caffè* and fresh brioche, not like that sludge and rubbish in plastic." He sat back and stared at her. "My, but you are lovely."

She felt a flash of heat. "Why do you say that when it isn't true?"

He shook his head with a melancholy look. "You still sell yourself short, don't you?"

She turned and yanked the door handle. What right had he to pronounce on who she was or wasn't, what she did or didn't think of herself? No, she thought. It was a trap into disclosure, a perk she wouldn't offer and he didn't deserve. She got out of the car and slammed the door.

He got out and motioned to the side of the café. "That way." He closed the door and walked across the street through a gravel courtyard to the open section of the bistro, its tiny takeout window unseen from the street.

"If proprietors need business, why do they set themselves up like this?" she asked. "Nobody can tell they're open."

Her father shrugged. "It's off season. The owners need a break from the riff raff, the *marocchini* who don't spend money but walk the beach hawking wares."

He tapped the small black and silver bell that sat on the splintered window ledge.

A robust middle-aged woman appeared at the window, her small dark eyes alert above plump tan cheeks. "Ah, *prego,*" she said with something like relief at seeing them. She wiped her hands on the white apron in a gesture that appeared to be more out of habit than cleanliness.

"Two espressos, *macchiato,* please," her father said. "And a brioche for my daughter."

The woman nodded and smiled but with a quizzical look, perhaps taking her for a foreigner as had the woman on the train. She had been mistaken for French on another visit, too, to St. Peter's in Rome, in a moment that hadn't set at all well with her mother.

Antonia looked her up and down with a tsk. "It's that light skin and freckles, like your father," she accused. Standing straighter, she walked out into the sunlight that burnished her naturally olive skin, a byproduct of what hereabouts was referred to in dialect as *bass'Italia,* lower Italy.

"Good day," Gia said in proper Italian.

The woman's smiled broadened. "And to you." She wiped her hands again and went to the coffeemaker. "Please, accommodate yourselves." She gestured to a smattering of empty chairs and tables with a view of the azure sea.

She watched as her father extracted a sheaf of napkins from the dispenser, went to the nearest table and pulled out from under it two white plastic chairs. He gave the chairs and table a swipe then stuffed the used napkins into the center hole that usually held an umbrella and stacked the others on the table. Taking a chair, he turned it toward the shore. So given the choice even now, he still preferred the sea. If she hadn't needed the fabric, she would have hailed a cab for the train station. She went over and took the other seat.

"So tell me *bella* what is this work that brings you to Italy?"

She gazed out at the water, striated in shades of aqua, sapphire, violet. She couldn't tell him why she was here exactly, but she had to tell him something to set off the subject of the material. His debt was greater than this, but it was a starting place.

"I'm here to see a prospective client. He's out on the West Coast but in Milan for Fashion Week. Friday is the only time we can meet."

The café owner brought a tray with two small white cups and matching saucers. The brioche in the little white dish exuded a warm, buttery aroma. "Enjoy, please." She set the tray on the table.

Running her finger along the stylish demitasse with the blue and white logo, she noted the lighter-weight ceramic. Better for warm weather, she thought, since it allowed the coffee to cool faster. It was probably less expensive to produce as well, to offset careless summer handling.

Her father leaned across the table and clinked his cup to hers. "Well, no matter the reason we're glad you've come."

She took a sip of espresso. Its fragrant froth melted into deep rich flavor that seeped into her core. She took a section of the airy brioche—sweet, light, flakey and probably a thousand calories. Taking a napkin from the stack, she wiped her fingers.

"I wanted to thank you for your gift." Looking up, she noted the pinprick of light in his eyes. "September can be chilly in Boston, as you recall, so the timing is appropriate. The colors, too, russet and amber in paisley. Autumnal, academic. Good work. And the yellow-gold in the center of the repeat, very vibrant." She could see he was pleased that she not only liked the piece but understood the depth of the design.

She took a bit of brioche. "Even more interesting is the fabric. Light, touchable, wearable. The hem looks like yours, but the material ..." She looked at him. "Your background is in tailoring, not textiles."

He touched a gnarled forefinger to his lips, his eyes unseen behind the dark glasses. "I am glad to hear you liked the gift. As for the fabric ..." He gave a shrug. "I have always appreciated good material, as would any competent tailor." He looked out at the water. "We do still have a fair amount of talent here, in many areas."

"These other areas—they include textile design?" she pressed. "I know something of it from school, but it's such a specialized field, so intricate, an art really. Competitive, too."

He looked at her. "All fields have their struggles."

"Some more than others."

"You didn't stick with it, then? Textiles, I mean."

"I'm better at selling."

"Really? I wouldn't have guessed it of you."

And what could he have accurately guessed of her over a decade and a half of years and four thousand miles? "I liked it enough to buy a little shop in Boston, well, half-ownership. The shop is called Fiber."

He stared at her. "You are part owner of a fabric store?"

"Yes, I—we have some prospects that could offer wider distribution."

With their electrical problems and the sudden seeming unlikelihood of James Martell becoming a client, they had a greater prospect of closing. She felt the familiar churn in her gut, under that, jet-lagged exhaustion. They must talk more about the material and soon, but she was tired. And when she was tired, she had trouble analyzing a situation and trouble trusting her instincts.

She looked out at the sun lowering through gauzy clouds toward the horizon, the endless sea. "Looks like it's getting late. I wouldn't want your—Stella—to worry."

"Mah," her father flapped his hand. "Where can she go? I have the car."

"Still, I'd hate to make a bad impression. And even if nobody naps anymore, I could use some rest, maybe a bit of prosciutto and melon."

She saw him perk up at the mention of sustenance and the regional staples, unable to resist the perpetual lure of *la bella figura* and food.

"I suppose we should move along." He got up and took out his wallet. "We can talk more later."

"Let me." She reached for her bag. "After all, you're hosting."

He looked as if she had scalded him. "Hosts are for parasites. Go on to the car, I'll handle this."

He walked with an uneven gait to the secreted window. She took her bag and went across the beach road.

The white pebbled shoreline was struck with colorful closed umbrellas like furled party toothpicks. Under a pale sky, the Adriatic lay in quiet calm, the briny beach air infused with the aroma of roast fish, possibly the *sardelle,* fresh anchovies, she remembered from the four seasons pizza they specialized in here. With clams, mussels and—what was the fourth type of seafood? Her mouth watered. She would have to ask.

"Ready?" Her father stood by the car.

She went across the sidewalk and caught the toe of her flat in the nicked edge of the curb where the concrete had chipped away. Figured, she thought, no solid footholds here.

Her father came to her side. "Watch your step," he said taking her arm.

She pulled away. "I've got it, thanks."

Bracing herself against the hood of the car, she pressed the protruding flap back in place and opened the door.

Chapter 14

Her father punched the gas pedal, pitching the Pinto into the intersection and away from Marotta's city center toward the hills. She grabbed the dashboard.

Her father's laugh produced a coughing spasm. "You're still nervous about my driving?"

Who wouldn't be, she wanted to answer. "No, of course, not." She let go of the faded dash and made a show of wiping the dust from the discolored surface.

He glanced at her hand. *"Madonna,* Gia, what is that on your finger?"

The driver of an oncoming Alfa Romeo leaned on the horn. Her father jerked the steering wheel to the right.

"Watch it, will you?" she said, steadying herself. "I'd like to get there in one piece."

Her father looked again at her finger. "But that ring is for an engagement, is it not? Though the size of the stone—it looks like a quartz from the caves at Sassoferrato, though a lot more substantial."

"It is more substantial," she said, turning the stone with her thumb.

Her father looked at her, beaming. *"Madonna mia, bella*—you're engaged. But why did you not say something?"

"It's recent," she said, looking at him. "And I didn't exactly get the chance."

"Oh, my, wait till Stella hears! She was already planning a party, but this—ho, my, she will be over the moon. What does he look like, this fiancé, handsome, yes? And a nice man, I am sure. What kind of job? He does have one? But, of course, he must, naturally. My daughter would never marry one of those louts you see here, always waiting for the woman to do the work. Better yet, the mother. A dime a dozen, not even, the fellows here." He patted her arm. "Imagine, my daughter engaged. So, what is his name, this fiancé?"

"Peter, Litton."

"Peter—Pietro, the rock—he must be a rock, too, I imagine, for you to have chosen him. Dear heaven, what a thing—my daughter engaged!" He slapped the steering wheel, his grin pushing his sunglasses up the bridge of his nose. "Now we must definitely show you off—"

"I'm not here on display," she interrupted.

Nor was she a carnival pony to be led around to every relative in driving distance, she thought, as they passed razed grain fields centered with clusters of olive trees. But what did her father know of her, anyway? She looked back over her shoulder at what appeared to be a new entrance to an enlarged autostrada.

"But, of course." Giovanni laughed softly and shook his head. "Is good you haven't changed so much."

She looked at him. "What do you mean?"

"No, nothing, I just ... it's good you haven't changed into the type that looks for the limelight." He shrugged. "But we must all change somewhat, I suppose. I imagine I am not quite the same either." His thin lips rose in a half-smile. "For example, I am quite a bit younger and handsomer than you may recall, rather like all those stars with the facelifts, kept young by other means. But no matter." He gave a wave. "Look we are already at Cento Croci—almost home."

She looked out the windshield at the tall slender cross, one among countless others jutting up like scarecrows from the countryside, though the simplicity of this one offended less. They shot past a green road marker with white letters announcing the upcoming village.

"Castel Barberini has its own sign?"

"These days there is a sign for everything," her father answered. "Though not many pay attention."

"And those buildings on the left, they're new, too, aren't they?"

"Industrial parks. Paolo designed the one on the end—his first project, for a friend from these parts. *Madonna,* how the years have flown." He shook his head. "And how few remain. But you are still young and will have time to see family, those who count, anyway."

She looked out at the office building on the end, a rectangular affair in sage green with matching tinted windows that blended with the surrounding fields. As to family, there was no point telling him now she wouldn't have time. She barely had time for what she had come for—a look at Ordito Trama, the mill and the loom that had produced the fabric, information on the fiber content and weave, and the completion of her dress. It was more than enough for the few days she had without adding obligatory visits. She had a sudden sense of claustrophobia and went to roll down the window.

"No need for that, we're almost there." He pointed ahead to the right.

At the crest of the hill on the right, the castle that gave Castel Barberini its name was ringed by a refurbished wall of sand-colored brick shaded by scrub pine. This was the village of her father's birth, the place where he had remained despite the prophesy of too many tailors in Italy, where he inherited his parents' home, a small house in a row of small houses, a passable location for daily living but killing, surely, for business.

The clock in the old church tower chimed five times, a sound that ages ago had kept her awake marking every quarter-hour, half-hour and hour.

"Church bells sound the same," she observed.

Her father shook his head. "They only ring on the hour now."

He turned right onto the village's quiet main street where two ancient souls sat in wooden chairs under shuttered windows, an empty card table on the sidewalk between them. Where, she wondered, were the green juice glasses of homemade wine, the checkerboards and decks of playing cards? Where, too, was the laughter?

She looked away. Why, for God's sake, hadn't she simply rented a car and stayed in a *pensione* away from the decrepitude? They must have passed an inn on the way, an agritourism bed and breakfast. But it was too late for that now.

As if sensing her mood, her father patted her hand. "It will be all right."

She looked at him, hunched over the steering wheel staring at a street he traveled countless times yet still seemed to regard as a great unfolding mystery. With a grinding of gears, the Punto shot up the hill past the vacant piazza and a coffee bar that looked brand new.

Via Barberini with its white stucco façades and scarred wooden doorways was empty of the tweens and teens that had continually harangued each other in that intrusive and intimate way she recalled. In the open door of the cooperative market, stood a crone in a formless black dress with pinprick polka dots, an emaciated tabby slinking around the legs of a white plastic lawn chair. Her father steered the Punto sharply left into an empty gravel lot and killed the engine, exposing a silence so deep all she could hear was her uneven breathing.

"Here we are," he said.

She looked out the window at the stucco flat inside which Stella would be waiting, sure to hate her on site for making them late and perhaps for other things, doubtless a prescient sentiment of her two sons. Please, God, she wouldn't be here long enough to see them.

"You can get out now, we're here." Her father stood by the passenger side door.

Startled, she turned and fumbled for the door handle, which jerked from her grasp.

"Pull up slowly," her father said through the glass.

She did as bidden, opened the door and stepped out onto the dusty gravel.

Her father went around the back of the car and opened the hatch. "Largely the same, our little village, is it not?"

No, she wanted to say, it was not the same. Not the same at all. There was no perpetual clang of chimes, no one in the streets, no sounds of berating banter, no children, no ring-ring of bicycle bells or meep-meep of scooter horns, no familiarity. In point of fact, there wasn't much of anything.

Feeling drained beyond herself, she shielded her eyes from the slanting sun and heard the whine of a performance engine jut out from behind the brick wall that held the village in place. On the other side of the roadway a line of houses bordered row on row of fields that lay like a vast quilt across the bosom of the earth right down to the sea.

"Come," said her father. "This way."

She turned to see him nodding at the two-story house that abutted the brick retaining wall.

"Tomorrow we'll greet your Uncle Paolino and Aunt Eleda. Today, you need rest, so does Paolino. He had a stroke not long ago. The physical therapy tires him out in the afternoon."

Dazed at mention of her uncle and aching now with an unnamed and ageless grief, she clutched the orange bag and followed her father blindly around the side of the house.

The front door, cracked and splintered across its center, was darkened by the sun, the years of inherited legacy—her father from his mother, his mother from her grandparents. "Good fortune," he had affirmed in one of his letters, that it had been here for him after the tailoring business outside Marotta had gone belly-up so that he at least had a place to hang his hat. Were they only a failsafe, she wondered, this house and his return to the village, and no proactive decision at all?

Her father threw the bolt and opened the door into a darkened vestibule. Following him into the dimness, she was greeted by the pungent aroma of prosciutto and *casciotta* cheese that hung perpetually in the air and recalled Palm Sundays in Boston when her mother made Easter pies. A nervous sensation rippled through her.

"Well, and you must be Gia." A woman with hennaed hair frizzed at the ends hurtled down the stairway that divided what had once been two separate houses connected by a common center stairwell. *"Madonna,* how lovely you are."

Stella, Gia, thought, putting her arms out to deflect the strong embrace aimed in her direction. Her father stood aside.

The woman gripped her arms, subsuming her with what appeared to be appreciation. The woman then turned and frowned at Giovanni, clucking her tongue and ejecting a string of rebukes at his apparent failure to adequately prepare her for how attractive his daughter was.

How could he put into words what he didn't know, Gia thought, feeling a stiff, weary smile form on her face.

"Now come, *bella.*" Stella opened the door on the left and steered her into the kitchen. "You must be hungry," she asserted, gesticulating to the room, the white linen tablecloth and matching napkins, the white enamel cabinets, the small pantry, all while staring, assessing and by some strange and dubious grace seeming to find this new young woman interesting.

"My English not too good," Stella said with a firm shake of her head.

"No, it's fine. My Italian is passable, I hope," Gia said in a form of the language somewhere between dialect and formal address.

"Ah, *brava,* listen how well she speaks," Stella asserted. *"Mah, Gi!"* She turned to Giovanni. "You should have told me your daughter speaks so well."

Gia glanced at her father, still standing in the doorway and wearing odd look as if he was as surprised as she was at such a welcome. He gave a quick shrug as if to say he hadn't any intention of trying to guess at details about her of which he couldn't possibly be sure. Meanwhile, Stella rattled off a cacophony of commands.

"Yes, yes, all in good time," her father intoned. He opened the louver doors of the pantry and stepped up onto a wooden stool whose squat legs wobbled as he grabbed hold of a breadbasket perched on the top shelf.

Why not have the basket handy, Gia wondered. But Italian women had their own way of involving their men in daily life. Of which, keeping common items out of reach appeared to be one.

"Really, Gia, you must be hungry, thirsty, no? After the trip, I mean." Stella motioned to the table.

"Actually, I'd love some prosciutto and a glass of water, if you have it," she answered.

"Sure, sure, all you want." Stella flapped at the nearest chair. "We even kept the water in the *frigo* for you, I understand Americans like the water cool."

In a whirl of motion, she went back and forth and back and forth from refrigerator to table, adorning the white linen cloth with sliced melon bright as a sunrise, prosciutto slivered to near transparency, a plate of assorted cookies with the fragrance of vanilla sugar and poured dark chocolate, fresh crusty bread, mineral water—*frizzante* and *naturale*—since she hadn't been certain whether Gia preferred carbonated or regular—along with figs, a *crostata*—a flat tart made of apricot marmalade under a crisscross of homemade crust—and a bottle of light sweet wine just right for late afternoon and the precocious fall weather.

"There." Stella paused at the head of the table. "It's a light affair, but now you can sit and eat and relax." She pulled out a chair.

With the timing of laughter during communion, the front door buzzer sounded.

"*Cazzo,* company already?" Stella threw up her hand. She shook her head and nodded at the set table and empty chair. "Of course, everyone will want see you, Gia, but not today all right? Tell them another time, Gi, won't you?"

"Your wish." Giovanni bowed slightly and went out into the hall.

Through the kitchen door Gia could hear excited chatter that seemed to grow progressively louder.

"Sit, sit," Stella said. "Never mind everybody else. We're glad you finally came. Better late than never, eh?" She jutted her chin in the direction of the hallway. "Gi tells me you're here only a few days. Did you come just for work?"

Gia felt a flush creep from her neck to her cheeks. "Mostly for work, yes, but to see you all, too, of course. I manage a fabric store in Boston so it's hard to get time off." Instantly, she hated herself for caving in so quickly to the guilt-aimed interrogation that was stock in trade.

"Ah, well, it takes something else sometimes to give a push, no?" Stella sat back in the chair. "I have two sons—you'll meet them later—who are just the same. We parents push and push." She gave a wave. "But what are you going to do? They like the city, Roma, you know, so I can't force. And Gi," she shook her head. "He's not good for pushing."

"Isn't he? I'm surprised," she said, recalling how good her father had been at pushing when it was for something he wanted. She heard the front door close, the click of the deadbolt.

He came into the kitchen with a sigh. "Three people left in this town and two show up now."

"Nina and Roberta?" Stella asked.

He nodded, sliding out a chair. "They wanted to know how much rabbit you want."

Stella gave a wave. "Roberta knows how much we need for everybody and Nina never does anything but tag along." She turned to Gia. "They want see what you look like."

Gia looked at her father. "Who is everybody?"

"Massimo and Paolo are coming from Rome. They love rabbit. But don't worry." Her father seated himself and pierced a slice of prosciutto with his knife. "We have time before they arrive. For now, eat something—and more than just a few breadcrumbs."

After a late *pranzo* of more than she usually ate in a weekend, she was overcome by a fatigue so profound she felt she was sinking.

Stella peered at her from across the table and shook her head. "You look like a dishrag. Go upstairs and lie down, why don't you? I'll wake you later." She rose and went to the door. "We fixed up Max's room. Gi, put the bread away meanwhile, will you? It gets hard otherwise. Come, Gia, I'll show you upstairs."

Pushing herself up from the chair, she stood at the table and rubbed her eyes.

"Stella's right," said Giovanni. "You look a frazzle. A rest will perk you up."

"Yes, here, come with me." Stella led her out to the hall.

Gia followed her up the stairs to the landing. What was it about the way people here cared for others that subdued them to passivity? Well, forewarned was forearmed. For now, she was glad for a chance to rest in the privacy of her own quarters.

"Here." Stella pushed open the door on the left.

The cool darkened room smelled of lemon oil from the polished pine bureau, highboy and twin bed, its white cotton hobnail spread pulled back to reveal crisp linen sheets that looked freshly laundered.

"I hope it's okay," Stella added, expectant. "Gi put your suitcase by the bureau." She pointed to the dusty bedraggled luggage in the corner of the pristine space.

"It's perfect," she answered, unable to stifle a yawn.

"Good. Then for now, rest. Later we'll talk." Stella went to the door. "If you need anything, call." She pointed across the landing. "We're right there, very close now after so long," she said, closing the door.

She slipped off her flats. Unzipping her suitcase, she felt around for the pajama top and jogging shorts that served as sleepwear. At least with her own space, she could work and call Peter in private. She changed, put her watch on the nightstand and stretched out on the coolness of the sheets. Odd, she mused as she lay against the down pillows, to have people so near after being on her own.

She looked over at the tendrils of light that filtered through the shuttered windows. She should push back the slats, she thought, let in more sun. Maybe later, after some rest.

Chapter 15

Eyes encrusted with sleep, she woke to a cool, shadowy room tranquil and tidy, the faint scent of lemon. It couldn't be her bedroom or Peter's place . . .

She sat up—she was in Italy, her father's house, and she hadn't texted Peter to say she had arrived in the village. Nor had she reached out to Rafael. Her cell was dead. She tried to steady herself. She could email them from her laptop, assuming it still had power, assuming there was Wi-Fi, which there must be if Stella had a cell. Dear heaven. Stella . . . her father . . .

She threw back the covers and hopped out of bed. Fumbling in the semidarkness, she looked around for the carryall. She couldn't recall bringing it upstairs. Maybe her father or Stella tucked it away somewhere. She went to the window and pushed open the shutters.

She blinked, shielding her eyes from the light of early morning. How could it be daybreak? She just went to bed. She recalled Stella telling her to call out if she needed anything, the lulling sense of other people only a room away. She took her watch from the nightstand—two in the morning Eastern time.

She stepped back and looked around the knotty pine highboy. The orange bag sat atop the radiator. She took it down and reached down past the gum wrappers and unstamped train ticket, took out her cell and pressed the display. Nothing. The phone was as dead as it had been on the train.

She unzipped the outer compartment, took the charger and went to the wall socket. Two small round holes stared out at her.

"Dammit," she said softly.

Maybe the village cooperative carried chargers, or the salt and tobacco shop on the main drag that peddled everything from lottery tickets to phone cards.

She put the charger back in her bag and went to the window. Across the roadway, the sectioned fields lay across the landscape in the evergreen hue of early morning like a carpet. Fastened atop the opposing hillside the village of Monterado, a church tower also at its midpoint, was the mirror image of Castel Barberini. How much alike the townships were.

But, no, Monterado residents would quickly contend. Our piazza has a limestone fountain. Yours has no fountain. Our town has cobblestones in the center and down the main street, yours only in the center. Amazing how people could freight small features with so much meaning. She heard a gentle knock at the door.

Stella poked her head in, two thick white terry bath sheets draped over her compact forearm. "I thought I heard noises." She clucked her tongue. "I wanted to call you for dinner last night, but Gi said let you sleep."

She laid the towels across the back of the wooden chair and clasped her hands together. "Gi says you are engaged. How wonderful! Your boyfriend—is Italian?"

The last thing she wanted was to answer questions, especially personal questions, especially when she hadn't the energy or clarity of mind. She needed coffee and quickly.

"Peter? No. He's Irish and English. Catholic, though, on his mother's side." He was protestant on his father's side and nothing in between. But why go there now.

Stella nodded. "Good, good. Nice looking, yes?"

"I think so," she answered. So did everyone, women, men.

"You have pictures?" Stella looked expectant.

"I—yes. But they're in my phone and the battery's dead." She picked up her cell and held it out. "I need an adapter for the plugs here."

"Ah, yes, I'm sure we'll find one." Stella came and took her hand. "But the engagement ring, is—different, no? Gi said so."

"Yes, it is different." She held out her hand. It wasn't even an engagement ring exactly, not in the usual sense.

Stella led her by the hand to the open window. "My, yes. Is different. The stone, I mean." She looked up. "Is a diamond?"

"Yes, uncut. For my adventurous side, Peter said."

She turned the ring with her thumb. A particle of light touched the stone, illumining its prismatic color.

"Ah, yes, adventure," Stella breathed. "How wonderful. So now we must celebrate—have a party—no?"

"No. No party." She pulled back her hand. "I mean, you're doing so much already."

Stella gave a wave. "How many times do we celebrate an engagement? Well, today, people celebrate all the time, then they get a divorce. But not you, eh? You will be for keeps." She patted her arm. "Come, I'll show you the bath." She motioned through the open doorway to the hall. "Is in the middle, between the two rooms."

Gia followed her into the hallway. She would have preferred a cup of coffee, but a bath could work better to start. She could still smell the train trip in her hair, on her skin.

Stella opened the door to a narrow master bath, translucent white walls inlaid with glistening black and white tiles from chest height to the terrazzo floor, flecked with black, gray and silver under a white shag bathmat. At the far end beside the toilet sat a new bidet. A chrome shower nozzle hung over the white porcelain basin of the claw-foot tub.

"Or use the shower," Stella offered, apparently noting her interest.

"No—I mean, thanks, a bath is fine."

"Well, is up to you. Until the boys come for lunch you have all this to yourself." She went out to the landing. "They wanted to meet you before now, but better late than never. For me is nice to have another woman around. The men, they don't always understand everything. I should know. I grew up in Rome, with two brothers." She pressed the back of her hand to her forehead. *"Dio, che palle."*

Gia gave a half-smile. She couldn't recall hearing family members, even males, referred to as balls, but the concept had a certain accuracy.

She went back into the bedroom and took clean underwear and a pair of tan Capri pants and white cap-sleeved top from the suitcase, along with a pink cotton shrug and a bag of toiletries. She took a bath sheet from the chair.

Stella went to the window. "I'll close this. You have a nice soak. Then we go out. I could make the coffee here but is nice if you see the town a little."

Gia paused at the door. They really did seem to be making an effort, Stella and her father. "Listen, Stella, I just—I wanted to thank you for letting me stay. It's—you didn't have to."

Stella gave a wave. "Don't think of it." She latched the shutters. "Is the least we can do."

Taking her things, Gia went back across the hall where filaments of light threaded the slats of the unscreened bathroom window. Leaving windows open had always taboo here, akin to advertising. But when would she have such natural light and a view besides?

She closed the door and draped the towel over the rack by the pedestal sink. Hearing the receding slap of Stella's leather slippers down the stairs, she eased the shutters apart and secured the latch. The resplendent collage of sloping hills under the brightening sun lay corn yellow and earthen brown. She leaned against the cool marble ledge. What was it about beauty that hurt when one tried to hold onto it?

An elderly man in a tweed cap riding a rusted green bicycle peddled the strip of hard-packed gravel at the back of the house. Passing under the window, he slowed and tilted his head. She reached for the latch and pulled the shutters together. No point inciting rumor, especially here.

She turned the bath tap and opened a bottle of bath gel with an alpine meadow on the label and squeezed, releasing the aroma of lavender and olives. Shedding the pajama top and jogging shorts, she slid into the fragrant water and watched the play of light through the window. A current of air carried the faint scent of resin. Stretching her legs in the soothing water, she heard autos and motorbikes zipping by on the roadway below.

If she had the days straight, this was Tuesday. Raf would have met with the electrician yesterday, and Peter would be working with Olivia on the fundraiser, two days away. Closing her eyes, she saw again his image in the airport, sunlight streaming in behind him, the pressed gray flannel trousers and navy blazer, the white button down shirt, the sleek brown hair and blue eyes like slate. His arms around her before leaving, holding her tight then letting her go, touching his fingertips to her lips before leaving. Hopefully, Olivia wouldn't become too efficient while she was gone.

A claxon sounded with the attendant grind of downshifting gears. She sudsed her hair and body with the shower gel and rinsed under the chrome sprayer then pulled the chain on the cracked rubber stopper and let the cloudy water drain away.

She stepped from the tub and wrapped the towel around her, its thirsty fibers like bunting. She dried quickly, dressed and peered in the beveled mirror. In just two days, her bangs had grown longer on one side and her hair had faded to an anemic shade, an indictment of the cut-rate salon she had tried on the fly two weeks before.

She hurried across the hall to the bedroom where her inert cell lay on the bureau. She needed an adapter and quickly—but first, coffee. She dressed and slipped on the shrug and flats then went to the laptop and pressed the power button. Nothing. What a pain in the ass. She tucked her travel wallet in her pocket and went downstairs.

Stella and Giovanni stood in the kitchen, the green Formica table void of linens, plates and food.

"Now we take you for coffee," Stella said. "This way you see the village and the people sees you."

Giovanni looked at her. "You don't mind, do you?"

"No, sure, fine, whatever. I need an adapter or two anyway. I don't have the right plug, and I need to reach Peter."

"But what is the problem? My cell is just for local, but you can the phone here." Stella indicated a rotary dial wall phone whose canary yellow casing gave it a certain kitschy style.

"But it'll cost a mint." She was already putting them out, and a regular call during peak hours would be through-the-roof expensive.

"Don't worry. Is important to keep in touch, specially now." Stella picked up the receiver and jiggled it.

"Then let me reimburse you." She reached in her pocket for the wallet.

"Absolutely no." Stella jiggled the receiver again. "Just call. Is early, but your fellow, he will worry otherwise, no? *Dai,* go on, we wait outside."

She glanced at the oven clock—just after nine here so around three in the morning back home. Still, Peter had probably tried texting or calling only to find her unresponsive.

"You're sure you don't mind?"

"*Mah,* don't be silly." Stella pushed the receiver into her hand. "*Dai,* Gi, get the key. We wait out in front."

Giovanni took the house key from the wall peg. "Give your intended our greetings. And tell him he is more than welcome to visit. We would love to meet him."

Smiling in a distinctly false way, she picked up the receiver, which felt heavy as a hand weight. "What's the country code for the states?"

"One," said Giovanni. "But dial zero first."

She stared at him.

"What? I used to dial quite often, you recall."

Yes, he had called often, until her mother died. Forget it, she thought. This wasn't the time. She held the receiver and started dialing. Each rotation brought a set of corresponding clicks. This would take forever. She turned and smiled so broadly her cheeks hurt.

"Come, Gi, let's give some privacy." Stella tugged the sleeve of his windbreaker.

"Patience, will you?" Giovanni took his hat from the back of the chair and donned it at a rakish angle. "We'll be outside."

"But no rush, *eh?*" Stella said, pushing the door open. "Talk long as you want."

Chapter 16

Gia heard a final series of clicks then dense silence. One of the rare occasions when her parents had offered their shared recollections was of a time when few homes here had phones and only the local bar offered a reliable hookup to the outside world.

Her father had mused on this memory in the kitchen of the *pensione* they rented that last long summer, a tender expression in his eyes as if from his padded red vinyl chair he could picture an entire gallery of such remembrances. At the time, she had envied him memories that stirred such fond emotion, though perhaps it wasn't the memories she coveted but his ability to safeguard something of value her mother couldn't take away.

"Cristo, Giovanni," Antonia cut in while he contemplated the quiet joys of earlier days. "You're staring with your mouth open like you've just seen la Loren."

Her father had responded to this rebuke and reference to the legendary Sophia not by pointedly ignoring her mother, but worse. He simply failed to realize she was there, a gaffe that repeated pleas for forgiveness hadn't undone.

"Gia, is that you? Where are you?"

"Peter?" she said, startled to hear a live, if groggy, voice. "I'm at my—I'm in the village."

"I'm glad you're okay. I texted, left messages …"

"Sorry. My cell and laptop are dead, and I don't have an adapter. I'm just going to get one."

"So where are you calling from?"

"The house, the kitchen, actually. My—they're outside waiting to take me for coffee."

"How are things?"

She rubbed her eyes, feeling suddenly worn. "Well enough, I guess. Stella's nice." She heard what sounded like a laugh. "What's so funny?"

"Nothing. It' just, you sound like you were hoping she wouldn't be—nice, I mean."

She stared at the receiver. Usually, she valued his candor, but at the moment it grated an exposed nerve.

"How's your father?"

"Okay, older. All right, though." Far as she could tell. "What about you? How's the event planning?"

"Fine. Everything's fine. Now all I need is you."

She felt a sinking sensation in her knees. Hadn't they settled this before she left? But Peter didn't do guilt. She changed tack. "I wish I were there."

"Really?"

"Of course, what a question."

"I could still come visit. After the dinner, I mean."

"No, it's fine. I mean, I'm fine."

"I was thinking of me, really. Selfish, I guess."

"No, not at all. I just meant—" She heard rustling and envisioned him at his place on the shore in the queen size bed stretching his tanned legs under the white down comforter she sometimes found too warm.

"I know what you mean," he said. "So everything is coming along?"

"Yes, or it will soon." She felt a spurt of anxiety. Things had better go well and soon; time was precious and wasting. But there was still protocol here, especially in someone else's home. "But appearances still come first." Even if the value of such appearances in such a paltry village was hard to gauge.

Through the shuttered window she heard her father's guttural intonation and Stella's muted laughter. "Sorry, I need to go, they're waiting." She heard a profound quiet on the other end. "Peter, are you there?"

"I'm here."

His tone sounded strained. Was it uncertainty or doubt? Or maybe just tiredness. It was, after all, very early in the morning there. "Is everything okay?"

"It's fine. It's just—I miss you, is all."

"I miss you, too. A lot."

"Well, that's good to hear. I—"

"I know. Me, too. Listen, I'll call again tonight. I should have everything up and running by then. *A presto.*"

"What does that mean?"

"It means talk to you soon."

"Fine. But Gia?"

"Yes?"

"Don't change too much while you're there."

"I won't," she said with a smile. "Now get some sleep. *Ciao,*" she said and hung the receiver back in the hook.

Out on the narrow sidewalk her father and Stella stood chatting, the closed doors of the ancient row houses on either side of the *viale* like aged dominoes. In summers past, the doorways had been open and overflowing with family—the aged looking for one more chance to reminisce, the children escaping their stifling cocoons, teens darting down to the commons to plan the evening run to the discotheque.

This morning the only person on the street was a dark-skinned child training to pedal uphill on a two-wheeler with a soft front tire. While her father also watched the boy, Stella nattered on about the crumbling façade of the house across the way. At Giovanni's nudge, she stopped.

"Ah, there you are. So, you had a good chat?" Stella asked with a wink. "How is the fiancé? Missing his girl, I bet."

"Perhaps the conversation was private, my pet." Giovanni poked his forefinger into the bowl of a briar pipe.

Stella tossed her head. *"Mah,* how formal we are all of a sudden." She came and linked her arm in Gia's. "So here is our little village." She swept her hand across the breadth of the narrow street like a game show host as they strolled down the sunlit cobbles. "Of course, hardly anyone is around anymore. There is so little work here. Everyone has gone to the city or abroad."

As they neared the piazza Gia heard the sound of children playing. "Is the kindergarten still there?"

"And still run by the nuns," Giovanni answered over the sound of singing.

Near the end of the street a window opened. An elderly woman in a black headscarf leaned out to shake a red checkered tablecloth.

"Lina," Stella called out, pulling Gia closer. "Do you know the daughter of my husband?" she asked in dialect.

The old woman stared out the unscreened window as if at an exhibit under glass. Seizing the moment, Stella presented her more formally as Giovanni's well-educated—and engaged—daughter who had taken time from the rigors of an important job in Boston to spend a few days with her papa.

The woman blinked and nodded. *"Piacere,"* she said with a withered smile devoid of teeth.

The only other aperture was the set of double doors to the beauty salon. Inside, the stylist stood behind a patron in a plastic smock expounding into the frontal mirror the need for a more seasonal shade of brunette, especially if one was a bit more mature, say, than the average teen with pink hair.

Stella scrutinized Gia's roots and uneven bangs then poked her head in. "Luciana, excuse me a moment. I have someone for you to meet." She drew Gia inside and introduced her this time as a harried stepdaughter only in town a few days. "Can you do something here?" She nodded at Gia's hair.

How in the hell had she even noticed, Gia wondered, feeling a smile stiff as ultra-suede form on her lips. Or had the gall to comment on, for that matter?

"Certainly, there is time," said the stylist, who apparently was also the owner. For both color and a cut tomorrow morning, if this was convenient.

That would be fine, Gia heard herself answer.

"See? We will do for you even better than in America," Stella affirmed, still staring at her roots. "Is important always to look your best, no?" She turned. *"Grazie,* Luciana. Gia will see you tomorrow afternoon."

The salon owner smiled and nodded. Still dazed, Gia mimicked the gestures while Stella led her out across the street.

"See over there," she intoned, pointing. "I used to go to the *piazza* every day when I first came here, to hear news of the region. And over there is *Sant'Antonio di Padua,* the church. On the other side is the café. That is new, completely." She drew her closer. "I don't mind saying, my Paolo remodeled it, top to bottom. He would have redone the priest's quarters, too, but they took too long with the approval. Eh, Gi, is true, isn't it?"

She nodded at Giovanni, who stood puffing on his pipe by the window of the ultra-chic coffee bar, its stucco exterior painted a shade of pale cream. Her father took up his pipe, Gia recalled, whenever he was edgy or needed a diversion.

Stella shook her head. "Why do you stand there leaving me to recount all the news?" She turned to Gia. "Come, we'll go inside, get some coffee and a brioche." She pushed aside the green spangled plastic strips that hung in the doorway to deter flies.

Gia watched her go in while her father tapped the bowl of his pipe against the window ledge. Was there a reason he hadn't made the introductions on the street?

"Let her do the talking for now," he said, reading her thoughts. "You and I will have our time. Go on," he said, pushing aside the green plastic.

Inside, the café was bright and cheerful, with immaculate white walls and tiny hanging lights in the shape of stars. Tall treated-pine stools stood at the bar, with small square white tables at varied angles. Only one table was occupied, by two men chatting, one in a fitted khaki shirt, the other in a charcoal gray crewneck cotton-poly sweatshirt. Gazing out the picture window, they spoke in undertones over cups of cappuccino.

Stella leaned over the counter. "Please, Dino, when you have a moment? Three cappuccinos and three brioches." She glanced at the men then went to an open table at the other window.

The spangled green strips parted again, for a youngish man with a styled goatee and receding hairline. The kind brown eyes behind the fashionable copper frames looked vaguely familiar.

"Ah, Stefano, good to see you," Giovanni said.

"And you, my friend."

Giovanni moved aside. "I don't know if you remember my daughter."

Gia felt a lurch in her gut and a rush of adrenaline. This was one of the faces on the About page of the Ordito Trama website. The operations director.

Stefano smiled and came to the bar. "I do, actually," he said in perfect English. "You're in Boston as I recall, yes?"

"Yes," she answered quickly. Realizing she was staring, she wondered whether to say how she recognized him.

His smile softened. "You don't remember, do you, the last time we saw each other?"

She struggled to recall the place and time but couldn't. "Not that meeting, sorry, no. But it's been a while since I was here last."

"And the meeting I'm thinking of was even longer ago. We were learning English at Maestro Tarini's house at the end of the lane."

"Gia made her confirmation here that year, too," Giovanni added.

This she did recall. She was nine at the time, and in a fleeting moment of unity her parents had decided she should study the Catholic catechism in the states and be confirmed in Italy. Now the only shreds of the visit she recalled with clarity were the unseasonably cool rainy days, and the white confirmation dress and matching white bridal lace head-covering her father made. And having to memorize one of the church's many creeds and not getting it right. But she couldn't recall the ceremony or the man standing here at the bar, though then he would have been only a boy.

"I'm sorry," she repeated. "I'm a bit hazy this morning—jet lag and no caffeine. But I wonder—"

"Time is always so short when one is visiting," Giovanni cut in. "And Gia's time is even shorter this visit. Do you think you might have a few moments later for a little tour of the mill? She's in fabric sales."

"A tour would be wonderful," she affirmed. She would need a lot more, but a tour would be a start. "Can we come by after coffee?"

"Perhaps we should let Stefano say when is best," Giovanni interjected. "Though perhaps prior to a shift change, so Gia can see the full operation."

"It would be my pleasure." Stefano nodded at the barista. "Let's say today at eleven, before the lunch break. My father will be thrilled for a chance to show the place off." He leaned across the counter to take an ironstone mug of steaming caffè latte from the barista. *"Grazie,* Dino, precise as always." He turned, holding the steaming mug. "When you're always on deadline, it's good to have a standing order."

Stella walked over with a swagger. "Ah, Stefano, good to see you looking so fit. The work must agree with you, even with the problems. You may be interested to know Max and Paolo are coming today. I'm sure Max, especially, will be glad you're well."

Stefano's smile was benevolent. "You must be happy to have the brood all together. Give Max and Paolo my best." He turned to Gia. "See you at eleven."

"Looking forward to it," she said, already ticking off in her mind the mills back home that could use Ordito's process to yield as much fabric as fast as possible at the best price.

Chapter 17

In the darkened foyer of the house, the piquant aroma of casciotta still lingered from the day before and, it seemed to Gia, from many days before. Her stomach rumbled. She could ask for a sliver of prosciutto and a slice of melon to offset the tremors from the coffee and brioche, even more her excitement over the prospect of seeing the mill. But it would be rude to ask for more than her hosts provided, and why waste time when it wasn't food she wanted.

Stella paused in the entryway under the denuded bulb. "Sorry the cooperative doesn't have the element for your computer. I guess is enough they still carry the cheese we like."

She could try the tobacconist across the road for the adapter, but first she wanted something else. She turned to her father. "I'd like to see the workshop."

Stella gave a laugh and pinched her nose. "The only thing to see there are antiques. With the mold, I sneeze every time I go in."

"Then don't go in," Giovanni offered.

Stella waved the snub aside. "But why do you want to see it, Gia? Is just an old workroom."

Yes, but it was his workroom and connected somehow to the creation of the scarf and why he sent it. "Personal reasons," she said.

Stella tucked her chin and looked at Giovanni. "Okay, sure. Make believe is your house. Gi can give the tour. I'll go see Roberta and Nina." She gave Giovanni a look.

"Good idea," he answered. "And take your time. Now you're sure, Gia, you want to see the old room?"

She stared at him. "How many times do I have to ask?"

Stella turned, her mouth slightly open.

Opening the front door, Giovanni took Stella's arm. "Go on, talk with the girls," he said, steering her out.

Once they were outside, Gia stepped back into the hallway. She could hear the torrent of Stella's concern over her stepdaughter's unexpected poor humor. Had they done something out of place, offended in some way? Nothing to get upset over, Giovanni affirmed. Gia had work to do and was tired on top of it. Go on, he urged, they would be here when she returned.

The door closed and the bolt snapped shut. Giovanni came back in, his face sallow in the wan light. There was a glint in his eyes.

"Now if you just want to see the place out of formality, don't feel obligated, eh," he said, watching her face.

Don't worry, she wanted to say. There was no obligation, on her part. "I just want to see where you work," she answered. "Or is that not allowed?"

"Of course," he replied. "Come ahead." He jiggled the loose doorknob until it caught then flicked on the light.

The overhead fluorescents blinked twice from behind the discolored plastic panels then emitted a low buzz and tinged the room pale yellow. A century-old cast iron treadle Singer stood against the wall, gold filigree logo emblazoned across its black enamel arm. A settling crack ran from under the machine's foot pedal across the room to under the shuttered front window where the sheen of the speckled terrazzo had worn away. Bits of fabric and buttonhole thread matted the fraying bristles of a wicker broom propped up against the corner. The air in the room carried the pong of cleaning fluid and stale vapor from the steam presser.

He couldn't still be fitting suits in here, Gia thought, looking at the three-way mirror, a chink in its beveled edge, that sectioned off the fitting area. Alongside the mirror stood a cloth and wire tailor's dummy. Beside it, the cutting table held a pincushion and magnet, the rusted tin of buttons and a tatty fabric brush.

For all its shabbiness, the place retained a certain order, the feeling of habitation, as if someone still came in on occasion to satisfy some solitary creative urge before venturing back out into the world.

She turned. "You don't still make suits, do you?"

Giovanni's laugh was truncated by a coughing spasm. "Who wears suits anymore? Today, everybody wants comfort, no matter how frowzy it makes them look." He motioned to a chair by the Singer. "Sit down, why don't you. Tell me of your work."

"I'd rather hear about yours." She slid the heavy chrome chair with its cracked red vinyl cushion out from under the sewing machine and sat. "You know that scarf really is quite something. The colors and pattern, the feel—all very different from what passes for quality women's wear material these days."

Giovanni shrugged. "You're in the business. Surely you have resources."

"Not for cloth like that."

"So what is it you want?" He moved the wooden stool from the workbench. "Given your demeanor at the café, there is something and some urgency."

Sitting there just the two of them, she felt the impulse to unburden herself, confide in him, though he didn't deserve her confidence, the trouble Fiber was in, her persistent doubt as to its future. She saw in his face that he intuited something of her thoughts.

"You don't have to tell me, if you don't want." He turned to the leather-bound writing pad on the cutting table.

She watched him toy with the pad and pencil. He knew more about clothing and tailoring than she and more about that material. He also understood how business here worked or didn't. And she hadn't much time.

"The meeting this Friday came about through my design professor, who's pretty well-connected. One of his contacts is James Martell."

Giovanni hoisted himself up onto the stool. "Martell, well, interesting background. You're aware of his nickname?"

She recalled Roccia mentioning it some time ago. "I believe so, yes." Martell had been known as the hammer, ostensibly from a stint as a manual laborer before going into fashion. Though few would have the nerve to call him that now, to his face, anyway. "He has a reputation for being relentless when he wants something." Though so did a lot of people.

"You believe he wants something from you?" Giovanni took the pipe from his pocket. "Don't worry, it's just something to hold. I don't usually smoke in here." He stuck the pipe stem in the side of his mouth. "What have you to offer, if may I ask?"

"Something new, I hope," she said, watching him. "Before I left Boston, I showed Martell the scarf in a video meet. He was impressed."

"It's an intriguing sample."

"It's not yours, is it?"

His gave a weedy smile. "What makes you say so?"

She gave a laugh. "You're a tailor, for God's sake, not a fabric designer." She looked around. "Not even tailoring anymore, from the look of things."

"And you think I had no hand in creating the piece?"

"The hem was yours."

His laugh relaunched the coughing spasm. He took a square of white cotton from a box of scraps behind the button tin and wiped his mouth.

"As for the design of the material," she continued, "the tertiary colors and warm tones could carry the fabric from late spring through summer and autumn. And the repeat, with that sunflower motif, is inspired, a subtle stamp of *il bel paese*. The hand has the feel of cotton voile but gauzier, almost vintage." She paused.

"There's something else going on, some fiber in the warp I can't identify." She saw his slight smile. "Whatever it is, the woman who wears a dress of that fabric will feel the difference. It's stylish and low maintenance, and she'll be spoiled by it. And while you're—you were a decent tailor—textile design is out of your wheelhouse."

He smiled, pipe stem clenched in stained teeth. "So what is it you're looking for, exactly?"

"I want the fabric and at a good price. And I want Fiber in distribution, internationally." In reality, they needed Martell or the shop was done. "I—I'm not ..." She wondered how much to disclose, how far in to admit him. "In reality, we're at a turning point. I'd like Martell as our first big client."

He took the pipe from his mouth. "Shall I open a vein, too?"

"Just the *tessuto* is fine. And as I said, at the right price." It would be best if he believed she would buy the material from Ordito, rather than simply nicking the fiber content and process for another mill to duplicate.

He looked at her as if trying to gauge whether all that she had said was true and how much more there might be to tell. He rose and put his pipe in an alabaster ashtray. "If you're really set on working with the mill, we'll see what we can do."

He returned the stool to the workbench and stood near the mirrors. He had never been tall, but alongside the tailor's dummy he appeared shorter than she remembered, his few remaining hairs barely encircling the crown of his head.

"I'll need more than just seeing what can be done," she said.

He shrugged. "You have a tour of the mill. Start with that. Stefano was right when he said his father loves to show it. Give Angelo the respect by allowing him." He tilted his head and gazed at the light through the shuttered window. "Perhaps it's best we leave now. We can go by the castle on the way." He turned and studied her face. "You could use a drive in the country, not to mention a bit of sun."

She stared at his pale cheeks. "I could use sun?"

He shrugged. "Perhaps we both could."

She got up and slid the heavy chrome chair under the Singer. Why was he willing to help? What did he want in return? As to the scarf, the originality of the pattern and repeat meant it had likely been designed by someone, at a studio perhaps, few of which were co-located with the mills that produced their concepts. She hadn't been inside a fabric design studio since college, but if he believed he would gain favor by acting as a go-between, she had no intention of obliging.

"Maybe it's better if I go to Ordito on my own," she said, watching him. "You've introduced me to Stefano. If the studio that designed the fabric is onsite, he can make the introductions."

The thin skin under his eyes crinkled. "You think this will come about without assistance?"

"Why not?"

He grinned. "Ah, *cara,* how you much you have to learn."

She felt the heat rise from her neck. "I've learned a hell of a lot in sixteen years." Like the fact that it was her mother, not he, who had stayed. "If you think that confirmation dress meant something—"

She stopped. He was baiting her, looking for confrontation. She could feel it, see it in his eyes. And she had neither the energy nor the future prospects to waste by giving in.

"So where is the mill?" she asked. From the website photos, it looked to be just down the main road from the village.

"You recall the Della Bastias?"

"Old Giulia's still alive?" If so, she would be well over a hundred.

"Not anymore. When she passed, the land went to Angelo, as her only son. He applied for a dispensation from the *commune* to add an office and renovate the old cow barn for commercial use. He finally got the approval last year." He nodded at her feet. "You have other shoes?"

She looked down at her flats. "Why? These are fine."

"Suit yourself." He opened the workroom door and went out to the foyer. "We should get a move on before Stella returns." He took his hat from a peg by the door.

"Didn't you tell her we'd be here when she got back?"

"We'll call it an error in calculation," He opened the front door and let in the brightness of late morning. "Turn off the light on your way out."

Reaching for the switch, she had a nearly overwhelming urge to recount his many other errors in calculation, but he had already stepped out onto the sidewalk. She flicked the switch, returning the workshop to silent darkness.

Out the street a black Mercedes turned out of the gravel lot alongside the house and chugged down the hill. Under the cornerstone of the *viale* an elderly man sat on a green lawn chair.

"I see Girolamo is out again this morning." Giovanni gave a nod. "You may recall the stone mason who went to earn his fortune in the states." He turned. "Close that, why don't you, I've got the key."

Pulling the door shut, she saw that Girolamo, who looked to be ninety-plus, had cocked his capped head at the mention of his name.

"That you, again, Don Giovanni?" Hands trembling, the old mason gripped the chair and raised himself with muscled forearms. "And who is with you? I hear a new anthem around here these days."

"My daughter, Gia. Remember, I mentioned she was coming?" Giovanni turned. "Come along, I'll introduce you."

Across the *viale*, the old mason tipped his black laborer's cap with its bit of red kerchief and tilted his head like a finch seeking a crumb. The texture of the seasoned oak cask at his side, the recurring pattern of weathered brick at his back, his artful pose in profile would make an alluringly practical deconstructed overshirt, she thought. Open down the left with three red toggle buttons on the collar, possibly in sand-colored, crinkled silk-cotton voile.

"You go ahead," she answered. She wanted her sketchbook and the box of scraps from the workroom.

Chapter 18

Giovanni drove the Punto up around toward Castello Barberini, which crowned the village's highest point. What would his daughter think now of the battlement and residence, stable and gentleman's farm that traced its lineage to 1314? The date was only an estimate, of course, since records were hard to come by, and no one seemed to care much for the precise year construction had been completed. And he had already written her that the tours of the castle had largely ceased, since most of the rooms were closed and the nineteenth-century mahogany pieces in the antechamber and parlor had little history or value.

"So what do you think?" he asked, as they drove past the fortification's eroding outer wall.

"Too bad that travel agent from the states backed out of buying. She could have made it a resort."

The woman's intentions, Giovanni was not alone in thinking, had been unrealistic from the start. "She came to her senses when she realized her so-called bargain would cost a mint to renovate and that people go to the shore on holiday," he noted. "Though that plot of land in back with the orchard is still lovely. You know Girolamo has a stake in it."

His daughter turned in his direction. "Why, is he royalty?"

"That bit doesn't belong to the Barberinis." Giovanni pushed the sun visor of the windshield down against the glare.

"So why doesn't he sell?"

"Tenacious old rook. Told his offspring they could wait until he was in the grave to rob him."

The road curved along the backside of the village past empty chicken coops and ramshackle houses with barrel tile roofs and patches of emerald-colored moss mortaring the cracked cement walls. Then all at once the roadway emptied onto a rutted country lane lined with blackberry brambles stippled with small white flowers. A yellow finch darted across a field of tall grass to the shelter of an olive tree that offered its silvery leaves to the passing breeze. When they reached the top of the hill, Giovanni downshifted.

"What's that?" Gia pointed to a prominent peak in the distance. "Monte Catria."

She shaded her eyes. "I don't remember seeing it before." She nodded at the horizon. "The mountains either."

To the west he could just make out the jagged blue outline. "The Apennines. Your mother and I always brought you here in summer, the heat and *foschia* obscured the view."

She turned and looked at him. "Was it at all hard for you here?"

"What do you mean?" He turned left at the road sign.

"Starting over after Mom and me. I mean, did you find it at all difficult to stay without us?"

Why was she asking this now, he wondered, since he had answered this question and sundry others like it so often and in so many ways in his letters. Though perhaps there was no statute of limitations on the desire for understanding and for meaning.

Guiding the Punto down to the main road, he took a white cotton handkerchief from his pocket. "I didn't start over really, just went on with life."

"You mean she chased you?"

He smiled slightly. "I could tell you I was better looking then." He swiped at his damp forehead under the hat brim. "But you still have your memory, and your eyes are still good enough that you don't need glasses. Besides, I don't like to lie," he added with a faint grin.

He stuffed the handkerchief back in his pocket and shook his hat, stained at the sweatband, out the car window. "In reality, Stella's husband was dead, and she had two sons to raise. And I was alone. Your mother never met anybody?"

"She never let herself," Gia answered quietly.

Before Antonia took his daughter back to the states, she told him she had never loved him, never truly cared for him, that he had essentially been a ticket, a way to remain in the states. Then she called him a failure as husband and, worse, a failure as a father, accusations that didn't stop at the shoreline of the ocean's breadth of distance between them. But what benefit could there be in spinning out these darker yarns now?

"I suppose she swore off men?" he asked.

"And a lot of things."

"It often happens that way." He turned right onto the main road and accelerated in front of a three-wheeled cart kicking up dust, its outer tire dragging the shoulder. "First you shut yourself to one person, then another, then this experience, then that. It's a contagion, really, once it begins." He looked at her. "Do you miss your betrothed?" he asked as they stopped at a traffic light.

"I—yes, I miss his company. He wanted to visit, spend a couple of days with me, meet you all."

She must have told him not to, he surmised, staring out ahead at the roadway. "Then why not have him come, if he's willing? We can make room." He glanced over and saw her shaking her head. "Why not?"

"Too much to do before Friday. And you can't honestly want another person in that house with Stella's sons coming. She'll implode."

Giovanni raised an eyebrow. "Not if it's a man."

"Well, it's moot now. Peter knows there's no time. He was happy to set a wedding date."

"He's Catholic, you said?"

"On his mother's side. His father was British and protestant. William died when Peter was twenty."

"And Peter—is he—was he ever married?"

"His first wife died—ovarian cancer."

Giovanni clucked his tongue. "Very sorry. And children?"

"Mattie couldn't conceive. That's how they found the tumor."

He shook his head. "Very sad, unfortunate."

"He's not unlucky," she countered. "And I don't believe in luck. People make their own choices."

"You think life is so singularly determined?" he asked, squinting up at the traffic signal while trying to see her from his periphery.

"You can't just make any decision you want and pawn the consequences off on somebody else."

He glanced at her over his sunglasses. "How long have you been engaged?"

She shrugged. "Peter gave me the ring just before my birthday, but we've been together two years. Why, what does it matter? He loves me."

He had wanted to ask what date they set for the wedding, but her comment snatched the wind from his sails. Clearly, she didn't believe that he, too, might love her, however poorly.

"One thing to consider," he said as the light changed. "It's best not to appear overeager with Angelo. He and Stefano are looking to grow Ordito, but a thread at a time. And no one wants the authorities in these parts thinking anything interesting is going on—anything they might want to be part of."

"People here still grease the wheels?"

"Grease, daughter, is what turns the country, when it turns at all. You should hear old Girolamo grouse about it. He calls the government a band of bloodsucking thieves and the populace even worse for bending over for it, though they're hard-pressed to do much else." He stopped the Punto alongside a cracked cistern. "The mill is just ahead." He pointed to a green and white glass-front office that formed the crosspiece of a long rectangular building. A dirt path on the right led to the grange.

"You may vaguely recall that longer section in back as the original mill," he said, pointing. "The office is new. The old cow barn was renovated for the studio. It's there on the right."

She stared out the windshield. "Wait, I remember this, the farmhouse, I mean." She pushed her face nearer the glass. "Can you pull in the drive?"

He turned into the visitor parking. "Now don't jimmy the door handle or you'll jam it. Pull up, slowly."

He stopped the car and watched as she got out and walked over the singular fig tree that stood resolutely on a mound of earth.

"They used to have cows here," she called out, a breeze ruffling her hair. "Oxen, too. We had lunch in the kitchen, and you could still smell the manure and hay from the stalls."

He, too, recalled that blistering summer's day. Angelo's wife, Franca, serving thick-crusted bread with rinds of cheese and calmly shooing away the bluebottles that lit on the heart of pine table, the plates, the food. He got out and walked over to the tree.

"I had my first taste of wine here," she said, gazing out over the field that ran alongside the grange. "It was strong. Homemade, if I recall."

Yes, he thought. That was old Giulia, who every year made wine, opaque and golden, and poured it from a green glass demijohn. That particular day after lunch there had been plump juicy peaches fresh from the trees, the best fruit in recent memory the countryfolk said.

A man with wiry black hair threaded with gray and combed back off his forehead came trotting out from the cow barn, his white shirt sleeves rolled under to reveal tanned forearms.

Giovanni hurried across the grass. "Angelo—" The rest of his words were lost in a gust of wind that soughed through the stand of cypress alongside Ordito's front entrance. He stopped and half-turned in Gia's direction. *"Mia figlia,"* he said loudly, nodding, my daughter, from America.

Angelo nodded and with a grin wide as a weaver's shuttle went rushing across to where she stood. Taking her face in his hands, he gave her a kiss on each cheek. How glad he was to see her, he exclaimed in formal Italian, especially after so many years—and, my, what a pretty young woman she had become. How proud he was to be a relative.

"Piacere," she answered. "It's good to see you, too, after so long." She looked at Giovanni, who hurried up to them, out of breath. "We're related?" she asked softly in English.

"His father and mine were second cousins, once removed."

"So what does that make us, third cousins, twice removed?"

He gave her a piqued look, which she ignored.

She and turned to survey the hillside. "The property is lovely, Uncle."

"Yes," Angelo answered with a wry smile. "The land still has beauty. Now we hope to get even more out of her."

She turned. "Stefano promised a tour of the mill. Can we take a look?"

Giovanni put his hand on Angelo's shoulder. "You will excuse my daughter. These people from Boston—too forward and too impatient to await a proper invitation."

"Nonsense," said Angelo. "I am honored. Stefano has a bit of a mess to work out in the laboratory so I will show you around." He led them across the parking lot through the double doors of the main building to the glass front lobby. *"Avanti,"* he said, ushering them into the central office.

A young woman in slim-fitting beige jeans and matching denim jacket sat at a glass desk, framed documents on the wall behind her. She had headset in one ear and a computer in front of her with a large flat screen showing what looked like shipping schedules.

"This comprises our headquarters." Angelo gestured to the vast length of building that ran behind the office. "Plus weaving, warping and quality control. The dyeing is separate. There we have the laboratory."

He stood by the window. "As you can see, Beatrice is checking the timetables. Your father tells me you have done some textile design, yes?"

"No. I mean, I studied, naturally, but I didn't finish the program." Her face colored as she tried to smile. "I'd like to go back and learn more. It's fascinating."

"Well, no time like the present," Angelo asserted. "Ordito's capacity, for instance, is five million meters a year in yarn-dyed and plain-dyed wovens. The fabrics are cotton, linen, nylon, poly, rayon, viscose and, of course, blends. Our prices are reasonable, and we produce only quality. For inspiration, we'll visit the studio."

He nodded at the double doors. "Initially, we thought to add the studio to the laboratory. But Stefano suggested converting the old barn. More of an organic feel, he said, since that is our direction."

He smiled. "We have many goals, but we also retain our roots. For example, when the wind changes direction, the smell recalls the days when cattle roamed the property. It makes us feel Mamma, all of the Della Bastia line, is still with us." He hitched up his trousers. "We'll see the design work after we tour the warping."

Glancing at Gia, Giovanni saw in her eyes a look of determination and something else, a foreboding expression, present also in the rigid way she held herself.

"Maybe we should we see the studio first," she prompted.

"Perhaps, Angelo, you could explain a little of your shipping process," he said, cutting her off. "Especially for samples, for example, for a rush order of new fabric."

"Certainly," Angelo said with a nod. "We keep samples of most of our fabrics on hand to send immediately. And our production line has some flexibility. We can produce new samples in a week, two at most. We handle bulk orders, too—with scheduled lead times, minimum quantities, that sort of thing."

"Sounds well-run," Gia said. "Would you mind if we see the warping before the weaving?"

Angelo looked at her. "Yes, if you wish. This way." He led them down a long corridor past the weaving and through another long hallway. "Let me get you some headphones. The noise is quite loud back here."

"No," Gia said. "I mean, thank you. I want a good sense of how things run." She turned to Giovanni. "You may want a pair."

He smiled. "I, too, will be all right." At least for now, he thought.

"This way, then." Angelo led them through a set of double-wide swinging doors.

Chapter 19

Gia stood in the doorway of the mill. Out on the floor the warpers cast their thread as if across another dimension of time and space. She had felt the same sense of awe when she first saw warpers in action with Don Roccia at a Connecticut mill that had come back online under new ownership.

"Really something, aren't they," Roccia had enthused.

She had watched transfixed at how the high-speed machines translated the ancient craft of weaving into the modern day with a timelessness quality. When she turned, she saw Roccia watching her as if searching for something, something he wasn't sure she understood or yet possessed.

"I see your daughter is one who truly appreciates what we do here." Angelo winked at Giovanni. "Stefano tells me you are in fabric sales back in the states."

"Yes, and we're always interested in new material." Unable to hold his gaze, she looked away. "Of course, what you do here is more than that—it's an art."

Angelo beamed and nodded. "Let me show you around. You, too, Gi, since you are essentially one of us."

Squiring them past the high-speed sectional warpers, Angelo spoke in reverent tones of textiles as the basic composition of life—the warp like the Della Bastia line, the crisscrossing weft their creativity. At each stop, he introduced a worker and assistant because each machine, he felt, needed a backup as adept and familiar with the job as the operator.

"Most of our people have been here for generations," he said when they reached the end of the line. "Some jest that they know more of their work than of their families. In reality, they are only half joking."

By the last introduction, Gia felt a whelming sense of sheltered inclusion. Yet, years ago she had only the notion of a factory, a memory vague and indistinct, one not worth retaining.

She turned to Angelo. "I imagine the dye process is remarkable, too. The colors in the scarf my father sent are lovely."

Angelo gave Giovanni a sly grin. "Your daughter has a good eye. Let me show you where it was made." He led them down the far end of the mill floor to a sectioned storage area set apart for samples and remnants.

She looked at the varied assortment. "You keep a good amount of samples on hand. Where is the material for the scarf?"

Angelo looked at Giovanni, who stood by a sample rack of shiny jacquards, specially woven fabrics using cotton, poly, blends. "You didn't explain about that?"

"I felt the finished product would mean more if Gia first saw how the material was created. Would you mind?"

"Not at all. The loom is this way." Angelo brought them to a chamber whose doorway and interior looked to be made of reclaimed barn board from the old stalls. He gave a nod. "Have a look inside."

Gia peered through the doorway. A young woman with long, dun-colored hair tied back with a scrap of plaid material stood working intently at an ancient hardwood handloom, her feet pressing the pedals up and down, her hands expertly threading the repeat of a pattern for a shimmering viscose jacquard in midnight blue and liquid silver-white translucent as moonlight.

She turned to Angelo. "That loom—it looks antique, eighteenth century?" She had seen one like it at the textile museum outside Boston, but on display, not in operation.

"This," said Angelo with obvious delight, "is my son's joy and pride. One would need the patience of a saint, or in this case of Chiara there, to make sure each thread is in its rightful place."

Gia stared at him. "This where the fabric for the scarf was made?"

As if from one end of a very long tunnel with a pinprick of an opening at the far end, she saw Angelo slowly nod. The whoosh of her breathing echoed in her ears. Handlooms produced only half a yard of fabric a day.

"Is the scarf the only example of that particular material?" she heard herself ask.

"No," said Angelo. "We have more in the storeroom—a couple of yards."

She pressed her fingers to her lips. A couple of yards was nowhere near enough for the style of dress she had designed to showcase the fabric's movement for Martell. And she wanted a sample to bring to the states for analysis. She looked over and saw her father watching.

"Is there a problem?" Angelo asked, looking from one to the other.

Feeling lightheaded, she stumbled back out to the storage area. Angelo and Giovanni followed. She braced herself against the wall of reclaimed wood and tried to gather her thoughts.

Angelo looked at her. "Is everything all right?" With a confused expression, he turned to Giovanni.

She, too, stared at her father. "I don't know if anyone mentioned it, but the fabric shop I manage is looking to expand into distribution. I showed the scarf to the head of a women's wear house in the states, and we're meeting in Milan to talk about a possible order. The meeting is Friday."

She felt as if the floor had cracked in two, leaving her teetering at the edge of a gaping fissure. "I told the prospective client I would show him the material. I also planned to surprise him with a dress made from the fabric so he could see how it moves."

"But there could be enough for a dress," Angelo said, consolingly.

Maybe, she thought, but not for all the rest. "But not for a line of dresses—next fall," she said slowly. "Assuming the client likes the sample." To meet the deadline, Martell would need to begin the run before he returned to the states.

"*Accidenti.*" Angelo ran his fingers through his hair. "No, there is not enough for that, at the moment." He pressed his fingers to his chin. "Listen, I understand your concern, especially with this meeting coming so soon. But maybe we can do something, if there is a bulk order coming."

Gia turned to her father. "You couldn't have warned me?" she said in English.

"You didn't mention your prospect until this morning or the dress until now," Giovanni answered calmly. "And as I said, I thought you should see the place. Meet the people, get a sense of how they work."

She had a sense that she was screwed, she thought, trying to quell a rising feeling of panic.

Angelo put his hand on her shoulder. "Listen, I can see your concern. So why not stay for lunch? Perhaps we can work something out."

"I am sorry, cousin, but we can't today," Giovanni cut in. "The boys are coming from Rome."

"Then come tonight," Angelo insisted. "Stefano leaves tomorrow for a *tintoria* near Modena that uses a new organic dye. But today he is in the laboratory here and always comes over for supper. If he can help or if I can, we will."

Gia rubbed her brow where a dull ache had lodged. The words brought little comfort, but Angelo seemed earnest and there was no other option.

"*Dai,*" Angelo urged, squeezing her shoulder. "Don't despair. We'll figure something out. At least you have material for some sort of a dress. The rest we can work on."

Gia looked at her father. This was his doing, duping her into coming to this God-forsaken place. And for what, more humiliation? Even as she tried to tamp it down, somewhere in her consciousness the thought bubbled up that it was she who had decided to come here and for her own ends.

"Please, don't worry," Angelo counseled. "Come back this evening. We will look at everything from the beginning." He hitched up his trousers. "When my Franca passed two years ago, it was just as we were building the studio. When it was finished and she wasn't here to share it, I have to say, I felt like giving up. But together we made it work, and to keep going became our motivation, what we needed to keep creating."

Giovanni patted him on the back. "And now we must be going, cousin, home to lunch. The boys are due to arrive any minute. Come, Gia, let's get a move on."

She gazed through the wood-framed doorway at the ancient loom and Chiara working with such precision that it was hard to tell where her labor ended and the labor of the loom began. If such unity had produced the fabric, how would she get enough for a dress, a sample for Martell and more to gauge the fiber content? Even if she could learn the blend and the source of the unidentified yellow-gold thread, no process could create all she needed.

She turned to Angelo. "Thank you for your time," she said, barely above a whisper. "We'll try and come back this evening."

Chapter 20

Stella hung up the wall phone. "Paolo just call. The boys will be here shortly. They would have arrived already, but there was traffic in Senigallia."

"Ha," said Giovanni. "The only traffic is with that new girl of Paolo's, with the green hair and the earring in her eyebrow. Lives on the beach in one of those tourist tents. *Rumena,* too, not even Italian. But the little idiot is nuts about her. *Mah,* these artistic types." He turned to Gia. "Did I mention your stepbrother is an architect?"

"I believe so," Gia said, vaguely recalling through a throbbing headache a description in one of his early letters. Paolo as a child using blocks and a colander to create such a distinctive form of dwelling the family still touted it at gatherings.

"And did I say how stiff the competition is here for architects? They're a dime a dozen. And to think, that *ruffiana* could throw him off what little track of work he has."

Such concern and over someone she didn't know, she thought, as she watched her father hang his hat behind the door. Though he certainly made knowing his business. And it must have taken some sort of courage for a man alone to bring home a new wife and two boys. The younger might possibly adjust to a new father after losing one he might not well remember, but the older would be able to recall.

Stella took a towel from the rack. "Oh, Gia, I was talking with Roberta about the party, and she says nobody in town carries gadgets for phones or computers, not even the tobacconist."

Well, that cinched it. She put her wallet back in her pocket. Now she would have to find a ride to Marotta. She stopped. "Wait, what did you say about a party?"

"*Merda.*" Stella covered her mouth. "I let the cat out of the hat. Was supposed to be a surprise."

She looked over at Giovanni. "Didn't I say no party?" she said in English. But her father was peering intently in the pantry apparently examining a stack of serving dishes.

"But we must to do something," Stella pleaded. "How you can be engaged without a celebration?" She put her hand on Gia's arm. "If you lived here, we would end up doing the whole wedding. This way is easy and we want to do—really."

An added incentive never to live here, she thought, if this was what people did when asked not to. Her thoughts flicked to Angelo and the mill, the impossibility of the tasks ahead.

"I need air," she said.

"But the boys will be here any minute." Stella turned to Giovanni. "Gi?"

"It has been a busy morning," he said, closing the pantry door. "Perhaps Gia needs a moment. Out back by the wall there is a bench." He nodded at the kitchen door.

"I won't be long." She took her shrug from the chair back.

She let the kitchen door swing shut on Stella's protests, which mingled in the hall with the aroma of garlic, onion and roasted vegetables. They must be lunching in the dining room. And since the kitchen bore no evidence of cooking, Stella must have ordered out. With a gnawing nervousness in her stomach where hunger should have been, she shut the front door, her mind racing through alternate dress designs that would work with less fabric.

She went around the house and across the gravel to the retaining wall where the warmth of the midday sun radiated from a cascade of brick steps cut into the hillside. How precise the stairwell was now that it was redone. She again caught a whiff of resin, from the stand of umbrella pine whose raised roots clawed the knoll. How often she had hidden beneath the pines with assorted cousins, planning, scheming, imagining.

Had all of them left for the cities, she wondered, feeling a sudden and unnerving wave of sadness at their apparent desertion. In her mother, a similar sorrow had mingled with bitterness each time Antonia conjured the past, a ritual she conducted with disturbing regularity.

"But all Dad did was ask if I wanted to stay in Italy," Gia said during one of their more memorable arguments back in the states.

"Your father begged you to stay," her mother accused. "He did nothing of the sort with me now, did he?"

"How would I know?" she answered, defiant. Caught off-guard, her mother stood momentarily silent.

"Well?" she said, pushing it. "How would I know what you two talked about? I never heard the conversations. All I have to go on is what you say." She had never taken this tack before, and a new possibility began to emerge. "How much of what you've said is even true?"

In one deft movement her mother gave her a slap then clasped her arms across her meager breasts, her mouth in a thinly drawn line. Afterward, they studiously avoided the subject. Though in front of the few people still left in their lives, her mother had upheld the *bella figura* of the self-sacrificing single parent all while her ex made a new life for himself back in *il bel paese* that didn't include her.

The low rumble of a car engine and heavy tires crushing gravel reverberated off the brick. A black Mercedes pulled alongside the two-story house abutting the back wall. The sleek dark sedan stopped at the far end of the lot away from the chicken coop.

A man got out and looked across the way, something recognizable in his long angular face, the straight sandy hair, layered and reaching nearly to the collar of his tailored shirt. Wearing a chunky, polished-steel timepiece at his wrist, he lowered the tinted designer shades. *"Non é possibile—Gia?"*

Alessandro Cantoni, she thought, though it couldn't be, could it? The boy her cousins had nicknamed Alex was Paolino's son gone away to school to become, what? She couldn't recall. An attorney, a financier? Something consequential with that car, the watch and shades.

Yet, she recalled his parents as plainspoken and hospitable, even after Paolino made it big in pork, such a good salesman he could vend even the squeal of a pig at a good price. His butcher shop and spotless packing plant so clean they shone. Paolino himself had worn nothing but white linen suits. His wife, Eleda, lauded for the sweet fragrant afternoon tea she served her guests in translucent floral china cups along with aromatic biscotti.

Alex came and gave her an embrace and a kiss on each cheek.

"Ciao," she said, feeling her vocabulary evaporate in the scent of clove and sandalwood that rose from his shirt collar.

He held her at arm's length. "You've hardly changed," he said in English that held only the trace of an accent. "Did you know I have only just returned from New Haven? I'm working with a clinic there."

God, Yale. "Right—you're a physician."

"Neurology, we're developing a new Alzheimer's treatment. You in America, you're always slow when it comes to medications and procedures. *Beh,* how do you find it here in Italy now? Not like it was, eh? Everyone's left, moved away. No one likes the towns anymore, too empty."

"Deserted," she agreed, her throat suddenly taut. Had her fugitive cousins found the village so void of anything worth staying for, family included? She turned quickly and wiped her eyes.

Alex put his hand on her shoulder. "Everything okay?"

"Fine." She brushed her face with her hand. "I'm just tired. The flight was long, so were the never-ending bus and train rides—" She tried to smile.

He notched his fingers under her chin. "Hmm, I see fatigue, yes, but maybe something more?"

She laughed and turned away. "I need a tissue, Doctor, not a physical."

He clucked his tongue. "If you knew who is trying to help you, you wouldn't be so quick to dismiss. But here," he said, handing her a pocket tissue thick as percale. "How long are you in town? Your father said just a few days."

"I leave Friday morning," she said, freshly appalled at the lack of time and awkward in his amber gaze. How was it that he had this coloring? Not like her father's family, whose darker features reflected their ancestry from the Catalan of Spain.

"Too bad the time is short," Alex said. "Still, we should get together."

"That would be nice. Oh, and do you know where I can get an adapter? The one I have doesn't work here, and nobody in town sells them."

"You can get one in Marotta or one of the PC places on the main road. If not, there's the mall. If you're around tonight, I can take you."

The church tower chimed the midday as a tan Fiat 500 rounded the corner, sending a shower of stones in the direction of the Mercedes. A pebble bounced off the back left fender.

"*Mah,* who is this Cretan?" Alex strode to the black sedan, now sporting a fine coating of dust across its rear panel.

A tallish slender youth with tight brown ringlets and a red bandana tied kerchief-style spilled out of the 500's driver side. A shorter more robust man with a trimmed beard and thick black hair in waves emerged from the passenger seat.

"Ha, I might have known." Alex said with a laugh. "I don't imagine, Gia, you've yet met your stepbrothers."

She stood mute as marble as the young man in the kerchief, who must be Paolo, rushed at her, grabbed her arms and planted an earnest kiss on each cheek while chattering a string of greetings and queries all in a breath.

Behind him the older Massimo walked slowly, deliberately, wariness in the round black eyes.

"Welcome," he said, holding her lightly and brushing her cheeks.

"*Ciao,*" she said, appalled at lapsing into monosyllables when abruptly surrounded by males.

"And you?" Massimo said, clasping Alex's hand. "Still playing the part of doctor?"

"Max, Paolo," Stella called out, coming apace across the gravel. "And Alex—*Dio,* what a reunion!"

Watching Giovanni trundle along behind Stella, Gia stepped back against the side of the house. Hatless in the bright sun, her father ran his hand over the dome of his head, now turning a light shade of pink. He walked up to Paolo and said something she didn't catch, his face showing concern, possibly over the lateness of their arrival or Paolo's Romanian girlfriend. Paolo, however, flapped his hand, dismissive, as if to say Giovanni worried too much. Then he put his arm around his shoulders in a gesture that looked oddly American, his youthful smile dazzling as sunlight.

In the far corner of the lot, the screen door of the two-story house banged open. Out came an older man with snowy hair and a white and blue pinstriped shirt with short sleeves and linen slacks the color of churned butter. Favoring his right side, he moved gingerly with the aid of a mahogany walking stick.

Gia turned to Alex. "Is that your father?"

Alex looked around. "Ah, yes. *Babbo* had a mini-stroke three months ago, but he's coming along. *Dai, Papà,* look who's here."

Matching Paolino's measured pace, Gia walked slowly across the gravel. The last time she saw her uncle was after that interminable summer and the autumn rains, just before she and her mother left the country. Antonia had been wrong in how she remembered the departure, Gia thought now. Her father hadn't asked, he had begged her mother to stay, offering six months, just the remaining school year, to try a move here since Gia's classes back home had already started. Her mother, however, had irrevocably refused.

"No more," Antonia had replied. "You don't get your way no more."

But so what? Her father still shouldn't have let them go. Even if the finality of her mother's words had intimated more than the rejection of an extended stay.

"Everything will work out," Paolino had said after lunch that one day and the argument that propelled one parent out of the shoreline rental to the sands, the other into the bedroom behind a slammed door.

In the abruptly tranquil kitchen, Paolino had sat stirring his espresso. "And if they don't—" he said, seeing her disbelief that her parents would ever patch things up, "you can always come back. You hear? Always."

Balling the tissue up in her fist, she clasped Paolino's shoulder in a consuming desire to hold onto someone, something.

"Zio," she said in a hoarse whisper, pleased to have remembered this one word in the absence of so many others.

Paolino nodded, the right side of his mouth curved slightly downward.

"He still has trouble speaking," Alex said, gently patting his father's shoulder. *"Eh, babbo,* you have to practice," he said in dialect. "He's afraid to talk, afraid he will embarrass himself. I keep telling him, the best place to recover is with family."

Gia held Paolino's arm. "We two," she said, speaking slowly and motioning to both of them. "Will practice together, you and I."

"See, *babbo?"* said Alex, with a smile. "Now you have a partner in crime."

"Alex, Paolino," Stella cut in. "You must come for lunch. Eh, Paolino, *dai,* come—bring Eleda."

"The next thing you know she'll invite the village," Alex said with a grin. "Sorry, *Zia,* I can't stay. I'm on call and *Papà* needs his noonday meds. But we will see each other tonight. Then, Gia, I'll take you to get the adapter. Here's my cell." He took a card from his pocket. "Meanwhile, get some rest, if you can with all this noise." He grinned and kissed her cheek. "You'll take the prescription, yes?"

Chapter 21

"Dio, Stella, but you have given the local oven enough business for a year," said Giovanni, who nonetheless appeared pleased with the baked eggplant, sautéed green beans and tomatoes in an olive oil and cognac glaze, roast rabbit and broiled beef filet, each in individual tins queued up on the sideboard of the small formal dining room.

The white linen tablecloth under the diminutive crystal chandelier gleamed as brightly as the suits Paolino once wore. Yet, how pale he looked today, Gia thought, standing awkwardly in the gravel lot behind the house in the stark midday light. She had hated leaving him just as in summers past she had hated leaving his lively home, with all manner of cousins going and coming, for the exile of whatever isolated efficiency by the sea her father had scavenged.

But Paolino was in good hands, with a son who was both a doctor and a specialist to affirm his improving health. Somehow she doubted that Alex's optimistic tidings were part of the usual false party line physicians and family here gave ailing relatives, stealing their dignity and in dire circumstances usurping their chance to reorder their affairs. Old Girolamo was right, she mused. In varied forms and ways, hereabouts there were still thieves aplenty.

"I think they did okay with the food this time," Stella said, taking a serving fork from the black lacquered breakfront. "Anyway, is best to leave the cooking to those who know, I always say. And the boys don't like what I make anyhow." She looked at Giovanni. "Or you either, for that matter." She poked him in the side with the handle of the fork then thrust it into the slightly charred vincisgrassi.

"We might like your cooking," said Giovanni. "If you deigned to do any." He put the tin on the table.

"Listen who's talking," Stella bristled. "When was the last time you boiled water?"

"Careful," Max warned. "We don't want to be caught fighting on Gia's first day with all of us."

"By all means," said Paolo. "Let's wait till we've eaten. We'll have more strength to argue." He took the seat opposite his brother.

"Here, Gia, sit next to Paolo," Stella directed. "Paolo, where are your manners? Pull out her chair."

With a flourish, Paolo rose and swept his hand over the seat cushion. "So, shall we treat you as the *principessa* in the fairytales?"

"Better not," said Max. "Those were ill-mannered stepchildren with ulterior motives. Besides, we don't want to forfeit a firsthand account from Gia of life in the states. We hear you are ever more divided over immigration, which seems odd to us here being a peninsula with easy access for all manner of people. Don't you find it degrading, having all those foreigners taking such advantage?"

"*Dio,* Max," Stella cut in. "How many times must I say it? No politics at the table."

"And no religion either," Paolo cut in. "Unless somebody can explain what the hell is happening in Rome."

Stella snapped to attention. "What, you don't like this pope either?"

"What's the difference, Mamma, who's wearing the mitre when the cardinals rule the day, and everyone knows it except, apparently, you." He turned and grinned. "*Caspita,* Gia, but we've done it now, eh? We've stunned you into silence when what we really want is to hear your thoughts of us. How long has it been since you were last in Italy—fifteen, sixteen years?"

"Is that what we want, little brother?" asked Max. "Yet another pronouncement from someone who doesn't know us well enough to say?"

Paolo turned. "What is it you fear, Max, that a non-Italian might understand us too well? Do you know that in my field of architecture the curator of the Biennale wanted an Italy exhibit because he considers us crucial to the world's culture, even if we haven't used our potential? His words not mine—and he's Dutch."

"For the sake of all that's holy, Paolo." Stella cuffed him on the arm. "Stop talking just to air out your mouth and pass the vincisgrassi. What we should discuss is Gia's engagement. *Bella,* show the boys the ring."

Grateful for a change of emphasis if not topic, she worked the band around her finger to surface the diamond and held out her hand.

Max leaned across the table. "Hmm, different. What is the stone?"

"A diamond, just uncut."

"Tell him what your betrothed said when he gave it to you," Stella prompted.

"Peter said it's for adventure." It wasn't quite what he told her, but considering Max's inclination to prejudge she didn't feel forthcoming.

Paolo took her hand and turned the ring under the light of the chandelier. *"Originale,* compliments to your mate. Clearly, he has discerning taste." He smiled, still holding her hand.

"Stop mooning and pass the pasta," Max cut in. "And besides, you only have eyes for Ana now, isn't that right?" His smile was thin. "Don't look so affronted, little brother. It is the truth, isn't it?" He drew nearer the table. "Now, Gia, what is most important, I think, is what brings you to Italy. The situation isn't ideal at the moment, as you have no doubt noticed. Perhaps an earlier visit might have been better?"

The electrified silence behind his words made her head buzz. Yet, despite the mention of truth, it seemed last thing anyone here wanted. Should she tell them anyway, get it out in the open? She looked around the table. Her reasons for coming would only validate Max's cynicism and disillusion Paolo. She glanced at Stella, whose erect posture and bowed head gave the appearance of prayer, probably for a swift change of subject. Her father, at the head of the table, sat focused on delicately excising a singed corner of noodles.

"I'm here for more than one reason, Max," she said, reaching for the bottled water. "The most pressing of which is work. I'm meeting a potential client in Milan on Friday so I thought why not visit everyone in the meantime."

Max's pensive expression seemed to indicate he was weighing this response.

"As to returning sooner, some things take time. I think, anyway." She poured a glass of the chilled San Pellegrino. While the subject would likely surface again later, this was a start.

"So, Mamma," Paolo cut in. "Where is the wine for our guest?"

Stella pressed her palm to her brow. "I completely forgot. We don't usually have wine with lunch."

Giovanni pushed back his chair. "Don't worry, pet. I believe we still have a Sangiovese set aside."

Watching him rise from the table, Gia wondered at the fact that he hadn't joined the conversation, though he had at least been present. Now she faced a table of strangers. Once the door closed, Max leaned forward.

Paolo half-turned toward her, blocking him. "So, Gia, we hear you design fabric. Is that right?"

"I wish," she said with a smile. "I've studied textile design, but it's such a complex field I didn't think I could do it justice." The veracity of the observation and her unexpected relief in saying it surprised her.

Max took the bottle of water. "Perhaps you could go for further study?"

"I could, but fabric design is both art and science. In fact, I was just reading of a manufacturer who digitally prints cells on material that is then grafted onto skin."

Max looked up. "Now there is a worthy endeavor."

"Sounds like your line of work," Paolo noted. "Did you know, Gia, that Max here is a design engineer? He has this idea that one day computers will be worn, like clothing."

"Really?"

She looked across the table at Max gazing down at his plate. Was it humility she saw in his face, shyness, a covert interest in further discussion? She felt a tangle of emotions and something vaguely like anticipation at talking more about the subject.

"Here we are." Giovanni held a bottle of wine whose contents under the faceted glimmer of the chandelier glowed a radiant shade of garnet.

"Ah, good, I'm glad we still have a bottle." Stella turned and drew a corkscrew from the drawer of the breakfront.

"You should know that this is made from grapes that grow on the very hillsides of Pesaro." Giovanni looked closer at the bottle. "And still good, I believe."

"Why wouldn't it be?" said Paolo. "What kind of wine gets worse with age?"

"Beaujolais nouveau, for one," Max answered in a light tone. "And it's not just certain wines that worsen with time."

Gia looked up and catching Max's sideways glance noted the ghost of a smile.

"Let's drink to Gia's arrival at last and her engagement," Stella said, raising her glass.

"And to better times here at home," Max added.

"And to all of us being together," Paolo chimed in.

Giovanni stood by his chair. "Let's also drink to a hopeful future."

"What I hope, with fervor, is that you make a dent in this food," Stella chided. "Now dig in and focus on the task at hand."

Despite the hearty appetite of two young men unlikely to cook for themselves, two older people who apparently enjoyed a meal most when it came from someone else and a sleep-deprived visitor, the tins on the sideboard still looked as if they awaited guests.

"*Dai,*" Stella urged. "Will no one eat anymore? What's wrong? Wasn't it good?"

Paolo blew out his cheeks and stretched. "It was fine, Mamma, considering the oven hasn't varied its menu in recent history." He pushed back his chair and turned. "Now, Gia, how about a trip to the beach?" He put his hand on her shoulder.

She looked at her father. "I was thinking of maybe taking a ride back up the road."

Giovanni looked up. "You can't—I mean, it's not advisable. Everyone will be busy. This evening is better."

Paolo squeezed her shoulder. "You could use some sun, and my closest comrades hang out at the shore. You can meet everyone."

"That's right, don't waste time looking for work. Spend it doing nothing," Max put in.

"Spending time with people is not nothing, brother. And it's area in which you especially could use improvement."

Gia stole a glance at the dining room door. What she ought to do was go upstairs to the privacy of the bedroom and sketch alternate dress designs that needed less material.

Paolo gave her another nudge. "Come now, how many chances will we have to spend time together?"

She turned and looked at him. Did he pull that puppy face on her father when he wanted something? Somehow she couldn't feature Stella falling for it.

"I suppose I could squeeze in the time," she said. She could do the redesign quickly tonight once the laptop was up and running. "Do you want to come, Max? The weather is perfect."

Paolo waved his hand. "It's not worth bargaining with someone who perpetually has better plans, though God alone knows what they are."

"Well, since you've extended such a gracious invitation—" said Max.

"Then you'll come?" Gia nodded. His expression seemed to indicate some desire, even if he was unwilling to concede it.

He gave a narrow smile. "Another time, perhaps."

She looked at Paolo. "Actually, I don't think I can go either. I didn't bring a bathing suit."

"Not to worry," said Stella. "You can borrow mine. Is new."

"Good luck keeping yourself in it," Paolo said, with a sideways glance. "It will be a bit abundant in the upper regions."

"Now, I could take offense at that," she said with a grin.

"Perhaps it is I who should be put out," Stella asserted. "But life is too short for offenses, eh?" She gave Max a nudge. "Come, Gia, you will like the suit. Red polka dots, quite youthful."

Chapter 22

The shore road shimmered under the autumn sun as the temperature in the Fiat rose like the heat of a kiln. Gia wiped her forehead and rolled down the window. She couldn't glimpse the sea from the flat strip of autostrada but could feel its pull like an outgoing tide.

Paolo glanced at her. "How did you ever manage the heat of summers here?"

"We stayed at the shore. I love the water, especially the Adriatic."

"And you are just now returning?" He made a tsking sound. "Maybe you wouldn't have come even now if not for work." He stopped at the intersection of Cento Croci. "Don't worry," he said, gazing up at the traffic light. *"Babbo* hasn't been speaking ill of you. He just wished you had come back sooner."

How did he know what her father wished, she wondered. But it was unreasonable to believe that in sixteen years her father hadn't unburdened himself with Stella and shared something of his former life with Paolo. Though somehow she had trouble envisioning Max inspiring confidences.

She looked out the window at a strip mall that managed to appear both recently built and a sixties throwback. "It wasn't the right time," she said.

"Were you awaiting an engagement to announce?"

She looked at her hand, the stone in bright sunlight radiating a dull fire. "Maybe there needed to be more than one reason."

"The only one you've mentioned so far is your job."

She looked at him. "Isn't that the main interest these days, work?"

Paolo pursed his lips as the light turned green. "Some of us seek more than labor just for the sake of it, or the money."

"Such as?"

"A future, for one." He took a right onto a side road.

"I agree," she said, though the tone of her voice sounded less than certain.

"Well, don't you have one—a future, I mean. With your business prospects and a man. You love him, I trust, if you're engaged."

She felt a tightness in her throat just under the jawline. In the ebb and flow of this other world and the other lives in it, Peter somehow seemed farther away. But she loved him, her agitation the aftereffect of too little sleep, too much food and nerves.

She clutched the straw beach bag with embroidered Shasta daisies borrowed from Stella. "Would you mind taking me to get an adapter? I forgot to buy one before I left." It might be better to get one now instead of waiting till this evening.

"You want to go now?" Paolo steered the Fiat up a narrow road that wound tight as a clock spring around the steep hillside. "Alex said he would take you tonight, and I've texted my friends to say we're on our way. Though if you need one sooner than this evening we can stop in Senigallia on the way back."

"That would be fine."

She pitched back against the seat in the centrifugal force of the roadway's upward coil. At the top of the hill, the byway leveled out to a plain, the sea beyond it ultramarine and glistening like shantung silk.

She stuck her head out the window. "Would you mind, I mean, could we stop up here for a minute? I know your friends are waiting—"

"No worries, the view from up here gets to everyone," he said, conciliation in his tone.

He glanced in the rearview then swerved onto a rutted turnabout apparently forged by others with the same notion. He stopped in the middle of the semicircle. She got out and went across the dirt tracks to the edge of a razed cornfield.

Down on the shore road cars and motor coaches were en route along the pebbled coastline from Rimini to Ancona to destinations of apparent import. Inhaling the tang of sea air, she felt the penetrating warmth of the sun. What was it about this place that despite one's best defenses still invaded the soul?

"A euro for your thoughts."

She turned to see Paolo leaning against the car, an inquisitive expression in the probing green eyes.

"You're lucky to live here."

He laughed. "If you were staying more than a few days you might not think so. There is little to inspire and even less opportunity, no matter how strong one's ambitions."

"You consider yourself ambitious?"

"I meant you," he said, grinning.

"You think I'm ambitious?"

He shrugged. "Maybe it isn't ambition so much as longing. But this is something I understand. I feel the same about my work, in a way."

She turned and looked out to sea. He might be right about the longing, but it was more an ache for something she had known once and now felt was out of reach. Looking around again, she saw his evident satisfaction that they had seemingly shared something he felt he understood.

She walked back to the car. "Your friends are waiting."

He grinned. "If you say so, princess."

"Don't call me that. Max is right, it's obnoxious."

"He didn't say it was obnoxious. More an off-putting designation when one seeks information. And is this what we have to look forward to now, your taking my brother's side in a debate?"

"I take the side of whoever's right," she said, smiling.

"Okay, if that's how you want to play it." He shoved the Fiat into gear and turned out of the overlook. "Now you'll see the fastest route to Senigallia."

Taking his foot off the gas, he let the Fiat careen down around the hillside. With the sensation of being airborne, she felt like her stomach had detached and wafted off to an unknown location. Only when they slowed for an intersection on a suburban street at the base of the hill did it return.

Looking around, she saw that the crossway sectioned off one of Senigallia's most thickly settled residential areas, part of the city she never saw because they had always stayed at the beach. A place like this would have been better, she thought, gazing at the apartments, *villettas* and condominiums speckled with brightly colored geraniums in terracotta pots, equally varied children romping in fenced-in playgrounds. In a place like this, she might have found friends.

"The business district is that way." Paolo pointed down a side street. "We can stop on the way back."

He jammed his foot on the gas through the intersection and down the busy street only to come to a screeching halt behind an articulated autobus that immediately expelled fumes from its exhaust to be sucked in through the Fiat's front vent.

She coughed and leaned out the window. Out in front of them, the Via Raffaello Sanzio ran perpendicular into the heart of Senegallia, the seaside resort whose port had been settled two thousand years ago. Somewhere nearby the Cesano emptied into the sea.

"See that fortress?" Paolo pointed across her to a battlement designed in an odd conglomeration of cylinders and squares. "*La Rocca Roveresca*—quite a combination of styles, don't you think? After the beach we'll go for a slice and have a look."

"After a lunch like that, I have no interest in pizza," she said.

But the traffic light turned green, and her words were lost in the blare of car horns and the crush of pedestrians clogging the curbsides. A woman in a navy pants suit sped past on a red Vespa. Behind her, a Nordic couple wearing t-shirts, white tube socks and tan leather sandals rolled placidly past on a tandem bicycle. They must come here a lot, she thought, watching the couple glide by in perfect unity.

"Our part of the beach is this way," Paolo instructed.

Turning left at the intersection, he drove parallel to the shore. At the next light, he turned right, narrowly missing an elderly man in tinted sunglasses, his shirt open nearly to the waist revealing his bronzed chest as he coasted past on a woman's bicycle.

Gia instinctively pressed her foot to the floorboard as the Fiat veered left. "You are old enough to drive, right?"

Paolo gave her a disgusted look. "I am old enough to have finished the Milan Polytechnic—with honors." He pulled the Fiat into an empty parking space in a line of empty parking spaces.

"I thought you and Max lived in Rome."

"You don't pay much attention to *Babbo's* letters, do you?" He flipped the visor down over the windshield.

"Sorry. Guess I misunderstood." She put her hand on his shoulder. "I'll pay more attention next time."

"Let's hope. And lock up, will you? This rattletrap isn't much, not like those emissions nightmares you have in the states, but we value it. Ah, look—" He pointed past the windshield. "Ana and Luca."

Out on an expanse of hard-packed sand wide as a tarmac a young woman and man sat on straw mats, legs crossed, faces turned upward to the blue.

"So now I'll have a chance to meet Ana with the green hair?"

"The color is teal," Paolo corrected. He grabbed a towel from the backseat. "I see *Babbo* has been talking."

"How do you know your mother didn't rat you out?"

"I know my parents." He rolled up the towel and stuffed his mobile into a black fanny pack. "Come, I'll introduce you." He got out of the car and waved. "Hey, Ana, Luca—vagabonds—have room for two more?"

Chapter 23

"Hey, Gia, dive in, why don't you?" Paolo called out from where he sat on a straw mat in the sand with Ana and Luca, all wading sandals and colored flip-flops cast aside.

"You're daring me?" Gia held the top of the red polka dot bikini where she had hastily basted it.

"Yes," Luca shouted, vigorously nodding his shaved head. "We're holding our breath to see if that top stays up."

Gia tightened the straps of the bikini and waded farther into the shallows, gasping at the unexpected chill.

"Cold, eh?" Paolo called out. "You all boast of the icy Atlantic, but we have our own chill here, no?"

"And sharks, too," shouted Luca.

"Stop it, you two," Ana said. "Don't let them scare you, Gia. Go for it."

"I intend to," she said, grinning. "Because the water is a lot colder back home, and the only sharks around here are on land."

Bracing herself, she waded out to the sandbar. *Accidenti,* but the water was colder than she expected and far more than she recalled, although the prior beach excursions had been at the height of summer.

The year she turned sixteen she used her birthday money to buy a modest two-piece swimsuit in pastel rainbow shades. On hitching a ride to Marotta with two female cousins, she found other more brightly attired sunbathers lounging along the pebbled shore like swatch book samples and paddling in shallows warm as bath water.

Wading out past the sandbar, she felt the chill grip her ankles. In seawater up to her waist, she bounced up and down on the balls of her feet, drew in her breath and dove down beneath the surface. The bracing cold slid over her like acetate lining. Once submerged, she opened her eyes and swam farther out.

A shaft of sunlight gleamed in the translucent green, illuminating particles of the sparkling sand she kicked up from the seabed. A school of small silvery fish darted toward her then away. She lunged after them, flexing her legs in swift scissor kicks through the chillier shadows to a bright column of light.

It was on that earlier beach day in Marotta that she first met Alex. Lying on a towel after a swim, she was lazily watching passersby when a tall youth a year or two her junior stepped lithely over the cement wall, poker straight sandy hair nearly to his shoulders, his expression guileless.

Once over the wall, he saw her, his eyes first on her face then traveling down to the square-cut top of her bathing suit, his look registering first surprise then approval. Her curves didn't turn heads, especially compared with the topless blonde on the adjacent stretch of sand, but in that moment she saw herself as he had, a young woman worth appreciating.

She felt the increased pressure in her lungs and pushed through the column of light to breach the surface. Inhaling deeply, she sank again, threw her head back and flipped her hair out of her eyes. Standing on the sandbar, she felt the saltwater clog her ears and her nose begin to run. She hastily ran a hand across the bikini top and felt it still in place.

"Hey, princess! What are you doing, trying out for the Olympics?" Paolo stood on a narrow line of wet sand holding a beach towel.

"And you said I couldn't brave the cold," she said with a shiver.

"That isn't what I said at all. But isn't that the way with you Americans—making everything a competition. Come out before you freeze."

She waded in to the shallows and trudged up the shoal, coarse with broken shells. "Like I said, the water back home—"

"I know, I know," he said, handing her the towel. "The waters of the Northeast are cold all year except a day or two at the end of August when you can swim without risk of hypothermia."

She shook herself and took the towel. "How do you know?"

"Surely you don't think Pappa waited for you to arrive to tell us of where he lived?" He rubbed the terrycloth across her shoulders.

"I guess not."

There were benefits, she supposed, to having a forerunner fill in her background, though her father couldn't have told them much lately since she hadn't answered his letters.

"So, have you finished proving yourself?" Paolo prompted.

"I'm not trying to prove anything," she answered, enfolding herself in the towel's scratchy warmth. "But since I'm here, why not take the opportunity?"

"So you're an opportunist, too?" Paolo queried, grinning. Freed of the red kerchief, his glossy brown ringlets blew back in the breeze.

"Why not, if the time is right?"

As if from the stratosphere, the thought of Fiber hurtled back into her thoughts. Raf deserved a call to confirm that she was still alive and working to get the fabric.

"Listen, Paolo, do you mind if we go downtown now? I really do need that adapter."

"Okay, okay. My, but we're anxious." Linking his arm in hers, he steered her across the pebbled sand. "Well, our Gia has survived," he said, letting her go. "And apparently not much the worse for the cold."

Luca rolled over. "O, intrepid, welcome back." He sat up and saluted. "So what do you think of your initiation into the Adriatic's depths?"

"With barely five feet of water and a sandbar, these are hardly depths." Ana tucked her long slender legs into a lotus position. "Don't mind him, Gia, he's the old man of our little band and ex-military besides. But, Luca, must you keep reminding everyone with the gestures and that hat? Don't you feel relieved that conscription is over?"

"Of course," Luca agreed. Raising his dark compact body, he shook the sand from his camouflage cap. "But with time and repetition, some things become habit."

"Never mind your habits." Paolo squatted next to Ana and picked up the fanny pack. "And cover that bald head before you blind somebody. We need to make a quick stop in Senigallia so Gia can get a charger for her computer."

"Now?" Luca groaned and lay back down. "I need sleep."

"Perfect, you can nap in the backseat. Come, *cara.*" Paolo pulled Ana to her feet. Even without sandals she stood several centimeters taller than he.

"Have it your way," said Luca. In one swift movement, he sprung from the mat to his feet. "But there better be a slice of Romeo's four seasons in it."

Gia took her t-shirt and shorts from the plastic bag and slipped them over the bikini. The mention of the shore's famous four seasons pie conjured a vivid recollection of *sardelle,* muscles and two types of clams, all fresh. The remembrance made her mouth water despite the heavy lunch.

She wiggled her feet into red flip-flops, also borrowed from Stella. "All right, count me in, but just one slice."

"Ah, see how you foreigners all flock around when it comes to food," Paolo said, rolling up his mat. "But who can blame you? Our fish is the best." He took the roll and started for the car.

"I don't know about that," she called out. "Boston's pretty well-known for fish, too, you know."

"Not like this," he answered. Opening the Fiat's hatch, he chucked the roll inside. "These were caught this morning."

Gia felt her stomach rumble despite the copious lunch, the salt water swim having piqued her appetite.

Ana gave her a nudge. "Don't let his goading get to you. He does that with people he likes."

She smiled. "I'll keep that in mind."

"All right, ladies," Luca said, taking their arms. "Our chariot awaits. Shall we?"

Paolo opened the car door. "Luca, you and Gia are in back." Fastening his seatbelt, he glanced in the rearview. "Everyone comfortable?" He nudged the 500 into gear and pulled out of the row of empty parking spaces.

"Try to avoid the main drag, Pao," Luca said over the headrest. "This time of day it's clogged as an eighty-year-old artery."

Paolo glanced in the rearview. "Now what have I warned everyone about backseat drivers?" He drove back under the overpass. "Gia, keep him busy, can't you?"

Luca turned and looked her over. "So, tell me about this phantom fiancé," he said, moving closer.

"Sure," she said, thrusting her outstretched hand between them. "Here's the ring he gave me."

They turned left at the traffic light onto the Raffaello Sanzio and drove over the Misa River to Senigallia's downtown. Drawn along by the vortex of traffic, the Fiat surged around the rotary onto a side street near the city's historic midsection open only to foot traffic.

"We'll park here," Paolo said. "The walk will do us good." He got out and opened the passenger's side. Ana took his arm, her height, olive skin and jet hair with its teal streak affecting the look of a graceful peacock.

Luca linked his arm in Gia's. "Listen, we're buddies now, right, you and I? So don't mind me. I always say you can't have too many friends." He slid his mirrored sunglasses down to reveal deep-set brown eyes earnest as a doe's.

Gia shot him a half-smile. "Why not?" she said as the traffic light turned red and the pedestrian walk sign began blinking.

"Stop fooling around you two and come along," Paolo urged. He rushed across the street, tugging Ana behind him.

They paused at a line of arches that separated the thoroughfare from the city's inner sanctum.

"You must admit it's beautiful, no, our Senigallia?" said Paolo. "One of my favorite small cities. Look there, Ghinelli's Foro Annonario, neoclassical forum, designed in the 1800s."

"Stop playing tour guide, Pao, and let's get some food, eh?" Luca prodded.

Paolo reached across and patted Luca's belly. "Are you quite sure you need it?"

"What need? I want. You can give a tour and get the charger after. It will be easier to think on a full stomach."

"Fine. Since you know Romeo's so well, lead the way."

"All right, everyone, follow me. It's just through here." Tugging Gia's arm, Luca drew her across the cobblestones, worn smooth with millennia of passing feet.

They walked in among the cool shadows of the Doric columns to a diminutive but eloquent piazza. Here the street noise fell away, and the diffused rose light of late afternoon slipped quietly into the square. Gia slowed then stopped. How could anyone live each day with such articulate splendor and not respond to its eternal invitation to pause and reflect?

Luca, still single-minded, tugged her across the square. "Look, there's Romeo's." He pointed to the street corner and a building with a phalanx of windows. "And it's not even crowded."

They walked into the pizzeria and stood at the bar. Gia reached in her shorts pocket for her travel wallet "Let me get this, please."

"Forget it." Paolo put his hand over hers. "Your money's not good here."

"That's right," Luca echoed. "Only Paolo's euros are acceptable. And hand over some napkins, too, would you, Pao, while we're waiting?"

As Paolo reached across the counter, two youths strode in, each wearing a blue and white soccer jersey struck with a gold crest on the chest. Laughing, the shorter youth looked down the bar in their direction. Taking note of Ana, he turned and nudged the taller teen, who paused inside the doorway, his bronzed cheeks flushed.

"Well, and what have we here?" Flattening the vowel sounds, the taller youth tilted his head. "Is this a *romena* I see?" Staring her up and down, he came closer. "My, but you're a reedy one, not like those squat little vagrants they usually export."

Luca looked at Ana. "Is he talking about you?" he said in a loud voice. "Because it sounds like he's talking about you."

"It doesn't sound much like a conversation," Ana answered calmly.

"What's that you say, *romena?*" the bronzed teen asked. "You know what conversation is?"

Luca nudged Paolo. "She's your girlfriend. Are you going to let him talk to her that way?"

Paolo put his arm across Ana's shoulder. "Do you want me to? I could, but you remember the last time."

A thickset man in a stained white chef's apron came from behind the counter. "What is this? What is happening here?"

Luca moved toward him. "Ah, Bruno, friend, do you want me to deposit this rubbish outside?" He nodded at the youths. "No charge for the cartage."

Bruno shrugged Luca's hand away. "I think you are the ones who should go. You and your friends." He turned his back to Ana.

Luca stared at him. "Us, what did we do?"

"Go on now, take your crew." Bruno gestured to the door. "We can't afford trouble."

"What trouble?" Luca persisted. "We're paying customers. Not like these freeloaders."

The tall youth laughed. "And what will you pay with, old man, your army pension?"

In one agile motion, Luca lunged forward. "You think you're something in that prep school getup? What will you amount to when your parents can't support you any longer? What will happen then, eh, lovely boy of the household?"

The teen took a step, but Bruno blocked him. "Come, Luca, show some understanding. You know this won't do."

Luca looked at him and nodded. "You're right. It won't do, not for me, not after serving this country for cuckolds like you." He edged past the proprietor. "Come on, kids, looks like we're no longer welcome."

Paolo took Ana's arm, but she stopped in front of the taller youth. "I'm sorry," she said, sincerity in her tone.

The teen's face was a mask. "What are you sorry for, *romena?* You can't help what you are."

She looked him in the eyes. "I'm sorry for you."

The youth's face hardened. "And why would the likes of you pity me?"

She looked at the emblem on his shirt. "Because you believe that a person is what others say. I hope one day you realize it's not so."

The teen's bronzed cheeks flushed a deep rubicund shade, the vein in his temple pulsing. "What is this you're giving us, eh *romena*? A sermon? Go to church, why don't you. Maybe you can justify your existence there." He cursed her, but she had already turned and walked outside.

The derisive laughter from the bar pulsing in her ears, Gia followed them out to the piazza. She took Paolo by the shoulder. "What the hell was that?"

"A way of life, apparently," he said, resignation in his voice. "Do you envy us our lovely land now?"

"This has happened before?" she asked.

"Just recently, at a club on the beach."

Luca put his hand on Paolo's arm. "Sorry, comrade. I never thought we would have this problem here, not with Bruno."

"Why wouldn't you expect it here?" Ana asked. "Your friend is just as afraid as everyone else, even those boys."

Gia stood beside her. "What are they afraid of? They have everything."

Ana smiled softly. "In Timisoara, where I'm from, just before the Revolution some years back there were riots. A man had publicly criticized the Communist regime. But as a man of informed belief, he took the people to task, too. He said they no longer knew their rights—as humans. It was like a pail of cold water. Eventually, the people woke up and started thinking again."

Chapter 24

"Ah, Gia, how was the beach?" Stella stood at the pantry, anticipation lighting her unlined face. "Everyone liked the new bathing suit, am I right?" Hand on her hip, she regarded Gia's hair, still limp from the shower.

Gia stared back at her. Despite its slimming navy shade, Stella's poly-blend wrap dress was too tight across the bust and too short for a woman with fleshy knees.

She turned away. "The beach was nice. The suit held up fine." No one had commented on its attractiveness, only whether it would slip off in the water, which, thank heaven and tightly stitched basting, it hadn't.

Yet, even without looking she sensed this wasn't the enthused response Stella wanted. Neither was it the highpoint of the afternoon. But how could she explain what happened at Romeo's? Although her mother had regularly denounced the country for its countless transgressions, the confrontation made her wonder how Paolo could resign himself to a bias that so warped the fabric of daily life.

"If the beach was so nice, why do you and Paolo look like something the cat dragged in?" Giovanni queried. "What happened down there, anyway? Did his girlfriend dump him?"

Gia turned. "Why don't you ask him if you're so interested?" Feeling irritable and chilled, she drew the pink shrug tighter across her chest.

"I will," said Giovanni. "Soon as I get the chance," he added in an undertone. He reached for the car keys on the wall peg "You're sure you want to go back out now? It might be a bit—early."

"Why, where are you going?" Stella questioned. "It's getting near dinner."

Giovanni consulted the clock on the stove. "It's only five-thirty."

"Then let's leave now," Gia put in. "That way we'll be back in time for supper." She couldn't imagine sitting down to another meal, but a sense of urgency would get them out of the house.

The kitchen door opened, and Max stood on the threshold, his pitch-colored eyes observant. "Did you have a good swim?" he asked, examining her hair.

"The water was colder than I expected."

"It can be chilly this time of year and after the rains."

Her thoughts flickered back to the close of the last visit, the constant autumn drizzle, the drop in temperature. "So I recall."

Max looked at Giovanni, the keys in his hand. "Going out?"

"Della Bastias'—Gia wants to see the old farmhouse."

"You were just there this morning," Stella put in.

"I imagine, Gia, you have seen our little mill." Max took a cluster of grapes from the fruit bowl. "I wonder if they got the certifications. They will need them, if they want to compete on the global market and do it ethically. Of course, if the overriding concern is profit, such validations may not be of interest."

Among the documents hanging on the wall behind Beatrice's desk, Gia thought she saw a confidence in textiles cert. "I would hope the Della Bastias run a mill with all those goals," she said.

"Hope is one thing," Max countered, plucking a grape. "Confirmation is another. And regulations hold people responsible for what they produce."

"From what I see, the Della Bastias are responsible—"

"Listen, Gia," Stella cut in, "why don't you and Gi go back to Ordito now, before supper. Then your mind will be at ease, and you can enjoy your dinner."

"Good idea." Giovanni slipped the car keys in the pocket of his windbreaker. "If we go now, we can avoid the traffic."

"*Perfetto,*" Stella affirmed. "Meanwhile, Max, come have a look at the upstairs faucet. Is leaking like a sieve again, and with more people in the house I don't want to worry. Gi, you and Gia go and bring back an appetite. We still have a mountain of food from lunch."

"We won't be long," Giovanni said and went quickly out into the hall.

Ignoring Max's calculating gaze, Gia went out after him. Though she had instinctually defended Stefano and Angelo, and Ordito's practices, Max had a point. Not only would the right certifications reveal Ordito's goals, they could be selling points for Martell. She shut the front door behind her.

"Thanks for getting us out of there," she said, walking behind her father to the car.

"Thank Stella," he replied, unlocking the door. "And don't underestimate her."

"I'm not." She jiggled the passenger's side handle.

"Because she has more on the ball than you may think. And don't prejudge Max either." He leaned over and pushed the door open.

She climbed into the seat. "What is it with you? I'm not judging anybody. I just believe the Della Bastias run a clean operation, and around here that's saying something." She gripped the dash as he threw the Punto into gear and swerved out of the gravel lot and down the hill to the main road.

"These days it's saying something anywhere."

"Agreed, so what's the problem?"

"The problem is, you don't know the people here. Take Stefano and Max, for example. They were fast friends once, like brothers. They even went to the same university, Sapienza in Rome, Stefano for biology, Max for computers."

"Sounds like a match made in heaven."

"Interesting you say so. And it was—till they had a parting of the ways."

"Over what?" She closed one eye as they zigzagged from the main road onto a gravel shortcut and around a pothole so large the Punto could lose a wheel.

"The sector where Stefano studied was called the Biology and Biotechnology Department Charles Darwin."

She looked at him. "Don't tell me. Max had a problem with the Darwin part?"

"*Brava.* Max is like many of his generation here. Very live and let live, until you cut cross the more conservative views of the church."

"I'm surprised he didn't argue Paolo's comment on the pope."

"In this the two might agree, since this pope has said, in public anyway, that evolution doesn't contradict biblical teaching. And since Paolo was swift enough to steer the conversation to Italy, Max's rebuttal went to national pride."

She stared at him as he veered right into Ordito's driveway. "After what I saw today, that's more offensive than I can even begin to say."

Giovanni parked the car and killed the engine. "What happened down at that beach?"

She shook her head. "Ask Paolo, if you want to know. And if you're really so concerned about bias, don't prejudge Ana."

She looked over at the old farmhouse. With the strength of the remaining daylight, no lamps yet burned in the grange windows as they had in times past. Ordito's glass front office, however, was ablaze with light, and Beatrice still occupied her seat at the desk. The designers were probably working, too, but before she visited them she needed as much of that fabric as they had on hand. She should have asked for it this morning, but her thoughts, not to mention her emotions, had been in a whorl.

"Ready?" Giovanni asked, interrupting her rumination.

She opened the car door. "Ready or not."

The horizon behind the Apennines was cloaked in violet, and somewhere under her nervousness she felt excitement over the meeting with Martell, a man grounded in the commerce of fashion who still sought new talent, fresh ideas. It was this pioneering spirit that drew her to him and the apparel house he built.

Watching her father walk up the path, she ached to share these thoughts, reveal her dreams, if not her hopes. But mistrust barred the way, making her feel oddly cut off—from him, this new family, her laptop and phone, even, she realized, the outside world and the man who in six months she would marry. She should have told Peter to visit after all, but she had too much business here of too deep a nature to resolve in the company of outsiders. Feeling the chill of the falling dusk, she buttoned the toggle on the shrug and followed her father to the farmhouse door.

He rapped on the screen. *"Permesso?"* he said, pushing it open.

"Come," Angelo beckoned, standing at the counter. "Sit, make yourselves comfortable." He motioned to the vacant cane chairs gathered round the heart of pine table. "Stefano will be here shortly. A little wine?"

"A small glass," said Giovanni.

Angelo took a green glass demijohn from a bottom cabinet and poured an opaque golden liquid that looked to be the same homegrown vintage she remembered. If it was as strong now as then, she would soon feel too indolent to think straight.

"Thank you, no," she said.

"A bit of cheese?"

"Yes, *grazie.*"

Angelo took a round of casciotta from the sideboard and a paring knife from the drawer. He stuck the knife in the center of the cheese with a practiced hand and broke the round apart, releasing the aroma that infused every kitchen in the region.

"Here, Gi, see how you like this." He set the casciotta in the center of the table. "It's from Urbino. Look at that texture."

He slid out a chair and sat beside Giovanni. As the two talked of the need to continue buying local produce, Gia only half-listened.

She had a decision to make. It would be more ethical, faster and probably easier to work with Ordito than to try and duplicate the fabric content and a production process that from what she had seen this morning couldn't be easily replicated, if at all. Besides, Angelo didn't deserve reprisal. Her father was another story, a discussion to be had once everything was settled. He had clearly assumed the visit to the mill and its family of workers would bring her around, as if he had known all along what she might be planning. So what if she did sign Ordito? She could convince Raf of its viability—assuming the mill had the organic side of the equation right. As to her father, she would deal with him, too.

She heard footsteps. Stefano pushed open the screen door, his copper-framed glasses pushed halfway up his forehead and looking as calm after a day in the laboratory as he had in the café this morning. Seeing him unruffled, she wondered if his composure, more than his beliefs, was what had piqued Max.

"Good evening, Giovanni, Gia. I'm glad you've come."

"I apologize for the hour," Giovanni said quickly. "Rest assured we won't presume on your hospitality for a meal."

"You're always welcome." Stefano took a juice glass from the cupboard. "Gia, I was thinking you might recall our first meeting if I mentioned that Maestro Bedoni called on you to read to us youngsters in English so we could hear the words spoken correctly."

Ah, yes, she did remember. She had gone to Bedoni's little brick house with its battered red wooden doorway wedged in at the end of the lane where the maestro taught a gaggle of elementary school children a variety of subjects. He had called her in to read—she couldn't recall which text, only that she had read poorly.

She felt her cheeks flush. "I do remember. And what a poor job I did. I'd never read aloud for a command performance."

"Well, I'm glad the memory returned." Stefano tipped the demijohn and poured a finger of wine into the glass. "As you see, we're not fancy around here." He slid a chair back from the table. "I understand you have an interest in a particular fabric."

"The shop I'm part owner of in Boston wants to grow the business toward distribution, internationally. I had a chance to demo the scarf my father sent to a prospect, and he's interested. But from what I hear, you don't have much of the *tessuto* on hand."

"Not at the moment, no. It has experimental fibers we were still working with at the time."

"And it's handloomed."

"Yes, but now with the new yarns we could duplicate its qualities."

As she sat thinking, she could hear the faint thrum of the warping machines through the screen door. "I have other concerns as well," she ventured.

Stefano took a sip of wine. "Which are?"

"Getting samples quickly enough and being able to mention certifications—Fairtrade and sustainable, possibly organic, assuming the experimental fiber is organic. The prospect is looking to start a women's wear line he can call organic, or at least move in that direction. The faster we can catch and hold his interest in this area the better." Having saved this detail until now, she heard the satisfying scrape of wood on terrazzo as Angelo and her father drew their chairs closer.

Stefano swirled the pale liquid in his glass. "Well, we're already a Fairtrade shop, and we have the confidence in textiles cert. We're also working toward sustainable. Organic, however, is more difficult."

"How long do you think those last two certs will take?"

"*Mah,* Gia, how is this a fair question when you haven't placed an order?" Giovanni cut in.

"Let them talk," Angelo affirmed. "We may as well put all the punch cards on the table, if you'll pardon the expression."

"My thoughts as well," Gia said, glancing at her father. "And while we're face to face." She turned to Stefano. "In reality, Fiber, my shop in Boston, is a small house, so we need every selling point we can get. We also need your absolute best turnaround—on samples and bulk—not to mention best pricing. Uncle Angelo tells me we can count on all these elements."

Stefano smiled softly. "You come right to the point."

"Since we're laying our cards out, can you legally call the new fabric organic?" From her periphery, she saw her father put his head in his hands and Angelo nudge his arm, ostensibly urging for calm.

"There are strict regulations for what constitutes a true organic farmer," Stefano said evenly. "For example, they are not allowed to grow genetically modified crops. So the best approach, the honest one, is to tell your prospect precisely what we have now and what we are working toward. This will show goodwill and our trajectory. You can also rightly say the fiber is natural." He looked at her closer. "Who, may I ask, is the prospect?"

She crumbled a bit of cheese onto her napkin. "Since we haven't yet signed a contract, I can only say he's the owner and founder of a top women's wear line based in the US, one still known for fair prices *and* good quality."

"At least we have these things in common," Stefano said with a smile.

She gave a nod. "Then let me make a suggestion. Let's talk best pricing and delivery for samples and put some scenarios together for larger quantities. And don't let me leave here without the fabric you have already on hand." Out of the corner of her eye she saw her father shake his head. "You have my word—I won't approach another mill."

Stefano gave her a probing look. "I don't suppose you're doing all this just for the challenge? I hate to say it, but Americans have that tendency."

She grinned. Seeing him at this moment and hearing the aspersion, though more tactful than Max's and not completely unfounded, she could well imagine how the two might have once been close.

"I'm not interested in the fabric because it's a challenge," she replied. "I'm interested because it's different, unique. I believe in it and in Ordito."

Chapter 25

"Gia, psst, come here a moment." Stella stood in the kitchen, a half-filled tin of green beans left over from dinner on the table, the phone receiver pressed to her chest. "Someone is calling for you. Says his name is Rap, Rafe—I think is about work."

Bautista calling Italy on his nickel? She felt lightheaded as the heat rose from her neck. And here she had just been talking costs and schedules without having consulted him. Feeling like a miscreant, she took the receiver and covered it with her hand.

"I'm sorry, would you mind?" She nodded at the kitchen door. "It's my business partner."

A vague look of surprise crossed Stella's face. Clearly, she hadn't expected to be told in her own kitchen regarding her own phone that she couldn't listen in.

"I'm sorry, but Raf can be—hard to deal with sometimes." She offered a grim smile.

If he was calling the number she had left expressly for emergencies, it must be bad news. Like maybe the city's Public Works department had finally had Fiber condemned. But keep a good thought, she chided herself.

"I may have to talk a little—louder—than usual." She arched an eyebrow.

"Ah," Stella said, expressively. "One of those." She covered the green bean tin with tinfoil and nudged the kitchen door open with her hip. "I'm down the hall if you need me."

She waited until the door swung shut and put the phone to her ear. "Raf," she said, forcing a cheery tone. "How are you? Sorry I haven't called. My cell is dead. I'm just off to get an adapter. I didn't have a chance to get one before I left."

"I'm not surprised." Bautista's voice was loud, his tone hot as a *balut* in the shell. "You were in such a hurry to get out of here. You at least brought the laptop, didn't you?"

What an idiot, she thought. She held the receiver from her ear. "I'm working on getting the fabric, if that's your concern," she said, hoping to steer him toward the real purpose of the call.

"The material, the material. Of course, I'm worried about the material. And about you caving in to those damn relatives."

"You mean you called just to check in?" she said in falsely genial tone. "That's so thoughtful."

"I'm not checking with you. I'm checking on you. What the hell is going on there?"

She paused. How much of what she accomplished should she reveal? Less, she thought on instinct, since she could always add more later.

"I've been doing just what I said I would," she answered firmly. "And I have both the fiber content and the process." The boast wasn't quite a lie. She did have an idea of both. The fact that Ordito still retained the actuality was beside the point.

"Don't tell me you've signed something. You haven't, have you?"

"Of course, not." While this, too, was true, if an order materialized and was big enough, telling Bautista why Ordito was the house of choice would be infinitely easier. "So, what happened with the electrician?" she asked sweetly.

His uncharacteristic silence set off a fluttering in her chest.

"Well, the good news, if there is any, is that Sullivan, the bastard, says the problem is fixable."

She squeezed her eyes shut. "The bad news?"

"It's gonna cost us."

She felt her stomach heave. Was it her imagination, or had he emphasized the "us"? She opened her eyes. "How much?"

"Six grand to rewire the closet."

She rubbed her forehead, which had broken out in a light sweat. "Hey, you there?"

In the harsh searching light of this revelation, the trip suddenly seemed imprudent. She had simply been too set on achieving her own ends to see it. She leaned against the window sill.

"What is it? You're thinking something. I know you're thinking something. I can smell the smoke from here. Eh, Falci, are you there?" Bautista shouted.

"I'm just wondering—how feasible all this is over here."

"Are you insane? The only chance we have is that order. It's a must-get."

"I don't imagine the insurance will cover anything."

"Well," Bautista said slowly. "I do know a guy—"

"No," she said, firmly. "No guys. The fix has to be legal." Funny how from a distance she not only saw her flaws with greater clarity but his, too.

"Then put together what you need, make the damn deal with Martell and get the hell back here."

She stared up at a stain in the far corner of the ceiling that looked oddly like the one at Fiber and wondered vaguely if the upstairs leak had spread beyond what Stella had surmised.

"Falci, what the hell? Silence costs, you know."

"I heard you," she said. "I'll get the deal done."

She was in too deep now to do otherwise. At least the conversation with Stefano had been hopeful, and there was something to be said for working with people she could trust.

"Actually, Raf," she said, forcing a change of tone. "I'm glad you called." Given the sudden hush of dead air, she had caught him off-guard. "It will spur me on."

"Well, then, maybe this is worth it to reach you in that hole."

"I'll call when I'm in Milan."

"Call with good news, or you'll—"

"Talk soon," she said with more hope than she felt and hung up before she heard his reply.

She got up from the sill and gripped the chair back. The subsuming exhaustion had returned, compounded by having lived through more in a day than what back home would have served for a month.

She glanced at the clock on the stove—nearly eight here, around two in the states. She could try calling Peter, but he would be busy solving his own problems. At least she couldn't be roped into those, too, though as the thought occurred a question rose in her mind.

Had her father felt the need for distance from the mounting difficulties with her mother, with her? The tightness was there again, the strained sensation down the back of her throat. Could she ever come to some form of acceptance at having been left, ever find a way to make the kind peace with it that was more than momentary?

At least with the day nearly over, she had only the adapter to get. And then? If she had the energy, a few new dress designs and a few hours' rest before a very early morning.

In the lingering stillness, she realized she no longer heard voices from the dining room. She went out to the hall and heard the muted sounds of a colloquy out behind the house. She walked down the hallway to the screen door. Out on the patio, Max sat holding court in a circle of torchlight with her father and Paolo, joined by Paolino and Eleda. She opened the screen door.

"The problem of immigration is not only one of law but of vigilance," Max intoned in formal Italian, forefingers tented to his lips. "And it must begin with better policing of the borders. As it is, the country is one long open coastline where nearly anyone with a boat can drop anchor." He looked up. "Ah, Gia, your leaders say the same of Mexico, no?"

Dear heaven, she thought, moving cautiously to an empty chair. "Well, it's a complex subject—"

"Max, why harp on something that has become a way of life," Paolo said over the soft chirp of cicadas. "And I doubt Gia would agree with such a narrow philosophy, anyway."

Max gave a laugh. "Ah, little brother, you say this because you have a vested interest in seeing the borders remain—shall we say—porous?"

"No, we shan't say. And as usual you don't know the half of it. You've no idea what it is to be a stranger here."

"Neither do you, little brother, unless you count the Milan bar scene at two in the morning. And we are not talking of a few instances or a girlfriend from across the Adriatic. We are talking about this country opening itself like a prostitute to anyone who comes along."

"*Basta,* Max," said Giovanni. "Paolo, don't egg him on."

Shaking his head, Max looked over at Paolino and Eleda, who sat calmly listening. At the sound of flapping mules and scattering gravel, they all turned.

"Ah, finally, Stella with the gelato." Giovanni rose. "Where on earth have you been, woman?"

Stella strode to the patio table, red leather mules smacking the soles of her feet. "What do you mean where have I been? I been getting an assortment of desserts for this motley group." She set the tray on the table.

"Here, eat before it melts," she urged. "And stop whatever foolish talk you've started. It never solves anything. Paolino, Eleda, did anyone ask if you want gelato? No, right? Well, no matter, I brought enough for everyone. Gia, pick something—we've got the good chocolate. Try the cone with the nuts." She turned to Paolino. "How about a cup, Pao, it's easier to eat than something on a stick. Vanilla or chocolate?"

Paolino's face displayed a peculiar look as if he was unable to decide.

Stella picked through the assortment and found a cup of vanilla and chocolate swirl. "How's this?"

Paolino cleared his throat. The small gathering instantly grew silent. Suddenly self-conscious, he hesitated.

How was it that the ballsiest of the Cantoni family could allow the stares of others to cow him? Gia felt the urge to tell him to forget everybody else, to not allow himself be confined in a silent prison.

As if sensing her thoughts, Paolino looked across the table with a lopsided smile. *"G-razie,"* he said, taking the gelato. "It has been— long time."

Looking at him askance, Eleda's eyes filled. She snatched a paper napkin from the stack Stella set on the table. "Do you know how often I have cajoled, coaxed and threatened this man to speak on his own?" She wiped her cheeks and gave her husband of forty-something years a cuff on the arm.

"Is right," Stella agreed. "No more excuses now, eh, Pao? We know you can talk, so no more babying."

Surprised that her uncle would take such a public scolding, Gia started to speak, but Paolino gave her a look. Another time, the expression in the clear blue eyes seemed to say. We'll deal with this one-upmanship at another time. She watched as he clasped the chair arm with the iron grip that had been mythic before he went into the sales, when he could still butcher a hog quarter in minutes, the same grip with which he clutched the mahogany cane.

Finishing her ice cream, she heard the sound of heavy tires and the crunch of gravel echo off the retaining wall. Squinting in the semidarkness, she saw the sleek black Mercedes sedan glide to a stop. Alex got out and locked the car. Pushing his hair off his forehead, he checked his watch.

"It's late, eh, doctor?" Stella said. "And you've surely missed dinner. But tonight we can offer a repast fit even for someone of your stature. Have a seat and I'll prepare a plate. We still have everything from lunch—vincisgrassi, eggplant, beef—"

"Why must you feel you should feed him, Mamma?" asked Max. "Isn't there anyone at his home to do it? Or is Nicoletta in Rome visiting her sister again?"

"My dear wife," Giovanni said, pinching Max's arm, "is right about a feast, primarily because she was not the chef." He got up and took a folding chair out from under the eaves. "Please, Alex, sit."

"Perhaps I will for a moment." Alex took the chair beside his father. "But I'll pass on dinner, Stella, though not for the cooking. An American pharma took us to quite a large lunch. We have picked up your bad habits in the states, Gia. Fining at a chic little eatery known more for its location than the food."

She balled up her napkin. "So, all those visits to the states to show off your knowledge and the only return is from a drug company?"

"Oh, your doctors come over, too, to learn from us." He took a cup of vanilla from the remaining assortment.

"How else would they acquire the latest methods?" Max queried, dropping his plastic spoon in the empty gelato cup.

"*Caspita,* why don't you stop," said Paolo. "Haven't we had enough national sentiment for one day?"

"How would you know what's enough?" Max turned. "Come to think of it, we are still waiting to hear what has been eating you since you returned from the shore." He looked across the table. "Gia, care to enlighten us?"

She shrugged. "It's not my story."

"*Brava,* sister," said Paolo. "Keep your own counsel."

"Here, here," said Stella. "To strong women." She raised her vanilla cone topped with chocolate and peanuts. "And to the men who keep them satisfied—if they know what's good for them."

Alex laughed. "Now there's a tough act to follow. Gia, still need that adapter?"

"God, yes," she said, quickly.

He scooped the last of the gelato from the cup and took a napkin from the dwindling pile. "Well, then, off to the mall. No point searching the main drag." He got up and stood by Paolino. "So, *Babbo,* you practiced speaking today?"

Paolino's eyes crinkled. He leaned sideways and looked up at his son. "I—make progress," he said slowly, raising his cone.

"Good, maybe tomorrow you'll say even more."

"Yes, he will." Eleda patted her husband's bristly cheek. "And maybe you'll shave, too." She looked around the table. "Listen, why doesn't everyone come for dinner tomorrow? Gi, I'll make the homemade fettuccine with the fresh tomatoes and the *bistecca.* That way we'll appease even the American appetite."

"Oh, but we couldn't impose," Stella said, giving Giovanni a look. "Not with so much food still left here."

"Speak for yourself," said Giovanni. He turned to Eleda. "How is eight o'clock?"

"Make it seven. We have early eaters among us. Alex, can you tear away from the office? You're at the surgery here in town, yes?"

"Yes, but the time depends on the patient schedule. Why don't I play my part by ear, as the Americans say." He took out his key. "Ready?"

Gia felt in her pocket for her travel wallet and cell. "Set."

"Now don't let that fancy limousine go to your head," Max cautioned. "Not all of us here are so blessed."

"Nor we in the states," she answered. *"Ciao,* all, see you later."

"We'll leave the back door unlocked," Giovanni said.

Stella waived her plastic spoon. "I am not leaving that door open. With all the riffraff around. Give Gia the key."

"It's inside."

"Uffa. Here, Gia, take mine." Stella took a key from the gold chain at her neck.

"How is it, Mamma, you're so quick to give her a key and I must beg?" Paolo cut in.

"Because Gia is responsible and will come home at a decent hour."

Max started to speak, but Giovanni squeezed his arm. "Now, Gia, make sure you get the right adapter. You have to call that fiancé of yours."

"I will." She would call or text tonight even if the hour was late, since the time difference favored Peter's side of the ocean and it would avoid interrupting the day tomorrow. She waited while Alex clicked the car doors open. "Do you always lock up here?"

"Force of habit," he said and went around to the driver's side.

Chapter 26

She sat in the cushioned seat of the Mercedes surrounded by the pleasing aroma of fine leather in a soft shade of dove gray.

Alex turned the key in the ignition. The CL responded with a low growl. "Ready?" A gentle whoosh of cool air puffed into the cab.

"Let's go," she said.

A surge of anticipation cast her back to her last summer here, when she and her cousins had piled into the miniscule Fiat of a friend just old enough to drive to the beach and the nearest discotheque.

"Sagittarius isn't still there, is it?" she asked.

Alex tapped the gas and put the car in reverse. "It's called something else now, Sahara, I believe." The engine rumbled as the tires pawed the gravel. "You remember the ceiling?"

"How could I forget?" Painted pitch black with small white lights in the shape of the archer, it had been designed to resemble the one in Grand Central Station. "We had our first dance there."

He turned in the semidarkness, the side of his face illumined by the indicator lights on the dash.

She smiled. "You don't remember."

"You were wearing a short white shirtdress with a red belt and red Bandolino sandals."

She laughed. "Wow. Photographic memory, or is something else going on?"

He squeezed her hand. "I've a good memory," he said, guiding the CL out of the village center to the thoroughfare. "Remember the music?"

"Mostly American and three years behind the times. Until they played Elton John's 'Candle in the Wind,' after Princess Di. Heartbreaking. Oh, and that one song. I loved that one—a dance song. Italian, French, both, some English, too, I think. What was it?"

"*Lasciati Tentare.*" He hummed a snatch of the refrain. "Great song, we still love it."

Across the road she could see the lighted windows of what were once farmhouses. "Not much time now for dancing."

"We have more important things, so we tell ourselves." He waited for a line of cars to pass then turned left onto the main roadway. "How did it go today?"

"All right, I think."

He glanced at her. "Just all right?"

"There was some progress." She thought of the meeting with Stefano, the myriad plans for tomorrow. "That's what I want to believe, anyway."

"Are you afraid to be encouraged?"

"I don't want to count my chickens." She looked out at the darkness dappled by the headlights of passing cars. "Something happened today in Senigallia."

He looked at her. "Tell me."

"We went to the beach. It was lovely, perfect weather." She gazed at line after line of strip malls along the thoroughfare and wondered vaguely how much business they did.

"You were lucky to get the time." He stopped at the traffic signal by a corporate park. "Who took you, Paolo?"

She smiled. "Good guess."

"He loves the water, says it's the only place to really relax. Though what he needs to relax from I have no idea." The light turned green. He tapped the gas and turned onto an unlit stretch of backroad that wended like an asphalt river through flatlands and cornfields outlined in silhouette by the glow of a quarter moon.

"We had a run-in at Romeo's."

"*Dio,* you're not here two days and already problems?" He fed the CL gas as they took a sharp curve.

"Not me, Ana."

"Paolo's girlfriend? Now what's she done?"

She looked at him, but his expression in the dimness was hard to read. Did he think the same of foreigners as those prep school snobs?

"She didn't do anything. These two boys, private school kids and privileged from the look of them, came in like they owned the place and started harassing her. Luca wanted to shut them up, but the owner told us to leave."

"That Luca really has a set, especially now that he's out of the military."

Around the next curve she saw a restaurant set in on the upward slope of a hillside, the name *Mezza Luna* in blazing green neon.

"Luca didn't do anything. He didn't get the chance. God, Alex, you sound like Max—"

He reached for her hand. "I'm not accusing, I'm just saying, Luca likes a bit of action now and then. Gambles, too, cards usually. He's gotten behind on the rent a few times." He looked at her. "You realize I grew up with these people. You're just getting to know them, but I know them well."

She looked out at the roadway, now perforated by the glare of orange streetlights alongside a roundabout. "Maybe, but there was no reason for what those kids said."

"They're resentful. Foreign nationals are taking people's jobs, their livelihood—"

"It wasn't that class of people, and these kids didn't look like they'd done a real day's work in their lives. And what gives them the right to threaten people, anyway? Just because they have money, go to a fancy school?" She looked out at what appeared to be a truck stop. "Luca's right, we'll see how well they manage when they have to shift for themselves."

"Is that what you wish for them?"

She shook her head. "I might guess you'd defend them. The upper class is your bread and butter."

"Now wait a minute," he said, slowing for the four-way stop. "Surely, you know I'm still a country boy at heart?"

Looking at him in the glow of the dash lights, she could see the contour of his smile. "We'll see about that." She looked out the window as the car slowed to a stop. "Why are all those women in the road?"

He drove slowly through the intersection and past a weigh station. "They're *lucciole*. How do you say it in English?"

"Fireflies?"

"Prostitutes. Transvestites, most of them."

"Out here, in the middle of nowhere?" Where on earth would they get business, she wondered.

"Why not? There's less competition, and they're largely left alone. It's safer, too."

"They're not afraid of the *carabinieri?*"

He laughed. "A number of police are customers. And the others, well, they usually get a cut. That way everybody's happy."

She sat back and stared out the window. Several of the workers looked Moroccan, possibly Nigerian. One well-muscled transgender in heels and pale knit pants tight as a second skin wore a gold lamé top that glittered in the orange light.

She looked in the side mirror as they passed. She must have been down this shortcut years ago with her parents but couldn't recall having seen anyone on the roadside. Then, again, they had usually driven in daylight, and she would have been too young to know what she was seeing and too disinterested to care. Even now it was hard to grasp, and she felt a sadness as if for some lost something she couldn't name.

Alex touched her arm. "Surely you've seen prostitutes in Boston."

"In the Combat Zone, but that's mostly cleaned up." Rising real estate prices had edged out most strip clubs and adult stores, but a lot of people there had wanted change and believed it possible. "Where are they from, anyway?"

"Morocco, Ethiopia, Mali—wherever they're running from."

"So they are running."

He looked at her. "Everyone is running, from something."

She remembered Max mentioning his wife. "You, too?" Instantly, she regretted the intrusion. "Sorry, I shouldn't have asked. It's not my business." Or Max's either.

"Don't be sorry, it's true. Nikki is a lively attractive woman with her own interests, compelling qualities that are sometimes more sought after than beauty. She comes here when she feels like it, which may be less often but is the price one pays for freedom. Like you, for example."

She looked at him. She hated to ask what he meant.

He smiled and squeezed her fingers. "What I mean is, you say you're here for work and seem quite involved in fabric and sales. Yet, you have that diamond on your finger—an unusual style, I might add, and kudos to the designer. And if it's the choice of your fiancé, well, then he, too, must be interesting. Yet, you are here and he is not."

"He owns a string of language learning centers. They're nonprofit, and the annual fundraiser is this week. They can't afford to not have it, and he can't afford not to be there."

He gave her hand a light shake. "I'm not accusing, as you so often seem to think. Merely observing, as is the way with a good physician, so I'm told." He took his hand from hers and downshifted. "You're quite apt to take things personally."

So she was told. Looking out the windshield, she saw the two-story mall looming in unexpected brightness like an amusement park above the residential area. The upper deck was encircled by stores with names she didn't recognize, all lit up in glaring red neon.

She turned. "After this, can we see what Sagittarius, I mean Sahara, looks like?"

He laughed. "It won't be the same."

"It would be a diversion." Suddenly, she didn't feel like going right back to the house.

He laid the back of his hand against her cheek. "You should call it an early night and have a good sleep. It will take the edge off that melancholy. We can stop by Sahara after the engagement party."

She pulled back. "They're not still having that. There's hardly time—"

"There's always time for celebration," he said, turning into a parking space at the end of a row.

Chapter 27

There were more than enough hours in a day and days in a year to do a bit of housekeeping, but Stella usually conducted a thorough cleaning of their little place only in the spring. Giovanni felt the reason was to compact the chore into a single annual event, and just as well. The lingering smell of lemon from all that furniture polish she used in deference to Gia's visit made his sinuses tingle and drain, and more this evening than at any other time.

Against the backdrop of whitewashed walls, the knotty pine dresser and highboy, night table and headboard inherited from his mother gave the bedchamber the feel of a monastery. And why Stella had gone through the trouble of deep cleaning it all was a mystery. Still, they had only decided—no, Stella had only decided—the room assignments at the last minute. Her final decree was that they would keep their bedroom, Gia would have boys' room, and Paolo and Max would stay in the downstairs *sala,* whose sofa opened out to a double bed.

"The *sala* has the little TV," she had affirmed. "In case the boys want to watch something late. And it's closer to the kitchen if they want a bite."

Yes, Giovanni thought, and it was closer to the door in case they wanted to go and come as they pleased instead of spending time with family.

"Now this is Gia's first visit so don't expect too much from everyone," Stella had expounded when he hadn't immediately agreed with her arrangements. "The boys are used to being with each other, and your daughter will want time to herself at night. Besides, the boys' usual room is closer to the bathroom."

It was hard to argue with this logic, Giovanni felt, primarily because it was logic, with no connection to sentiment. What he wanted, however, was for Max and Paolo to spend more time together with less fussing and to spend time with their stepsister without it being mandated like a court-ordered sentence. At least Paolo was making an effort. With Max, anything more than the minimum could be too much, since he formed his own brand of relationships and in his own time. Not to mention that the affiliation with Gia was, for all of them, a work-in-progress. He covered his mouth and sneezed.

Stella shifted from her reading. "Didn't I tell you this morning if you're coming down with something use the decongestant?" she said over the red pince-nez glasses. "You don't want bronchitis like last year." She put the splotched, dog-eared issue of *Oggi,* snagged from the local salon, on the nightstand. "There is some in the medicine cabinet."

He put his hand on her arm. "It's nothing, just a reaction to that damn lemon stuff you've sprayed all over the place."

She sat upright. "What do you think, the house cleans itself?"

"Not at all." He would never think such a thing, especially of this house or this housekeeper. He looked sideways at her, her hennaed hair secured by bobby pins at the temples to keep the sides from puffing out. "And take those pins out. Flat sides make you look like a fish."

She put her glasses by the reading lamp with a grunt. "You, Signore Falcini, are a pain in my rear." She took out the bobby pins and put them with the glasses. "Well?" she said, turning to look at him. "What have you to say for yourself, eh?"

The embroidered rose pattern that ran from the mandarin collar of her nightgown to the yoke had frayed at the vine just above where her bust line pressed against the transparent cotton. He rolled to his side, reached over and gave a squeeze.

"What do you think you're doing?" she breathed. "What if Gia comes home early, or the boys?"

He gave a slow massage, pleased at her response. "Let them get their own girl," he said, tugging at the hem of her nightgown.

The clock on the church tower chimed eleven. Stella lay slumbering on the overstuffed mattress, one leg on his. He pulled the nightgown over her rounded backside and gave it a pat. Mumbling in her sleep, she rolled onto her stomach.

He felt his nose prickle again and pinched the bridge. He should open the window, get some air. Slowly, he slid his leg from under hers then went to the shutters and fingered the latch. Stella would have a cow if she saw the slats open even a little—too big a risk of catching cold from the night air or, worse, letting in bugs. If so much as an ant appeared after such a transgression, she would immediately claim the house was infested, and he would never hear the end of it. He left the latch in place.

Not ready to return to the confines of the antiquated double bed, he tried to marshal his thoughts. But despite his efforts, they raced like hounds back to the morning car ride to the Della Bastias' and Gia's question about what it was like for him here after he decided to stay. It wasn't an unusual query, of course, but he had felt something in him harden. Perhaps what really bothered him was what she hadn't asked—why he never went back to the states. After sixteen years, the question still ate at him, often at unexpected moments.

He glanced at Stella on the bed sleeping soundly as a fallen log, her soft snore like the soughing of the wind though an umbrella pine. Yet, despite her invasive tendencies, so much like Antonia at times, he was glad he had remarried, for with Stella there was laughter.

The church clock bell struck eleven-thirty with a bong. He peered through the window at the flashes of headlights. Though it wasn't overly late, he found himself wondering why Gia wasn't yet home. The needling sensation rippling his spine was unfamiliar, the rising concern for a daughter after years of boys largely raised by someone else. And with affection and food and threats of *la frusta*—the strap—which Stella never used, though Max might have benefited from more than just a scolding, if he was any judge.

How had Antonia raised Gia, he wondered. For all his years of infighting with his ex and their subsequent divorce, Gia didn't seem too damaged. Though under the surface, the drive, the hunger to prove herself, there was a sort of erosive vulnerability.

And now she was late coming home when she knew as well as he or better the work she needed to do tomorrow to make that sample dress. He hunched and looked through the louver, a coil of worry tightening his gut as it had with Antonia toward the end.

"Strega," he muttered, that witch of a woman. Stella murmured something unintelligible and turned onto her side.

Yet, it was Antonia who, despite her continual fears of imminent catastrophe, had ministered to Gia amid an alarmingly extended bout of gastritis after an early trip to Italy where his relatives had fed her everything from polenta to pumpkin seeds. My God, what had they been thinking? What had he been thinking, letting them stuff a two-year-old so? It had taken a yearlong diet of little more than white rice to effect a cure, and he still didn't know if she could tolerate whole grains.

Oddly, this was one of the few calamities for which Antonia hadn't blamed him. She knew how people here did and overdid, killing in kind with generosity and guilt. But her understanding had been fleeting, the anxiety ongoing.

"Get more rice while you're out," she said after half a year of keeping Gia on the same regimen. "We don't want to set her back another six months now that she's finally moving her bowels better."

He listened dimly as cars whizzed by on the roadway below and burped up acid. Was this how his ex had felt over the years, the eroding apprehension and knotted gut? When they were together, she had worried enough for both of them until it wore him out, until he could find solace only here amid the multitude of hills and cousins where his concerns could be diffused and he could find rest from the relentless pronouncements of doom, proclamations of his varied and evidently limitless inadequacies, all of which had made life a seemingly unbearable burden at best and hell at worst, the raising of a child either way an impossibility.

He heard the crunch of gravel, the low vibrating thrum of a car engine and the sound of heavy tires coming to a stop in a shower of small stones. He looked at Stella still sleeping but hadn't the stuff to force himself back under the covers. He heard a car door open, then another and the sound of feminine laughter.

Was this his daughter's laughter? He thought so but couldn't be sure. How was he to know, anyway, since he hadn't heard her laugh in a dog's age, couldn't have recalled the sound if his life depended on it. And now here she was laughing in the dark with a man who, besides being a cousin even if of some distant lineage, was an attractive doctor with a marriage, it had become known, that was a question mark. All this with his daughter engaged to some phantom fiancé in the states.

He listened to the man's voice—it sounded too deep to be Alex. Though perhaps voices deepened in darkness. He heard a car door close then silence then indecipherable words intoned between a man and a woman, apparently bidding each other goodnight. How intimate they sounded, or were such tones with men usual for his daughter?

He didn't know this either, he realized. And in a surge of sentient comprehension that crashed over him like a breaker, he realized, too, that there were vast numbers of things about her he would never know. He belched again and pressed his hand to his belly. Perhaps he should just go back to bed, since the advent of all this awareness had nauseated him and given him a headache.

Above the low rumble of the car engine, he heard a car door close. Over on the bed Stella snorted and buried her face in the pillow. He heard the engine rev then fade.

He really should go to sleep, he admonished himself. Yet, even as he thought this he tiptoed like an automaton to the bedroom door and put a foot in one of his worn calfskin slippers. He paused, knowing from long years of experience in going downstairs for the occasional smoke of his pipe in the small hours that the slapping sounds of the leather soles against the terrazzo stairs would wake most any sleeper.

He eased his foot from the slipper and picked it up along with the other. Then gripping the doorknob, he slowly pulled the bedroom door down and back to avoid the consequent creak that in the stillness would sound like a gunshot. He opened the door slowly and standing at the top of the stairs slid his feet into the calfskins. He listened and heard the key click in the lock.

With a squeak, the front door opened, and Gia stood at the threshold. She looked up, the door ajar behind her.

"Close it," he said in a loud whisper. "You'll let in the bugs." He noted her hand still on the knob. Even in the dim light of the stairwell he could see her defiance. "Suit yourself," he said and turned.

He heard the door close with a thwack, the shot of the deadbolt reverberating like a report. He turned to see her still at the door.

"Don't tell me you were waiting up." She looked aloft up the stairs like a ziggurat.

He soft laugh was derisive. "Has it occurred to you that those here have their own lives, ones that have nothing to do with yours?"

"That thought occurs all the time—I have a lot of reminders."

She was in a mood, he could tell. But despite the trembling in his belly from lack of sleep, nerves and some anger, he would not, he told himself, rise to the bait. He felt the jittery sensation travel from his paunch to his torso. His blood sugar must be low. He really should have had a snack before bed.

"Don't start," he cautioned.

"Why not?" she answered, her voice rising. "Is it inconvenient?"

"It's late," he said, softly. Perhaps if he kept his voice muted she would lower hers.

"So you were waiting up."

He stood on the top step, tottering slightly. "You know he's still married?"

She stared with a bewildered look as if his face had gone out of focus. "What the hell are you talking about? I went for an adapter not a quick one in the back of a Benz."

He gave the air a swat. "Now isn't the time."

"Then when is, the time?"

"It's late. Go to bed, get some sleep."

He shouldn't have started this, but something had compelled him, urged him to express himself. Perhaps so she would reveal herself, even badly, in some manner of connection.

"Where are Max and Paolo?" she asked.

"Paolo went back to Senigallia. Max is up at the circle playing cards."

"When do they get in? I want to call Peter."

As well you should, he wanted to say, and had the sense that she knew his thoughts.

She smiled, clearly reading him. "When do they get in?"

"Max, around midnight. Paolo—who knows. Regardless, they're sleeping in the *salotto,* behind the dining room. They won't hear."

"Perfect. I'll just get a glass of water." She turned and went into the kitchen.

Yes, he thought, it was all so perfect. Max would return punctually as always. Paolo might stay out all night for all he knew. And his daughter would be up until who knew when talking with a future husband he had never met and might never know. Perhaps by morning they would all turn into pumpkins.

Chapter 28

Filaments of light threaded through the shuttered windows. She pressed her fingertips to her eyelids, sore and stinging from too little sleep. If she kept eyes closed, she could see last night's fragmented dreams flicker past like the frames of a silent film where she labored like a sweatshop worker to finish the dress. What was it that had lurked in the shadows behind the exertion and deadlines? The feeling of judgment.

She sat up and kicked back the sheet. What her father had accused her of, her and Alex. "Was he kidding?" The four stucco walls around her remained silent and white, resolute and unmarred by transgression.

She bunched the down pillow and shoved it behind her. Had her father forgotten she was an adult? Or had he simply defaulted to the nasty habit of Italian mothers and, apparently, fathers to perpetual worry?

"Try empathy, for a change," she croaked, her throat scratchy.

But this species of parent viewed empathy as dangerous ground. It implied identification, a loosening of boundaries, a measure of parity even, as might befit a grown woman who in one sense might be a peer.

When the family left Boston for Italy that last summer, her father had spied a wallet-sized snapshot she had tucked inside her passport holder. The photo was of a high school boy, a keepsake he had given her for the trip. The straight black hair and wide mirthful blue eyes made him look so American, so normal. Just before the plane's overhead lights dimmed for sleep, her father had gaped at the photo and at her as if she had escaped the confines of childhood without permission.

He nodded at the picture. "We will talk about that later."

Then he signaled the flight attendant for an extra blanket. Once in Italy he forgot the photo, the talk, everything except being here, the raising of a daughter left on the cutting table like an unfinished garment.

"The hell with him." She reached for her cell on the nightstand and switched on the bedside lamp.

What a blessed vision to see the working display and apps, the messages and texts from Peter. There was nothing more from Raf, who after the uncharacteristic call would be too proud to contact her again—until Milan and only if he didn't hear from her first.

God, Wednesday already and still so much to do. She trundled out of bed, grabbed a towel from the chair and slipped quietly across the hall.

Closing the bathroom door, she opened the tap, splashed water on her face and brushed her teeth. In the mirror, she saw a face pallid as the day she arrived, any glow from yesterday's seaside jaunt having dissipated in the frenzy of intervening hours. She took the scrunchie from her wrist and pulled back her hair. Today she would have it cut and colored by the local stylist, whom she hoped was as competent as she seemed.

She slung the towel over her shoulder, went back in the bedroom and unlatched the shutters. Sunlight cascaded in the window and illuminated the green and gold patchwork hills under the cloudless Sistine blue. She leaned against the sill. If she had time, she would ask Paolo to take her on a drive farther up in the hills, past all she had seen so far, past all she knew. A Vespa buzzed by down on the roadway under the retaining wall. From downstairs in the flat, she heard the echoed scrape of chair legs on terrazzo and smelled the rousing aroma of coffee, one redeeming feature of morning in a household.

She changed into tan cargo shorts and a white t-shirt and opened her laptop. It had been worth buying a second adapter to keep both devices charged. This spark of Solomonic brilliance emanated from

Alex after she impulsively bought a pair of taupe peep-toe pumps she saw in a window display on the mall's second floor.

"We'll take a second adapter as well," Alex told the tech store clerk. "No sense doing without if you don't have to."

Feeling a sweaty relief when her desktop appeared, she double-clicked the folder she created on the plane and opened the files. Each drawing showed a modified sixties-style swing dress with band collar, long sleeves and fitted bodice, the full skirt accentuating the fabric's movement. In one version, she added a hemline ruffle for flounce, but it was overkill and with the limited quantity of material, impossible. What mattered was showcasing the fabric—lightweight, breathable and able to retain saturated color, all while its cloudlike quality held a weave tight enough not to be transparent.

She unplugged the laptop and felt the same spurt of excitement as when the scarf arrived, as if she had finally found something worth representing, something of value.

She tucked the laptop under her arm and pushed the shutters wide open. A breeze rushed in carrying air fresh as a mountain spring. She breathed deeply. Ah, coffee. And a slice of melon, even a sliver of prosciutto.

She slipped on her flats and went downstairs, nudged the kitchen door open and put the laptop on the counter.

"Good morning, late riser," said Max, sipping *caffè latte* from an ironstone mug the color of cream. "Have a good sleep?"

"I closed my eyes, anyway."

"Mamma went to pick up the bread. She left the coffee on the stove. There's melon in the *fridge*—you say *fridge* in the states, don't you?"

No one she knew used the term, a holdover from a bygone era. "Sure," she said, opening the Frigidaire. She put the plate of melon on the table, where Stella had left a jar of fresh fig preserves, a container of natural honey and a platter of pink, thinly sliced prosciutto.

Max nodded to the variety of food. "Looks good, eh? You won't find bacon and eggs here. With such a diet, it's no wonder you're all obese and obsessed with cholesterol."

"You're thinking of my father's generation," she answered. Nobody she knew ate like that. She glanced at his feet on the opposite chair. "We don't have time."

Max shook his head. "As evidenced by the laptop you seem to have slept with under your pillow. If you're not careful, you'll go the way of the Japanese with overwork."

Feeling raw from lack of sleep, she put the dish down. "All right, Max, out with it. What's bothering you? You've had something stuck in your gut since you got here. You Italians are good at talk, so say it, if you have something to say. Here's an opportunity."

Max set his coffee down on the table. "You really want me to speak?" he said evenly. "To say what I think? If this is truly what you want, then I can tell you that what I think is this. Despite years of letters and possibly as many gifts—though we didn't hear it from *Babbo*—we haven't heard from you at all. Yet, suddenly you are here. Why? Because, it would seem, you have a need and believe your father can fill it. And this is precisely what I have said about Americans. You are always looking for what you can get from others, with little thought for them or anyone else."

"Yet, I wonder," he continued. "Has it occurred to you that perhaps your father wouldn't say no to your request, whatever it is, because he can't refuse you no matter what you ask and, by extension, Mamma wouldn't either? Even if it costs a good bit of their savings to throw this engagement party, though we've never seen this man you're to marry, not so much as a photo, only a ring he had made for you. I wonder, do so many people cater to you this way that you have come expect it of everyone?"

She turned to the coffee warming on the cooktop and reached for the carafe, her hand trembling. "Well, that was quite a speech," she said, her back to him. His delivery was so compact and eloquent, she envisioned him practicing in front the television whenever the news was on.

"But it's true, isn't it? You would never have come if you didn't need something."

She turned. "What do you know of it? Did your father decide to take off for some foreign country and leave you like you never existed?" The mug clattered as she set it on the saucer. "Well, did he?"

Max opened his palm and looked at it as if playing a hand of cards. The click of the front door bolt echoed in the foyer.

"In a manner of speaking, my father did leave for a foreign land, if you consider death as such. This is, if one believes such things." He looked at her. "Except that in the case of death there is no return."

Stella shoved the kitchen door back with her hip, in her arms two wax-paper bags of bread, the smaller bulging with rolls, the larger with a loaf sticking out. Protruding from the string bag slung over her shoulder was a wedge of cheese and two bunches of Muscat grapes, one green, one red.

Max shook his head. "Honestly, Mamma, must you always buy the cheap fruit?"

"Ha, listen to him." Stella put the bags on the counter. "Whoever doesn't work around here doesn't eat. Eh, Gia, what do you think?"

"It all looks good to me." She turned and forked a slice of prosciutto onto a plate with a piece of melon. "You won't mind if I bring this into the workroom, will you, Stella? I'm running a little late this morning."

Stella paused. "Sure, but here, take a *pagnotta*." She put the bag of rolls on the table.

"Thanks, no, this is enough. And thanks for the coffee." She set the mug on the plate and slipped the laptop under her arm.

Chapter 29

She stood in the foyer clutching the laptop, the coffee mug rattling on the plate where her hand still shook. She set the dish on the bottom step of the stairwell. What in hell was happening around here? After a sixteen-year hiatus, her father had become a parent, and a stepbrother she didn't know had taken her and the entire US to task. With neither had there been query or discussion, only decision and decree. Well, maybe Max had a partial point, but how could such a *cafone* be so astute?

She stared at the workroom door, rimed with a layer of dust and grit. She should have done this when she arrived. Now she felt weary, doubtful. But in that antiquated room was a vibrant, glowing *tessuto* from Ordito that embodied years of experience to create.

From the kitchen, she heard the muffled voices, conspiratorial tones, probably Max tattling to Stella about what a bitch she'd been. She heard a dismissive laugh and the scrape of a chair leg then shuffling. Not wanting to be caught eavesdropping, she tucked laptop under her arm and picked up the plate.

"*Permesso,*" she said, opening the workroom door.

The narrow bolt of fabric she had taken from Ordito yesterday evening with Stefano's permission lay on the cutting table. Alongside the table marking in a leather journal, her father sat blinking in the wan light of the extension lamp. It was hard to tell from where she stood and through his thick glasses, but the film over his eyes seemed dense, the left in particular. Cataracts, she thought, since the males in his family were prone to poor vision.

"So you are in here." She put the plate on the cart with the pushpins but kept the coffee. "You were up so late I thought you'd be sleeping."

Her father blinked again. If he was still vexed over the night before, he seemed to be controlling it. Steadying his hand, he guided the stub of pencil to its holder.

"Let's see the designs you've brought," he said, hoarsely.

She looked around. "Can we get more light in here? It's dark as hell."

He studied her momentarily over his glasses then got up and turned on the fluorescents. The glass tubes through the plastic casing cast their usual yellow tinge.

"Wow, that glare is worse than the dark."

"Now you see why I leave it off."

"Then can we open the shutters?" She saw a slight smile touch his face. "What's so funny?'

"Do you know how few of them here leave the shutters open, particularly in front? Stella says it draws flies. Mostly, she doesn't like the neighbors peering in. Well, she likes the neighbors and a good chin wag but not when she isn't expecting it."

"I can imagine. Hard to present *la bella figura* that way." She drank half the coffee and put the mug on the cart.

He looked at her. "You still don't understand that way of doing things, do you?"

"What's to understand? They like to make a good impression, however false."

"It's more that they fear a bad impression because it's impossible to dispel, even with a lifetime of trying."

"That's a lot to pin on appearances," she said, opening her laptop.

"Especially when pretense so easily becomes reality." Pushing back the shutters, he squinted in the lush morning sunshine on the glistening cobbles, the white and cream stucco houses.

She looked over at him. "Angle the louvers if the brightness bothers you."

"These bother me more." He flicked off the fluorescents. "Now bring that little computer over, and let's have a look."

She put the laptop on the table and examined the length of material. Its leading edge unfurled like a veil, the vivid fibers in shades of lemongrass and brick, the lustrous golden yellow and that ethereal silvery thread that lined the edge of the paisley. She felt a fluttering in her chest as she moved her finger over the mouse and clicked on the file.

"The designs are for a swing dress with a band collar, a full skirt to show off the material—" From her periphery, she saw movement in his face. "What?"

"It's good to see you excited about something."

"This is worth getting excited over."

"Only to impress Martell?"

"He's a big fish—"

"So you've said." He looked at her with what appeared to be unease.

"You don't think Martell is really interested, do you?"

"I—no, not at all. I am sure he is. It's just, with his reputation for deals and the rise and fall of designers, can such an imposing figure provide the kind of long-term relationship you're looking for?"

She put her hand on her hip. "That isn't what's bothering you. You think he won't be interested because I'm the one doing the showing." She saw in his discomfiture that he wanted to backpedal. "Don't deny it. You've lied enough already."

He stepped back. "What are you talking about?"

"I see it in your face. You never believed in me." She felt a feckless fury fueled by caffeine. "You don't think I can handle things, the shop, the negotiations."

"What are you saying? That's not so. I—it's Martell I don't trust." He put his hand over his mouth as if to stop himself, silence his pronouncements where her pride and self-doubt were involved.

"Why are you worried about Martell?"

"It's not just him. He's so high up. I'm concerned—"

"That he won't show up, screw me over, what? Don Roccia has known him for years, and Martel promised a viewing."

"I know. And I am wrong, I'm sure."

"You are wrong. If anyone can't be trusted it's you." She felt herself spiraling out of orbit, untethered to earth. "You never asked my mother to stay here. You waited until she left the house that day to try and convince me. You never made an effort with her."

He put his hand to the center of his head as if trying to keep it from lifting off. "That's not true. I most certainly did try. Not only then but before, every time we came to visit. She never wanted to discuss it. One time I thought she was softening. We drove down to Naples to visit her cousin Pompeo, the only family she had left. We drove all the way up to that blot in the hills in July only to learn he had left without goodbye, gone north for work, someone said. Milan maybe, or Switzerland. Your mother was so beside herself that he had left without a word she couldn't speak. After that she never talked of her family and was too proud to accept mine."

She gave a laugh. "Now that's a story I never heard."

"There are a lot of stories parents don't tell their children."

"Well, they should. I certainly heard how betrayed she felt. Over and over again. My God," she said, staring at him as if he had slithered in through a crack in the plaster. "You never came back to the states. My friends used to say, 'Hey, where's your father?' Like we'd lost a suitcase. Do you have any idea what that's like? In the beginning, whenever somebody asked Mom where you were she'd say, 'He's over there trying to start a business.' People just assumed at some point you'd ask us to come. Eventually, they stopped asking."

She stared unseeing at the outmoded room littered with tokens of a prior life. "I got so desperate for a friend to confide in I made the mistake of telling that guy I was dating—the dark-haired kid whose picture I carried. He broke it off, said his dad didn't think he should hang with a girl who didn't have a father. Didn't have a father, can you believe it? Not lost her father. Or whose parents were separated and getting a divorce."

She tore a section of pattern paper from the roll. Max was right, she had come here for what she could get. But, dammit, he owed her. She wiped her face.

He put the journal slowly down on the table, pressing the pliant leather hard with his palm. "If I had done as you say, tried to coerce you to stay here, don't you think I might have succeeded?"

She threw her head back and laughed. "Don't flatter yourself."

"No? You don't think so? You think I waited for your mother to leave that day so I could convince you to stay here? I waited to ask you again about staying because I saw how afraid you were to say what you really felt with her in the room."

"How the hell could you put me in that position?"

"What position? You were sixteen. I was giving you a say in our family, treating you like you had a brain, like what you want matters. You believe your mother did that? Why do you think she looked at you that way at the lunch table? She was terrified that for once you'd say what you felt. That you would disagree—with her."

He moved closer. "Tell me, why didn't you go into textile design?"

She moved back a bit and stared at him. "What?"

"Why didn't you finish college, go into design or dressmaking or fashion?" He gave the bolt of fabric a shove.

She wanted to reach for it, protect it. "Someone—another student stole my design."

"Someone stole your design? *Poverina,* cry me a river. You think you alone have suffered heartache? You don't think they took advantage of me when I tried to make a go of it here, that I didn't have to prove myself?"

"That's my point," she answered, gathering strength. "Where did all of that get you?" She wanted to shut her eyes to the reminders of the trade he loved but no longer practiced. "Don't you get it? I don't want to end up like this, like you. This—is what I'm afraid of."

He slapped the countertop. "Ah, now, there. At least you've said it—you are afraid. As afraid today as then." He took her arm. "Listen, you don't want this life? Fine. Then make a better one. But be honest. With yourself, of all people. Don't say you want a fabric store when it's not even second best and you know it."

She shook her arm free and stood back. "I know why you sent the scarf. It was the material. You hoped I'd come for the fabric. Maybe even sure. So, congratulations. You know something about me. Well, I know you, too. You asked why I didn't stay in school. Let me ask you something. Why in God's name, in sixteen years, didn't you once come home?"

"I've told you. Over and over—"

"No. In all those lists and letters over all those years, what you gave were excuses. But not one reason. Do you know I never let anybody, not even Peter, read a word of it? Not one word. I thought you were better. But this—this disgrace." She swept the room with a wave. "It's yours. But it's mine, too."

Hunched under the weight of what she'd been holding in, he sat back down. This was what she had never asked and why she never asked it. He had known it was coming, knew within him in a place he couldn't identify or name. Now it was here and she was right. In all those years, he said many things and everything, everything but one thing. He looked away, the stool beneath him unsteady. He held onto the table edge.

"When I decided to stay I—had my problems. But the family embraced me. More than I expected because they never liked your mother, southerners and all that. They helped me, and I began doing well. They introduced me around, got the word out. I had more support from them in six months—" He stopped, wiped his forehead.

"I lapped their attention like cream." He looked at her. "At first, I didn't return because I was angry with your mother for not staying. Then I had my own place, a new life, in some ways a better one. I felt—I was—free. For a while it went well, the work, the house, Stella and the boys. Then one by one, like a trickle, people left town. The styles became informal, the material inferior. Now when a garment ages, people discard it."

He looked around. "In the end, as you say, the business did not go well, just as some predicted." He looked at her. "But you are right. There is no excuse." He glanced at the narrow bolt of fabric, lovely, alluring, incapable of amends. "In the end, I didn't go back because even though I lost so many things, I had my freedom." His breath burned as when he smoked the cheap tobacco. "But you are right to be angry—and to be hurt."

She shook her head, her exhaustion deeper, heavier than on arrival, her rage imploding, taking with it her energy, her drive, even her desire.

She shook her head. "You still see Mamma as domineering and afraid her whole life. And you're right. But she could never be anything but who she was. She wasn't ambitious like you. She was afraid of the future, and that held you back. You hated her for it. Don't you think I felt that hatred, too?"

He gave his head a shake as if to clear it. He never once thought of himself as hating Antonia. And certainly never his daughter. But she was right, again. He felt as though his nerves were the thread in the warpers being thrust at a very high speed across a very great expanse. He wiped his eyes with the back of his hand. Should he ask forgiveness, remain silent, give her time? He hardly knew anymore what to do, what to say, what to ask. Though to walk away was inconceivable.

He looked at the fox cub face and pointed chin, the uneven ginger hair. "You know, in all my many letters I don't think I asked forgiveness, in so many words. I suppose I was afraid of that, too. It meant admitting how much I had failed, you, your mother. At least now I want you to know, to hear it. I have failed. I am—sorry."

She sank a little as though his remorse was also somehow hers. As for pardon, his admission was too stark to take in. Yet, in a sense she understood him, this diminutive man who wanted his place in the world. She, too, wanted a place and not just to fill the void created in some measure by his leaving. She thought of the tailoring shops in Boston where he and her mother had worked, one whose empty storefront she still passed. She thought, too, of Fiber. Whatever she did or didn't do with her life, did or didn't do with the business, she needed a foundation that was more than just what someone else hadn't done.

She patted her cheeks with her fingertips. "I—don't know about forgiveness—"

He smiled. "Take your time. Perhaps we will talk again, even if your days here are short."

The workroom door thrust open. Stella stood in the threshold, a navy cardigan over her arm, her hair brushed back.

"What in the name of the Madonna is going on in here? Gia, your hair appointment, did you forget?" She looked at Giovanni. "And what are you doing standing there?" Suddenly noting the open shutters, she gasped. "And the windows wide open. Close them before we become a breeding ground for every fly in the village."

Gia glanced quickly in the fitting room mirror. The last thing she needed was to delay work for a salon appointment, but her hair looked even more wretched in trifold reflection.

"Go on." Giovanni nodded at the door. "I'll get started in the meantime." Smiling weakly, he reached for her hand and giving it a small squeeze felt a tiny pulse in return.

Stella took Gia's arm. "Come or we'll be late, and I'll never hear the end of it. And get this place cleaned up, Gi. Maybe that way you can use it again."

He stood and watched them leave, Stella looking contentedly in charge, Gia looking frazzled but relieved that someone else had stepped in. Hearing the click of the front lock, he closed the workroom door and went quietly to the table. The handloomed fabric truly was distinctive, enchanting, but an idea was forming that would require a different material. More substantial but with good luster, from a different bolt.

Chapter 30

An undercurrent of autumnal chill stole across the stone courtyard, scattering the falling leaves and ruffling the branches of a bottlebrush in late bloom. The lowering sun across the fields lit the hillside villages like rows of votives.

They had eaten a hearty dinner of broiled *bistecca,* a salad of lightly dressed spicy arugula greens. To mollify the American appetite and Giovanni's, the *primo* was Eleda's homemade fettuccine, sunflower yellow from the yolks of fresh eggs and glistening in rich, fruity olive oil and garden-grown tomatoes. Now they sipped digestive limoncello from crystal glasses at the Cantonis' outdoor table.

"We never eat so much in the evening," Eleda said. "But for you, Gia—"

She smiled with such sincerity and warmth that Gia felt an inner tug that made her inwardly wince. Even Max had been convivial during dinner. Possibly since the nod to American custom yielded an excuse to eat pasta in the evening, which the suggestion of a spare tire at his midsection indicated he might enjoy on occasion. Paolo, on the other hand, ate the first dish sparingly and after devouring his steak stared at the sideboard.

"Mah, Paolo, you know how much good meat costs?" Stella scolded.

Without a word, Eleda rose and forked a slice of the robust beef onto his plate. "You forget, *cara* Stella, we still have friends in the meat business."

Paolino offered a stiff nod. "S-some even r-recall when pork was k-king."

Pleased with his returning boldness, Gia smiled across the glass-top table, marveling at the bristling white hair, the slate blue eyes with a reflected light that so caught at her she could barely breathe. All in all, quite a day. She drew the pink cotton shrug tighter around her shoulders against the evening chill.

"We made good progress today," Giovanni said, reading her mood. "Despite interruptions."

Stella dipped her head and securitized Gia's hair through half-glasses. "Yes, but how well you look *bella* with that color warmed up and the layers. When you go back to Milano, you will be glad you took the time."

"She will also be glad we took time to make the design changes," Giovanni put in. "Eliminating the sleeves on that dress, for one." He shook his head. "Skinny arms, indeed."

Paolo looked at her. "Is that why you wear that insipid coverup all the time?" He reached over and fingered the loose weave. "When you get home, burn it."

"Really?" she answered. "And your t-shirt? The smiley face went out with the last century."

"The swing dress is from the past, too," Giovanni noted. "But how well it works with the slit neckline—much more feminine than that band collar like a priest's vestment."

"Ah, Gi," Stella sighed. "Must you always push for better and better?"

"Is that not the point and challenge of tailoring—to work with imperfections? Including what my daughter believes is a shortage in the height department."

Max sat up. "What's wrong with her height? What are you, Gia, a meter seven?"

"Thereabouts." It was hard to tell since they were sitting, but he didn't seem much taller than she at five-five.

"But that is average height at least," Max affirmed. "Not short at all."

"Precisely what I told her," Giovanni agreed. "It was the other side of the family who were short—dwarves by comparison. Which means, Gia, that you can wear a richer color palette than pastels and earth tones."

"Like that shimmery Shantung swatch in the workroom?" She hated to think how that would look on. "I'd stand out like a stoplight."

She smiled at the ripple of laughter around the table. It was a feat to wield their sardonic humor instead of being on the receiving end. Still, she felt an odd pang at Stella's appreciative nod, a prick of guilt that with all they had done her party was still ahead.

"Stella, listen, about the party. Don't you think it's too much? With the time so short—" Recalling Max's earlier comment, she wanted to add and money so tight.

Stella tucked her chin. *"Mah,* what are you saying? Would you deprive us of this privilege?"

"But it's a lot to do, not to mention the expense."

"O, Dio. What expense? Who would say such a thing?"

She noticed Max stiffen and felt a flash of heat. "I know firsthand these affairs are pricey, and you've done so much already—"

Across the table, Paolino gripped the arm of the padded wrought iron chair. The effort to speak was clearly arduous, but he appeared determined.

"S-some years ago, Gia, I s-said you could always return here. What d-did you think it meant, if we couldn't d-do this now?"

She shook her head and looked from him to Eleda. "You're both in on this, too?"

She could see in their faces the desire to be part of the festivities, not as an obligation but as a way to give her something to remember them by, even as they would for their own children.

"Buona sera." Alex peered through the screen door.

Did he never get wrinkled, she wondered, noting the charcoal gray jeans and matching jacket slung over his shoulder. Or perform surgery, for that matter? She felt an annoying nervous sensation as he slid back the screen. The long-sleeved fitted shirt in powder blue cotton was so smooth it looked like silk.

"Good to see the veranda finally getting some use." Alex looked at his parents. "How long has it been since you've sat out here?" He laid his hand lightly on his father's shoulder. "I see I've missed a fine meal, too." He stooped to kiss his mother's cheek. "So, Gia, ready for a little ride?"

She looked around. "A ride? Where to?"

"Sahara."

"You mean it's still there?"

"In a manner of speaking. It has changed hands again, to LungoMer. The boys and I are taking you—our parting gift." He nodded at Max and Paolo. "Luca and Ana will meet us there."

Last night's conversation with her father suddenly sharp in her mind, she glanced at him across the table.

"Go, enjoy an evening out," he affirmed. "There will never be enough of them."

"So true," Eleda agreed, cozying up to her husband. "And while you spend your evening on the *riviera* we will spend ours under the stars."

Chapter 31

Gone was the smoke-filled discotheque with painted black walls and ceiling, twinkling overhead lights in the shape of the archer. In its place stood a rectangular nightclub in whitewashed adobe with aqua-colored, wavy-glass windows and brushed metal pendant lights. A narrow chrome bar bordered by white counter stools ran along the far wall. The tables and chairs in front replicated the bar's décor, with a small dance floor to the right.

From the deck overlooking the Adriatic, they could gaze inside the club through the picture window or out down the length of coastline where a breeze gently drifted in from the rippled sea.

"It all looks so different," she commented.

"And expensive," Paolo noted. He pointed in the window at the constellation-shaped luminary in the center of the club ceiling. "That Moooi alone is worth two thousand."

The waiter brought a tray of drinks. He set a Martini glass in front of Gia with a sparkling liquid the same azure shade as the Adriatic on a crystal day.

She lifted the glass. "What's this?"

"The LungoMer," said Max. "Signature drink. Blue Curaçao gives it the color and citrus flavor. The club owners created it. Only one is Italian, though. The other is French."

"I am surprised you're frequenting the place," said Paolo.

Max shrugged. "It's a good cause." He poured the rest of his pilsner, an artisanal brand whose front label bore only a number—09. "Ninth sign of the zodiac—in honor of the former club." He raised his glass. *"Buona fortuna,* Gia, in your work and aspirations."

"And your engagement," Ana chimed in.

"And to your fiancé," Luca added. "A fellow on whom fortune has already smiled."

"I don't suppose we could see a photo of this phantom," said Paolo.

"Yes, definitely." Gia put down her glass. "Now that my phone's charged." She reached in her bag. "See?" She handed the phone across the table. "He's real."

Ana angled the cell and peered at the display. *"Mah, che bello.* So debonair. He doesn't even look American."

Gia laughed. "I'll take that as a complement."

"Of course." She tiled the phone the other way.

Luca snatched the cell from her and stared at the display. "Hmm, looks okay, a bit Anglo perhaps with those eyes."

"Let me see," said Paolo. He took the phone and held it up for Max and Alex. "Looks quite refined," he said with a grin.

"He's British on his father's side and protestant. His mother was Irish Catholic."

Alex sat back. "That's a fine stew—no Italian in the broth."

"So what will your children be?" asked Max.

She looked at him across the table. "What do you mean?"

"How will you raise them—his religion or yours?"

She searched his face as though somewhere in the rounded cheekbones and slightly pug nose was the answer to this question and sudden innumerable others. Like how anyone could possibly live with someone else all the time, and how they would ever raise a family without some disaster along the way.

How would all this happen, anyway, she wondered. Peter and Mattie hadn't been able to conceive. What if Peter's first wife … Dear heaven, she would be his second. She reached for the Martini glass. What if his first wife wasn't the only problem? What if it was Peter, too? But this could be okay, she thought, her mind spinning like a carnival ride. She couldn't envision children now anyway, or in the immediate future, not until Fiber was resolved. And if she eventually went out on her own? Where would she go? Dear heaven, where were all these questions coming from?

She raised her glass for another sip, but the impossibly blue liquid suddenly seemed more for show, not for anyone to actually drink.

"*Dio*, Max, those are personal questions," Alex chided. "To be resolved between Gia and her intended."

"I don't think such questions should be asked at all," Luca chipped in. "Not until you have to face them. I mean, how can anyone possibly plan for every eventuality in advance? The options are too many to consider." He shook his head, fervor etched in the lines at his mouth.

Ana stared at him. "But you planned in the military, didn't you? I mean, how can you go out on maneuvers without planning? And these questions are even more important. Although concerning children, in America there is still some freedom of choice, including what to believe."

Paolo put down his beer. "Are you saying you want to change religions, not be Catholic?"

A soft smile rose on Ana's lips. "Does this surprise you? You know I have my own ideas."

As Gia listened, their voices ebbed, restituted by an incoming tide of memories, late nights and dancing down the single hours, the intimate magpie chatter of cousins telling tales of first times and first loves, revealing their sixteen-year-old selves in shared secrets and believing they knew then and forever who they were.

This night should be like those nights, she thought. They should stay up late and talk and bare themselves because this was what friendship was, what family was, love even, intimacy. These other discussions called for decisions, carried the ache of uncertainty or, worse, certainty, because with every choice came the inevitable loss and cost of all that would not be.

She felt an edge of panic, then anger. Why in heaven wasn't Peter here? Why hadn't he just come? Because, she reminded herself, she had told him not to, and he had listened.

"What about a film," Paolo said, looking at her. "They're showing a comedy at the Gabbiano, that classic *Pane e Tulipani.*"

Like a tidal wave, she crashed ashore. It was the wife in *Bread and Tulips* her father had held up as the epitome of a free thinker to entice her mother to move here. She felt her face blanche then a sudden chill.

Alex put his hand on her arm. "Everything all right? You look a bit pale."

"No, it's—I'm fine. I just remembered I have to call my business partner. And with the party tomorrow—" It wasn't true, but she needed an out.

"But surely this can wait," Luca cut in. "You can't allow work to spoil your last evening."

"Or your enjoyment," Ana echoed.

Looking around the table, she knew they wouldn't understand. Nor could she explain what she felt or why. And social graces still counted for more than candor, especially from guests.

"I don't know how to explain," she said.

"Perhaps I do," Max cut in. "There is much to finish and plan, perhaps even beyond the meeting Friday. And that takes time. It is the same with my engineers, especially if the project is difficult." He smiled slightly. "After the party you may not feel like working."

"How will you get back?" asked Paolo.

"I'll take her," Alex offered. "I need to give *Babbo* the lower dose statin anyway. This will save me going tomorrow."

Ana handed back her cell. "Do what you must. We don't want your last memories of the visit with us to be unpleasant."

"Well, if you must go, we must give the proper sendoff." Luca got up and held out his arms.

She rose to her feet with reluctance. This was the part of coming here she hated like a pestilence, the abysmal sadness of leaving with no guarantee of return. She felt like sitting back down, but Luca gripped her in a bone-crushing embrace and planted a kiss on each cheek.

"Let's exchange contacts." He nodded at her phone. "That way you have no excuse not to keep in touch."

"With apps that now let us call for free, how could she not?" Ana's eyes filled. She pressed the back of her hand to Gia's cheek. "Don't worry, with grace you will be back, and no one will stop you."

"Meanwhile, let's get your number." Luca asserted. "Put your contact information here."

When they finished, Gia slipped the cell back in her bag. "Paolo, Max, I'll see you at the house." She felt a hand on her arm.

"You realize it's better to leave with people still wanting your return."

The soft voice, if she could trust her ears, was Max's. She smiled weakly.

Alex took her arm. "We'll head up to the house. Ana, Luca, *addio.* I'll see you other two ruffians tomorrow." Drawing her arm tighter in his, he walked her down the deck and around the nightclub to the sidewalk. "Wait here a moment," he said.

Chapter 32

She waited on the front sidewalk while Alex went back inside LungoMer. In moments, he returned, tucking a black credit card into an ultra-slim black wallet. They never left a stone unturned here, she thought, with a smile. But she was proud of his thoroughness and certain he had not only paid the bill but left something on the tab for the other four to have another round or two.

Pausing a meter away, he stopped and shook his head. "You look the picture of dejection." He came and put his arm around her. "You know you can always return. Unless, of course, you're caught in some horrid scandal. Even then, perhaps especially then—"

She looked up. "That's what *Zio* said last time, and it took sixteen years to get back here. What if it takes that long next time?" She felt a stab of anxiety. What if her prospect didn't want the fabric, and it was never at all?

He tucked his fingers under her chin. "First of all, you can come back anytime because you have family here. You don't need the excuse of a client. And please, God, don't tell me you would stay with that business in Boston simply because you fear not having an alternative."

She felt a rush of emotion at how easily he read her. "No, of course, not. It's just—" She closed her eyes. "How is all this happening, and I have to leave just as we're all getting to know each other."

"Does that go for Max, too?"

She looked up at him, tall and substantial, haloed in the light of the streetlamp. "See how smitten I am? I'm even fond of Max."

He laughed. "Then you're besotted for sure."

"It's just, I feel like the things I want most all conflict with each other. I don't know how to sort one from the next." She pulled at the shrug's perpetually short sleeves. "Haven't you ever had to a tough decision to make with a p-patient?" she asked, her teeth chattering from chill and nerves.

"More than I care to admit," he said as they walked to the car. "Most recently, with my father. But a person takes one decision, then the next. You're letting everything in at once, as if all the concerns are of equal importance and must all be decided now." He held her chilled hands. "And you need something warmer, *carina,* than this little cotton piece. One thing you truly can't afford now is to get sick."

She gazed at his smooth light olive skin, the amber eyes filled with calm, the prospect of shelter. "Where do you live?"

"Just up the road. Why?"

"I have to go back and do some work but not just yet. Do you mind?"

"Not at all. We'll get you changed into something warmer."

Taking her arm, he walked her to the Mercedes and unlocked the door. "We'll even warm the seat."

They drove down the beach and turned onto the main road then into a roundabout ahead of a white Fiat that blared its horn.

"Pazzo," he said. "The drivers here are demented. Be glad you're not staying long enough to get out on the road."

"It can't be worse than Boston."

He laughed. "Now that would make an interesting comparison."

They drove past the center of Senigallia, whose blazing floodlights on the medieval walled palace and turret gave the effect of a life-sized postcard. Just outside the city, they turned onto a tree-lined lane fringed with low-rise condominiums and two-family flats. Imitation gas lamps with crested domes of frosted glass lit the quiet street corners. The Mercedes turned right into a tasteful quartier of ultramodern townhouses.

"My humble dwelling." Pressing a button on the dash, he drove past an iron gate and down into a covered parking area. "I hope you don't mind a short walk."

They walked up from the lot into a foyer of sand-colored marble. A smart-looking concierge in gray flannel slacks and a navy jacket of what looked to be cashmere stood at the polished cherry wood desk.

"*Sera,*" Alex said, nodding. "This way." He motioned her through the foyer to the elevator and pressed a button.

The lift door opened to reveal a bank of mirrors under recessed ceiling lights, appropriately dimmed for the hour. Despite the flattering illumination, her face reflected in the glass looked pallid, the legs protruding from the rolled-up cargo pants like milkweed stems. If only there was time for another beach run on a sunny day.

He pushed the fifth and last button. "My floor," he said as the door opened.

She followed him down the marble hallway. "Doesn't anyone else live up here?"

"I hope not. At the end of the day, I like my privacy." He slipped a plastic card into a slot beside the heavy lacquered wood door.

She paused at the threshold. "Alex?"

He turned. "Yes?"

She looked up at him, hesitant. "I was about to say I feel underdressed. But I guess that's what I'm here for."

"Don't worry about it. I'll put the coffee on. That will warm you."

They went inside and down a short hallway to the kitchen where a quartet of dove gray counter stools flanked a white quartzite center island.

"The housekeeper prepares everything for the morning." He lit the gas under the Moka on the brushed stainless-steel range. "Now let me see what's in the closet."

She ran her hand over the polished surface and gazed at the smooth white cabinetry. Who had chosen the sleek décor, Alex, Nicoletta or a decorator for hire? The only adornment with a color was a ceramic vase in ice-pop blue. The Moka made a whooshing sound, suffusing the air with the aroma of fresh java.

"I hope you don't mind." He held up a long-sleeved black hoodie imprinted with a Hard Rock Cafe logo. "It's not quite couture." He handed her the sweatshirt and took two gleaming black ceramic mugs from the cabinet.

"I didn't know you were into rock."

"A present for my nephew's birthday."

"Oh, Alex, I can't accept this." She held out the hoodie. "It's a gift."

"I can get another in a couple of weeks when I'm back in LA. Meanwhile, it's still a gift." He handed her a cup. "Cream and sugar?"

"Neither, I have a dress to fit into."

"You'll model it?"

"Hope so," she said with a feeble smile. Searing hot, the coffee possessed a charred earthy quality. She set the mug on the counter.

He took a coaster from the caddy. "Are you really so worried about Friday?"

"That, whether Ordito can deliver the fabric—" She shook herself. "I really do feel chilled. I should change."

"I'll show you to the bath."

He led her through a large open living room with a white, three-seat linen sofa and matching loveseat fronted by a curved glass-top coffee table whose lustrous silver and gold edging looked like satin ribbon.

"Wow," she whispered, gazing at the glimmering ceiling-to-floor silk drapes in a natural pearl shade.

"The bath is here." He opened the door to an airy space with full Jacuzzi, double sinks and a bidet, all framed in ice-pop blue tile.

"Now I really feel underdressed," she said, staring.

"You're never underdressed here at the Hard Rock," he said, closing the door.

She pressed the lock and took off her bra, t-shirt and shrug, all of which had absorbed the damp sea air like a sponge, something Angelo's fabric would never do. The tight weave and natural fibers of his material would wick the damp away, perfect for summer cruise wear. She examined herself in the massive mirror and shook her hair. The layers fell into place. Stella was right. At least her hair looked good.

Out in the living room Alex sat on the sofa, her mug on a coaster in front of the empty seat beside him. "Let's see you, then."

Feeling campy, she tossed her head and assumed a pose.

"Have you modeled? You're slender enough."

"But not tall enough."

"It's not always about height." He leaned on a shimmering silk throw slightly thicker and a shade darker in hue than the drapes.

She took the empty space, warmed from where he was sitting, and picked up the mug, coffee now cool. He laid his arm across the back of the sofa.

"That's the problem with these." He took her mug and set it back down. "They're lovely, but wait a moment too long and what's inside grows cold."

His lips brushed the apple of her cheek, the scent of his skin fresh as the sea. She leaned against him, his body long, sinewy.

"Do you have to get up early?" she asked.

"Don't worry about it," he said quietly, his lips brushing hers.

His skin felt warm, the light stubble reassuringly rough. His hand slid under the hoodie where her skin still felt clammy except for the press of his palm. His fingers slipped under her breast, sending a tingle down her belly. There was comfort in his closeness, reassurance in the orderly splendor of the surroundings, an established and well-defined space perfectly composed and distinctive, and one that belonged to someone else. She felt suddenly awkward, out of place.

"Everything all right?" he said against her cheek.

She laid her head in the hollow of his throat. "Sorry."

"You're uncertain," he said, stroking her hair.

She closed her eyes. "About a lot of things."

Chapter 33

Stella hovered by the breakfast table. "I thought I heard voices last night, Gi. Or did I only dream so?"

Who knew what she dreamed or didn't, he thought, soothing his aching fingers with the warmth of the oversized coffee cup. "I heard Gia come in," he said, not wanting to belabor the point and glad that this time he had occupied himself in other ways than worry.

"She came before the boys," Stella said, looking expectant. "Hope everything is okay."

"Why not?" he said.

He, too, had heard the arrivals and varied voices but told himself that whatever happened, if Gia wanted to talk, she would. She was, after all, a grown woman. He also thought he heard her chatting in her room, perhaps on the phone with her intended or that crude fellow she worked with.

"So what do you think?" Stella looked at him pointedly.

He took a wedge of late season cantaloupe, insipid in color and likely in flavor. "I don't know, Stel. What do you want me to say?"

"Well, you don't have to snap." Muttering, she gave him an astigmatic glare.

"What are you mumbling about?" He dumped the melon in his dish, the edge of the fruit marred by a sliver of rind where she cut it badly. "You know I can't hear when you mumble." Now he would not only need the fork but the knife to fix what she had botched.

"I said your daughter should be more considerate. Here the boys take her out, yet she returns with someone else."

He took the fork and stuck it in the fruit. "What do you mean someone else? She came home with Alex."

He hoped, albeit with trepidation, that his discussion with Gia the prior night, however inept, had impressed on her the boundaries here. Especially with the good doctor, whose relationship with his Roman wife was alternately convenient, strained or modern, depending on who described it. Yet, he had been right to warn Gia about other men. Fathers, after all, had instincts about such things. He cut away the bit of rind, but the serrated knife left a jagged place.

"You see what's happened now? Why do you never cut the cantaloupe properly?" He chucked his napkin on the table. "Or set the places with the right utensils? This knife is for meat." He got up and went to the counter.

Stella stared at him. "I am talking about your daughter, and you talk about meat? What's wrong with you this morning?"

He turned. "What's wrong with me? What's wrong with you? What are you worried about? That Paolo and Max might have been spied coming home without their stepsister by one of these hens with nothing to do but to watch out the window? Is this what concerns you—*la brutta figura?*"

Dio, but his head ached. Last night's southerly breeze had been as deceptive as all things from that direction, promising refreshment but ushering in warm humid air instead. Now his sinuses were clogged as a gutter pipe, and his hands were killing him.

He tugged at the drawer handle. "What's wrong with this?" Stuck, he thought, like everything else.

"Here, I'll do it." Stella rose and pulled the drawer open. "And what worries me is precisely Alex. You know how things are with Nicoletta. But if it's the flatware that worries you, maybe Mare Monte will do better. I am almost sorry now we planned this party, if the end result is everything ruined." She looked upward and crossed herself.

Giovanni stared at her, his jaw working. The paring knife felt thick in his fingers, swollen from the arthritis that had flared with the weather and more work than he had done in ages.

"*Mah,* you surprise me." He gave his head a shake. "Are you really so superstitious? Or are you worried Max will be offended? Because, of course, we could never have that."

Stella turned slowly and drew her lips in tight. "Is easy to talk when the one under discussion is not yours. Gia was gone from you when she was still a child, and when we came my boys were already in the stalk. That was my doing, not perfect, but I push myself. Even now I push, because sometimes a little guilt makes them think. But with you it is always the work, even now with your daughter." She flapped the air with her hand. "*Mah* what's the use. Better to get this hair combed out. Fix what you can, right? Isn't that what the Americans say?"

He watched her turn away, shaking her head and murmuring. Only on rare occasions did she use the "American" epithet, and she had stopped only just short of calling him one. She also barely sidestepped accusing him of being a delinquent parent, which he already felt and didn't need reminding. Yet, he seldom saw her cynical, which was infinitely worse than her barbed tongue. At least when she wheedled, she wasn't offended. But bitterness, whose end result he knew too well, was a thing he couldn't bear, not on top of everything else. This infernal party, his daughter leaving soon.

He grabbed a napkin and wiped his cheeks. "I don't know what's come over me this morning," he muttered. What in heaven was all this emotion? Gia had not even left yet.

Stella smiled softly. "Maybe you're just starting now to know your daughter, Gi. But I know my boys. Paolo bounces back quickly from an offense. Max doesn't recover so well." She took his napkin and wiped her eyes.

The gesture made him feel easier. "You realize he could use a kick on occasion."

"Ha, you say this, yet you are gentler with him than I." She paused. "You realize while we stand here jabbering there is only today with Gia and the boys and us. That's all, Gi, just this one day. Tomorrow your daughter leaves."

Barely able now to control himself, he wanted to sit and weep, and for as many years as he and Gia had been apart, though this would only waste the remaining hours without bringing the them one stitch closer. Looking at his wife, he saw she, too, knew this. He held her arms. "Long as you're not cross. I couldn't—I can't bear it, not with the rest."

She shook her head, smiling through the shimmer in her eyes. "You old goat." She pulled his head down and kissed his bald pate. "Now let me get this hair combed out. The ends are fried with the humidity. The coffee is on the stove."

He smiled and when she turned gave her a pinch. She swung around and threw him a look somewhere between grin and glower.

"What?" he said, his expression innocent. "Nobody's perfect."

The moment she left he heard the squeak of the bedroom door and soft footfalls down the steps. The kitchen door swung open. Gia stood there wearing a wilted look like one of those sparrows the mouser across the street deposited with regularity on the front mat. Unable to ignore the dark circles under her eyes, he tried to prevent the extent of his concern from showing.

"Sleep well?" he asked, casually. She wasn't sure how to take this query, he could tell, which made him want to bring her to the workroom now and give her what he made.

"Not really," she answered, eyeing him.

"I—thought I heard voices last night," he said, tentatively.

"I tried reaching Peter but couldn't. I ended up texting." She looked around. "Where's Stella?"

"Getting her hair combed. Have some coffee?" He gestured to the empty place setting. "We have a bit of time before we leave for lunch."

She went to the stove. "Max and Paolo up?"

"Not yet."

She turned. "I came back early with Alex, if that's what you're wondering. I was feeling a little overwhelmed. He had to give *Zio* some medication and offered to drive me."

He tried to keep his voice level. "Everything all right? I'm asking about you, not anything else."

"Okay," she said with a shrug. "I was thinking—I should go back to Ordito before I leave, just quickly, to see the studio."

He felt a smile form and ran his hand over his mouth. "Sure, why not?"

"I thought of asking Stefano while we were there. But it was late and designs are proprietary." And she wasn't sure then if he would let her in.

He shrugged. "Perhaps if you explain—"

"What? That someone nicked my design in college, and I haven't seen the inside of a studio since?"

He looked at her, the expression in her eyes, and saw that she still believed this was why she wanted nothing more of school, nothing more of learning a real trade. Yet, he had seen her watching Chiara at the handloom, had seen, too, the spark of interest in her momentarily unguarded expression, the longing that lit her face.

"What if I roust Paolo, have him go with you?"

"I—don't know. It's early, he's probably tired. Why would it matter to him, anyway?"

"It would give him a chance to show off a bit, since he helped get the approvals from the *commune* to convert the barn and gave some pointers on the interior. I believe the head of the design group is a compatriot of someone he works with." He turned and started for the door.

"Wait."

He paused, his hand on the knob.

"I'm not—I'm not sure I can go back."

He turned and saw the look on her face, the old malevolent fear that continually threatened. He went and leaned gently against the enameled countertop. It put his hip at a bad angle, but he tried to look comfortable, as if he had all day or a lifetime, whatever she might need.

"When you say go back," he queried casually.

"I mean, it's too late now to go back to school, to design. There's too much to know. It's been so long. I'd have to start over."

He wanted to tell her she was still young, that there was still time, that even if she married there was time. But the issue wasn't time. It was her self-doubt, the insecurity he, too, had felt and tried to dispel by staying here.

"Fashion, fabric, such complex fields," she said, talking softly. "Of course, if you don't care, it doesn't matter."

"But to you it matters." He saw her eyes brim but forced himself to stay where he was. "Let me get Paolo, for the very fact that it does matter."

There was so much he wanted to say, the importance of doing work that made a difference, if only to you, that if you did what you were called to do it was still work—because those fools who said that if you do the work you love you don't work a day in your life were idiots and wrong on top of it. No. If a person truly did the work he loved, somewhere along the line he would pay for it, and dearly.

He ached to push her to see this design thing through, to go back to school, find herself, for she would find nothing if she remained among those dusty bolts he saw all too clearly in his mind's eye. But looking at her, he saw her pallid with apprehension.

"Why not have something to eat with the coffee?" he said, his voice still calm. "Perhaps a bit of prosciutto and a slice of cantaloupe." This time he would cut it himself.

She gave the empty place at the table a longing glance. "Maybe I will." She looked at him. "So could you—I mean, would you mind waking Paolo?"

Chapter 34

Standing in Ordito's parking lot, she felt she must speak with Angelo before seeing the studio. She owed the mill's founder that much, even if it forestalled the necessary confrontation that would return her with unsettling clarity to the moment she learned her fabric design had become someone else's ...

Just the prior week she had bragged to a classmate of her idea for a commercial fabric to upholster the furnishings of a Dutch wind energy firm set to open a new office in Amsterdam. Her idea was for a nubby, reverse-weave fabric the color of storm clouds, silvery thread crisscrossed throughout to evoke the motif of wind turbines.

Literally, faster on the draw, the other student submitted his entry first using the same pattern, except with a lighter shade of thicker yarn to represent the turbines. On hearing the buzz his entry generated and seeing what he submitted, she dropped out of the competition. It was no consolation that the energy firm had sponsored the contest to get an original design for its décor for free. In a moment of pique, she later used her version of the fabric for the chairs in Peter's office.

"What are you waiting for?" Paolo prompted. "You heard *Babbo.* Departure for Mare Monte at eleven-thirty. Mamma is a shrew if she's late to a party."

As well she could imagine, especially if Stella was hosting. "With Stefano in Modena, I want to see Angelo first, get his okay."

Paolo's mouth gaped. "Then what in the balls am I here for, window dressing?"

"More for moral support." She paused, awkward. "It's just—things didn't go well in design school, a problem with a colleague appropriating a concept. Maybe you had it easier designing buildings."

He laughed. "No one around here has anything easy, in case you hadn't noticed. I'm only employed now because the firm I've contracted with is owned by the father of a school chum. That corporate building I designed was for him. But if you are so sensitive, maybe such a competitive field is not for you."

She felt as if he'd poked the place in her where fear lived. "Maybe you're right."

He put his hand on her shoulder. "Look, we creative types are sensitive. Even the implacable Ana needs a boost on occasion and from me, no less. So in this you are not original. I only hope your designs are inventive." He gave her shoulder a squeeze. "Courage, sister. And don't dawdle." Taking his cell from his pocket, he moved nearer the building and began scrolling.

Bracing herself, she turned and went inside Ordito's main entrance. After listening courteously, Beatrice put a call out to Angelo in the mill. She paused and pressed her earpiece.

"*Signore* Della Bastia asked if you could wait in his office, just there on the left. I will show you."

Beatrice rose from her desk, her tan eyelet jacket covering a crisp white cotton blouse atop brown skinny jeans. She went down the hall to a large windowed space with a distressed pine desk that looked to be a family heirloom and a set of comfortable leatherette chairs in soft vanilla that framed a coordinating couch.

"Please, make yourself comfortable," Beatrice said, indicating the couch. "May I get you a coffee?"

"No, but thank you."

Too antsy to take advantage of the coffee or the seating, she stood and stared out the tinted windows. What would it be like to work with designers in real time and the latest software when she was so far behind it was as if she'd fallen into a crack in the earth? But evasion would only lengthen their lead, and she had always been more energized by live work than the classroom.

"Good day, Gia." Angelo stood at the door. "Did we miss anything last night," he asked, concern on his face.

A thought suddenly arose. She must see the studio, but she wanted another look at the loom.

"Would you mind, *Zio,* if I saw the jacquard again? I'm sorry to be abrupt, but we're nearly out of time. And I have great respect for your tradition here." She nodded at the desk. "This piece. Was it in *Zia* Giulia's family?"

Angelo's face softened. "Over a hundred years." He tapped the doorframe. "Follow me."

He led her down a maze of hallways and past the warpers to the chamber framed in reclaimed board, now empty. The girl with the dun-colored hair was no longer at work, her feet no longer pressing the pedals, her hands no longer expertly threading the blue and white repeat on the now silent loom.

She turned. "Where is Chiara?"

"Gone home for the day," said Angelo. "The job wasn't very big."

She swallowed against the tightness in her throat. "Could I?" She gazed at the loom. "I'd like to see it up close."

"Certainly, just be careful near the harness."

She moved nearer to the loom, eighteenth-century Venetian, its metal jacquard the brain that read the punch cards and created the pattern. Each thread went through part of the harness, the holes in the cards determining which parts moved up, which stayed down. Speeds might have increased over the decades and the technology had changed, but the rudiments of weaving remained.

Of course, Chiara had finished the job, she thought, staring at this link with the past. Angelo couldn't let someone else continue because the repeat would be altered. Everything from the loom's setup to the pattern was unique to the weaver.

She turned. "The job Chiara was working on, who was it for?"

"We create some of the cloths for the church," Angelo said. "Mostly tea towels for the kitchen, hand towels for the bath. They order the communion linens from a supply house."

Was there a trace of irony in his tone? For although the church still bought the odd dishtowel from Ordito, whoever was charged with ordering the altar cloths, corporals and palls used a commercial source. Even the mill's paltry order was likely to be donated. She thought of Fiber, the meeting tomorrow night, and felt torn between this place and that, the design of fabric and of fashion. If she ever did return to school, how would she decide?

She looked at Angelo. "Do you have any samples?" For a reason she couldn't discern, she wanted to see them, touch them, take one home, though only for herself.

Angelo looked around. "Normally, we keep a few. But it's not a new job so everything from the run is at the church."

She felt a pull, a longing as if to complete some primal rite left undone. She saw Angelo's almond-shaped eyes crinkle at the corners.

"Listen, *Zio,* I'd like to see the studio before I leave, if you will allow it." She felt herself faltering. "I should have asked last night. But such work is proprietary, and I didn't want the designers to think I was there for the wrong reason." She took a breath. "It happened to me once. I wouldn't want to do it to someone else."

Angelo nodded, his eyes on hers. "Such things happen in this field. Other fields, too, more often than one imagines. But they shouldn't happen, should they?"

She smiled. "I didn't think so."

He put his hand on her arm. "Perhaps one day we will work together," he said with a half-smile.

She blinked away the emotion that brimmed her eyes. "Then would a quick visit be all right? I would love to see what you've done with the stables. I still remember the oxen, the lunch that summer with *Zia* and the *casciotta.* I first tasted wine there, too, from that same demijohn."

Angelo smiled. "You know Paolo helped get the plans approved."

"I know, he's waiting outside. Do you mind? I can't ask you to take more time. You've already done so much."

Angelo gave a quick bow. "Who better?" He gave her a bright peck on each cheek. "I wish I could be with you this afternoon, wish you good fortune."

"With Stefano away, you're needed here." She felt her eyes well again.

He pressed his fingers to his palms "Then, *Addio, bella.* Shall I show you out?"

"Thank you, no. I know the way." She blew a kiss.

Outside the mill the Apennines were obscured by *foschia* and a long narrow bolt of low-hanging clouds.

Paolo hurried toward her. "You got the okay?"

She nodded. "We're set."

"Let's go." He hurried her around the mill down the path to a squat stone building. *"Permesso,"* he said, raising the latch on the wooden door.

Feeling as timorous as on the first day of design class, she followed him inside the old stable whose stonework had been painted a brilliant reflective white. Tiny hanging lights with bare uncoated bulbs shed unsparing brightness in every angle. Four designers sat at white Lolly drawing tables such as Paolo might have chosen as a nod to his architect roots.

Two designers perched on padded high-backed swivel stools sat running software for design, editing, loom control and the jacquard process. Another stared into a computer screen showing varied fabric weaves and textures. Still another examined options for dobby and jacquard fabrics with an inset window displaying pattern processes.

She wasn't surprised at the illustration and photo software, but seeing the designer with her phone out, she realized that mobile apps had also come of age.

At the computer screen, the designer who looked to be the capo held an iPad and stared at them, a startled expression on his face. Color printouts were tacked to the corkboard walls around him; swatches and scraps of fabric covered the exposed surfaces.

"Good day, Franco," Paolo said. "I want to introduce you to Gia, my stepsister. Please excuse our barging in. Gia is down for a few hours and begged to see your place. She has a design background, but I promise she won't steal your ideas. She only wanted to meet the curator of that marvelous scarf." Paolo turned. "Gia, Franco Matteoli, co-founder and principle of Ordito Trama Studio."

Franco unfolded his tall slender frame from behind the desk, his cropped silvery hair, slate blue eyes and gunmetal glasses giving him a steely quality. *"Piacere,"* he said.

She held out her hand. "Pleased to meet you as well." She looked at the iPad. "You like the new indie apps?"

"I'll leave you to talk shop." Paolo turned toward the pretty young designer with long black hair and deep-set hazel eyes still holding her cell.

"You do recall Ana, right?" she whispered, with a nudge. "Whose email and cell number I have?"

"Don't worry," he said, grinning like a rake. "I know my place." He went to the girl's desk. "So you're new here since last year?"

"If you're a designer and working on your own, this app works well," Franco noted. He turned the iPad. "It does scale, direction, color, repeat. Then you apply the designs to a figure, see how the print looks on a garment."

She felt the adrenalin pumping. This meant a designer could edit a piece for a collection with enough speed to pace the imagination. Yet, she still felt the underlying pull of the *tessuto.* Beside her, Franco was still speaking.

". . . a good tool for us here in this small office. So you're in design?"

"I started but didn't get as far as I'd hoped. I'm in sales now, but I may go back."

"Someone nicked your work?"

She felt herself blanche.

Franco gave a wry smile. "Aside from the relentless pressure in this business, theft is the commonest reason for people getting out. But the field can always use good representatives, if they know the products."

"Gia?" Paolo held up his cell. "It's eleven, we have to get ready." He gave her t-shirt the fisheye. "You of all people must look decent."

She turned to Franco. "Could we exchange contact information? I'm meeting a prospective client in Milan tomorrow who would appreciate your work."

Franco's laugh had an ironic tenor. "There are thousands of afficionados in Milan, but why not, you never know."

Chapter 35

Standing in the foyer outside the workroom, Gia felt her cell vibrate. She took it from her pocket and checked the display. Peter texting all was well, everyone was busy with tonight's fundraiser. Everything still okay there? All good here, she texted, keep her posted. In the colliding of two worlds, she felt her excitement over the studio dip. What were the odds of going back to school for anything, fashion or design?

Her father opened the workroom door, an eager expression on his face.

She slipped the phone back in her pocket. "I know, I know, I need to get ready."

His gaze took in her shorts, t-shirt. Well, what had he expected her to wear? She hadn't planned on celebrating anything here and no idea which of her very casual clothes would work for the engagement lunch. The new dress was for Martel, and the thought of trying to baste one of Stella's frocks into a wearability made her cringe.

Giovanni took her arm. "Let me show you something."

Pushing the workroom door open wide, he went to the clothes rack, unzipped a gray garment bag and took out a short A-line dress in crimson Shantung silk. Even in the dim light the fabric's nubby hand and visible grain radiated a luster all the way from its mandarin collar down to the fitted bodice and cutaway armholes to the slim skirt and narrow scalloped hem ruffle.

"What's this?" she asked, staring.

He held the dress to the light. "What does it look like?"

She looked at him. "Who is it for?"

"Well, I'm not wearing it."

"But how—when?"

"Go try it on."

She stared at the dress. She would never have chosen such a vivid shade. Yet, the rich warm hue would enliven her complexion, and the simple style would be flattering but not overly feminine. She ran her fingertip along the ruffle.

He gave the hanger a shake. "Take it upstairs, try it on."

She took the hanger and held the garment in front of the mirror.

How had he known what to create? This man barely taller than she and nearly bald with weak eyes and slack arms protruding from a threadbare cotton shirt, an aging man who for all his effort at connection still felt and would always feel at times like a stranger as all fathers must sometimes seem even to daughters who grew up with them, a man who for his all shortcomings still apparently and infuriatingly knew her, perhaps in a way she had yet to know herself.

"Go on," he said. "Take it."

Still hesitant, she draped the dress over her arm. The deep red silk glimmered softly. She turned and started up the steps then stopped, turned and came down. The strong embrace on offer was of the sort bestowed more frequently at the close of letters than in person.

"Thank you," she whispered and rushed upstairs.

Sitting in the front seat of the Punto, Stella turned again to look her up and down. "So, Gi, why you don't make a dress like this for me, eh?" She swiveled toward Giovanni. "And the color," she enthused, reaching around to finger the skirt ruffle. "Who would have thought, Gia, that such a shade would suit you?"

Gia glanced at her father, who eyed the roadway looking self-satisfied. "He would, apparently."

She crossed her legs away from Stella's reach and looked out at the rough fair hills sweeping down to the Adriatic, sparkling in the sun. How was it possible to long for a place as if or even more than for a lover, she wondered. Out in the blue a fishing vessel trolled along, its low hull only just darker than the waves.

"O, *Dio,*" Stella said, glancing in the side mirror. "I hope my feckless son doesn't drive so close like that in the city."

Gia looked around and saw Paolo hunched over the Fiat's steering column seemingly mesmerized by the Punto's rear bumper. She gave a broad wave to get his attention. As if disengaging from autopilot, he grinned and waved back. Beside him Max sat stoically.

The Punto crested the hill nearly airborne then wafted down the other side and turned sharply right onto a rutted dirt access road. A quarter kilometer up on the left stood a small country manor in shell pink stucco with a brick-red barrel tile roof and long narrow windows, plank shutters stained the same red brick shade as the tiles. The Punto skidded into the circular gravel drive and stopped at the front entrance.

Giovanni turned. "So, Gia, what do you think?"

"What do you mean, what does she think?" Stella cut in. "She has seen nothing yet, nor has she tried the food." She opened the car door and disgorged herself from the bucket seat.

"She can still appreciate the view," Giovanni called out as Stella walked across the driveway in a wrap dress of restful forest green poly and flipped her hand without turning.

Gia leaned over the passenger's seat. "She's not angry because you didn't make her a dress, is she?"

He dismissed the notion with a wave. "She is only annoyed because she adores red but looks like hell in it. Clashes with the hair." He turned to look at her. "So, really, what do you think?" He nodded at the house. "It is a good location, no?"

It was same insistence on agreement he had mandated every time they toured a property he fancied. She wrapped her arm around the seat back. "Why, did you buy it?"

"If only," he muttered, gazing heavenward. "The shoreline climate prolongs the season so the owner makes good money even at the holidays. Takes groups, too. People who like organic food. Doesn't pay the staff well, though. Or so I hear. Come, let's look around." He opened the door and hurried across the drive.

She slipped her feet back in the peep-toe pumps and smoothing the dress got out of the car.

Apart from the black wrought iron ornamental planters replete with red geraniums that flanked the marble steps, the edifice was unremarkable. Though the stucco appeared recently refreshed, the tile roof devoid of cracks and mold. The windows looked clean, the shutters freshly stained. Overall, it seemed less like an eatery or inn and more like a house and in better repair than most of those her father had explored, many of which had no real elegance, just a tumbledown quality that seemed to justify his interest, as if fixing them up would earn him the right of ownership.

She walked around the side of the manor where the hillside curved down to a cove where the blue-hulled trawler was now anchored. She had to admit that, structure aside, the location was first-rate, as it had been with most of his selections. Houses, haberdashery and waterfront, old habits, she thought, breathing in the invigorating air that rose from the sea.

Behind her, the cream-colored Mini zipped down the dirt road and rumbled into the driveway. She turned to see Paolo wave out the window then kill the engine, raising a rooster tail of dust and grit. The vehicle coasted to a stop, and though she half-expected a coterie of clowns to exit only Max got out. He closed the door and walked toward her, black waving hair buoyant in the breeze.

"Well, what do you think?" He gestured to the property. "Not a bad position."

"Not at all," she answered.

He turned and looked down the length of shore. A light chop had come up with the wind. "So much open coastline," he murmured, shielding his eyes. "Makes us as vulnerable now as during the war."

She turned to look at him. Despite his comparative youth—he must only be a year or two younger than she—and not knowing war firsthand, he seemed determined to commemorate its desecration as had her mother, along with her vilification of Mussolini and that "damned 'Itler."

"Have you studied history?" she asked.

The ghost of a smile appeared in his eyes, seeming to indicate he had somehow lived it.

"One doesn't need formal study to know our conflicts. The village elders remember, the few still left. The middle-aged don't want to know. The young don't care. Though they may come to care soon enough, when we're overrun and making a decent living becomes impossible." He nodded at the fishing boat. "They will wait until evening to bring ashore their cargo. And it will not be *sardelle.*"

She looked out at the boat bobbing on the waves. It could be carrying almost anything.

"*Bella!* Don't tell me you're assessing the property for a potential buy."

She turned to see Paolo had abandoned his red kerchief and exchanged the smiley face summer T for a long-sleeved black Henley. His brown ringlets blew back in a gust, revealing trimmed sideburns.

"Of course, if you're bitten by the speculation bug, I can help remodel," he coaxed.

He pressed his arm to hers. "Imagine—a Palladian window there on the right. Too fancy? A simple floor-to-ceiling affair then, with mullions or divider frames. Or, if you prefer, just individual panes. Inspiration from the sea and enough natural light for your designs." He gave her a nudge. "You could deduct everything as a business expense. With that dress and hair, the shoes, you'll rake in the orders."

He was a charmer, she thought, with a smile. "Houses are a vice I've managed to avoid."

She looked over to see Stella standing with her father, who took in the manor and adjacent field with the sweep of his hand, she nodding as he spoke. There was a time he wanted only assent; now he seemed content for someone to listen. Maybe if her mother had listened instead of always saying no ... But after the many decisions he made without her, she hurled the word with the regularity and force of habit. The sense of place and attendant longing she felt in the car returned. She tucked her hair in the collar of her dress and started for the house.

"Don't tell me you're not going to buy," Paolo called out.

She waved without turning. "Maybe after I sell the fabric."

"I'll take that as a verbal contract."

He could take it however he liked, she thought, and found herself craving an end to the luncheon before it even began. The thought of being confined by polite chatter and endless eating felt like a jail sentence.

She heard a muffled reverberation like low thunder and turned. The black Mercedes sedan rose over the hill, its heavy tires clawing the furrowed road, the four heads inside bobbling back and forth. She couldn't bring herself to look at the driver but could clearly see the blonde in the passenger's seat. Dear God, would this waking nightmare never end?

The Benz glided to a stop at the head of the drive. The front door opened. Alex stepped out wearing a white oxford shirt and charcoal gabardine slacks. The driver's side back door opened. Paolino emerged, aided by the mahogany cane.

He hobbled gamely to the passenger's side and opened the door. Eleda, wearing a lightweight navy suit and pale silk blouse, stepped out. Alex walked around to the blonde, who stood nearly as tall as he in second-skin slacks of blinding white cotton twill. Her boat neck pique cotton top in white and navy horizontal stripes accentuated the protruding collarbone, a feature Gia had always envied.

"What do you want to look like that for?" her mother had exhorted. "Those models with the bones sticking out look like a plucked chicken."

Yet, she had envied them and was appalled to find she still did.

Alex took the blonde's hand and led her down the uneven drive in heels as spiked and narrow as nails. Yet, she looked quite capable of managing even without his aid.

Gia felt her face crease in an involuntary smile taut as a starched collar. The image flared in her mind. She must look an idiot. Like an automaton, she stuck her hand out and jolted forward in the new pumps only to trip over air.

"Dear Gia," Alex intoned, sounding pastoral. "How wonderful to see you—you look lovely."

With surgical swiftness, he moved her extended hand aside and kissed her on both cheeks. Meanwhile, she felt the blonde staring and looked over his shoulder to see Paolino escorting Eleda down the drive, each apparently holding up the other.

Alex stepped back and took the blonde's slender hand. "You remember Silvana."

Gia stared, blinking. Had she gotten his wife's name wrong, or was this his girlfriend? God, he had a nerve. Her smile grew stiffer.

He leaned in slightly. "My sister," he said, softly.

"Oh, my—yes, Silvana," she said, quickly. "Alex's sister."

She stepped around him with haste to give the beauty with a face like an actress an air kiss on each cheek. She couldn't identify the fragrance that delicately lingered, but if sunlight were a scent, it would be this.

"Piacere," the blonde said, politely.

The courtesy in her tone carried a certain diffidence. Had she been pressed into service for the occasion? Still, she felt exquisitely relieved Nicoletta hadn't come. Maybe she would survive this torment after all.

"Ah, everyone, welcome." Stella tottered down the gravel drive smoothing her hair and dress. "The boys are on the veranda. Paolino, Eleda, so wonderful you are with us. You, too, Alex. Silvana, a vision, as always." She moved deftly among the four, giving each an embrace. "Everyone, use the walkway there on the right. Gia, *cara,* you come with me."

Stella took her arm and walked her up the flagstone path past a garden of late season squash. "All this today is for you," she crooned, squeezing her arm. "We hope you enjoy."

The veranda, stretching the length of the house in back, was arranged with wooden trestle tables in a U formation that allowed everyone a view of the sea. Each trestle was set with vintage white linen cloth and white Lastra dinnerware. Absent was the once de rigueur array of dishes and flatware at each place, though the sleek five-piece stainless exuded an ethereal quality.

"We were skeptical of such an unassuming arrangement," Stella said as they walked up the stone steps. "But Alex convinced us." She turned and gave him a wide but reticent smile, seemingly to indicate that if he were wrong, he would bear the blame.

Alex flashed a brilliant grin. "I had it on good authority. Giovanni told me."

Stella turned and shot Giovanni a glance with pursed lips then steered Gia to the middle of the center table. A tall slim man with neatly trimmed gray-black hair came out a side door.

"Good afternoon." Bowing slightly, he turned to Stella. "*Signora* Falcini. We're so pleased today to host you."

Stella puffed out her chest. "We have heard good things." She glanced at Alex. "I am sure they are all true." She turned and gave Giovanni the fisheye.

"I am Tonino, the owner. As you may know, we specialize in *frutti di mare.*" He nodded at Gia and motioned to the server.

"Fruit of the sea," she said, gazing at the water. The breeze carried a faintly briny aroma infused with undertones of grilled seafood in butter, garlic and white wine. "Smells wonderful."

"What may I get you to drink?" Tonino asked.

"A glass of white?"

"We have a Fontanella Bianco from Goretti."

"Two glasses," said Stella. "Water for Gi. He is watching his alcohol intake. The *naturale,* not the *frizzante,* for the water. He doesn't need the gas, right, *amore?*"

"The natural, yes. But put some wine in it," Giovanni directed. "Life is short."

"Let's have the Fontanella for everyone," Alex put in. "So we can offer the guest of honor a proper toast."

Tonino hesitated momentarily then took in Alex's mode of dress, the watch. "Certainly." He motioned to the drinks server, who had emerged from the other side door with an empty tray.

"Let's everyone take our seats," Stella instructed. "Gia, your place is in the middle there at the head table with Max on the right, Paolo the left. At the table on the right, Silvana you are next to Paolo, with Paolino in the middle, Eleda on the end." Stella turned. "Alex, you are beside Max here, and I am in the middle. Giovanni is there on the end."

"Wonderful." Giovanni stepped aside so that Paolino could use his free hand to help Eleda to her seat.

"You realize we're an odd number," Max said, taking his chair.

"But we're a multiple of three," Stella pointed out quickly. "That makes us lucky."

This anti-curse formula was one Gia had never heard and Stella had likely fabricated on the spot to avoid an ill omen.

Two servers appeared from the left side door with wine for everyone and water for the table. Fingering her ring, whose diamond had slipped around and made it hard to hold a glass, Gia took the Fontanella, Giovanni the tumbler of wine and water.

"Shall we offer the first toast?" Giovanni said, raising his glass. "To the bride to be—a long and happy life."

Gia felt her stomach drop to the vicinity of her knees. Over the past days and in numerous and varied circumstances, real and imagined, she somehow hadn't thought to picture herself as a bride.

"Salute, bella." Alex touched his wineglass to hers.

The whirl of toasts and clinking glasses was followed by an appetizer of mixed seafood crudité and a *primo* of *tagliolini* with prawns, after which Paolo pushed back his chair as the server came to remove Gia's empty dish.

Max leaned toward her. "You notice the boat is still there. Yet, we have no *sardoncini.*" He nodded sideways at the second server, who appeared too swarthy and hirsute to be Italian, even from the south.

Catching Giovanni's eye, she rose and put her napkin her chair. "I think I'd like a little sea air."

"But the mixed grill is coming," Stella said, bristling.

"Perhaps that's w-why she needs air," Paolino observed.

"Maybe we should get some, too," Eleda said, patting her broad waistline.

"You have no need of air, too, do you?" Paolo leaned nearer Silvana, who smiled demurely.

"That's about all she lives on," Alex answered.

Gia paused by her father's chair. "Want to come for a walk?" she asked softly.

He looked up and hesitated then noted her expression. "Perhaps a stroll, to aid digestion and allow the servers to clear." Patting Stella's knee, he rose and laid his napkin across his chair.

Gia walked ahead along the side of the manor past the garden and paused on the flagstone path. "What would you think about coming to the wedding?"

Giovanni stopped. "It would be wonderful, of course. But this is up to you and your intended." He looked at her closer. "Why, what is it?"

"Peter sent a text just before we left. He didn't say much, just that the fundraiser is coming along. Of course, I know he's busy."

Giovanni shook his head. "But something is bothering you."

"I know I told him not to come—"

He took her hand. "But that would be wonderful, if he came to see you and met all of us."

She knew she should nod and agree, but her time here was short. Still, now that she had come to know them, somewhat anyway, maybe it would be easier, less pressure, if Peter did meet them now instead of after they were married. Yet, somehow the timing didn't feel quite right either way.

"What is it?" Giovanni pressed. "I can see something is off."

"It's just, I'm only now starting to find my way here, with everyone, the work."

Giovanni glanced at the veranda where two servers had brought platters of mixed grill. "Let's walk a bit further so we don't risk Stella sending the wait staff after us."

They walked along the windward side of the manor, where the afternoon sun glinted off the water and the breeze carried the fragrance of late season orchids.

"I'm sorry," she said. "I shouldn't keep you."

He put his hand on her arm. "You're not keeping me. And I understand you want to find your way. But must it be on your own, without help?"

"Maybe, yes. If it's truly to be my way. But it's more than that. I feel like I'm on the edge of something—"

"And you want it to be your discovery, not someone else's."

"Is that so awful?"

He smiled. "Then maybe it is best to learn now instead of later who you are, what you want."

She gazed out at the water. "Maybe it was seeing Angelo again, Stefano and the mill, the studio. I'm starting to feel something again." She looked at him. "After you stayed, Mom kept a pretty tight rein, on everything. Then after she died, I met Peter. He had just lost his mother. We had so much in common—"

He touched her cheek. "You realize, *cara,* that when it comes to relationships and the future everyone with a brain has some doubt."

She looked out at the anchored boat tossing in the waves. "The day I met Peter I was at Haymarket picking through produce, thinking how the colors and shapes would make an amazing fabric pattern. He saw me eyeing the vegetables and thought I was a chef. Can you imagine?" Across the sandbar under the shadow of drifting clouds, the shoals had taken on a violet hue. "We started talking, I started feeling there might be more than to life than Fiber and Front Street."

That day she hadn't wanted to return to the tiny North End co-op in the baked-in summer heat and had walked down to the harbor to watch the cruise boats motor in and out of port under the hail of wheeling gulls. She felt then that she had met someone who might come to mean something and she had. Yet, looking back now from the vantage point of time and distance, the period of reflection seemed limited.

"For the first time in a long time, I've had time to myself here. Or maybe it's less about time and more about opportunity, for discovery." She looked at him. "I may want more of that when I get back."

"So tell him. You are not the first to have such feelings."

She looked at him. "You and Mom?"

He kicked at a small stone that lay in the grass. "I should never have let the relationship go so far—"

"Why did you?"

He shrugged and gazed at the sea. "I feared not having options."

Chapter 36

She stood in the upstairs bedroom, the splendid inner ache like a kind of dying. Yet, the luncheon had gone better than she hoped, with everyone enjoying the view, the superb seafood, each other. Even Paolo so glowingly praised Mare Monte after his fourth glass of Fontanella that she had wanted to slip out to the Punto and drive away, though the restaurant's owner took the effusion in stride.

Precisely because the gathering had gone so well, she couldn't grasp that tomorrow morning she was leaving. To offset the growing unease, she took advantage of the sun still streaming in the bedroom window to pack. Looking around the tidy but barren space, she felt aimless, adrift. She hung the pink shrug on the back of the chair and slipped quietly downstairs.

From the foyer, she could hear the television in the backroom, a game show, from the raucous laughter that echoed down the hall. Had it been the news, she would have assumed Max was still home. If not, Paolo might be alone. She tiptoed past the dining room.

Paolo lay on the couch in the small den staring at the TV screen smiling vaguely at the blonde hostess who eerily resembled Silvana.

"I see you're busy," she said.

He looked up, dazed. "Gia, come sit." He patted the sofa cushion.

When she made no move, he looked at her closer and pressed mute. "What is it? What's going on?"

She wasn't sure how to begin. "Would you mind taking a walk?"

He looked at her vaguely as if movement was a foreign concept. "Where to?"

"Just the church. I'd like to see it again. I heard you renovated the priest's quarters."

"Ha, those projects require a sanction from the Vatican. I just remodeled the café. Before that, it was the afterhours men's club. Even now the older folks still gather there. But if you want company, we can walk up to the piazza. With so many strangers passing through the area, the church is usually locked."

He shut off the TV and put the remote on the end table. "Max plays cards with the sacristan. He will have the key."

"Thanks," she said. "I'd hate to walk up and not be able to get in."

"Neither do you want to deal with Max and a bunch of old men. Not that I blame you." He got up and went to the backdoor. "Let me just tell the parents. They're out on the patio."

"Would you—I mean, could you tell them where I am when you get back? We won't be long."

He looked at her. "Well, if you're looking to be secretive, let's take a stroll."

She walked with him down the quiet cobblestone street. With no one else about and little ambient sound to muffle their footfalls, she found herself stepping lightly.

He gave her a sidelong look. "What are you doing, playing the ballerina? Or are you planning to break into the church and get arrested? Because let me tell you, that's not the way to stay, if that's what you're after."

She looked at him. "Am I that transparent?"

He shook his brown curls, now back under the red kerchief. "With so much ahead, how can you not want to go back? Here, let's cross over." He nudged her across the street, the conversation's depth apparently more than he could manage on a still-full stomach.

Inside the café, the small lights shone like tiny stars. Over by the window Max and three older men had pulled together two small tables and sat playing a hand of *briscola*. Max looked up as did the others, who by their expressions seemed more appreciative than he of a female visitor.

Max nodded and looked back down at his cards. "You know my brother, Paolo."

"Of course, but who is with him?" said a man in an olive drab shirt.

"Our stepsister, Gia," Paolo spoke up. "We are looking for the church key. Vittorio, you have it with you, right?"

Vittorio hadn't taken his eyes off her, his expression a mixture of suspicion and fascination. He pushed back his cap. "What do you want to go in the church for?"

"Maybe she wants to pray for a blessing," said the older man at the table.

"I'm getting married." She held up her hand and waggled her ring finger. "We were thinking of having the wedding here," she added, lying with abandon. "But my fiancé and I live in Boston. I was confirmed at Sant' Antonio's and would like to see it again."

This at least was true, and she derived pleasure from their shocked expressions. "It would be lovely to see the inside before I leave, even for a few moments."

She smiled broadly as if to say, how could a loyal sacristan deny a good Catholic the privilege of viewing the local *chiesa?*

Vittorio got up and scrutinized her afresh as if under the fitted t-shirt and cargo shorts she might be concealing a weapon. "Hold my place, will you, Rico?" he commanded the man on his right.

Rico proffered a lopsided grin. "I hold onto nothing but my cards."

She glanced at Max to confirm that these were the thoughtful historians he mentioned as being eager to preserve the past. Max, however, kept his eyes on his cards.

"Your turn, Leo," he prompted, ignoring her.

"This way." Vittorio pushed the green plastic strips from the doorway.

Outside along the horizon the setting sun cast a violet veil over the Adriatic.

"I guess you won't need me," Paolo affirmed, heading for the sidewalk.

"Unless you want to give a tour," she said with a smile.

"As I said, there is no business in churches less you are in the in crowd. Right, Vittorio?"

Vittorio shrugged. "I only work here." He motioned to the large front door.

"*Ciao bella,*" Paolo said with a nod. "See you at the house. Meanwhile, don't do anything drastic, like join an order or something." He threw a quick wave and walked back up the street.

"I will keep the door unlocked while you are inside." Vittorio pulled out an ancient ring of equally ancient keys. "I can see from the café when you come out. And stay in the sanctuary, no going around back."

He hadn't said, around to the priests' quarters, but she wondered if that was what he meant.

She raised her ring finger. "I just want to spend a few moments in quiet." She pushed the diamond around to be visible. "We'll be busy with the wedding arrangements when I get home so the solitude would be nice," she added, surprised to find the words true.

When had it come to this, she wondered, as Vittorio put a large black iron key in the lock. Even in a sparsely populated village they locked the local house of worship. Across the piazza, an old woman in a shapeless black dress stood in the shadow of the façade as if waiting.

The sacristan opened the door and motioned her inside. "I am just across the way," he reminded, pocketing the keys.

She nodded and went inside. A cool, incense-suffused dimness pervaded the sanctuary, the ambient light through the stained glass windows speckling the long empty rows of polished oak pews with rainbow hues. Down along the narthex, tiers of candles gleamed in votives of ruby-colored glass.

She tiptoed to the back pew and sat at the end. The woman in black slipped in and went down to what was likely her usual seat at the front left. Another gray-haired member of the faithful in a black lace head covering crept in to a place on the right. As her eyes adjusted to contour of light and shadow, she looked up at the faded ceiling fresco, an ambitious depiction of angels in soaring flight amid pallid rays of golden sun and a deity whose glory lay obscured under dingy white clouds and cracked paint.

Recalling bits and pieces of the confirmation ceremony, she remembered the day as wet and unusually dark, the fittings for her dress and twitching before the three-way mirror in her father's workroom.

"Do I have to wear this?" she asked as he hemmed the stiff white crinoline so that it wouldn't peek out from under the hem. She pulled at the waistline where it chaffed her skin. "It's itching the hell out of me."

Her father looked up. "Don't use such language. It's not becoming."

"To what," she asked. "The dress?"

He had been the one to push for her confirmation here, she recalled, viewing the mirror within the frame of memory. She'd had to memorize what felt like the entire Catholic catechism and one of the world's many creeds and recite it all in Latin. The priest who came to hear her had taken pity when he heard her struggling with the language and ultimately had her recite the text in English, allowing a passing mark even though she gave the Apostle's creed instead of the Nicene.

"Your mother's not much for tradition," her father had said, taking a pin from between pursed lips and straightening the hem. "She doesn't care a fig for *la chiesa.*"

"Neither do I," she answered.

He crouched at her side. "Maybe someday you will." He pressed the pin into the crinoline.

She sat back against the wooden bench. Tomorrow morning, she would leave for Milan, Sunday for home where Peter was waiting, where she had a life and a place of her own, a job and a wedding to plan. She leaned forward over the narrow railing. A wedding to plan, a meeting with Don Roccia and James Martell and a wedding to plan, a fiancé who loved her and a wedding to plan.

She imagined a celebratory dinner at an elegant little North Shore inn with close friends and work associates, since neither she nor Peter had family there. Then what? Peter had asked her more than once to move in, since they were together on weekends anyway. But this would be marriage, a continual mutual intrusion and sequestering of each other's lives. How would that work? Peter wanted children but she didn't, not yet, though surely with time.

Something within had her feeling unsettled. Was it the marriage contract, the legal side of the arrangement? Though her parents hadn't stayed together, she didn't doubt Peter. If anything, she trusted him more than she did herself. She sat back. What was it about her that she didn't trust? Was it her fidelity, her work with Fiber, the ability to deal with Martell? It could be any of these things or all of them. Yet, as she considered each option in turn, tried each like a key in an unfamiliar lock, none seemed to fit.

A priest in a black cassock entered the front of the sanctuary, genuflected at the small altar and crossed to the far side of the church and the confessional.

Everything would be fine once she left the village, she told herself, exited the vortex of rural life. Once she reached Milan, she would be fine. The meeting with Martell would renew her momentum, the feeling of reality. She gazed up at the ceiling, the faded fresco of angels amid dimmed gold, the muted representation of the figure of a man, hand outstretched across the cosmos.

Chapter 37

Eight o'clock Friday morning and she was nearly ready to leave. She had tried texting Peter but got no response. No news on the fundraiser should mean it went off as expected. Still, it wouldn't hurt to check again.

She took out her cell. Me again, she texted, feeling foolish. Hope everything's okay. Text when you can.

She looked out the bedroom window at Paolino's house, the Mercedes parked near the wall and away from the chicken coop. She turned and slipped quietly out of the bedroom and down the stairs past the kitchen, out the front door and around the side of the house.

Standing at the Cantonis' backdoor, she heard the low hum of male voices. What was she doing here feeling awkward and hugely embarrassed, an intruder in the life of a family that wasn't hers? Hadn't they all said goodbye yesterday?

Before she could turn to leave, the door opened. She stepped back. Alex stood on the threshold, Paolino behind him looking pale in the small circle of daylight that illumined his oval unshorn face. From the little kitchen off the hallway, she heard movement, the bustle and clatter of dishes and daily life.

"Gia," Alex said, surprised. "Please, come in." He stood aside.

"No, I was just—I wanted to say goodbye, again," apparently. She smiled at Paolino. Why were these people so hard to leave that each farewell brought more sadness? From her periphery, she saw Alex watching.

"C-come in, Gia, p-lease," said Paolino. "Eleda is in the k-itchen."

232 • ADELE ANNESI

"No, I—it's near time to go. I just wanted to see you again." And hear their voices and have them tell her once more that she could always come back. Was this why she came, what she needed to hear?

Eleda peered out from the kitchen.

"*Zia,*" she said. Emboldened by her aunt's timid smile, she stepped in the doorway. "So good to see you yesterday. I just wanted to say thank you, again."

Eleda's smile deepened. She shook her head. "The time was too short." She came over and patted Gia's hand. "Come again, soon, eh?"

"I hope." She turned to Paolino.

A faint glimmer shone in the bright blue eyes. He drew near and bussed her on each cheek, scraping her skin with his stubble. "I will miss you," she whispered, squeezing his hand tighter than she intended. She turned quickly to avoid Alex's eyes.

"Wait a moment, Gia. I'll walk you out," he said. "Tomorrow then, *Babbo,* all right?" And don't worry, Mamma. His postnasal drip is late season allergies, not a cold."

She pushed the screen door open, pressed her fingers to her eyelids and walked blindly to the wall. She felt Alex's hand on her arm.

"Listen," he said, turning her around. "You really can come back anytime. We will be here."

She looked up. "Will you? All of you?"

"What do you mean, all of us? Are you worried about your father?"

"Dad, *Zio*, everybody." She shook her head. "It's just—I hardly ever come here and when I do it ends in unfinished business. There's never enough time to know everyone. We humans deserve that, don't we, having someone take the time to know us?"

He put his arm around her. "You have just described one of the reasons I went into medicine. It wasn't just for the sick because they are sick but because they are human and deserve time and attention, as do their families. And if people do not believe that anxiety and dementia grow worse for lack of human contact, they're fooling themselves."

She looked at him. "So what should we do?"

He laughed. "My dear Gia, what would you have us do, stop time?"

"Yes." She cuffed his arm. "Let's do that. Let's stop time. Right here, now. So what if the world has to wait? What, I'm serious."

He stopped laughing and squeezed her shoulders. "It's not time you want to stop, is it?"

She felt the tension again in her neck. "I don't know what I want."

"Then as we said at LungoMer, you must learn. Listen, you know why any doc worth his salt tries to get his patients to relax, gives them water, talks to them a bit, pats their hands? It's because any procedure, especially one that is invasive, is more painful when the patient is afraid, when they resist. Moreover, fear doesn't always yield an accurate diagnosis." He looked in her eyes. "Whatever you must learn will hurt more if you fight it."

She shook her head. "But I don't even know what I'm fighting."

"Then open yourself to finding out, especially here." He pressed his palm to her chest.

She laid her head on his shoulder. "I wish you'd come with me."

"I will try to come to Boston for a visit. I usually go to LA but Mass General is doing more in neuro, and one of the stroke docs is Italian. So who knows, even I may learn something." He smiled. "And now I have someone from whom I can bum a room—as you say." He nudged her arm. "Now take this."

She took the crisp white cotton handkerchief he produced from his pocket. He must buy them by the score, which made it clear the kind of news he often had to give his patients.

"Gia! What are you doing out here?"

She looked to see Stella hurtling in their direction, red mules clapping her heels as she strode unevenly across the gravel.

"The boys want to say goodbye." She motioned to the house. "You already said your farewells to this bunch yesterday. Sorry, Alex, but we must get a move on. Now hurry, Gia, or you will miss the train."

She gave Alex a helpless look and handed him the hankie.

"Keep it. And here again is my cell," he said, producing another card from his pocket. "Now you know I mean it when I say we'll keep in touch." He gave her a firm hug and a kiss. "Good luck in Milan."

"Quickly now," Stella said, taking her arm. "Everyone is waiting."

Giving her face a swipe with the handkerchief, she forced herself to look ahead.

In the kitchen, Max stood at the sink draining a cup of coffee and looking like this was more his usual morning routine than sitting at the breakfast table. Paolo, however, sat slowly peeling a fig.

"I guess it's time," she heard herself say.

Paolo looked up with an odd expression, sadness, fatigue, apathy? Her emotions were raw and playing tricks so it was hard to tell, and she hadn't known him long enough to be sure.

He put his fork down and got up. "Ah, *cara*," he said softly. "Feels like we have known each other longer than a few days. Before you know it Ana and I will come visit Boston. We may even bring this lout."

He nodded at Max and gave her a hearty embrace and a kiss on each cheek. She heard Max behind him clearing his throat.

"Max," she said trying to smile. "I guess you and Paolo go back today, too. After all, you have work to do like everybody else."

"Well, not quite like everyone," he said with the same ghost of a smile. "Many others are not as fortunate." He stepped closer. "But if we have work we love, we are blessed. Don't you think so?"

He gave her an unexpectedly strong hug and lightly touched his cheek to hers; she was surprised at the softness of his skin.

"Let us know how things fare with the business," he said, letting go.

Stella cuffed him on the arm. "More important, send pictures of the wedding,"

"Why don't all of you come visit?" she asked, fumbling for the hankie. "I—Peter and I would love to have you. We would invite you to the wedding, but it will be small." She turned to Stella. "We could go shopping at Faneuil Hall. It's in the heart of the city. You could buy a red dress."

Giovanni stood in the doorway. "The bags are in the car, including that orange monstrosity."

Wiping her eyes, Stella grabbed his arm. "Gi, what would you say to a trip to Boston?"

He stared at her. "Now?"

"Why not?" She winked at Gia. "What's the matter, you don't want to go?"

"It's fine. Long as Gia is there, we don't need a special occasion."

"I think we need to get going," she cut in, the front of the pink cotton shrug now thoroughly damp. To the rag pile with it, the minute she got home.

"Then let's go," Giovanni said, adjusting his hat.

The Punto was the only vehicle in the lot besides the Fiat. The black Mercedes was gone. She hadn't even heard him leave.

Giovanni reached for the door handle. "Let's open this, get some air in." He glanced at his watch.

"What are we waiting for?" she asked.

"I took the dress to Stefano while you were at the church last evening."

She felt a cramp grip her stomach. "You're kidding, right?"

"It needed a quick once-over with the steam iron."

She stared at him then turned to the street, but it was empty. She started for the sidewalk. Maybe Stefano had a flat or stalled out somewhere.

"Ho, there, ready to go?"

She turned to see him walking briskly up the cobbles carrying the dress in a clear plastic bag and holding it by the hanger.

"Thank God." She let out the breath she'd been holding and took the hanger. "Do you mind? I mean, can I have a look?"

"Sure, but Giovanni was right. A good steam with an overnight set always helps. But if you want to see it—"

She glanced at her father. "No, it's fine. Can I—do you mind if I take it?"

"All yours," Stefano said with a smile. "May there be many more."

"Here's hoping." She took the garment bag and started for the car then turned and gave him a hug, American style, and a kiss. "Give one of those to your father, too, and thank you both."

"*Piacere.*" He lifted both hands in the double ciao of departure and stood alongside Max and Paolo.

Stella went to the Punto's passenger side. "Gi, can you put the one garment bag inside the other? I want to say *addio* to our girl." Stella took hold of her arms. "I hope it wasn't too hard, being in the middle of nowhere with us crazies."

Blinking, she tried to smile. "Not at all." It hadn't been so bad, she reasoned, perhaps because she had thus far survived.

Stella tilted her head. "We are glad you came. Call when you get to Milano. Remember, you are always welcome."

She nodded as Stella clasped her tight and let her go. Her father stood by the open driver's side door.

"*Addio,*" she called out.

She blew a kiss to the four of them. In less than an hour, Stefano would be back at the mill, Max and Paolo would likely leave for Rome, and Stella would walk down the hill to the cooperative as if she had never come. How in heaven could she stand it without them all?

"Set?" asked Giovanni, his hand on the ignition key.

She nodded. "We're already late." She took her sunglasses from the orange bag and waived, the darkened lenses easing the sting and glare of daylight. She turned again and wiped her face.

The main artery into Marotta was congested, a conveyer belt for every lorry in the region. She kept her eyes off the hillsides that sheltered the surrounding fields and focused on the asphalt stretched out ahead.

"Can't you go any faster?"

"And where would I go faster? These idiots are clogging the place." Giovanni cursed as the truck in front of them veered off at an intersection without signaling. "*Cretino,*" he shouted, "from a long line of *Cretini.*"

She tightened the already tight seatbelt and closed her eyes as they headed straight for an elderly man on a Vespa who loudly condemned them and their lineage. Maybe they wouldn't make it to Milan after all and would meet their end here. Keeping her eyes closed behind the dark glasses, she felt the car finally slow then jerk to a stop.

"Let me find a place to park," Giovanni said.

"We don't have time." She grasped the door handle. "Let me off."

He turned. "I can't leave you in the street. Let me pull into the parking." He gunned the engine and lurched through the intersection as the light turned green.

"Perfect," she barked over the din of city traffic, grabbing the door.

"*Dio,* Gia, wait for me to stop at least."

He maneuvered the compact into a spot marked for drop-offs. As he opened the door, a *carabiniere* in a blue cap and shoulder holster strode toward them. Giovanni kept the motor running and got out.

"We're not staying," she told the officer in formal Italian. "Jerks," she muttered in English.

"Good God, Gia, don't stir anything, please. Half of them know English now." He pushed back the seat. "Let me get the suitcase. You get the garment bag."

On impulse, she opened the carryall and quickly checked for the red plastic travel wallet that held her passport and plane ticket, a task she should have taken care of at the house. Her heart hammered in her chest. Where was the damn wallet?

"What are you doing?" Giovanni asked from behind her.

She shoved aside the mini-umbrella and found the wallet underneath, the passport and ticket inside. "Nothing. I'm set."

She hoisted the orange bag and saw her father staring at her. His eyes seemed clearer this morning, the strain of the past days perhaps relieved by her departure and no more close work on dresses. A garbled squawk erupted from the loudspeaker. She shook her head. "I have to go."

He moved closer. "Call from Milan."

She nodded. "Listen, I can't begin to say—"

She looked at his face, the vertical lines in his cheeks, the pallor under the small patch of stubble he had missed while shaving, the age spots from too many years and too many days by the water he loved. She draped the garment bag over the car door and put her arms around him.

"Thanks," she whispered, feeling the pressure of his palm on her shoulder.

He stood back and held her. "Listen, the meeting with Martell—don't push too hard. I mean, don't look eager. If it's not him, it will be someone else." He gave a wan smile. *"Beh,* what do I know? Your bullying worked with me."

She smiled and heard another squawk from the public address system. "I'm sorry."

"I know." He draped the garment bag over her shoulder. *"Addio, bella."*

She shoved the orange bag up her arm and swiveled the suitcase. *"Ciao,"* she said, folding her fingers. "See you."

He waved. "Go on," he added with a sideways look at the *carabiniere,* who had lingered within earshot. "I'll just wait a moment," he told the officer. *"Mia figlia."*

She hurried up the front steps and into the ticket office. A dark-skinned woman with an infant draped over her shoulder stood in line. She got behind the woman, tilted her suitcase upright and laid the bag on top. Speaking in clipped English, the woman asked for tickets to what sounded like Bergamo. The ticket agent shrugged and turned aside.

She moved around to the window. "Bergamo, right?" she asked the woman. The child on her neck gazed up with drowsy dark eyes. "Bergamo, yes?" she repeated. "You and your daughter?" The little girl appeared too young for school. "One way?"

The woman nodded and put a selection of euros on the counter.

The ticket agent sat staring.

"Look, *signore,*" Gia said in Italian. "You will have to deal with us for two more hours if you don't get this customer two tickets to Bergamo now, one way."

The agent glared at her.

"Or I could get the *carabiniere* from the parking lot." She smiled. "He seemed quite attentive when I was out there just now." She batted her eyelids, a gesture she loathed and couldn't recall ever having used before.

The agent muttered and turned. "Get back in line. This woman is ahead of you."

Gladly, she thought, stepping aside. *"Prego,"* she said with a nod to urge the woman forward. She stepped up to the window. "One to *Milano Centrale."*

The agent gazed at the computer screen and slowly keyed in the information. A man in a gray tailored suit filed in behind her.

"Can we get a move on here?" she said in a loud voice and perfect Italian. She turned and rolled her eyes at the man, gave a side nod at the agent and slid the euros under the window. The agent counted them and peered at one of the bills.

"Mah, signore, please," said the man in the suit. "What do you think, the *signorina* printed the bills in the cellar?"

She smiled benevolently as the agent deposited the bills in the cash drawer and handed over the ticket. "Thanks," she said in English as a train whistle split the air.

She started to ask if it was the Eurostar to Milan, but after this episode the agent was sure to give the wrong information. She turned to the man behind her. Eurostar *Milano Centrale?"* She nodded toward the whistle.

"Let's hope." He turned to the agent. *"Su,* step it up."

She rushed to the stamping machine.

"Always get your ticket stamped *before* you board," Paolo had reminded her last night, twice.

The train whistled again as she rushed down through the underpass and up the stairs on the other side. On the last step, the garment bag slipped from her shoulder. She hoisted it and rushed up to the platform as the Eurostar pulled in. The woman and child stood at the other end. The man in the suit walked up as the train slowed to a stop.

Leaning from the railcar doorway, the conductor waited till the train came to a squealing halt and swung down. She draped the garment bag over her arm and dragged the suitcase behind.

"Milano Centrale?" she asked.

The conductor nodded and moved aside. She heaved the case up the steps and climbed aboard. Checking her ticket, she found her seat halfway up the car on the aisle. She gently folded the garment bag and set it in the overhead. A woman in the opposite aisle seat wearing a silk leopard print blouse noted her gear with a frown.

"And never leave your bags in the aisles or on the seats," Paolo had also warned. "They frown on that."

She gave the woman a broad smile, swiveled the case and moved back down the aisle to the luggage compartment and shoved the piece alongside a large rubberized red case with a Gucci tag. At least this was a Eurostar, spacious and air-conditioned, not a cattle car.

She moved to her seat and peered out the window as the train clacked out of the station. Down in the parking lot, her father stood watching each railcar as if to catch a glimpse of her through one of the darkened windows. She leaned across a vacant seat, but the train zipped past before she could wave. It had passed too quickly, she thought, looking through the glass as they moved from Marotta's downtown. All of it had passed too quickly. She went to her seat, took off the shrug, rolled it into a ball and shoved it under her neck. Her back to the aisle, she gazed blearily out the window as the train rolled past a carapace of hills under a bank of clouds.

Chapter 38

She stretched and opened her eyes to see rain pelting the window and soaking the planed countryside as field after verdant field of rice rolled past under a mantle of gray. She straightened against the balled-up shrug. An older man with silver hair sat across from her unwrapping a *panino* of prosciutto and mozzarella. Her mouth watered.

"In the café car," he said, nodding behind him and biting into the soft white roll.

She smiled briefly and looked around. The woman in the leopard blouse adjusted a pair of reading glasses over an iPad. She should try texting Peter again, she thought, and turned to see the man across from her nearly finished eating. Better to wait and call from the privacy of her hotel room. She could call her father then, too, let everyone know she made it.

She glanced at her watch then out at the rain and the passing landscape, fewer hectares of farmland now between one municipality and the next.

When she was nine, her father had insisted on visiting a cousin, second or third in lineage, who had gone to seek his tailoring fortunes in Milan. The cousin owed money to more than one family member back *alle Marche* and was no longer in their good graces. Yet, they still held a grudging respect for a man who had the nerve to leave the village, one of the first to do so, and found work as a cutter in a men's suit factory at a reportedly tidy wage.

She felt the heat rise in her cheeks at the recollection of her father's visit to his relative's workplace. The cousin had met them in the parking lot, hadn't even invited them in, affirming that, yes, he was doing well. Almost before her father could ask, he added that there were no job openings at present, nor were there likely to be anytime soon.

"You see," her mother said once the cousin—what was his name—went back to work without even offering a coffee. "I told you there was no use. And just as well. You think your cousin found his fortune? Look at the place."

She hazily remembered a long low brick building, rows of small, square wired-glass windows effecting the look of a penitentiary. God, her father did have nerve, she thought, watching heat lightning flash across the clouds. Showing up on the fly barely ahead of a phone call warning the cousin—what was his name, anyway—they were coming. Why had he bothered? The chances of finding work were so slim.

The man across from her wadded the plastic wrap from his sandwich. She pressed her hand to her stomach to silence the rumbling and noted the café car icon above the carriage door, the up arrow pointing to the back of the train. She got up and took the carryall from the seat.

After a *panino* and caffeinated diet soda, she felt marginally better. The sky had lightened, and the steady downpour had diminished to a drizzle. Beside the carriage door the lighted display showed *Milano Centrale* next. As if by an innate call, people began gathering their belongings. The man across looked up as she stood.

"Going on to Paris?"

"Just to Milan."

He raised an eyebrow. "You're not French?"

It was the fair skin and smattering of freckles, and the ginger hair. "Italian," she said, feeling only slightly disingenuous in not saying Italian-American. "My great grandmother may have been French. Her maiden name was Simone."

"Ah," the man responded, as if to say he thought as much.

"Is Milano the last stop?" she asked.

"Should be," the man said as the train slowed.

She looked out the window at the rows of track in cross-stitch patterns. Shouldering the carryall, she reached overhead for the garment bag and went to end of the car. The vast rubberized red case with the Gucci tag blocked her suitcase. The automated loudspeaker confirmed *Milano Centrale* was the next and last stop. The train slowed. She inched her suitcase around the red one.

"What are you doing there?"

She turned. The woman in the leopard blouse stood in the aisle.

"Just moving this." She tugged her case by the handle.

"What do you mean, touching someone else's things?" The woman's voice rose.

She reached for her suitcase and pulled it free from where it was jammed against the side of the compartment.

"But do you see what she is doing?" said the woman to a growing audience. "Where is the conductor, anyway? This isn't how things are done." Craning her neck, she looked down the aisle.

The train lurched as she swiveled her suitcase. She regained her footing as the conductor came up beside them.

"Look, here," the woman said. "Look what she's doing." She moved aside so the conductor could see.

Gia righted her case and held it. "The only problem here is that this woman's luggage has taken up nearly the entire storage. Tsk," she said, clucking her tongue. "Is that size even legal for this type of trip?" Tilting her head, she gave the woman an accusing look.

The conductor looked at the case then turned and began lecturing the woman and everyone in earshot on the ills of bringing oversized luggage on an in-country trip, without paying the tariff.

"You realize there is a fine for this," Gia heard the conductor say as she moved past the line of passengers waiting for their bags while the Eurostar rocked into the station past a cluster of rusted freight cars on a spur of tangled side track.

The train jolted to a stop, convulsed then rocked again, wheezing like a giant bellows as the brakes clamped and held. After a final jolt, she steadied herself and dragged the suitcase to the exit. How she longed for a shower and room service, if not takeout from the nearest locale.

The carriage doors opened onto the platform. She dragged the case down the steps and hoisted it with the garment bag onto an auto-porter. She put two euros in the slot and heaved the cart nearly onto the foot of an older gentleman with a red and green plaid scarf.

"Sorry, *scusi,* " she said. Rolling past him, she ignored his shouted pronouncements on intransigents and sped away.

The humid air of the arrivals area under the domed roof reeked of diesel. She rolled the cart down the breezeway, through the glass doors and along a jammed aisle to a sloped side passage parallel to the massive main corridor. Searching for an exit, she wondered with a twinge what Alex was doing this evening, whether Nicoletta had arrived from Rome. What did it matter, she chided herself. Either way, he was with family.

Out in the street the mentholated air was saturated with the sound of car horns. A pair of skyscrapers under construction loomed on the horizon under a dome of clearing blue.

"*Tassi,* " she called out, waving down a cab that stopped across the road. Several people queuing up at the stand closest to the station turned as she rushed across the thoroughfare.

She tugged the cart to the back of the cab and hoisted the suitcase in the open trunk. She put the garment bag beside her on the seat with the carryall.

"Eurotel Rho," she said.

When she arrived at the hotel, at the marble counter stood the same concierge, attired now in a gunmetal tunic and matching stretch pencil leg slacks, her stilettos bright red.

"I was here earlier in the week," she said. "The name is Falcini."

Flipping back her tawny hair, the woman looked at the computer screen. "I believe you have a message."

Her father must be concerned to have called already. "Giovanni Falcini?"

The woman looked up. "From that gentleman."

She turned. A tallish man stood in the lobby wearing a navy cashmere jacket and tailored white shirt. She blinked and squinted, but he still stood there.

"I thought I'd stop by," he said. "Maybe take you to dinner. Know anyplace good?"

Chapter 39

Standing in the gleaming marble foyer, Peter looked immaculate and sleek as a diplomat. She felt the concierge staring as he moved closer. How had he gotten here? When had he gotten here? He was really here, right? She felt a whelming unease but no desire to display it.

He drew near, pulled her close with a kiss then drew back. His steady gaze touched off a fluttering in her stomach and a feeling of vertigo.

"You're really here," she said, barely above a whisper, her voice dry as rustling leaves.

"You're surprised," he noted with satisfaction.

"Well, what did you think?" She felt her face grow warm and kept her back to the front desk. "Where are you staying?"

"With you, I hope," he answered.

"Well, sure." She lowered her voice. "It's just—I really wasn't expecting you. But I guess that's obvious."

Her quick laugh had the squeak of panic. She looked up at the slate blue eyes. Had he gotten taller? Glancing down, she saw the same half-inch loafers in black glove leather he usually wore.

"What is it?" he asked, following her gaze. "Wrong style for the fashion capital?"

"Not at all," she said, staring. "It's just, you seem different, taller—I don't know." Still gawking, she was intensely aware of the exhibition she was providing for anyone who might wander past. She steadied herself. "How long are you here?"

"Till Sunday, same as you, just leaving on an earlier flight. I couldn't get a seat on yours." He turned to the woman at the counter. "Could you have our bags brought up, please?"

"My pleasure," said the concierge. Pressing her earpiece, she spoke in flowing Italian. "The porter will bring up your things. It will just be a moment. Here are your keycards." She handed them to him across the desk.

"*Grazie* and can you suggest a place for dinner? Something casual but appetizing. Though I'm sure anywhere here would be fine." He offered a smile.

She found herself still staring with a strange mix of awe and envy at this other side of him, the self-assurance his upbringing provided regardless of the venue or role. She thought of Alex and shook her head to dispel the image.

"For outdoor dining with an artisanal flair, there is a mozzarella bar on Via Mercato. It has good food, a casual atmosphere, just right for a first time in the city."

"Is it obvious?" he asked with a grin.

The concierge smiled as the porter went behind the counter to retrieve his suitcase. The porter started for hers and the garment bag.

"I'll get that." She draped the bag over her arm.

"Let me." Peter reached out to help.

"Thanks, no. Sorry, the dresses are in here."

"Shall we?" Peter nodded to the porter, who wheeled the brass luggage cart around and down to the lift.

The porter pressed the lighted elevator button. The door slid open to the glow of recessed spotlighting reflected in a full mirror. Facing the glass, she saw Peter behind her. The memory of Alex's condo flashed in her mind with such intensity that she thought for a moment it had shown in the glass. She turned quickly as the elevator closed.

Peter took her hand. "Everything okay?"

"Fine, I'm just really surprised to see you." Stupefied was more like it.

The elevator door opened to the second floor. The porter rolled the luggage cart down the hallway to room two-thirteen, took out a keycard and slipped it in the slot.

Inside the room, the brass bedside reading lamp had been lit, creating a pool of soft light. An extra set of fresh white bath towels lay on the quilted teal bedspread. The thick matching drapes were drawn nearly closed, their sheer midsection letting in a shaft of afternoon light and the sound of rush hour traffic from the street below.

How well-planned this was, she thought, as she hung the garment bag in the walnut armoire. She recalled the self-satisfied look on the concierge's elegant face. Peter must have notified the hotel he was coming. She waited while he tipped the porter, who bowed slightly and closed the door.

She drew back the drapes. "So are you going to tell me how you managed all this?"

"I took the eight-thirty-five out of Logan last night." He put his wallet back in his jacket pocket. "Got into Malpensa around half-past noon."

"You look rested for having just arrived."

"And you look beautiful," he said, softly. "Of course, I can't tell you that very well all the way over there."

"But the flight must have cost a mint. Did you book it before I left?"

"I used credit card points and frequent flier miles. And, no, I didn't reserve it beforehand. It was spur of the moment. Though if I didn't know better—and at the moment I'm not sure I do—I'd think you aren't glad to see me."

"Of course, I'm glad. It's just, as I said before I left, the trip is business."

"And, what—no friends or family allowed?"

"No, it's—"

"You don't have time? Time is short, Gia, a fact I know better than most people."

"I know. I'm just not sure how much time together we'll have here." She tugged at the drapes, feeling the stiffness of the commercial fabric.

"So, what? You're worried about being available? What have I asked since I got here, Gia, except to let me into a little of the time you do have."

"I'm sorry. I didn't mean it that way." She moved closer. "It's just that there's so much to plan. And I'm nervous, more than I realized." She let out her breath and felt the tightness in her chest ease.

He came and put his arms around her. "A case of nerves means you care."

"Maybe too much." She laid her head on his shoulder and heard cell in the carryall vibrating. She buried her face in his shirt. "Honestly."

"I suppose you should get that."

She went over and took the cell from her bag. "It's Don, confirming tonight with Martel, at the Pinacoteca di Brera. The Sala della Passione at nine." She looked up. "Want me to see if he can get you in? There are drinks in the Cortile. You could take a tour."

"I'm sure I'll find something to look at," he said with a smile.

She texted, asking to bring a friend. "He says, 'More, merrier.'"

She texted the acceptance and waited. "We're set." She saved the invite code and set the cell on the nightstand. "And now I have the right dress. Two, in fact. My father made one for me."

He moved closer. "At the moment I'm more interested that we have two days in Milan together—two for two."

"Wait," she said. "I'm doing the math."

He smiled. "Look out, we're in trouble now."

"Careful," she chided, poking his side. "Or I won't bring you. And I really think you'll enjoy it."

"This is what I enjoy," he said, drawing her close.

She glanced at the radio clock on the nightstand. "It's nearly four. The show is at six. And I need to shower before I put on that dress. Wait till you see it—"

"I'd rather see you." He slipped his hand under the t-shirt. "And we can still have that shower." He cupped his hand to her breast. "Two birds and all that."

"Yes, but the time—"

He slipped her straps down over her shoulders. She unbuttoned his shirt and pressed against him.

"So you have missed me," he said, softly.

"Maybe, a little," she murmured. "But you'd better take that jacket off. Cashmere and water don't mix."

Chapter 40

The bistro in the intimate residential quarter near the Via Pontaccio offered cozy outdoor tables and temping dishes featuring fresh mozzarella. At Gia's suggestion, they opted instead for pizza with zucchini flowers, *burrata* and anchovies from Cetara, the crust made with stone-ground flour from a family-run mill in Padua.

After sipping an evocative Pinot Bianco from Lombardy and smoothing the protective white linen napkin on her lap, she thought of Ordito and Castel Barberini and what felt unnervingly like a homeland and one she would soon leave behind. As they left the bistro, she consoled herself with the knowledge that this evening, at least, was still ahead.

"So what do you think?" She glanced at her reflection as they walked down Via Brera past a line of windows marking the Brera Academy of Fine Arts. In the clear pane of glass, she noticed Peter wearing a slightly piqued look.

"You've asked a dozen times," he said calmly. "But, yes, you look lovely. Roccia will love the dress."

"It's Martell I'm worried about," she said.

And he should love the fabric, too, she thought, feeling her spirits lift at the sight of the russet and amber paisley, the yellow-gold of sunflowers at its center. She told her father that the woman who wore a dress of this fabric would feel the difference, and she did.

They stopped in front of the late-Baroque style Palazzo di Brera, erected over the remains of a fourteenth-century monastery. Maybe it was a good omen that tonight's meet would be held in a space comprising some faith and many cultures and venues—a Palazzo and museum, two academies, a botanical garden and an observatory—all underscoring the smarter side even of clothing, a kind of sweet spot between couture and covering.

They walked in through the Cortile d'Onore, with its symmetrical columns and arches, and ascended the broad stone steps. A well-muscled security guard stood in the upper portico wearing a snug black dinner jacket and checking cell phones.

Well, here goes, she thought. She took her phone from her bag and pressed the side button. Nothing. She pressed harder, then again, but the phone was as dead as the day she arrived. She stepped aside to let a group of four behind them pass.

"What's wrong?" Peter moved around beside her.

"My cell's dead. I can't access the confirmation." In the frenzy of seeing Peter and their hours together, she must have left it on and unplugged.

"See if the attendant has your name."

"Fine, but walk ahead of me."

She stepped in behind him. The attendant gave Peter a searching look and moved around to his side.

"*Buona sera,*" she said. "I wonder if you have reservations for Falcini and guest?"

"No confirmation?" asked the attendant.

"I saved the email to my cell, but my phone is dead." She showed him the darkened display.

He gazed just below her neck, disapproval in his narrow black eyes.

"I'm here for a meeting tonight with James Martell," she said, her voice rising squeakily in a panicked note.

Peter stepped around her. "Good evening, speak English?"

The attendant offered a toothy smile. "A leetle, yes."

He moved closer. "You know the problems with mobile phones. Especially American models. If you need a reference for tonight, I'll give you my cell number."

Gia stared as he offered his phone, whose home screen wallpaper was a photo of him smiling in front of Litton Learning—a really good photo.

She tugged his sleeve. "What are you doing?" she whispered.

He shook her hand away. "You won't misuse the number now, will you?" he queried, with a grin.

"Of course not," the attendant affirmed in an answering leer.

"My friend and I thank you."

The guard glanced at Gia. "Ah, the friend, yes, very good. Take the walkway on the left, not so many people."

Gia stared at Peter as they went down the walkway. "Well, that's a side of you I haven't seen."

He took her arm. "I figure I'm here so I might as well be useful."

"Not that useful," she said.

The columns of the Cortile's upper portico gleamed under a line of angled overhead spots. There must have been a fashion exhibit earlier, given the rows of empty chairs, the white catwalk runner rolled up and shoved aside. Down in the courtyard visitors strolled past the statue of Napoleon in the guise of Mars the Peacemaker. Echoing through the open corridors were the strains of a string quartet and a suite by Arcangelo Corelli that subsumed with its resonance conversations she couldn't make out, perhaps echoing others over the centuries that had meant the ascent and dissolution of so many aspirations. She turned back to the stone staircase and the way out.

Peter held her arm. "You're not leaving, are you?" He squeezed gently. "I'm not."

She stopped and looked at him. "Maybe I don't want this," she said, her voice unsteady, her emotions unnervingly raw, overwhelmed by the surroundings, those in the arts who had come and gone or hadn't been at all. She thought of Max, his falling out with Stefano over Darwin while at university in Rome.

"I mean, why go through the hassle?" She recalled her father and the botched attempt to garner a tailoring job at the suit factory. "It's just the rag trade after all." Her voice sounded shrill against the melodic violins.

He searched her eyes. "Is that how you feel, really?"

It was how she felt but not all that she felt. Fabric and fashion meant more than she could express, more even than this night.

Yet, she couldn't help feeling that the part that meant more was somewhere else. But if not here, where?

"Listen," he said, drawing her close. "Try not to look at this one evening, this one event, as if it's your whole career."

He had a point, she reasoned, as she took in the calm blue eyes, the smooth skin. So why couldn't she shed the fear that her future hung precisely in the balance of this night?

She stepped back and slipped her arm in his. "Just don't let go."

They walked down the portico past one bust after another commemorating those who once graced these halls and were now elevated above all human height and reach.

"I'm feeling really short right about now," she whispered.

"All the better to fit into tight places," he answered, steering her back around toward the drinks table. "These look interesting."

He ushered her to a Plexiglass tabletop set on a row of miniature columns that evoked the style of those in the Cortile. Among the crystalline glasses of varicolored liquids she found nothing familiar and would have given anything for a white wine, something recognizable, simple, homemade even. The closest in appearance was a glass at the far end with contents the color of champagne.

Holding the glass by the bowl, she turned and took a sip and noticed the server trying to hide a smile. The bitterness of what tasted like straight grain alcohol set her teeth on edge. Reluctantly, she swallowed, choking slightly.

Peter took the glass. "Not something you'd recommend?"

She coughed. "All sensation, no flavor."

He took a drink the color of Green Chartreuse. "Mm, melon. Not bad."

Figures, she thought, and looked down the portico, now thick with people and the drone of multilingual conversations. She looked around again and saw Peter head-to-head with the drinks server, who appeared to be disclosing the secret of whatever was in the glass of green liquid he now held to the light.

Great. And right after he'd promised not to leave her. She looked down the portico and saw a tall trim figure gliding in her direction, dark almond eyes trained on her face. Heavens, she thought, observing Don Roccia's attire. The man was a slim-fitted work of catalog art, from charcoal wool sport coat and cotton dress shirt to pinstripe woolen trousers, none of which looked Italian except, she suspected, the black leather dress shoes.

"My, but aren't you a picture in that dress." He took her by the arms and bussed her on each cheek. "I can do this now since you're not my student. At least not this evening."

"Don't be so sure," she said spontaneously.

"So you are here to learn—good." Roccia offered a smile. "And this must be your intended." He extended a long-fingered hand to Peter, who had materialized at her side. "I had a feeling when you asked for a second invite this was why."

"Pleased," Peter said, somewhat stiffly holding out a hand.

She suppressed a grin to see him finally less at ease than she and short of words.

Roccia turned. "So, *bella,* ready to meet the man of the hour? Apologies, I should say the other man of the hour. Would you mind, Peter, if I borrow your girl? We have a meeting in the Sala, but you can stroll the Cortile and the Palazzo. I believe the museum is open as well. There's much to see, and we won't be long."

Her heart thumped against her ribs. "You won't mind, Peter, will you? We really shouldn't be long."

"Not at all." He kissed her lightly. "I'll take a tour and come back for you." He nodded at Roccia. "I hope the meeting goes well. I wouldn't want my girl disappointed."

She noted his cautioning look with surprise. And though she might have done without the overprotection, it felt good to have someone watching out for her.

"Not to worry, I'll take good care." Roccia offered his arm. "The Sala is this way."

He escorted her down the portico to a smaller interior room whose blue-gray walls and notched high ceilings had the feel of a cloister. The surrounding gilt-framed paintings dominated by shades of royal blue and ruby exuded a regal quality.

"James is down there on the right." Roccia nodded. "I'll introduce you."

Following his nod, she felt she would have recognized Martell without the indication. Wearing tapered black wool dress pants and a simple white cotton tuxedo shirt, he was no taller than those around him. But he was larger, broader, without the svelte silhouette of a model but with the form of a man firmly established, his sun-soaked skin stretched like leather over broad flat cheekbones, the long deep lines of a lightly pocked face a testament to one who hadn't followed the crowd, who still smoked and drank grappa and, it was said, gambled more than a little and not only in business. He certainly did so with his apparel lines, raising them up to stand on their own and, if they disappointed, letting them fall. The industry had seen several of his smaller startups tumble over the years because he was willing to wager on the spark of an idea that might or might not ignite. It was an admirable quality, to risk working with those still finding their way.

Martell stood near the front of the *Sala* talking with a tall, handsome woman in a silk jersey wrap dress in black, violet and aqua. The woman looked familiar, but she felt unnerved enough already and kept her eyes on Martell. Roccia went to his side and at a break in the conversation smiled at the woman and put his hand on Martell's broad shoulder.

"Sorry to interrupt, James." Roccia nodded toward her. "This is the young designer I've been telling you about."

From her periphery, she noticed the woman beside Martell look her up and down. She felt her body go cold.

Martell gave a nod. "Leigh, good to catch up." He gave the woman an air kiss on each cheek. "You'll come see us at Maggiore this week?"

"Of course," the woman answered in softly accented English. She signaled a young man in a deconstructed black jersey jacket waiting patiently nearby. "Nari, let's see what's in the main room."

As the woman left and Martell turned to give her his full attention, she wanted to tell him not to bother, that all this had been a mistake and he could go back to talking with the woman whom Gia presently recognized, most recently from a special on legendary designers of women's fashions. Before she could entreat Martell for pardon and escape, Roccia intervened.

"Gia is trying her hand at dress design, fabric design, too. Her family is in the business."

"I recall the video," Martell answered.

She felt herself go from chill to electric panic, though Martell didn't seem to notice.

"With a last name like Falcini, her roots are here in Italy, too," Roccia continued. "The Marche region."

"Lovely area, very pastoral." Martell looked at her closely. "My people are from Calabria, the toe of the boot. I always say this is why I can't get enough of the sun. The original name is Martello."

Gia smiled in spite of herself.

"I see you've heard of it," Martell said, genially.

"I might have caught something about it somewhere," she answered, captivated by his warm candor. "And thank you for taking a few minutes. I know business isn't usually done this way, but I wanted to wear the dress for the design and the fabric. You mentioned having resources, but I hope you'll consider the advantages of a smaller supply house."

Martell raised a broad tanned hand to his cheek. "Well, then." He waggled his fingers. "Let's see you."

With a quick nod, she lifted the hem of the dress and began to turn, watching as in slow motion one person after another looking then staring in her direction as she completed the circle to again face Martell, who still nodded, still looked appreciative, but with seemingly clairvoyant scrutiny in the deep brown eyes behind the thick glasses.

She felt a lump the size of a nectarine form at the back of her throat and in that instant saw everything—the dress, the design, the fabric, herself—reflected from his veteran vantagepoint. She tried to swallow, moisten her throat, which still felt raw from whatever was in that shimmering but deceptive drink.

It might hurt less, be less humiliating, she intuited quickly, if she were the first to express what she saw so clearly.

"It's not—quite what you're looking for, is it?"

Martell's smile bore a sympathetic quality. "You may have heard the adage that you need to know a thing in order to throw it away. You've come this evening with two goals, the dress and the fabric. As to the dress, you've chosen a swing style—I imagine to showcase the material. But the piece feels constrained, limited, almost incomplete, though the tailoring is good." He paused, leaning back. "The result is functional and feminine. Not quite original."

He reached down to finger the material. "Now the fabric, I admit, is lovely. And you may know that we're creating a line that can support an organic label. But we've just contracted with a mill that's already approved."

The full import of his words struck somewhere just under her midsection. She suddenly felt like sitting down, but the nearest chair was out of reach.

"You took a chance coming this evening," Martell said, still looking at her. "Which, though precipitous, shows courage. But look around, Ms. Falcini, at the masterpieces here." He gestured at the works that graced the *Sala's* walls and high ceiling. "You're Italian. You comprehend this level of artistry. Doesn't it stir something in you to create your own *capolavoro,* whether dress or textile or both?"

She felt cut to the quick. Yes, she wanted to say, this was precisely what she wanted. "Thank you for your guidance, Mr. Martell," she said hoarsely. "And your time."

"Not at all and you do have a start here." Martell reached down again to touch the material.

"Thank you, James," Roccia cut in. "I'll just walk Gia out to the Cortile."

Martell took her hand. "Try me again when you can do an entire collection."

Roccia took her arm and turned her around toward the exit. "Buck up," he said in an undertone. "He doesn't meet with just anyone and he's offered good advice—strive for originality. It was for this that Brera was created—"

She tried to take in what Roccia was saying, to hold on to it. But being surrounded by those who had long since gained and surpassed their pinnacles pushed the summits out of reach.

Roccia walked her by a knot of people arguing over whether the ubiquity of video would obliterate the future of painting and led her to a vacant section of railing between two arches.

"I'm sorry tonight didn't go as you hoped," he said, still holding her. "But you did get a meeting. And James meant it when he said try him with a collection, if you opt for design. But you know what this means—"

"Back to the classroom and the drawing board?" She looked him full in the face. "After that last fiasco?" And which drawing board in which class, fashion or fabric?

He took her hands. "I know you think I should have intervened that time with Larsen, but you shared your idea voluntarily, before you even finished the design."

Yes, and she had been stubborn enough to try the same tack here at even greater risk. Feeling utterly degraded, she took her hands form his and pressed her fingers to her cheeks.

"Don't despair." He gave her a quick embrace. "Had you been successful so early you might have wondered for the rest of your life if it was a fluke. And the textile design you did then was commercial, not apparel, for which you have more of a knack and an interest. Now at least you're inspired. And, I believe, for a better reason. Don't let tonight ruin that."

He consulted his watch. "I must get back. But Peter will arrive shortly, I'm sure. He's a catch, by the way." He looked at her. "You'll be all right?"

"I'll be fine," she said, swallowing hard.

He stepped back and blew a kiss. "We'll talk again in Boston."

She watched him go then turned and looked out over the Cortile, the symmetry of its columns and arches under the indigo sky. Dear heaven, what would she do now, she wondered amid the music of the strings, the murmur and hush of the remaining visitors. She couldn't imagine creating again, anything, ever. Maybe she should step away from design and textiles all together, but the thought of it, the searing reality of what it would mean or wouldn't, hurt even worse.

Chapter 41

Last night's sleep had been elusive, the hours having ebbed away like a tide that left behind only a barren strip of shore. Now she stared blankly out the lobby window at the traffic buzzing past the street corner consoled only minutely by the activity.

She turned to the young man at the desk whose fair etched features resembled those of the concierge. "Please, would you mind calling a taxi?"

He nodded and pressed his earbud.

"Any idea where you'd like to go?" Peter asked, looking relaxed in jeans and a white cotton button-down, shirt sleeves rolled under.

"No idea," she said.

After his best effort to put her at ease in the privacy of their room, his soft smile in the brightness of the lobby made her feel unsettled. She looked out the window at a pasta delivery truck halted at the corner, of the handful of other vehicles the only one to obey the red traffic signal.

"But I can't go home with nothing."

He put his arm around her waist. "You have a lot more than nothing to show for the time here. You saw your father, met his family, visited the mill. And Martell did say to try him again."

Another audience with Martell—she winced. It would take months to create a collection. And meanwhile? What of Fiber, Ordito? She had talked last night's meeting up to the stars with Raf, to whom she owed an accounting of the result. Yet, Martell hadn't even inquired after the source of the material. "Precipitous," he had called the encounter. She felt a pang at the truth of it. That he had remarked on her courage was barely noteworthy.

She pressed her fingers to her temples. "I have no contract," she said, feeling the weight of reality.

"*Signorina,*" said the desk clerk. "The taxi is waiting."

"Thank you." She looked at Peter. "Are you willing to go with someone who doesn't know where she's going?"

"Maybe we have that in common." He opened the glass door to a bright, noisy day whose autumnal coolness carried the aroma of leavening bread.

The cab driver looked in his rearview. "Where to?" he asked in English with a lilting North African cadence.

"Where do you suggest?" Peter asked.

The driver blew out his cheeks. "There are many places, many places." He scratched his forehead under the visor of his cap. "Very near are the Duomo and Vittorio Emanuele Gallery, also the da Vinci Museum. The Castello Sforzesco is not far, nor La Scala. And there is shopping."

She leaned over the seat. "Can you take us to the canals?"

The cabbie cocked his head and nudged the cab from the sidewalk. "The *navigli?*" he asked, waving out the window at the driver of the parcel truck behind them to pass.

"Yes, can you take us?"

"Certainly, but there are two—the Naviglio Grande and the Naviglio Pavese. The Naviglio Grande is more scenic."

"Then let's try the Pavese," she said, sitting back. "Fewer tourists."

The driver smiled in the rearview. "It's a bit of a ride, but we'll put the pedal to the metal." Gunning the engine, he turned right at the light.

They passed the Libraccio Libreria, which she always had to remind herself meant bookstore and not library, swept past the Zona Risorgimento and the Boccone University and zipped down the Strada Provinciale.

As they merged onto a straight section of roadway, Peter edged closer and squeezed her hand. "Sorry things haven't turned out as you hoped."

She wanted to confess her utter shame at having tried to prove herself using the same rash method that sank her design in college but couldn't manage it. "I pushed things way too far, too fast."

He looked at her. "Wasn't it Roccia who suggested the meeting?"

"Yes, but clearly as a consult, not a business prospect."

She felt her face grow hot at how eagerly she had flaunted what she felt certain was the perfect complement of design and fabric. Maybe if she had modified the dress to a tunic, added matching bell bottoms like a sixties' pants suit. But the time was short and so was the material. And here she had assured Martell he wouldn't be disappointed. Oddly, he hadn't seemed to be. But why would he be? He hadn't been thinking business at all.

She looked out the window as the driver turned off the Provinciale. "I can't go back like this."

"Can you get a later flight, try to work out something else?" Peter asked.

"I could plead hardship," she said with a laugh. "A matter of life and death." It didn't feel far off the mark.

"Does Fiber have the budget for a flight change?"

She looked at his face in the strobe of late morning light between buildings on Milan's south side. "No. And with no contract, no future either."

The driver slowed as they turned onto a boulevard lined with bars and cafés whose netting separated outdoor seating from the street and passersby.

"The Pavese is on the right," said the cabbie, swerving past a line of parked cars to a miniscule space just large enough for a scooter.

"*Grazie.*" She reached in her bag.

"Let me." Peter handed the driver the fare plus a ten euro note.

"Many thanks, my friend, many thanks." The cabbie handed the receipt over the seat back.

She slid the orange bag back onto her shoulder. "Thank you," she said softly and squeezed Peter's hand.

Getting out of the cab, she went to the small rise of the bridge that was barely perceptible to passing motorists. Yet, the canal beneath had once served as a main artery of commerce and livelihood, the route by which textiles went out to the world.

On either side, the narrow waterway was lined by apartment buildings of varied colors and epochs and clogged with outdoor eating areas, a floating restaurant and bar, and a houseboat.

She couldn't have arranged this trip worse if she tried, she thought, looking out at the jumble, the opaque water running past. She had been out her depth from Roccia's first mention of Martell. Yet, instead of taking steps in keeping with her stride—or in this case, with the actual opportunity, not what she imagined—she had compounded the challenge.

Paolo's voice echoed in her thoughts. "Isn't that the way with you Americans—always making everything a competition." Yes, she thought, especially with herself. She felt Peter's arm around her.

"I'm here, you know," he said against her cheek.

She leaned closer. How different life would be on a houseboat, she thought, gazing down the canal. Though when had anybody last used one to actually go anywhere? She thought of Alex, his townhouse, functional, secure, elegant and belonging to someone else.

She turned. "Why do you love me?"

He looked at her. "What do you mean? Why shouldn't I love you?"

"But why me and not someone else?"

She thought of how they met, how quickly they had clung to each other as if each had believed their meeting was more than chance and hadn't wanted to learn otherwise.

He shrugged. "I love you because you're pretty, smart, you have a sense of humor, sometimes." He smiled.

"I'm not looking for a resume."

He moved closer. "All right. Then I love you because you can think for yourself, because you have a lot of life in you."

Curious, she thought, since at the moment the feeling of being alive seemed singularly absent. "It all sounds so neat, so logical."

"I'm nothing if not logical," he said with a half-smile.

"And thorough."

He straightened, looking resolute and buttoned-down. "I didn't rehearse the answer, if that's what you mean."

"I know." She put her arm around him. "You're too honest for that. It's one of the things I love about you."

He looked in her eyes. "You make it sound like that's not enough."

The clatter of plates drifted over from the café across the street.

"Maybe it's too much. Too safe."

"But shouldn't there be some safety in the world?" he countered, the sun catching the glint of auburn in his hair. "Shouldn't love be safe, some of the time, at least?"

She smiled softly. "It isn't, you know." She searched his face. Did he know it? Did he realize love wouldn't be any safer with her than it had been with Mattie?

He pulled back. "What is this, Gia, some kind of test?"

"Not a test, just questions." She looked out at the water. "Funny, but the last thing I wanted when I came here was questions. I wanted to just know—why my father let Mom and me leave, why he stayed, never came back to us. I wanted the fabric, too, to know how it was made." She looked at him. "I wanted the process so I could have another mill make the material for less. I told Raf I'd do it. In fact, he's expecting it. That's why I came."

He looked at her warily. "That doesn't sound like you."

She gave a half-smile. "But it is, me."

He stood stiffly, a guarded look in his eyes. What else did she see there? Fear, disdain?

"Payback for your father staying," he said as if to provide an alibi, an out for her culpability.

She shrugged. "Partly." She looked down the canal. "But I wanted controlling interest, too, if not in Fiber, then in the future." She felt him draw closer, felt his heat intensified by the sun off the water nearing zenith.

"So, what do you want now?"

"A lot of things. I just can't quite see how they all fit."

"Do you have to know all that now?" he said, taking her hand. "Because you're asking the same questions I'm asking. You with Fiber, me with the learning centers. We can find the answers together."

He had a point. Their circumstances were similar, and they could work things through together.

She turned. "Let's get coffee and something to eat." The sunlight on the Pavese like a mirror had sapped her energy.

Chapter 42

After brunch at a bakery that served *al fresco,* they hopped the tram to the city center. Along the Via Fiori Chiari, Gia paused at the window of a storefront. Inside, a cluster of young people sat on stools in rapt attention as a woman with jet black hair in a tight chignon and a tape measure around her neck gesticulated at a tailor's dummy, a female form with a cast iron skirt.

The woman pointed to the dummy's bustline, swept her hand across her own upper body then gave a series of signals in the direction of the street. Finally, pointing at the students' sketchbooks, she nodded at the door. One by one the youths hopped off their stools, several pausing momentarily at the front window. The woman turned to the casement and glared, annoyance tensing her face.

Gia turned. "Do you mind? I'll just be a minute." She stepped around the hurrying students and stuck her head in the door. *"Scusi,* sorry to interrupt. Is this a class?"

The woman heaved an exasperated sigh. "If you are a student, you are a month late for the start of this course."

"I'm not a student here." She looked around at the remaining fresh faces. "But *maestra* would you mind if I ask—why the storefront and not a studio in a school?"

"But this is a studio, and it is part of a school," the woman countered. "The New School of Design, *Moda e Tessuto.* And where should we have class except where we can see the human form?" She waved at the window and the street beyond. "That is our classroom, an integral part of our studies." She stared out at the sidewalk. "Is he yours?"

Gia followed her gaze to Peter standing near the corner. "If I can hold onto him in this city."

The woman turned and gave her an appraising look. "Then keep yourself young—and interesting."

"I'll try," she said with a smile. "Again, sorry to interrupt."

The woman nodded. "Come back and take a class, if you're interested in clothing the human form."

"*Grazie,* I'll see what I can do."

She went back out to the sidewalk. If she did enroll in classes, how long would it take before she could create as Roccia and Martell did, even as her father had once?

"Is it sewing class?" Peter asked.

"Tailoring, for design." She looked back in the window as the last student filed out to the street. "They focus on the human form."

"So do I." He put his arm around her as they walked to the corner.

As they waited for the pedestrian signal, she looked up at him. "Do you—I mean, would you—" She saw a shadow darken the slate-colored eyes. "I mean, would you hate me if we changed the wedding date, pushed it back a couple of months?"

He paused and drew a breath. "How did I know you were going to ask."

She took his hand. "It's not what you think. I just—I want more time."

"Is that all?" he asked softly.

Looking at him, she knew he was thinking of Mattie, his fear that even with a younger woman there wouldn't be enough time.

"Let's cross." She linked her arm in his and drew him across the boulevard past a quadrangle of shops to a small courtyard and a wrought iron bench.

Out along the sidewalk foot traffic had picked up, each passerby with a story and a form, and all of them needed covering.

"I have so much to learn," she said softly as a dark-skinned teen with long dark hair and tattered stonewashed jeans hurried past clasping an infant in powder blue bunting. "No wonder I didn't stick it out at school."

"You had a lot on your mind," he said, taking her hand. "Your mother was sick. You were working—"

She saw the look of empathy in his face. "I had a chance to work with a professional who knows the industry—fashion and textiles—and really learn something. But I was afraid, of how much I didn't know." Worried about being weighed in the scales and found wanting.

When her mother first passed, she hadn't felt the fear. With the long-held restraints gone and the inherited anxieties seemingly buried, she felt euphoric, liberated. Just as her father had described of his decision to remain here.

But for him the freedom was real, if purchased at a price, and for a while he made the most of it. For her, the sense of liberty quickly morphed into a pernicious disconnection, disorientation. Her mother, with her many fears, had been oppressive, but she always knew her mind. With the past and attendant boundaries gone, she discovered she didn't know her mind at all.

Peter squeezed her side. "You want to take classes again."

"I, yes—maybe. I don't know." She felt the warmth of his fingertips.

His smile was lined with fatigue. "You know I want to say yes, sure, let's wait. If that's what you need."

She drew closer. "But you can't. You wanted more time with Mattie, and you're afraid you won't have it with me either."

He turned and looked out unfocused at the street. "I did everything," he said, quietly. "The doctors, the clinic. I begged her to try the experimental treatment—to not give up." He closed his eyes. "Do you know what it's like having someone not love you enough to fight to stay with you?"

She took his hand. "I don't think that's what Mattie felt. Sometimes we can't control what we fear. You think Mattie didn't care enough, but maybe she was just afraid." Or tired, or hopeless, any number of things or all of them. "From what you've said, it sounds more like Mattie couldn't take anymore and was honest about it." She pressed her palm to his. "There's something I think I need to tell you."

He turned and looked at her, his face blanched. "What?"

What should she say, what could she say? She hadn't thought of what to tell him or how. In reality, she hadn't thought to tell him at all, and she hadn't planned on seeing him here.

"You met someone else," he said, stoppering her silence to fill the void as he had when he gave her the ring.

"It was more a reunion."

"You mean, like a class? You didn't go to school here."

"I hadn't seen him in a decade. We were kids then."

"But you're adults now."

"He's married," she said, discarding the niceties. "I could say it was a vulnerable moment." Or that she had been lonely. And while both of those things were true, they weren't why she sought Alex's company. "I didn't want to face—"

"You didn't want to face me, is that it?"

"I wasn't thinking of you. I didn't even know you'd be here." She looked at him carefully. "You know, you didn't exactly ask me to marry you."

He sat back. "So you slept with someone because I didn't put a proposal in so many words?"

"Four would have been enough."

"You weren't ready to hear them."

"So you chose the easy way."

"You slept with someone else."

"I held someone else, kissed someone else. I spent time with someone else because I wanted someone else's life, because I couldn't envision my own."

He took his hand from hers and closed his eyes. "Sounds like we have some things to work out." He looked at her. "The question is, do we work them out apart or together?"

She held out her hand and gazed at the ring, the opalescence of the uncut stone glimmering faintly in the brightness of the afternoon.

Chapter 43

Giovanni sat in the kitchen, the plate of leftover prosciutto now dried but the figs from the last morning of his daughter's brief and strenuous visit worth savoring. Sitting here alone, he felt her departure like an undertow. It was just as well Stella had gone to midmorning Mass, even if she went less for God and more for gossip, because this also gave him rest, a chance to pause and think, as there was much to consider.

First was his pleasure that Gia had generally gotten on well with Stella and the boys, though Stella could hold a conversation with a lamppost, and Paolo could find worthwhile qualities in any female. Yet, the relationships had taken on a heartening familial quality. Even Max seemed to have largely cottoned on to his stepsister despite the intervallic diatribes to which he subjected nearly everyone anyway. This, Giovanni felt, was a test of how far he could push a relationship. Gia, however, had appeared to hold her with him and Paolo, too. For a more objective assessment, he sought out Stella after the boys left on Friday.

"I know why you're hanging around," she accused, knowing him better than to think he was lingering about the kitchen to help clean up. "You want to know what the boys think of Gia."

It was hard to keep from smiling at her candor, usually intended to get everyone's cards on the table sooner than later. How different she was from Antonia, he marveled again, since his ex had ever been ready to wield the knife over a playing hand, with a twist for good measure.

"Well, then?" he prompted. "Don't keep me waiting." He needn't remind her that dragging out the tale would do no good since no amount of effort would entice him toward the sink.

"Well, then, in my opinion we survived well enough. Of course, the boys said little to me directly," she added with a coy smile. "But before they left, I heard them talking in the *sala.*"

"And?" he queried, imagining her with her ear to the bottom of a glass against the family room door. "Out with it."

"They made the same comments in private as when we were all together. Paolo thinks Gia is quite genuine. Max thinks that so far she seems okay, though it was hard to tell from a very limited first meeting. Max's words, not mine."

He had smiled then, because this was as close to a rousing thumbs-up from Max as anyone would get.

"So are you satisfied, you old goat?" Stella prodded.

He was satisfied and content. Since, as she said, they had all survived and were little the worse for wear because of it. Even Stefano and Angelo seemed to think well of Gia, Angelo especially.

"She is shrewd enough to get along even here if she wants," he observed, lauding Gia's canniness. How he had drawn this conclusion he hadn't let on, and Giovanni hadn't pushed.

Looking at the clock on the stove, he wondered whether she was yet at the airport and whether once she got there she would lose herself in busyness or balk like a donkey as he had when faced with the prospect of returning to a life he no longer wanted. On boarding that last return flight before he decided to remain, he could barely get himself on the plane let alone in his seat, certain with each passing moment that the aircraft would implode, obliterating his prospect for an eventual last bid for freedom.

But for Gia the flight home could offer a chance to mull the days and decisions ahead. Would she stay with that fabric shop? Who knew? He found himself wishing her fiancé had ignored her admonition and come for a visit. He would like to have met this Pietro who had chosen such an unusual ring that seemed more an homage than an engagement.

The ringing of the phone caught him so by surprise that he jumped.

"*Cazzo,*" he said, cursing it soundly. He got up and gingerly raised the receiver. "*Pronto?*" he said and heard the single word response. And in the background what sounded like a bustling international terminal. "*Ciao, bella,*" he said, trying to keep his tone calm.

"I'm at the airport," she said, sounding out of breath. "I was going to try the cell, but I wasn't sure it was handy."

She probably meant she hadn't wanted to reach Stella instead. He looked again at the clock. A bit early for departure. "Everything okay?"

"So far—Peter's here. He came to see me. His plane leaves in a few minutes. I came to see him off."

He sat in stunned silence at his sixth sense or however many senses parents displayed when something unseen by human eyes was happening with their children. Unfortunately, these intuitions were rarely accompanied by instructions.

"How are you?" he asked, trying not to query her with the implied insistence that she be all right.

"I'm all right—"

He heard her pause and wanted desperately to ask if she was sure she was okay. Instead, he toyed with the section of fig still on his plate.

"Is Peter with you?" he asked casually.

"He's in the men's room."

"Have you—talked with him?"

"Yes."

O, Madonna, but the glacial speed at which she was revealing information was killing him. "And were you able to come to a resolution?" he prompted.

"He's willing to give me time, which I need because the meeting with Martell didn't go well. I mean, Martell was kind enough, but he said the dress design wasn't original. He appreciated the tailoring though. As for the fabric, he never asked. Just said try him again when I create a collection. God knows when that will happen."

"I understand," he affirmed and paused, hating his silence and fearing it, as if he must supply a response, especially if she didn't have one. But this particular answer wasn't his to give. He heard a call over the loudspeaker in the background.

"Did you make any other contacts?" He heard static then silence. "Gia?"

"One, some weird stylist I met at the fashion show when I first got here. I have his card somewhere—Erno Prati?"

The name wasn't familiar. But there were so many in fashion these days, especially up north. "Why not give him a call before you leave?"

"I might, if only to hook him up with Ordito. I'm—thinking of going back to school."

"Wonderful," he exclaimed before he could stop himself. "I mean, if that's what you want, of course," he added, adjusting his tone.

"Dad?"

He smiled then covered his mouth to keep from gushing. "I'm here," he said evenly as his eyes brimmed.

"Peter said we could postpone the wedding."

He had assumed this was what she meant when she mentioned the allowance of more time. But if she was bringing it up again, there must be something more.

"But that's good, isn't it?" he encouraged. "You can focus on school." He could tell from her silence that this was not good, or perhaps not good enough. "You want more than time."

"I think so."

He toyed with the fig, twirling the bit of neck that remained. What was it she wanted him to say? There was something in particular, he was sure of it. He stared at the fig, overripe now in late September, a plump little fruit with a nice tough rind just right for protection.

"Perhaps you could talk with Peter again, tell him what you feel. You're not married yet. The choice to stay in the relationship is as much yours as his." He paused and thought he heard her sniffle.

"Dad?"

"Yes?" He grinned, loving the sound of the word, and wiped his eyes.

"Zio Paolino said I could always come back. Do you—I mean, would you say the same?"

He felt so elated she would even ask that he opened his mouth but for a moment couldn't answer.

"Of course, you can always return. Though I wish you could see me say so, for you would see how much I mean it. And one day, God willing, you will see. But for now, you must believe only my word that, yes, you can come back, always, anytime. I'll send a letter—in case you need it in writing."

He heard her laugh, raw and exhausted but mirthful. "And, Gia, your time here was not a waste, in any way."

"Then tell Stella thanks, again. And give my regards to Max and Paolo. And come to Boston, all of you, if you can."

"You never know but what we might and Paolo for sure. He is already boasting of how the architecture is worth seeing because it represents so much of American history. Though, to be fair, at the time he was looking online at a group of college girls walking through the Common." He heard what sounded like a short laugh but couldn't be sure with all the clamor in the background.

"Dad, I—"

He heard her pause again and knew in his soul what she wanted to say—that she loved him and would miss him, that she wanted him to tell her he loved her and would miss her, and to return quickly, on the next train even. More than anything he knew she wanted a guarantee that there would be a next time and that somehow during that time nothing and no one would change or leave—all the longings no one had a right to expect yet were human to want and expect and hope for all the same.

"I know," he said. "I feel the same."

"I'll call when I get home."

"I'll be waiting. *Addio.*"

He heard a click then silence. Replacing the receiver, he imagined how difficult it would be to have the conversation with her intended but even more so, he thought, to have her dream of working with

Martell dashed. But she had wanted to impress him almost at any cost and far more with the fabric than with the design of the dress.

Well, she would have her work cut out for her back in the states, he thought with a wry smile as he took another fig. At least now she knew what she must do and why, whether she liked it all or not.

Peeling back the thick rind, he wondered if while waiting for departure she would reach again in her bag for the padded pouch, take out the scarf and hold it to the light. It wasn't the timing of the gift he had wanted her to appreciate or its insulation from the chill. Nor was it the vibrant pattern or the vivid shades or marvelous hand and breathable wearable qualities she might always admire. The draw was not in these things or in the beauty of the piece but that all these qualities had come together to create a story she could step into.

Chapter 44

The sudden morning downpour ended to reveal a sunlit October sky dotted with high white clouds, and on the pavement a glistening sheen. Walking down Commercial Street, she felt the lift that came from having successfully mediated between Erno Prati, head *stilista* for Trentino Alta Moda, and Ordito Trama. Although Prati admired the fabric of the scarf, he appreciated the mill's virtues even more, especially its move toward organic certifications. This made the initial excruciating mediatory call from Malpensa worth it, a strike while the steam iron was hot.

The boost of having facilitated such a connection was just the reassurance she needed before what would shortly be her second confrontation with Raf since her return. He was even less likely to relish today's little summit than the news that Martell was a no-go. She hated to recall Raf's tirade at that bulletin, though the altercation had strengthened her resolve.

Anticipating the moment, she felt her adrenalin surge with a vigor so like her mother's frenetic energy that she had wanted to bury it at Antonia's passing to avoid being consumed. Yet, she needed this part of herself just as she needed her father's perpetual yes to the newness of life.

Pausing momentarily at Fiber's front window, she breathed in the city air, suffused with the smell of exhaust. She looked inside the shop and found it already lit. She had come in late for once and without advance warning. She could see Raf standing at the back counter piled with the swatches she had left, unwilling finally to pick up after him.

Opening the door, she went inside.

"You're late," he asserted, not looking up.

She walked down the center aisle past the protruding bolts of fabric to the counter and took a manila envelope from her bag. "For you," she said, handing it across the tabletop.

He looked up. "What's this, another wonder scarf?"

"It's my share of this place."

He blinked bloodshot eyes behind the contacts. "What do you mean, your share?"

"I'm leaving." She held out the envelope.

He paused then snatched it, folded back the metal clasp and looked inside, turned it upside down and shook it. The title transfer and quitclaim deed fell onto the counter; her attorney had taken care of the rest. He stared at the papers and looked up.

"These are what you're giving me? Papers and no contacts? You owe me a hell of a lot more than this."

"You've got that right," she answered. "I owe you a lawsuit for not disclosing the extent of the electrical problems when I bought into this hole."

Bautista blanched under the baked-on tan.

Her attorney had apprised her of the options for redress, but the value of liberation was beyond price. "Let's wait, Jake," she told him. "Before we call in the big guns."

"I want the Italy contact for the fabric," Bautista insisted.

She smiled. "I don't think so." He had pressed her for this information from the moment she returned from Milan, payment for failing to secure Martel. But if she couldn't make a go of broader distribution with Fiber through Ordito, she sure as hell wasn't putting the Della Bastias in Bautista's sweaty little grip.

He moved around the counter. "You know you can't just walk away like this."

He was, if nothing else, predictable, she thought, recalling her mother's warning.

"Those petty hoods are all alike, runts that yelp loud because they don't have the size. Don't fall for it."

She took the keycard from her bag. "You'll find all the accounts in order on the upstairs computer."

Bautista glared. "What the hell did you do, plan all this while you were with those dagos?" He moved closer. "That's really what you went for, isn't it? Tell the truth."

In one sense, she couldn't honestly dispute this point since the further she went from Fiber the easier it became to imagine a different life. She found herself recalling Senigallia, the confrontation at Romeo's with that prep school brat and Ana's grace under pressure.

"I'm nothing if not a planner," she answered evenly.

"You realize I know where you live," he said with a sneer.

She laughed. "Then you're the only one because I don't live there anymore."

She had skipped the usual real estate hassle by walking down Hanover and stopping in a few places to drop the word. The effort had yielded the sale of the co-op to an eager young first-generation Italian-American looking to move back near family.

"Well," she said, shouldering the orange bag. "I would say it's been a pleasure, but—" She put the keycard on the counter.

"You'll regret this," Bautista said, spitting a little. "You know sales is all you're good for."

She stopped. This, she realized, was the other reason he had sold her a share of Fiber. It had been an easy buck from a young woman who didn't believe in herself.

She looked at him. "You know, Raf, I might have thought that, once."

She turned and went to the door. Behind her she heard Bautista call first her immediate family then her entire lineage into question. Closing the door, she walked out to the street.

For an instant, she felt the same incipient doubt she felt on quitting school and again on buying into Fiber. But this was different, she thought, and kept walking. This time she was going on to more, not less.

She walked over to Haymarket and the Green Line, got off at the Museum of Fine Arts. Crossing the Avenue of the Arts, she thought of Peter. What was he doing now, she wondered, though she no longer had the right to ask. Once she thought she saw him in Faneuil Hall as she caught the fleeting glimpse of a navy cashmere jacket but not the man wearing it.

The last time she saw him was at Malpensa, the blue ring of alpine peaks in the distance over his shoulder. Knowing what she was about to do, his earlier question came to mind. "Do you know what it's like having someone not love you enough to fight to stay with you?" But they weren't married, and if she didn't love him enough it seemed better to say so now.

"I am sorry," she said as they stood at the far end of the terminal.

He shook his head. "Nothing to be sorry for."

She moved closer. "I'll call when I get back—"

"No," he said. "It's fine."

It wasn't fine, she thought. Yet, she couldn't halt what she had put in motion, couldn't stop herself reaching for the uncut stone that had slipped around her finger out of sight. Taking his hand, she pressed the ring into his palm and clasped his fingers.

He took the ring with bloodshot eyes and slipped it into his pocket.

She wanted to look away. "I'm sorry—"

He pressed a finger to her lips, turned slightly then straightened and walked ahead to the gate.

A passel of what appeared to be aspiring models, slender and carrying designer overnight bags, brushed by. A tall blonde paused to watch as he passed. What had she done? There wouldn't be another like him, but this wasn't their time or place.

She walked into the Museum of Fine Arts café where Roccia sat in the glass-enclosed courtyard.

He looked up from his San Pellegrino and half-rose as she approached. "Back from the dead?" he said with a smile.

She laughed. "You don't know the half of it." She hailed the waiter and ordered a coffee then leaned over, tenting her fingers.

"What is this?" Roccia queried, his voice rising. "A naked ring finger?"

She gave a half-smile. "I've quit Fiber as well."

He looked elated. "I knew it," he said, grinning. "Now I can get you back in the program, my class—"

"I'm going on," she cut in. "But not here." There was a sense of satisfaction in watching him deflate. He hadn't been obligated to step in and advocate for her back in college, but he hadn't been overly concerned either.

He leaned closer. "Where will you study?"

"You'll have to come see," she said, smiling. "If you can leave Maggiore long enough to slum it in downtown Milano."

It was interesting, she thought now as she held up her sketchbook and the design inspired by Castel Barberini and the old stone mason, that none of her work reflected the life she had just left, though maybe one day it would, after enough time passed.

Taking her sketchbook, the *maestra* held it at arm's length. "Well," she said, squinting. "It isn't the worst thing I've seen." She tilted the pad sideways. "But you're so literal in your translation. Plus you're straddling the fence again, mixing print—which would work better for a blouse—and this side-button style, which with the toggles is better for a jacket. Pick a piece and commit—shirt or jacket, color or solid. And consider the material, since you're so fond of fabric."

Jacket, she thought, taking the sketchbook as she looked out the studio window, having been warned that November in Milano meant fog. The jacket would be made of thick cotton waffle cone weave and the rich yellow-gold of sunflowers, with black inset stitching and red wooden toggle buttons.

It was the first piece of the series she had visualized unexpectedly and almost in its entirety before leaving Malpensa while looking out the airport window at the distant peaks.

The collection would be for women's day-to-evening apparel comprising a midrise, basket-weave pant cropped above the ankle whose repeat echoed the weathered brick of the stone mason's flat, a sleeveless shift dress in ultramarine silk shantung, a belted pants suit in sand and ultramarine, a square neckline dress in a translucent shade of foam green with a sheer matching shrug, for which Paolo would certainly give her flack. There was also a silvery dress like the shimmering *sardelle,* a short A-line skirt and matching jacket for the diminutive but eloquent piazza of Senigallia and a rosy-hued, day-to-evening short dress with a ballet feel that evoked the city center in the diffused light of late afternoon.

The other images that had flashed in her mind—the sectioned fields and sloping patchwork hills, the curved road that ran behind the village, the country lane lined with brambles and stippled flowers, the yellow finch and grassy field, the lone olive tree, leaves shivering silver in the wind. All these could yield an affordable, easy-care collection with clean lines and a tranquil feel. A careful choice of complementary fabrics would elevate each design, this time without overpowering it. The final piece, inspired by an elegant Senigallia townhouse, would be a stylish but functional reversible trench in silvery taupe.

At first, she considered grouping the pieces by location—village, hills, shore and sea—but that wasn't the way to tell the story. The tale must unfold as those in the *bel paese* and everywhere now lived their lives, in snatches and stolen moments and extremes, and rarely in a discernible sequence. She would take Martell's suggestion to create a *capolavoro*—the Mare Monte collection, if not exclusively for James Martell, then for another house or for the sun glinting off the Adriatic, the waves that stroked the shore, insistent, lulling, the life of fruitful labor whose time always seemed too short to spend..

ACKNOWLEDGMENTS

My thanks to the following:

Acorn Storiers' Barb Wanamaker and Jillian Ross for their longtime friendship, support, love and wisdom.

American Woolen and Kliton Shqina for his time and expertise in describing how mills work.

The Angeloni, Angerosa, Artibani, Bacchiocchi, Carboni, Frattini, Malatini families in Italy for their fine example of the distribution side of the business, continual hospitality and open hearts.

Banksville Designer Fabrics and Larry Shapiro for his expertise and candid take on today's fabric shops and his appreciation that the best part of the business is finding great fabric.

Robert Cox for his encyclopedic knowledge and love of literature and learning.

Connie Keller, sister in the faith, longtime friend, writing colleague and member of Wellspring Writers' Fellowship, for her faithful love and wisdom.

Hazel and William Kessler for their fellowship, wisdom and friendship.

Hollis Seamon for her take on strengthening the manuscript.

Pete Nelson for his fine mentoring and example as a writer.

Peter Selgin for his astute and unstinting initial guidance on writing and the writing life.

ABOUT THE AUTHOR

ADELE ANNESI is an award-winning writer, editor and teacher. She is the author of *What She Takes Away* (Bordighera Press, 2023) and co-author of *Now What? The Creative Writer's Guide to Success After the MFA*. A founder of the Ridgefield Writers Conference and Muse & Music Evening Cabaret, a book editor for Word for Words, LLC, and a former development editor for Scholastic Publishing, Adele has published varied works with *34th Parallel, Authors Publish Magazine, Dawntreader, Feile-Festa, Fresh Ink, Fringe Blog,* Hamline University's *Lit Link, Hotmetalpress,* Jane Friedman's Blog, *Midway Journal, Miranda Literary Magazine, Orca, The Pittsburgh Quarterly, Pyramid, The Ridgefield Press, Washington Independent Review of Books,* and *Southern Literary Review,* where she served as managing editor. Her work has been anthologized for Chatter House Press and Fairfield University, where she received an MFA in creative writing. Her essay on Italian citizenship is among the Clarion Award-winning Essays About Life Transitions by Women Writers, and she received the Editor's Choice award from the National Library of Poetry. Adele's sudden fiction has been adapted for the stage by Joanne Hudson, and she has served as poetry and short story judge for the Danbury Cultural Commission.

Adele led a fiction workshop on scene development for Manhattanville College MFA in Creative Writing. She teaches fiction and creative writing for Westport Writers' Workshop, where she mentors emerging and established writers in long-form fiction. Adele is a member of AWP, Acorn Storiers, the Connecticut Authors and Publishers Association, the Historical Novel Society and the Ridgefield Historical Society. She is also a film screener for Ridgefield Independent Film Festival. Her long-running blog is wordforwords.blogspot.com, and her website is adeleannesi.blogspot.com.

VIA Folios

A refereed book series dedicated to the culture of Italians and Italian Americans.

ANNIE RACHELE LANZILLOTTO. *Whaddyacall the Wind?*. Vol. 159. Memoir.
JULIA LISELLA. *Our Lively Kingdom*. Vol. 158. Poetry.
MARK CIABATTARI. *When the Mask Slips*. Vol. 157. Novel.
JENNIFER MARTELLI. *The Queen of Queens*. Vol. 156. Poetry.
TONY TADDEI. *The Sons of the Santorelli*. Vol. 155. Literature.
FRANCO RICCI. *Preston Street • Corso Italias*. Vol. 154. History.
MIKE FIORITO. *The Hated Ones*. Vol. 153. Literature.
PATRICIA DUNN. *Last Stop on the 6*. Vol. 152. Novel.
WILLIAM BOELHOWER. *Immigrant Autobiography*. Vol. 151. Literary Criticism.
MARC DIPAOLO. *Fake Italian*. Vol. 150. Literature.
GAIL REITANO. *Italian Love Cake*. Vol. 149. Novel.
VINCENT PANELLA. *Sicilian Dreams*. Vol. 148. Novel.
MARK CIABATTARI. *The Literal Truth: Rizzoli Dreams of Eating the Apple of Earthly Delights*. Vol. 147. Novel.
MARK CIABATTARI. *Dreams of An Imaginary New Yorker Named Rizzoli*. Vol. 146. Novel.
LAURETTE FOLK. *The End of Aphrodite*. Vol. 145. Novel.
ANNA CITRINO. *A Space Between*. Vol. 144. Poetry
MARIA FAMÀ. *The Good for the Good*. Vol. 143. Poetry.
ROSEMARY CAPPELLO. *Wonderful Disaster*. Vol. 142. Poetry.
B. AMORE. *Journeys on the Wheel*. Vol. 141. Poetry.
ALDO PALAZZESCHI. *The Manifestos of Aldo Palazzeschi*. Vol 140. Literature.
ROSS TALARICO. *The Reckoning*. Vol 139. Poetry.
MICHELLE REALE. *Season of Subtraction*. Vol 138. Poetry.
MARISA FRASCA. *Wild Fennel*. Vol 137. Poetry.
RITA ESPOSITO WATSON. *Italian Kisses*. Vol. 136. Memoir.
SARA FRUNER. *Bitter Bites from Sugar Hills*. Vol. 135. Poetry.
KATHY CURTO. *Not for Nothing*. Vol. 134. Memoir.
JENNIFER MARTELLI. *My Tarantella*. Vol. 133. Poetry.
MARIA TERRONE. *At Home in the New World*. Vol. 132. Essays.
GIL FAGIANI. *Missing Madonnas*. Vol. 131. Poetry.
LEWIS TURCO. *The Sonnetarium*. Vol. 130. Poetry.
JOE AMATO. *Samuel Taylor's Hollywood Adventure*. Vol. 129. Novel.
BEA TUSIANI. *Con Amore*. Vol. 128. Memoir.
MARIA GIURA. *What My Father Taught Me*. Vol. 127. Poetry.
STANISLAO PUGLIESE. *A Century of Sinatra*. Vol. 126. Popular Culture.
TONY ARDIZZONE. *The Arab's Ox*. Vol. 125. Novel.
PHYLLIS CAPELLO. *Packs Small Plays Big*. Vol. 124. Literature.
FRED GARDAPHÉ. *Read 'em and Reap*. Vol. 123. Criticism.
JOSEPH A. AMATO. *Diagnostics*. Vol 122. Literature.
DENNIS BARONE. *Second Thoughts*. Vol 121. Poetry.
OLIVIA K. CERRONE. *The Hunger Saint*. Vol 120. Novella.

GARIBLADI M. LAPOLLA. *Miss Rollins in Love*. Vol 119. Novel.
JOSEPH TUSIANI. *A Clarion Call*. Vol 118. Poetry.
JOSEPH A. AMATO. *My Three Sicilies*. Vol 117. Poetry & Prose.
MARGHERITA COSTA. *Voice of a Virtuosa and Coutesan*. Vol 116. Poetry.
NICOLE SANTALUCIA. *Because I Did Not Die*. Vol 115. Poetry.
MARK CIABATTARI. *Preludes to History*. Vol 114. Poetry.
HELEN BAROLINI. *Visits*. Vol 113. Novel.
ERNESTO LIVORNI. *The Fathers' America*. Vol 112. Poetry.
MARIO B. MIGNONE. *The Story of My People*. Vol 111. Non-fiction.
GEORGE GUIDA. *The Sleeping Gulf*. Vol 110. Poetry.
JOEY NICOLETTI. *Reverse Graffiti*. Vol 109. Poetry.
GIOSE RIMANELLI. *Il mestiere del furbo*. Vol 108. Criticism.
LEWIS TURCO. *The Hero Enkidu*. Vol 107. Poetry.
AL TACCONELLI. *Perhaps Fly*. Vol 106. Poetry.
RACHEL GUIDO DEVRIES. *A Woman Unknown in Her Bones*. Vol 105. Poetry.
BERNARD BRUNO. *A Tear and a Tear in My Heart*. Vol 104. Non-fiction.
FELIX STEFANILE. *Songs of the Sparrow*. Vol 103. Poetry.
FRANK POLIZZI. *A New Life with Bianca*. Vol 102. Poetry.
GIL FAGIANI. *Stone Walls*. Vol 101. Poetry.
LOUISE DESALVO. *Casting Off*. Vol 100. Fiction.
MARY JO BONA. *I Stop Waiting for You*. Vol 99. Poetry.
RACHEL GUIDO DEVRIES. *Stati zitt, Josie*. Vol 98. Children's Literature. $8
GRACE CAVALIERI. *The Mandate of Heaven*. Vol 97. Poetry.
MARISA FRASCA. *Via incanto*. Vol 96. Poetry.
DOUGLAS GLADSTONE. *Carving a Niche for Himself*. Vol 95. History.
MARIA TERRONE. *Eye to Eye*. Vol 94. Poetry.
CONSTANCE SANCETTA. *Here in Cerchio*. Vol 93. Local History.
MARIA MAZZIOTTI GILLAN. *Ancestors' Song*. Vol 92. Poetry.
MICHAEL PARENTI. *Waiting for Yesterday: Pages from a Street Kid's Life*.
   Vol 90. Memoir.
ANNIE LANZILLOTTO. *Schistsong*. Vol 89. Poetry.
EMANUEL DI PASQUALE. *Love Lines*. Vol 88. Poetry.
CAROSONE & LOGIUDICE. *Our Naked Lives*. Vol 87. Essays.
JAMES PERICONI. *Strangers in a Strange Land: A Survey of Italian-Language
   American Books*.Vol 86. Book History.
DANIELA GIOSEFFI. *Escaping La Vita Della Cucina*. Vol 85. Essays.
MARIA FAMÀ. *Mystics in the Family*. Vol 84. Poetry.
ROSSANA DEL ZIO. *From Bread and Tomatoes to Zuppa di Pesce "Ciambotto"*.
   Vol. 83. Memoir.
LORENZO DELBOCA. *Polentoni*. Vol 82. Italian Studies.
SAMUEL GHELLI. *A Reference Grammar*. Vol 81. Italian Language.
ROSS TALARICO. *Sled Run*. Vol 80. Fiction.
FRED MISURELLA. *Only Sons*. Vol 79. Fiction.
FRANK LENTRICCHIA. *The Portable Lentricchia*. Vol 78. Fiction.
RICHARD VETERE. *The Other Colors in a Snow Storm*. Vol 77. Poetry.
GARIBALDI LAPOLLA. *Fire in the Flesh*. Vol 76 Fiction & Criticism.

GEORGE GUIDA. *The Pope Stories*. Vol 75 Prose.
ROBERT VISCUSI. *Ellis Island*. Vol 74. Poetry.
ELENA GIANINI BELOTTI. *The Bitter Taste of Strangers Bread*. Vol 73. Fiction.
PINO APRILE. *Terroni*. Vol 72. Italian Studies.
EMANUEL DI PASQUALE. *Harvest*. Vol 71. Poetry.
ROBERT ZWEIG. *Return to Naples*. Vol 70. Memoir.
AIROS & CAPPELLI. *Guido*. Vol 69. Italian/American Studies.
FRED GARDAPHÉ. *Moustache Pete is Dead! Long Live Moustache Pete!*.
    Vol 67. Literature/Oral History.
PAOLO RUFFILLI. *Dark Room/Camera oscura*. Vol 66. Poetry.
HELEN BAROLINI. *Crossing the Alps*. Vol 65. Fiction.
COSMO FERRARA. *Profiles of Italian Americans*. Vol 64. Italian Americana.
GIL FAGIANI. *Chianti in Connecticut*. Vol 63. Poetry.
BASSETTI & D'ACQUINO. *Italic Lessons*. Vol 62. Italian/American Studies.
CAVALIERI & PASCARELLI, Eds. *The Poet's Cookbook*. Vol 61. Poetry/Recipes.
EMANUEL DI PASQUALE. *Siciliana*. Vol 60. Poetry.
NATALIA COSTA, Ed. *Bufalini*. Vol 59. Poetry.
RICHARD VETERE. *Baroque*. Vol 58. Fiction.
LEWIS TURCO. *La Famiglia/The Family*. Vol 57. Memoir.
NICK JAMES MILETI. *The Unscrupulous*. Vol 56. Humanities.
BASSETTI. ACCOLLA. D'AQUINO. *Italici: An Encounter with Piero Bassetti*.
    Vol 55. Italian Studies.
GIOSE RIMANELLI. *The Three-legged One*. Vol 54. Fiction.
CHARLES KLOPP. *Bele Antiche Stòrie*. Vol 53. Criticism.
JOSEPH RICAPITO. *Second Wave*. Vol 52. Poetry.
GARY MORMINO. *Italians in Florida*. Vol 51. History.
GIANFRANCO ANGELUCCI. *Federico F*. Vol 50. Fiction.
ANTHONY VALERIO. *The Little Sailor*. Vol 49. Memoir.
ROSS TALARICO. *The Reptilian Interludes*. Vol 48. Poetry.
RACHEL GUIDO DE VRIES. *Teeny Tiny Tino's Fishing Story*.
    Vol 47. Children's Literature.
EMANUEL DI PASQUALE. *Writing Anew*. Vol 46. Poetry.
MARIA FAMÀ. *Looking For Cover*. Vol 45. Poetry.
ANTHONY VALERIO. *Toni Cade Bambara's One Sicilian Night*. Vol 44. Poetry.
EMANUEL CARNEVALI. *Furnished Rooms*. Vol 43. Poetry.
BRENT ADKINS. et al., Ed. *Shifting Borders. Negotiating Places*.
    Vol 42. Conference.
GEORGE GUIDA. *Low Italian*. Vol 41. Poetry.
GARDAPHÈ, GIORDANO, TAMBURRI. *Introducing Italian Americana*.
    Vol 40. Italian/American Studies.
DANIELA GIOSEFFI. *Blood Autumn/Autunno di sangue*. Vol 39. Poetry.
FRED MISURELLA. *Lies to Live By*. Vol 38. Stories.
STEVEN BELLUSCIO. *Constructing a Bibliography*. Vol 37. Italian Americana.
ANTHONY JULIAN TAMBURRI, Ed. *Italian Cultural Studies 2002*.
    Vol 36. Essays.
BEA TUSIANI. *con amore*. Vol 35. Memoir.

FLAVIA BRIZIO-SKOV, Ed. *Reconstructing Societies in the Aftermath of War.*
   Vol 34. History.
TAMBURRI. et al., Eds. *Italian Cultural Studies 2001.* Vol 33. Essays.
ELIZABETH G. MESSINA, Ed. *In Our Own Voices.*
   Vol 32. Italian/American Studies.
STANISLAO G. PUGLIESE. *Desperate Inscriptions.* Vol 31. History.
HOSTERT & TAMBURRI, Eds. *Screening Ethnicity.*
   Vol 30. Italian/American Culture.
G. PARATI & B. LAWTON, Eds. *Italian Cultural Studies.* Vol 29. Essays.
HELEN BAROLINI. *More Italian Hours.* Vol 28. Fiction.
FRANCO NASI, Ed. *Intorno alla Via Emilia.* Vol 27. Culture.
ARTHUR L. CLEMENTS. *The Book of Madness & Love.* Vol 26. Poetry.
JOHN CASEY, et al. *Imagining Humanity.* Vol 25. Interdisciplinary Studies.
ROBERT LIMA. *Sardinia/Sardegna.* Vol 24. Poetry.
DANIELA GIOSEFFI. *Going On.* Vol 23. Poetry.
ROSS TALARICO. *The Journey Home.* Vol 22. Poetry.
EMANUEL DI PASQUALE. *The Silver Lake Love Poems.* Vol 21. Poetry.
JOSEPH TUSIANI. *Ethnicity.* Vol 20. Poetry.
JENNIFER LAGIER. *Second Class Citizen.* Vol 19. Poetry.
FELIX STEFANILE. *The Country of Absence.* Vol 18. Poetry.
PHILIP CANNISTRARO. *Blackshirts.* Vol 17. History.
LUIGI RUSTICHELLI, Ed. *Seminario sul racconto.* Vol 16. Narrative.
LEWIS TURCO. *Shaking the Family Tree.* Vol 15. Memoirs.
LUIGI RUSTICHELLI, Ed. *Seminario sulla drammaturgia.*
   Vol 14. Theater/Essays.
FRED GARDAPHÈ. *Moustache Pete is Dead! Long Live Moustache Pete!.*
   Vol 13. Oral Literature.
JONE GAILLARD CORSI. *Il libretto d'autore. 1860 - 1930.* Vol 12. Criticism.
HELEN BAROLINI. *Chiaroscuro: Essays of Identity.* Vol 11. Essays.
PICARAZZI & FEINSTEIN, Eds. *An African Harlequin in Milan.*
   Vol 10. Theater/Essays.
JOSEPH RICAPITO. *Florentine Streets & Other Poems.* Vol 9. Poetry.
FRED MISURELLA. *Short Time.* Vol 8. Novella.
NED CONDINI. *Quartettsatz.* Vol 7. Poetry.
ANTHONY JULIAN TAMBURRI, Ed. *Fuori: Essays by Italian/American
   Lesbiansand Gays.* Vol 6. Essays.
ANTONIO GRAMSCI. P. Verdicchio. Trans. & Intro. *The Southern Question.*
   Vol 5. Social Criticism.
DANIELA GIOSEFFI. *Word Wounds & Water Flowers.* Vol 4. Poetry. $8
WILEY FEINSTEIN. *Humility's Deceit: Calvino Reading Ariosto Reading Calvino.*
   Vol 3. Criticism.
PAOLO A. GIORDANO, Ed. *Joseph Tusiani: Poet. Translator. Humanist.*
   Vol 2. Criticism.
ROBERT VISCUSI. *Oration Upon the Most Recent Death of Christopher Columbus.*
   Vol 1. Poetry.

CPSIA information can be obtained
at www.ICGtesting.com
Printed in the USA
JSHW020924290323
39629JS00002B/156